LORI FOSTER

SLOW *RIDE*

ISBN-13: 978-1-335-50494-4

Slow Ride

Recycling programs
for this product may
not exist in your area.

This edition published by arrangement with Harlequin Books S.A.

For questions and comments about the quality of this book,
please contact us at CustomerService@Harlequin.com.

® and TM are trademarks of Harlequin Enterprises Limited or its
corporate affiliates. Trademarks indicated with ® are registered in the
United States Patent and Trademark Office, the Canadian Intellectual
Property Office and in other countries.

www.HQNBooks.com

Printed in U.S.A.

To Allen, my crazy, wonderful, hilarious husband of over forty years.

Somehow you make every year better than the last—happier, easier, safer and more balanced. You may not be perfect, but you're perfect for *me*...since I'm imperfect, also. In fact, I think our faults complement each other.

I'm so very glad you switched history classes on the third day of our sophomore year of high school, and I'm doubly grateful my mother convinced me to give you a call. It's the best decision I ever made!

Here's to forty more!

Love you bunches and bunches,

Loretta

(Dear readers, any of you who didn't know that my full name is Loretta—though I've always been called Lori—probably haven't heard my husband talk to me. Check out my Facebook sometime for his amusing "Hey, Loretta" videos at www.Facebook.com/lorifoster.)

Dear Reader,

You know how brothers can be similar, but also... oh-so-different? Well, that's Jack and Brodie. You first met the brothers in *Driven to Distraction*, book one in the Road to Love series, aka Brodie's book. Each book stands alone, I promise you, but in book one you saw that while Brodie is all brash and brawn, Jack is a little more refined.

Or is he?

In *Slow Ride* you'll find that Jack's style differs from his brother's, his approach calmer and more polite. That is, until he meets Ron, Ronnie, Veronica—an ever-changing, ultimately independent woman who pushes all his buttons, a woman who wants him sexually but otherwise doesn't need his help, thank you very much.

For a man like Jack, a natural protector and a gentleman to the core, Ronnie isn't just a challenge. She intrigues him, gains his instant respect and steals his heart without even trying.

They're still feeling their way in a new relationship when threats appear—and the more basic nature of each is revealed.

I'm having a *wonderful* time writing this series with all new characters and a fresh new setting. I hope you're enjoying reading it, too! Please do let me know. :)

Happy reading!

Lori Foster

www.LoriFoster.com

CHAPTER ONE

RONNIE WOULDN'T HAVE walked into Freddie's, a dinky little honky-tonk bar in Red Oaks, Ohio, if she'd known a local's birthday party was underway. But hey, she needed a distraction and this seemed to be the only one available.

Seated on a stool, she lifted her beer to the loud toast made by a fellow in dusty overalls. Something about the birthday boy supplying corn to an upcoming festival. Ronnie wasn't sure. Small-town vibes usually eluded her.

And this town was smaller than most.

The main street began with farms that melded into small tidy houses lining each side, along with a few establishments, and abruptly ended with Freddie's.

God willing, she wouldn't have to be here long. Her employers had recently decided that she needed a professional courier to help acquire their purchases. Even though Ronnie was more than capable on her own.

Worse, the man they wanted to hire was, by all accounts, a super-slick, suit-wearing choirboy—and she wanted nothing to do with him. Tomorrow she would present the offer as directed, but with any luck he'd turn it down—and then she could get back to work.

Alone.

Until then, she needed to shake off the tension, or at the very least find a diversion from her thoughts. Thus her visit to this dive.

"Come on in," someone shouted. "There's still plenty of room."

Ronnie glanced up to see the newcomer—and was instantly hooked. Well, well, well.

This customer stood better than six feet tall. Messy light brown hair contrasted with heavily lashed, dark eyes. Two different paint colors splattered his T-shirt, and his faded jeans hung loose and low.

Hello, distraction.

She'd hoped a beer would take the edge off, but perhaps there was a better way to help her sleep tonight.

Swiveling to face him, Ronnie smiled. This was what she needed. *He* was what she needed. Her heart beat faster just thinking of the possibilities.

Allowing her gaze to skim down his body, she lingered in key, tantalizing places.

Straight shoulders.

Trim waist.

Delicious biceps.

Down to a flat stomach, narrow hips, and…a nice bulge in his softly worn jeans. Whoa.

A curl of heat teased through her system. Yes, she had a definite type, favoring rugged, rough men. *Real* men.

This one fit the bill to perfection.

Her gaze shifted to his hand. She noted the lack of a wedding band, but then a lot of guys didn't wear them. She never, ever got involved—even for one night—with men already in relationships.

Now, how to proceed?

When she looked back up to his face, she found him standing still, arms loose at his sides, feet slightly braced apart…staring at her with a very slight smile on his sexy mouth.

Terrific. They had a mutual attraction going on.

Playing coy, Ronnie slid her gaze away and faced the bar again, forearms folded on the counter. Awareness sizzled as she sensed his casual approach.

"Drinking alone?"

Mmm, that deep voice. So far, everything about him stirred her.

He kept a slight distance, not invading her space but still making his interest apparent.

Rubbing her thumb along the neck of the bottle, she glanced up at him. "Not if you join me."

Her invitation warmed those dark brown eyes. He settled on the stool beside her, turning slightly so that his thigh touched hers.

And just that, such a light touch, sent excitement coiling through her. As he ordered a cola and pulled-pork sandwich, she studied his profile: the masculine nose, sensual mouth, strong jaw, and high cheekbones. Oh, those darker-than-sin eyes and lush lashes...

His gaze cut her way. "Have you eaten?"

She lifted the beer. "Moved on to dessert." No, she wasn't a heavy drinker, but he wouldn't know that. Let him think what he wanted. She didn't care.

"New to the area?" he asked.

"Just passing through." Somehow she'd make that true. But what if he was a local? In the off chance Slick took the job tomorrow, she'd be in and around the area a lot—meaning she shouldn't complicate things with neighbors. She sipped her beer again, gauging how she'd ask, then settled on, "You work here as a painter?"

His mouth curled a little more. "No."

"Ah, somewhere else, then." Relieved, she let out a tense breath. "That's good."

He started to say something but asked instead, "Good because…?"

Ronnie waved a hand. "I don't want to start anything with the locals."

One brow cocked up. Eyes direct, he asked, "But you want to start something with me?"

She liked his confidence, the bold way he asked that, and she liked how he held her gaze. Why hedge? It was already getting late and the beer wasn't doing it for her. She dreaded the idea of sleeping alone. That was true for most nights, but as it sometimes happened, tonight was worse.

Tonight, memories plagued her. Horrid memories. She always fought them off the best she could, but some nights—like tonight—they wormed their way in. Company, along with extracurricular activity, would make them easier to deal with.

So she turned, sliding her knee along the inside of his and saying with suggestion, "I do. Something that could last the night?" Then she clarified, "*Only* through the night. What do you think?"

His attention roved over her, from her short pale hair in styled disarray, to the front of her sweater where her less than stellar boobs wouldn't impress a single soul, down her waist to her legs to her ankle boots. Those sinful eyes slowly rose back to her face. "There's a hotel a few miles down the road."

She knew that, because she'd rented a room there. "Perfect." Tipping up the beer, she finished it off and started to stand.

He grinned. "Mind if I eat first? It's been a long day."

Well. Well, *hell*. Here she was ready to rush out the door and he wanted to eat first?

Plopping her behind back on the plastic-covered stool and resting her elbows behind her on the bar, she waited as the steaming sandwich with a side of chips was set before him.

"You could get it to go," she suggested. "Eat it on the way, maybe?"

For an answer, he picked it up and took a big bite.

What. A. Jerk. Did she need a diversion this badly?

Her heart ached as she accepted the truth that, sadly, yes, she did.

She crossed her legs and swung a foot. "If I have to wait, you damn well better be worth it."

Nonchalance personified, he nodded. "I'll do my best."

Ronnie sighed out her frustration. She had the feeling his best would be pretty damn good.

JACK COULDN'T REMEMBER the last time he'd been this attracted to a woman...or when he'd had so much fun teasing her. The little beauty next to him was all but steaming, and still she wanted him.

A real boost to the ego.

And he wasn't at his best. He'd gotten a day off at the office, but he'd worked all morning on the yard, done a few roof repairs, and then painted two rooms. Hunger had driven him to Freddie's without showering, shaving, or changing into clean clothes first. Not his usual style.

Judging by *her* style, his present state of "worked all day on a rehab house" suited her. He cast another glance over at her and forced himself not to gulp his food. Petite women didn't usually turn him on, but God love her, she did.

She had this edgy style with platinum hair cut short

in the back but long in the front. The wispy bangs nearly hung in her eyes—soft gray eyes lined with kohl—until she ran her slender fingers through it, pushing it to the side. When she turned her head, it fell forward. No matter how it lay, she looked sexy as hell.

The pale blue sweater hugged her upper body, but not as tightly as those jeans hugged her trim little ass and crazy long legs. For a woman so small, she was put together really fine.

And she wanted him.

For *tonight*.

She wasn't local and probably wouldn't be around here again. Even knowing it was better that way, he couldn't deny the twinge of disappointment. He had a feeling he was going to enjoy her. A lot.

Suddenly she asked, "You're not involved, are you?"

"Romantically?" He took another massive bite. Freddie's had amazing sandwiches.

"Romantically, sexually, whatever. I don't want to step on any toes."

He swallowed. "Uninvolved on all counts." But he thought to ask, "You?" because he didn't trespass either.

"Free and clear." She fidgeted, toying with a dangling silver earring in her right ear. In her left she had a stud. Three fingers on her left hand sported silver rings, along with her thumb on her right.

Fascinating.

He watched her survey the bar, not with any real interest but just to track the movement of the party.

She had amazing skin. Peachy. Smooth. Natural skin, he thought, despite the loud eye makeup. Her brows were a medium brown, not that he needed to notice that to know she'd bleached her hair. Altogether, she gave off a confident, distinctive, sexy vibe.

He liked it. "What's your name?"

She immediately shook her head. "No names." Bringing her attention back to him, she scowled. "Hurry up already."

"What's the rush?"

Tucking in her chin, she gave him a killing glare. "Look, if you're not interested—"

"I'm interested." Jack shrugged. "I'm also hungry after working all day. Will five more minutes hurt?"

She seemed to be debating it, then with a deliberately flippant attitude, she said, "Whatever," and slipped off the barstool.

For a second, Jack thought she was leaving and he had to fight the urge to catch her arm, to dissuade her, to… convince her to stay.

Since when did he have to *convince* women? Not for years.

When she merely dug some change from her pocket, he relaxed. Sort of. But he did eat a little faster.

"The jukebox work?"

Jack nodded, swallowed. "But it's all country music."

"Of course it is." Wending her way around the crowds until she finally reached the old-fashioned jukebox, she studied the songs, slipped in the change, and smiled as music joined the din of conversation.

Jack studied her body as she started back toward him, the graceful way she moved while still being very aware of the press of bodies around her. She touched no one as she slipped this way and that, not even a brush of arms. Her sweater barely met the waistband of her jeans, and twice he got a glimpse of her smooth, pale stomach.

Fuck the food. He'd had enough.

Standing, he put some money on the bar and waited for her. If he wasn't careful, he'd get half hard just imagining what was to come.

Right before she reached him, someone said, "Hey, Jack. The house is looking good."

He gave an offhand "thanks," not even sure who'd said it. Everyone around here knew him, his brother, and his mother, and they were all friendly.

She stopped, her made-up eyes flaring. "Jack?"

He didn't have a problem with names, so he held out a hand. "Jack Crews. Feel like sharing now?"

Instead she slapped his hand away and surged forward in one big step, going on her tiptoes to glare up into his face. "You're supposed to be slick."

"I am?" This close, he could see her individual lashes and he detected the faint perfume of flowers—an odd contrast to her sharp appeal.

"Yes!" Dropping back, she gestured at him. "You are not supposed to be messy or rugged."

With no idea what was going on, Jack folded his arms and leaned back on the bar. "Is it against the rules if I'm all of the above?"

She appeared to be sawing her teeth together. "Thanks for nothing." Turning on her heel, she started out the door.

What the hell? Jack bolted after her, following her through the door and out to the walkway. "Where are you going?"

To the tune of furious stomping, she said, "The hotel."

Were they still on, then? Unsure, he offered, "I have a truck."

"Alone."

Yeah, that was plain enough.

He easily caught up to walk beside her. "So…that's it? You changed your mind and I won't see you again?"

She muttered something low and mean.

Jack leaned closer. "What?"

Halting, she stared down at her feet a moment, and when she raised her face, she looked *almost* calm again. "I'll see you tomorrow as a matter of fact." Her smile could wound. "At your office."

Jack still didn't get it.

"We have an appointment first thing."

"I have an appointment with Ron Ashford."

She held out her arms. "That would be me. And if you don't mind, I'd like to forget about this. Tonight, I mean. That we might have…" Lips compressing, she shook her head. "Just forget it." And with that she continued on her way, her behind swishing, her legs eating up the pavement.

Very slowly, Jack smiled. Forget about it? Like hell.

And damn it, now he *was* getting hard.

OF COURSE SHE hadn't slept. It had turned into one of *those* nights, the nights where demons visited and her skin itched while her thoughts traveled back in time to moments better forgotten. As if. Some things burned into the brain, branded there forever.

Sex usually helped and had the added benefit of giving her a warm body to snuggle against. Not being alone meant she wasn't as vulnerable, even if the person with her was a stranger.

But after the mix-up with Jack Crews, she didn't feel like searching out new game.

She probably could have found an agreeable man. After all, when it came to sex, most men were absurdly easy.

The problem was that after her high expectations for Jack, no one else would have measured up. A man like him would be a hard act to follow.

Now she was bleary-eyed, grouchy—and running twenty minutes late. Ronnie locked her jaw as she stared up the stone steps to the business. No one had told her she'd have to climb. She shook her fist at the imposing steps, put one foot forward—and someone beeped.

She swiveled around to see a superhunk in a red Mustang smiling at her. Oh, wow. Now if only she'd met *him* last night—

Through the driver's side window, he asked, "You going up to Mustang Transport?"

Ronnie nodded. "Who had the bright idea to build it *up there*? And why isn't there a sign warning people? What if I was old, or physically challenged in some way?"

His grin widened. A lethal grin that made her tingle almost as much as Jack had. "If you drive on around the bend, you'll see a road that leads you right up to the door."

She propped her hands on her hips. "Well, a sign saying so would be nice."

"Yeah, that's what my wife said, too."

His wife? Ugh. She dropped her hands. "She'd be right. Thanks for the tip."

Ronnie turned away, heading for her Chevy hatchback. Next to the Mustang, it looked pretty drab.

"I could drive you up," he offered. "I'm headed there myself."

She stalled with her back still to him. Her shoulders

might've cringed a little. *He's in a Mustang. Heading to Mustang Transport.*

Well, hell.

With a huff she faced him. "You're the brother, aren't you?"

With a grin that'd do wicked things to a woman's imagination, he confessed, "Guilty."

I just bet you are. She looked at her car, then his. "If I rode with you—"

"I'll show you where to go, then bring you back when you're ready. No biggie." He surprised her by getting out and circling around to the passenger side, where he opened the door and then waited for her.

Presuming she'd do as he asked.

Why not? Ronnie strode forward with a purpose—then paused again when she saw a gigantic dog sitting in the small back seat, eyeing her. "Uh…"

"Howler's friendly."

Since the dog's tongue was already out, lapping toward her in anticipation of giving her a wet lick, she believed him. "I love animals." She got into the seat, turning sideways to coo at the big dog.

His tail wagged so hard that it hit the seat with a loud thumping drumbeat.

Ronnie laughed. "Well, aren't you a sweetheart." She stroked his head, around his long ears and neck. "Is he smiling at me?"

The brother got back behind the wheel. "Probably. He digs the chicks."

"Chicks?" she repeated, her tone soft with warning.

Not that he took heed. He put the car back in gear and drove forward. "I'm Brodie, by the way."

Honest to God, she just didn't have the energy this morning to spar with a guy like him. "Jack's brother."

"You know Jack?"

"Not really, but I have a meeting with him this morning."

His brows climbed up. "You're Ron Ashford?"

"Guilty," she said, mocking him. "Ronnie to my friends."

"So why does the appointment calendar say *Ron*?"

Shrugging, she explained, "I use Ron for business contracts, so bozos don't dismiss me out of hand just because I'm female. Mostly I go by Ronnie."

Not in the least insulted by her bozo comment, he asked, "Not Veronica, huh?"

Some of her warmth iced over, but she hopefully hid it with a smile. "Well, Veronica is my given name."

"Used only by family?"

She gave a stiff nod. *Family...and reporters.*

That sexy grin of his returned. "Jack is going to be surprised."

No, he wouldn't, since he'd met her last night, but she saw no reason to clue in the ape. Already he'd turned the bend and drove up a road that circled around behind the business. Off to the side, Ronnie saw a looping track, then thick woods. The position of the business put them atop a rise overlooking the small town and guaranteed privacy from the rest of their neighbors.

She liked it.

In the light of day. She imagined at night it'd only feel dark, isolated, and creepy.

"Here we are." Brodie pulled right up to a door and turned off the purring engine. "I'm running late, so that means you are, too."

"Had a rough morning?" she asked him.

"More like a late night. Not that I'm complaining." He grinned with meaning. "You?"

"Late night, yes. Not so lucky with the reason why."

"Ah, too bad." He gave her a commiserating look. "Since it *was* something else, is there a way I can help?"

She almost choked. *If you weren't married, then yes, you could help.* But no, actually he couldn't. He was also Jack's brother, and he worked at the business.

His brows lifted. "Is your silence a yes or a no?"

"No—but thank you."

He nodded but didn't pry beyond that. "There should be coffee inside," he said, as if that'd make everything better. He started around to her door.

To do the gentlemanly thing? Ronnie gave the dog one last stroke and stepped out on her own. She would not start this meeting as the "little helpless lady."

Brodie didn't comment, he just pulled her seat forward and unfastened the dog. Howler unfolded himself from the car, long limbs going everywhere as he gained the ground and then stretched.

"How in the world does he even fit?" she asked, eyeing the small seat in back.

From some distance away, a deep voice said, "He considers it cozy."

It was a voice she recognized.

Slowly, Ronnie straightened and looked toward the office. There stood Jack, arms crossed over his chest, one shoulder propped against the glass entry door, his dark gaze direct and oddly suspicious.

Today he'd dressed closer to what she'd expected, in black slacks and a button-down striped shirt—but he wasn't *too* buttoned up, not with the collar open and the sleeves rolled to his elbows. Though a cool morning breeze played with his hair, it remained neat, and she could see from here that he was freshly shaved.

God help her, he looked even more devastating.

Resisting the urge to fuss with her hair, Ronnie rounded the car and started toward him. "Sorry I'm late. No one told me to drive around past the sign to enter."

Jack's gaze didn't waver. "I see you met Brodie."

Why was he almost growling? She wasn't *that* late.

Moving up beside her, Brodie asked, "You two know each other?"

She said, "Not really."

At the same time, Jack replied, "You could say that."

Alarm shot through her. Narrowing her eyes in warning, Ronnie turned to Brodie. "I ran into him last night. Very *briefly*."

"Yeah?" Brodie looked more curious by the second. "Where was that?"

"Freddie's," Jack explained.

"Ah." After his gaze bounced back and forth between them a few times, Brodie grinned. "Am I missing something?"

"As a matter of fact—"

"No," she interrupted, "you're not." Then with more vinegar, she asked, "Will we have this meeting in the yard, then?"

Without a word, Jack pressed the door open with one hand and waited for her to enter. He didn't leave her much room to get around him, and because she thought he did that deliberately, she got irate.

Her being irate was never a good thing. Couple it with lack of sleep and unrequited lust for his very fine body…

Pasting on a fake smile, Ronnie said, "Why, thank

you," as she moved past him. Very closely. Close enough that the side of her body brushed all the way across the front of his.

She felt him go still, heard his inhalation—and then the dog nearly plowed her over as he shoved in past her. Ronnie tripped forward but righted herself quickly.

"Sorry," Brodie said, still sounding amused. "Howler isn't the patient sort."

Jack still stood at the door, staring at her.

She stared back, trying to look smug so he wouldn't know how he affected her.

"Coffee?"

They both answered Brodie with an affirmative, and finally Jack stepped forward. "Through here." Pressing open an inner door, he waited as if in expectation.

"Thanks." This time she passed with plenty of space between them. Her heart could only take so much.

He closed the door and went behind a desk. "Have a seat, Ms. Ashford."

If he wanted a belated business tone, fine, she could handle that. It would probably make things easier for her. She crossed her legs and sat back in her seat. "Thank you, Mr. Crews."

Then he blew it by saying, "Your hair is different today."

Yeah, it was. Without any sleep to motivate her she'd only finger-combed it after her shower and let it dry naturally, meaning it hung in chunky layers to the side. "My hair is always different, depending on my mood."

Sitting forward, he folded his arms on the desk. "You look tired."

"Not at all," she lied with credible conviction. "I slept like a baby."

That dark, sensual gaze flicked over her, taking in her loose black sweater, then her jeans, and finally her boots.

His eyes met hers and he growled softly, "I didn't."

Damn, those two gruff words nearly melted her. Had he lain awake thinking of her, of what they might have done?

She knew she had.

Brodie shouldered open the door, three cups of coffee balanced in his hands. "Howler already a-t-e and now he's sleeping, so we should have a few minutes."

Jack took two cups from him and handed one to Ronnie. "Cream or sugar?"

"Black is fine." She glanced at Brodie. "You spelled that...why?"

"Because the dog is alert to anything that has to do with e-a-t-i-n-g. And his hearing is damn good." He drew a long sip and sighed. "At least he doesn't like coffee."

"Hmm." Ronnie wasn't sure if he was teasing or not. "So if I mentioned, say, a snack—"

"Don't."

The sound of claws scrambling on the floor came ahead of the big dog and a second later he skidded in, ears up, alert, his gaze darting to each of them expectantly.

Jack blew out a breath, opened a drawer, and pulled out a dog treat. He tossed it over Ronnie's head and into the hallway, but the dog moved so fast that he caught it.

Brodie said to Jack, "She's the type that has to test it, huh?"

And Jack, as if he knew her type, replied, "Apparently so."

Dazed by how fast that had all happened, Ronnie glared at both men. "Don't you—?"

"Shh," Brodie said, lowering his voice. "Of course we f-e-e-d him. You can see he's healthy. But to his mind, it's never enough."

"That's ridiculous—"

"It's a long story," Jack explained. "I'll tell you all about it another time."

She didn't intend to be with him long enough to hear a story. Though, damn it, now she was curious.

"The short version is that the dog was mistreated before Brodie got him, and now he's a little spoiled."

"Just a little," Brodie agreed.

This wasn't going at all as Ronnie had planned. She'd wanted to come in, state the parameters of the job, convince Jack he didn't want it, and then be on her way, confident of the fact that she'd spared herself.

She hadn't counted on meeting Jack in a different setting first, but she had.

She hadn't counted on wanting him, but boy, she did.

She definitely hadn't counted on liking them both, but as each second passed, that's what happened.

"Well, hell."

CHAPTER TWO

JACK COULDN'T STOP looking at her—and thinking.

About what might have happened last night if she hadn't learned his name.

What her trim body might look like under those clothes.

How her mouth and skin would taste and feel…

He almost groaned. It was like being offered a gift—then being told he couldn't unwrap it while it remained close to taunt him.

Even now, with her muttering to herself and looking more cross than usual, he still wanted her. That said something, since he was discovering that she wore that disgruntled look more often than not.

Maybe if he hadn't known her initial plans for him. Maybe if her frank honesty hadn't already appealed to him. Maybe if he hadn't already thought to have her—then he could put things in perspective. But it was too late for that.

Insane.

He'd never been a damned masochist, never enjoyed insults and barbs. He couldn't say he actually enjoyed them now.

But he did enjoy her. Every shift of expression, the way her slender body moved.

He imagined it moving under him and…

Clearing his throat, Jack asked her, "Something wrong?"

She ran her fingers through her hair, flipping it to the other side. "No." Abruptly she sat forward and drew a paper from her purse.

Not a briefcase. No, not for this lady. Her purse was more like a colorful bohemian sack, big and shapeless, which meant the paper was a little crumpled.

"Here's the job." She shoved the paper across the desk toward him. "The thing is, my bosses think I need someone to escort me to different pickups. But I don't."

"Why do they think that?" Brodie asked.

She flagged a hand, as if it didn't matter. "A few misunderstandings during exchanges."

"Like?" Jack prompted.

"Different things."

Jack frowned. "Be specific."

With an exaggerated eye roll, she said, "There was… an incident recently. The seller had more than one interested buyer, but I got there first."

"And?" Brodie now stared at her, eyebrows lifted.

"And I outran the jerk. End of story."

What the— "Outran…?" Jack asked.

"In my car." She huffed. "The important part is that I handled it. But now my bosses have the mistaken idea that the job requires someone more badass than me. And it doesn't. They pay well, but you really wouldn't like it. If you want, I can let them know that you're passing on the offer."

Jack stared at her, trying to absorb that diatribe enough to dissect the pertinent bits.

Brodie, no doubt equally thrown, gulped the rest of his coffee. After setting his cup on the desk, he turned his finger in the air. "Rewind a bit. Bosses? As in more than one?"

"Twins. Very eccentric. Goth-like." Her frustration pulsed in the air. "Collectors of *oddities*." She said the last with dramatic effect, as if doing her utmost to scare them off.

But Jack saw things other than her determination. Like how her fingers curled around the arms of the chair, so tightly her knuckles strained. And how the pulse in her throat beat a little too quickly.

Why fight working with him when she'd already made her attraction clear? He had a feeling she was apprehensive. About him. Of complications.

Maybe more.

Leaving it to Brodie to get a few answers, Jack sat back to look over the terms of the offer. He bit back a whistle at the hourly wage. Nice.

"I've dealt with some oddities," Brodie said. "Murderabilia, to be exact."

"Murderabilia?" she asked, with obvious surprise.

"Nasty business."

"Yes," she agreed with alacrity, latching on to his comment like a junkyard dog to a bone. "This would be similar, I assume. Very nasty. In fact, sometimes it's even dangerous."

Jack looked up. Their gazes met.

Her stubborn jaw tightened. "I'm completely familiar with it, of course, so I don't need any help, but they—"

"Your twin Goth bosses?" Brodie supplied, his humor barely veiled.

The way she'd described the men *was* humorous. He already had an image in his mind of two scrawny identical dudes draped in black and wearing eyeliner, reverently admiring a pregnant frog or something even more comically odd.

Bristling, Ronnie stood, flattened her hands on the desktop and leaned toward Jack. Storm clouds darkened her gray eyes to pewter and a wash of rose tinged her cheekbones. "Reject the offer and I'll be on my way."

His attention moved to her mouth, so close to his. An invitation? Another taunt? He breathed in the scent of warm womanly skin, the fresh outdoors, and citrusy shampoo.

Hanging on to his civility, he ruthlessly tamped down the lust and, ignoring her request, passed the paper to Brodie.

Huffing, she spun away, arms crossed tight, and glared.

Making his casual comfort a stark contrast to her antagonism, Jack sat back in his seat. "So your bosses want two badasses on the job?"

As if trying to figure out a puzzle, she studied his face, gave up on her anger, and dropped her arms. Silver bracelets on her left wrist jangled. Today she wore the rings on different fingers, but included multiple earrings in her ears.

"That was their wording, not mine." She'd tried to sound more composed, he'd give her that, but the indignation, and more, seeped through.

"They consider you a badass?"

Jack waited for her explosion at Brodie's question, but it didn't come. Apparently she saved all that sizzling heat for him.

"Drake and Drew know I'm more than capable of handling anything that comes up."

"And yet…" Brodie looked up at her. "You're here."

A flash of pain crossed her face, and damned if Jack didn't feel the discomfort in his chest.

Leaving his seat, he circled the desk and propped a hip on the edge. It brought him closer to her and also blocked her from Brodie's view. Gently, because he could see this mattered to her, he said, "Give me an example of what comes up?"

Shrugging one narrow shoulder, she said, "People try to ditch after they get the payment, without turning over the goods."

"We've dealt with that," Brodie murmured, back to perusing the particulars of the offer—or at least pretending to. It was a single sheet of paper, not a tome. Neither he nor Brodie were insensitive to distress, so Jack assumed Brodie had seen the same things he had—belligerence to cover insecurity, determination to conquer fear. Strength but also vulnerability.

Unlike Brodie, who was now married, Jack's attentiveness went beyond curiosity and compassion. He wanted her and by God, he'd figure out the quickest, easiest route to get them there.

Her chin lifted. "I was shot at once."

"Me, too," Brodie said, without much inflection.

Jack almost laughed. Ronnie was doing her best to turn them off the deal, but she didn't realize that Brodie took danger in stride, or that her efforts merely sharpened his interest.

Her jaw worked, her lips compressing as she tried to decide the next tack to take.

The concentrated expression amused Jack.

Until she said to Brodie, "Okay, sure, so you can handle yourself. I already knew that. But your time is mostly taken so the offer is for Jack."

Brodie looked up in surprise, then barked a laugh.

For his part, Jack locked his jaw to cover his irritation.

"That's funny?" she asked, her heavily made-up eyes narrowing.

"You think Jack can't handle shit?" Brodie still laughed, but managed to say, "Oh, honey, don't let the polish fool you. Jack's downright deadly when he needs to be.

For the love of… "What my brother means is that the threat of violence doesn't send me running, as you seem to think it would."

"Not *exactly* what I meant," Brodie countered, "but it'll do." He leaned forward to put the paper back on the desk. "I say go for it. Pay's good. Commitment isn't unreasonable." He eyed Ronnie. "Company might be a bit sketchy, but I figure you can—"

Jack gave him a shove that almost took him out of his chair. "You'll have to excuse Brodie. He's an ass."

Ronnie didn't appear to be listening to any of it. She dropped back to lean on the wall, her disappointment as loud as a scream. "You're accepting the job?"

"I'm considering it."

At that, she brightened. "What's the deciding factor?"

So she could sway him to the negative? To hell with that. He wanted her, but unlike his ape of a brother, he could and would handle things with a little more class, a touch of finesse. Since she'd already spelled it out last night, he knew that she wanted him, too, and that gave him extra confidence.

"C'mon," she said, impatient as ever. "What would it take for you to say no?"

Jack wasn't used to women rejecting him so thoroughly. He definitely wasn't used to it the morning after being propositioned.

Staring into her incredible eyes, the gray irises enhanced with a striation of darker hues, he wondered what they'd look like without all the makeup. If he stripped away her layers of clothes, washed away that painted veneer, and pleasured her until only a warm, naked woman was left... Would she be just as appealing?

He had a feeling she'd be even more so.

He casually straightened. "I want a trial run."

Distrust sparkled in her eyes. "What does that mean?"

"You pick a job and we'll handle it together." His gaze skimmed down her body, but only for a nanosecond. Doing his best to bank the heat simmering to the surface, he added, "Just to see how we fit."

Brodie choked, but Jack ignored him, his gaze never wavering from hers. He admired the way she didn't blink...even when her cheeks warmed. Even when her nostrils slightly flared. And her lips trembled.

"All right, fine," she burst out, throwing up her arms. "Is that it?"

Not even close. "I want to meet your bosses." Something troubled her, and if these supposedly Goth-like grown men were the cause—

She went from reluctantly agreeable to stiff with umbrage in a heartbeat. "Your contact with them would be through me." Her thumb landed against her own chest.

Jack couldn't help but look where it pressed directly between her modest breasts. At least until she dropped her hand.

"Ultimately they'd be my employers—so I want to meet them." He held out his hand. "Do we have a deal?"

The seconds ticked by while she considered him, a

dozen different scenarios flickering across her expressive face with obvious calculation. Finally, she asked, "Are you free to do the job today?"

He wasn't presently, but he could rearrange. "Sure."

A triumphant smile put a dimple in her cheek as she fit her small hand into his for a single firm pump. "Deal. We'll leave in half an hour."

RONNIE DID HER best not to gloat with her new plan. Mr. Sexy, as she was starting to think of him, would soon be over the idea of accepting the offer. She couldn't have asked for a better pickup to change his mind.

Plus, she now knew it had to be today. If she was forced to see him again, she'd cave in to the ever growing need building like a small volcano inside her.

She wanted him. Now that she'd seen two sides of him, the scruffy worker and the polished businessman, it was worse. She liked how he was with his brother. She loved how he was with Howler. She enjoyed verbally sparring with him, and she was *almost* relieved that he hadn't yet given up on the job—despite how she'd pitched it.

God Almighty, she wanted him *bad*. He infuriated her, and she thought about squeezing close to him. He smiled in mockery, and she wanted to lick that smile off his mouth. He stayed calm in the face of her irritation, and oh, how she wanted to rile him.

Worse than those physical reactions, when he joked with his brother, she had the urge to join in. When he spoke reasonably to her…she wanted to be reasonable back.

These days, she wasn't reasonable with *anyone*. Being unreasonable kept people from getting too close.

But…the way he looked at her really got to her. It was

as if he saw *her*, not just the person she presented, like he
could somehow read her past and understand her hang-
ups. It was both scary as hell and oddly sexy.

He'd be her match in bed, she sensed that much.
He could play all elegant and urbane, but she had his
number—Jack Crews would be 100 percent raw man
during sex.

Ronnie shivered despite the warmth of the car.

"Cold?"

More like so aroused she had to struggle not to squirm
in her seat. "I'm fine."

Sitting beside him in his *very* awesome yellow Mustang was a bit torturous. He was *right there*, close enough
that she felt the heat from his body. Near enough that,
when she drew a nice deep breath, she could pick up his
spicy scent.

She had the terrible suspicion that it was him, not co-
logne, that smelled so damn good. It was enticing enough
that her toes kept curling in her boots.

To keep herself from groaning, she needlessly repeated the directions to their destination. In just a few
more minutes, they'd arrive.

She couldn't wait to see how he handled things, and
to see how quickly he rejected the job.

If he did.

He *had* to.

So why was she already thinking that maybe, just
maybe, it wouldn't be bad to work with him?

*Because you're thinking with parts south of your
brain, that's why.*

Clearly, it wasn't only men who were sometimes ruled
by their bodies. Her body was making every attempt to
change her mind.

Traitor.

Every thirty seconds or so, Jack glanced at her. She'd almost gotten used to it. That is, if a woman could get used to sitting beside breathing, smoking testosterone.

After yet another glance—and a small smile—he asked, "You want to tell me anything about where we're going and what we're retrieving?"

No, she didn't. But so far he'd been completely agreeable, doing whatever she directed without fuss, so she supposed she could spare a few details. "We're meeting a familiar seller at the bar she runs. It'll be a piece of cake." For her, at least. Not so much for him.

"It's a woman we're meeting?"

Not just any woman, but Marge. Ronnie smiled in anticipation. "Yeah, so?"

"I figured you'd pick someone difficult. A problem to be handled."

And he thought he could handle any woman? What an egotistical jackass. It was all she could do not to laugh, but instead she put on a serious face. "You think women can't be problematic?"

"Of course they can, but unless she's a beast of a woman, I figure—based off everything you've said—that you would do all right on your own."

Ronnie refused to let his confidence in her ability soften her. Yes, it was nice that he acknowledged she might have some skill. And yes, it was extra nice to be respected on her word alone.

Because, seriously, he didn't know her. She'd done some boasting but he hadn't seen her in action. Yet.

Unless you counted her many fits of anger.

Ronnie sighed and forced herself to focus. She was fighting for her future here. If he didn't retreat, he'd try to take over her job and she'd be damned before she ever came under another man's thumb. "Ah, so you wanted me to put you up against a goon? Maybe some dude with brawling experience and death in his eyes?"

Jack laughed. "You say that with such relish, like you'd love to see me get my ass handed to me."

Actually, she didn't. She liked his face, perfect in its masculine arrangement with the strong nose, the low brows, and high cheekbones, and didn't want to see it rearranged. Not that she'd let that happen, but still… "So I know your brother handles himself well. The twins studied up on both of you before sending me on this useless errand."

She almost winced. Would he think she meant *he* was useless? Even she wouldn't go that far in her effort to turn him away. A glance showed he didn't look insulted, only curious, so she continued.

"I know all about the trouble Brodie ran into working for Therman Ritter." She also knew Brodie was exclusive to Ritter, which took him out of the running altogether, leaving only Jack.

A shame, since she and Brodie had hit it off, without all the chemistry mucking up her decision-making skills.

Not that it mattered really, because she didn't need either of them. She didn't need anyone. Eventually she'd prove it to everyone…herself included.

"It's public news," he said. "Not a secret."

"What about you, though? Yeah, I know your brother talked you up, but that's what brothers do, right?" A guess on her part, since she only had a sister and she couldn't imagine Skylar ever sparing her a true compliment.

Jack didn't take the bait. Instead of getting annoyed,

he grinned in a way that ramped up all that overwhelming sex appeal. "Believe me, if you hadn't already been hostile, Brodie would've run me through the wringer. He probably would've recounted every black eye I've gotten since grade school."

Oh man, when he piled on the down-to-earth charm, it did crazy things to her insides. Her brain skipped right past *I need to get rid of him* and headed into *Could it really hurt to get him naked?*

Not good. It *would* hurt, damn it.

It'd hurt if he stuck around and took over, as slick men like him always tried to do. And it'd hurt...if he didn't stay. God, sometimes she was just too pathetic.

She blew out a breath, determined to stick with her original plan. Working alone. And that meant, Jack and all his appeal had to go. "I wasn't hostile."

"That's a joke, right?"

She, of course, couldn't resist the bait. "So big brother had to jump to your defense, huh?" Even to her own ears, that sounded way too snide. She tried to moderate her tone to mere curiosity. "Does he always do that? Play protector?"

"Of course." Unfazed by her nastiness, Jack said, "He's the big brother," as if that explained it all.

She was still trying to comprehend what type of man made such an admission when Jack spoke again.

"You should know, younger brothers are the same. I've had Brodie's back more than a time or two."

No, that absolutely was *not* jealousy creeping around her heart, making it feel so damned heavy. What did she care if he had a good relationship with his brother? She *didn't.* Just because she and her sister had never gotten along...

"Turn here." Thank God the need for directions gave her something to do other than look inward. "You can park at the curb, just make sure you keep plenty of space from the motorcycles. They get really pissy if anyone hems them in."

Giving a low whistle, Jack took in the seedy area as he pulled into an empty space right in front. "You don't mean this broken-down building is a running bar?"

"Sure it is." Seeing the establishment as he might, Ronnie took in the half-painted brick facade. Puke-green paint, faded and dirty, had been haphazardly slapped around the blacked-out windows on the upper level. A slightly less pukey shade of dark, dull pink covered most of the bottom half. Grime-coated windows, one balancing a rusted, rickety air conditioner, hid the interior, but the black metal front door, dented in numerous places, stood open to allow cigarette smoke and other noxious odors to drift out.

There was no charming jukebox spinning a country tune, no happy din of conversation from friends and neighbors. All a passerby could hear was the low drone of drunken whispers and threatening connivance.

Two men slouching outside eyed the Mustang with flat, indecipherable gazes.

Hmm. In her haste to be rid of him, she hadn't considered the possible hazard to his car. It was such a sweet ride, she had sudden reservations. No way could she do that to him. It wasn't his fault her bosses wanted to hire him.

Damn her conscience.

"Tell you what," she said, unbuckling her seat belt. "You wait here and I'll take care of business. We'll figure out another job that we can do togeth—"

The sound of his door closing drew her attention and she looked up to see him walking in an unhurried, casual stride around the hood of the car.

The men who'd been watching became more attentive. *What the hell does Jack think he's doing?*

He opened her door. "You ready?"

Blinking up at him, Ronnie took in his styled hair, the crisp shirt, the nice trousers. He stood out in the worst possible way—an easy target.

She frowned. "Didn't you hear what I said?"

"I'm not letting you go in there without me," he replied in a low voice, "and I sure as hell won't leave you sitting out here alone, so…" He gave her a look and stressed, "Let's go."

A rush of anger wiped out her concern. Mostly. It took her a second of fumbling to get her big purse off the floor. In the process, she nearly dumped it, which wouldn't have been great considering she had things inside that she didn't want Jack, or anyone else, to know about.

Finally getting the strap securely across her body, she gave the car one last fond look, wondering if it'd ever again be the same, then stood to square off with him.

Even for a single trial-run job, he had to know that she was the one in charge. Not him.

"Later," she snarled, matching his low tone, "we'll discuss this idiotic idea you have that you can allow or disallow *anything* I do. But until then, just stay quiet and let me handle things."

The corner of his mouth twitched. "Yes, ma'am." He locked the car doors and gestured for her to lead.

Still, she noticed that he positioned himself to her side, a barrier to the two loitering men. She also noticed that he stared them in the eyes, his gaze daring and full of warning.

What. The. Hell.

Was he *trying* to start a brawl? She brought her elbow back into his ribs and hissed, "Stop that."

But damn it, he caught her arm and then didn't let go and she could either let him get away with it or cause a scene in a place where scenes were best avoided.

Worse than being outmaneuvered by him, though, was the fact that his hand was big. And hot. Power seemed to emanate from him, a raw type of strength that enveloped her in the same comfort as a security blanket.

Dangerous.

Waaaay the hell more dangerous than the thugs inside the bar who eyed them up and down, measuring their worth.

Ready to wrap up this ill-conceived plan, Ronnie made her way straight to the bar where Higgs handed out drinks.

A big man, both in height and girth, he could intimidate most people with a single look from his faded blue eyes. He kept numerous weapons behind the bar, including a knife, shotgun, and a clichéd wooden baseball bat. His brows and scruffy beard were brown, and she'd never seen him without a do-rag tied around his head. He changed them out like some men switched up neckties. It was Higgs's one and only fashion statement.

She guessed him to be midforties, knew him to be rattlesnake mean, and had, oddly enough, found in him an ally.

She slid onto an empty barstool between two slouching men, which forced Jack to release her. Leaning forward, she called, "Hey, Higgs. How goes it?"

He looked up and smiled, showing even white teeth. "Slow and steady. You?"

Nodding back at Jack, who loomed very close behind her, she said, "Training day, so it's a grind." *Take that, Jack.*

Higgs laughed. "You want a drink, girl?"

"Never on the job, but thanks." In a place like this, a smart person kept her wits razor sharp. "Marge around? She's expecting me."

"In her office. You can go on back."

"Thanks." She slid back off the stool and made full body contact with Jack.

The butthead didn't move.

His lower chest pressed her shoulder blades, and his thighs pressed her butt. Standing still, soaking in this one horribly timed moment of pleasure, Ronnie registered the differences in their sizes.

She glanced over her shoulder. "Wanna back it up?"

"Not really, no." But he did.

He didn't go far, just enough that she could catch her breath and get her brain functioning again. And still she hesitated.

"What are we waiting for?"

Shaking her head, Ronnie leaned back into the bar. "Hey, Higgs, there's a very sweet yellow Mustang outside. If anyone touches it, I'm going to be really pissed."

"Yours?" he asked.

"Same as," she replied, because that'd bring about quicker compliance.

"Consider it safe, then."

"You're the best, Higgs." Now *she* took *Jack's* arm—and she couldn't help noticing that his wrist was as thick as her biceps. Also hot. With a soft sprinkling of hair…

Stop it, Ronnie. Really, she didn't need to notice every little thing about him. So he was hot. Big deal. She'd known other sexy men. None like him, but still... She growled at her own distraction. "This way."

Leading Jack through the smoky bar, she ignored the blatant stares of curiosity and fervently hoped he did as well. This would not be a good time to mean-mug any-one.

Few people ever made it past the kitchen, but Ronnie was the exception since she did business with Marge. The hall was dark and narrow, hiding some of the more repulsive stains on the floor. The smell of the perpetually out-of-order bathroom assaulted her nostrils. Just beyond the ancient pay phone, she saw the closed wooden door with a peephole. "Stay quiet."

Jack said again, "Yes, ma'am."

If he "ma'amed" Marge, no doubt Marge would feed him his teeth. After she played with him, that is. Marge was as lecherous as they came.

And...there went her conscience again, pricking and prodding her determination.

A little late, but Ronnie finally admitted to herself that she'd overreacted by bringing him here. True, it'd be expedient, but there were other ways that'd cause him less embarrassment and be less of a threat to his person.

So she'd have to suffer him a little longer? He wasn't *that* bad. Eventually he would turn down the job, she felt sure of that.

Extremes like this weren't needed.

Relieved by her own decision, she turned to face him—and had to look way up. He was just so glori-ously big.

Of course, he was looking back down at her, too, and

they stood so close together, she almost forgot what she wanted to say. "Jack…"

He smiled.

"That damned dimple is overkill," she grumbled.

His brows climbed up. "Am I supposed to understand that?"

The door opening behind them cut off any reply she might've made. A very pissed-off person stormed out. Before Ronnie could blink, Jack had her behind him so only he caught the hard brush of a shoulder as the man plowed past.

Normally she'd have taken his protectiveness as an insult, because she really could take care of herself. She'd proven that plenty of times in her not-so-rosy past. But now, well, coming from Jack it just felt nice. Not arrogant as much as considerate. After all, he *was* a hell of a lot of bigger than her.

Marge's crackling laughter trailed the disgruntled guy, followed by her succinct "follow him," which meant yet another man trailed out.

As this one passed, he said back to Marge, "You have company."

Marge appeared at the door. "Ronnie Ashford, back for more?" Then her gaze bounced over to Jack, and her brows went so high they took the wrinkles from her eyes and drove them into her forehead. "Well, well. What have you brought me?"

CHAPTER THREE

JACK SAW THROUGH her ruse right away. She'd planned
this little field trip, but now had regrets. *Too late, Ronnie.* He'd let it play out and hope that, once they both
left hale and hearty, she'd have a little more faith in him.

Ronnie sat in a chair, arms crossed, long legs crossed,
eyebrows almost crossed, too.

Marge mostly ignored her as she circled Jack, once,
twice. She trailed talon-shaped red fingernails along his
arm.

Marge Mayer was quite the character. Six feet tall and
wearing heels, she looked Jack in the eye. Wide shoulders over a massive rack tapered to a nipped-in waist and
flared out again in ample hips, all emphasized by a low
cut, body-hugging red dress.

Jack had noticed all that when she'd first appeared in
the doorway. Since then, he'd kept his gaze strictly on
her face, especially with the way she sized him up like
a prime steak.

She probably wasn't more than fifty, but he sensed it
had been a hard fifty, leaving creases carved in an otherwise striking face. Her hair, dyed an unnatural shade
of strawberry blonde, did nothing to soften her features.
Her application of makeup wasn't as precise as Ronnie's,
making it look more garish. Lipstick bled into lip lines

and her fake lashes were so thick and long, he wondered how she could blink.

As she circled behind him, her boobs brushed along his back.

"Do you have it?" Ronnie asked, bristling with impatience, and maybe a touch of annoyance, too.

"What's the rush?"

"Getting late, that's all. I have other things to do today."

"It's on the way." Marge's hand boldly stroked over his butt, ending with a pat as she said, "You're a day early, or I'd have had it on hand."

Jack stepped out of her reach and turned to face her. Without saying a word, he drew a line, ending the nonsense.

Marge stared him in the eyes, only slightly deterred, then cut her gaze to Ronnie. "You'll leave him here."

Curious to see how she'd react, Jack held silent.

"No," Ronnie said, the word sharp, bit off between her teeth. "I won't."

Propping a hip on her desk, Marge smiled. "Why? Does he matter to you?"

Good question. Jack watched the way tension gripped Ronnie's body, how she struggled to keep her expression impassive. He'd give her points for a credible poker face, but he knew better. Marge and her bully boys might buy into the act, but he didn't.

Beneath the sardonic indifference, panic edged forward. He saw it in her eyes, in the subtle shifting of her hand on her purse.

Deciding to spare her, he opened his mouth—

And Ronnie snorted. "Actually, he matters to the

brothers. They hired him as the driver. You already know I prefer to work alone."

Admiration took him by surprise. *Good cover, Ronnie.*

It definitely *was* a cover. Somehow, he already knew she wasn't mercenary enough to sacrifice him—even if that had been her initial intent.

Yet Marge seemed to buy in. "You know how to drive."

"Right? That's what I keep saying, but I'm not the boss." Ronnie stood, moving closer. "Still, I need to keep him." She added with mock regret, "Sorry."

When she possessively slipped her arm around his, Jack almost grinned.

Almost. The fact that they were still on shaky ground kept any real amusement at bay. The two burly goons standing at either side of the door didn't help either. As if he could forget their presence, one of them made a production of cracking his knuckles.

Jack gave him a pitying look for the obvious display.

Cackling another laugh, Marge said, "I like him, Ronnie. Maybe I'll just borrow him for an afternoon?" She looked at his mouth. "What do you say, honey? You want a real woman instead of a scrawny bag of bones?"

Ronnie stiffened again, meaning the shot hit home.

"Tempting as this all sounds," Jack said, his tone flat, "I'm here strictly for the job."

Subtle signs of anger transformed Marge, hardening her gaze, putting a slight curl to her painted upper lip. She moved away from the desk, asking with lethal undertones of disbelief, "You're rejecting me?"

There'd be very few right answers, something Ronnie had probably anticipated. Was this her plan then, the way she'd chosen to chase him off?

Why, he wondered, did she want him gone so badly?

"Marge," Ronnie said with a touch of warning, one hand half inside her purse.

"If she doesn't shut it," Marge said to her lackeys while keeping her sharp gaze locked on Jack's, "shut it for her."

The goons stepped forward.

Jack considered a few scenarios, including demolishing them both for daring to threaten Ronnie. He discarded them just as quickly because he couldn't guarantee she wouldn't get hurt. Yes, he could handle the men in this backroom office, but there were other men crowded into the bar not so far away.

Satisfying as it'd be to level the bastards, he wouldn't risk Ronnie, so he shrugged. "Only because I'm loyal to the job. I was hired to see to a pickup—" he still didn't know *what* they were picking up "—and that's what I intend to do. No other offers, regardless of how tempting, can come before that."

Arrested, Marge weighed his words, some emotion contracting her features even more, honing them into cruel lines…until she gave into a rusty, robust laugh far more authentic than those that came before it.

The men joined in, roaring with hilarity while Ronnie stared at him. For his audacity? Or because she'd expected him to cower with fear?

Jack wasn't sure if the lady-boss's humor signaled death or reprieve, but while hoping for the latter he stayed vigilant, ready to react if necessary.

Wiping tears from her eyes without smudging her makeup, Marge said, "Oh, now that was slick. Very slick."

"He's known for being slick," Ronnie offered, releasing him now that the crisis had passed. "It's one of the things the brothers liked about him."

"I see why." Right in front of him, Marge rearranged her boobs, hiking them up and plumping them together, making sure plenty of cleavage showed. "This," she said to Jack, "is what you're missing. Few women are as gifted." After a pointed nod at Ronnie's chest, she waved off the knuckle-crackers.

The two goons snickered, earning a glare from Ronnie, but she didn't utter a verbal protest. Why would she bother?

At the first opportunity, Jack would find a way to show her the appeal of her slender frame. At the moment, though, his number one thought was that Ronnie dealt with these people on a regular basis.

Did her employers realize the threats, ridicule, and danger they exposed her to? If so, that would explain why they wanted her to have a driver.

And come hell or high water, it'd be him.

"Relax, Ronnie. Your man is safe enough."

Until Marge said it, he hadn't realized that Ronnie remained on high alert, too, poised to…what? Fight for him? With such a low opinion of his ability, it was no wonder she wanted to shake him loose. She actually believed she was better equipped to battle grown men than he was.

Sure, she appeared to be resourceful given she'd gotten through it so far on her own, but she was still half his size and that of the other men looming nearby. Hell, in many ways, she was actually delicate… And if she knew he thought that, she'd probably give him holy hell. With her prickly nature, she'd see it as a weakness, and he already knew she'd deny any hints of that. Just as she'd deny needing his help.

Getting her to accept him wouldn't be easy, but he'd figure it out.

Ronnie didn't know it yet, but her ruse had backfired on her in a big way. Rather than scare him off, the little show of danger had sealed the deal. He wanted the job—and he wanted Ronnie, too.

It was a decision he didn't make lightly. He'd long ago outgrown the sport of chasing women. They either came through easy agreement, or he moved on.

Nothing about this lady would be easy. It would take time and effort to win her trust, but already he knew she'd be worth the effort.

When Ronnie relaxed her stance, Marge headed across the room. As if nothing much had happened, she asked, "Something to drink?"

Jack said, "No, thank you." He didn't trust the woman enough to consume anything she offered.

Surprisingly, Marge poured herself coffee. Somehow, in this particular setting, he'd have bet on whiskey regardless of the time of day. After all, plenty of patrons filled the front of the bar and he was pretty sure they weren't having breakfast.

Ronnie, obviously, felt differently. "Thanks. I'll get my own." Her stride was that of a much taller woman as she joined Marge and poured herself a cup, this time adding both sugar and creamer. She gulped down half, her gaze meeting his over the rim.

She winked.

Jack didn't dare smile, but damn, she impressed him. Ronnie Ashford was a chameleon, changing from one second to the next depending on what was needed.

A short knock sounded at the door seconds before a man opened it and stuck his head in. "I have it."

"Good," Marge said. "Bring it in."

SILENCE STRETCHED OUT as Jack drove. Ronnie knew he had questions, accusations, demands, but the impossible man played mum, leaving her to stew in her own guilt.

Things could have gone south so easily.

If Marge didn't respect her.

If she didn't want to keep doing business with the brothers.

If Jack hadn't handled himself so calmly and, yes, competently. That's what really rubbed her raw. He hadn't needed her effort. To serve her own best interests, she'd stuck him in that untenable situation, and he'd have gotten out just fine on his own.

"You're going to break your teeth if you don't stop grinding them like that."

She shot him a look of acute dislike and then couldn't drag her gaze away. They'd just faced a very iffy situation and he didn't have a single hair out of place. He appeared as complacent as he had in his own office.

"I should have let her have you."

Amusement curved his mouth. "You're all ego, aren't you? News flash, Ronnie. It wasn't up to you."

Her thumb jabbed to her chest, an insubstantial chest that had just been thoroughly derided. Not that she wanted Marge's massive boobs, but seriously, a bit more wouldn't be bad. Hoping he'd believe it, she stated, "I'm the reason they backed off."

"Scared to death of you, huh?" That too-sensual mouth smiled, making her own mouth go dry in reaction. "I don't know if they fear you, but Marge obviously respects you, and that's probably more important. Have you tangled with them often?"

Her eyes flared. Compliments? Acknowledgment? How could she continue to blast him when *he* continued to be so reasonable? And why did she want to blast him anyway?

Because he's still here, still my problem, and it's my fault for miscalculating.

A deep breath, released slowly, helped Ronnie regain a modicum of composure. "Marge entertains a lot of men, one of them a detective. He often brings her memorabilia from different crime scenes, and when those items suit, she in turn sells them to the brothers. She'd probably get more if she auctioned them off to the highest bidders, but she says she likes keeping it simple, and the cop doesn't want his involvement advertised. So every couple of weeks she has something to sell. The brothers like buying things from her because the cop can verify authenticity."

"That envelope she gave you?"

"Right. It includes a pic the cop took of the crime scene, showing the item there." Ronnie dug it from her purse and pulled out the photo, showing it to him.

Without much interest, he glanced at it, then shook his head. "Pretty absurd, if you ask me."

Shrugging, Ronnie returned it to the protective envelope. In today's case, the item was a glass eye, cracked in two places. During a robbery, blood got in the eye and ran into the cracks, creating a truly macabre effect. "The intended victim of the robbery had a gun and happily blasted the thug—who expired on the kitchen floor."

"Marge said the shooter lost his eye in the process?"

"That's the story. The house has since been sold and the owner moved away."

"But the cop kept the eye?"

She almost grinned at his revolted tone. "He figured it'd sell."

"What will the brothers do with a cracked eye?"

"Display it." She half turned toward him, wondering if that was the key to making him back off. "They'll show you the basement when you meet them. They remodeled it to look like a creepy dungeon, all inky-dark, lit mostly with black lights, and weird stuff everywhere."

Showing a lack of interest in the basement, he asked, "When can I meet them?"

"Not until tonight." She lifted a hip to get her phone from her back pocket and checked the time. She had hours to spare, but what would be better? To engage him until them, pointing out all the reasons why he didn't want the job? Or should she take the time to be alone, to regroup and recover?

He settled it for her, saying, "Let's get something to eat. Breakfast has come and gone and it's time for lunch. I don't know about you, but I'm starving."

Her first reaction was to deny him, just because.

Because she didn't want to be agreeable. She didn't want to encourage him. She didn't want to be around him, torturing herself with what she shouldn't, couldn't have. She didn't want to like and respect him either. Unfortunately, she already did.

But a restaurant with other people milling around would be safe, right? Distracting, even. An empty belly left her frazzled. She'd think more clearly after eating.

Weighing the pros and cons, she chewed her lip a

moment, but a grumbling stomach helped decide her. "I could eat."

"Great."

After that short reply, the silence stretched out again, and this time it bothered her even more. Lack of sleep, hunger, disappointment all played against her.

To keep from staring at him, cataloging his every handsome feature, she searched for conversation and settled on, "Excitement always makes me hungry." That seemed like a good statement to segue into her own ability handling trouble, as she'd done at the bar.

Jack ruined her plans by asking low, "Sexual excitement?"

Damn him, just hearing that word *sex* from his mouth made her nipples tighten. And of course, that made her think of his mouth *on her* nipples and she breathed harder, her whole body going taut.

I have it bad. Ronnie closed her eyes, counting to five before opening them again.

And there was that small smile on his mouth, the bastard. He knew what he'd done to her. "Jerk," she muttered.

The smile widened. "It makes me hungry, too, just so you know."

No, she didn't want to know! Rushing away from that thought, she said, "I meant at the bar. The excitement of possible violence. It was close there for a minute or two. No one denies Marge. No one would dare—"

"I dared."

"—*and*," she continued insistently, "if I hadn't been there, you might've learned how the woman shows displeasure." Let him deny it like a sexist jerk. Let him downplay her influence. Then she'd—

"Ah, but you were there," he said, his tone gruff. "My white knight. Or maybe you're more like a bulldog? Facing off against bad odds, ensuring I made it out of there whole-hide. They do respect you, I could tell. That's no small deal. So how should I thank you?"

Was he mocking her? Of course he was. A big guy like him probably thought himself invincible. Well, she had an answer for him. "Refuse the job." *Let me continue plodding forward in life in the only way I know how—alone.*

"Can't do that. Name something else."

She stiffened. "That's all I want." It was all she dared to want.

"No," he said gently as he took an unexpected turn on the road. "You want me."

Her heart slammed still, then shot into a wild beat, emboldening her, making her reckless. Men were easily led by sex. Maybe she'd been handling this all wrong. Maybe she had a simpler resolution that would please them both.

"You're right." She tilted a little closer to him. "I do."

That simple admission had a startling effect on him.

His hands tightened on the wheel, making his biceps jump. A deep inhalation flared his nostrils. He subtly shifted his thighs.

Liking the signs of sexual excitement, she leaned closer. "I've wanted you since you first walked into Freddie's."

"I'm more than willing."

She counted on it. "I had planned to let Marge scare you off today."

"I know."

So he'd figured her out? So what. "I had a change

of…" Not heart. *Never* her heart. *God, do I even still possess a heart?* "Conscience. See, I figured you'd refuse, then she'd have had her boys work you over for the insult, and we'd have both been tossed out, you bruised and battered, me short one collector's item. You'd have surely quit, but then the brothers would've been displeased that I'd failed to collect, so I gave up the idea."

As he rolled to a stop sign, his gaze cut to her face. "You gave up the idea because you didn't want to see me hurt. Though I wouldn't have been, I still appreciate the effort. Now about that wanting—"

"You realize they were armed, right?"

"So were you."

She faltered for a reply just long enough for him to continue.

"But you wouldn't have needed a gun. You should know, Ronnie, I *do* appreciate your concern, but I could have handled them both."

"Bullshit!" Pointing at him, she said, "You might've done some quick talking, but it's because of me that they—"

He caught her hand, drew it to his mouth, and kissed her palm. "I already thanked you, right?"

Yeah, that right there, the hot press of his mouth to her ridiculously sensitive palm, stole her arguments and left her breathless. And he still held her hand, his big thumb now rubbing softly over the racing pulse in her wrist.

Lord. She swallowed and whispered, "I want you, Jack."

Voice husky and rough, he replied, "It can't be as much as I want you."

Actually, it had to be ten times worse, but she saw no point in debating it. "So let's do this." Saying it sent liquid heat burning through her limbs to pool in key places, places now pulsing with need. "Let's go somewhere," she urged, "get naked, make each other nuts—"

"Easily arranged."

"—and tonight I'll tell the brothers you didn't want the job." She held her breath. Hopeful. *Needy.*

He froze.

Oh no. *Please, please, please don't refuse me. Please just go along like a good boy.* Or a mega-hot man. Whatever.

Dying a little, she almost pleaded, "Say yes, Jack."

"We'll discuss it over lunch."

Until that moment she hadn't noticed where he'd driven. He was off the main roads, heading back toward the Mustang Transport offices. She pulled back. "Wait—where are we going?"

"Lunch, remember?"

Suspicion burned bright. "Lunch *where*?"

He turned down another side street—*away* from the business. Almost reluctantly, he admitted, "My place."

Hello, temptation. "Your place?" she croaked.

"Yeah." Brusque, he explained, "It'll give us some privacy."

If she got alone with him, she'd cave. She knew it. He probably knew it, too, but how dare he assume? She tried to sound cool when she asked, "Did you forget I'm armed?"

He gave a short laugh. "No."

The landscape changed from smallish houses close together to nothing but lush trees, a weed-lined gravel road, and nature.

When had dark clouds crept forward to hide the sun? Was that rain she scented in the air? And was the static she felt from an impending storm, or from Jack Crews with sensual intent?

Damn it, she'd always thought storms were sexy.

She definitely thought Jack was sexy.

And now, to be all alone with him like this... How would she resist?

"One thing you should understand, Ronnie. For me, no means no. You don't have to worry that I'll pressure you, or come on strong."

Oh, great. Now he thought she was afraid? "I'm not worried." No, it was her own inability to resist that concerned her, not an assault from him. She looked around. "Where the hell do you live? The woods?"

"Somewhat." Through a clearing up ahead she saw a quaint, farm-style house come into view. "Is that it?"

"Yeah. I'm remodeling it and there's still a lot of work to do."

"You live in a secluded paradise." Rain started, a light sprinkling that grew stronger in seconds until rain lashed the windows. The interior immediately fogged—probably from her accelerated breathing.

Jack smiled. "There are other houses." The wipers added a rhythmic thrum to the sound of the rainfall. "The mature trees make it seem more remote than it is." Rather than take the driveway to the front of the house, he pulled around back to a carport. "The garage is filled with tools, so Brodie helped me put up a shelter as a temporary place to park."

Ronnie was too busy removing her seat belt and looking at the incredible surroundings to pay much attention to where he parked. Until he turned off the engine. Then the feel of his attention enveloped her.

Her gaze shot to his. *Think of your future*, she told

herself. *Think of how he'll screw up the job if he sticks around.*

He'd half turned to face her, one forearm draped over the wheel. After his gaze traced every feature of her face with almost tactile concentration, he murmured, "We'll wait here just a minute to see if the storm blows over."

Here, in this small space? With only a console, their warm breath, and hunger between them? Did the man think she was made of stone?

She swallowed heavily, already tempted beyond measure. A boom of thunder resonated in her chest, and she barely noticed, not with her gaze locked on his and the tension ramping up with every heartbeat.

Suddenly she knew. No matter what happened with the job, regardless of how he might irk her, she'd never again experience sexual chemistry this strong, and she'd be a fool not to explore it.

She'd like to think she wasn't a fool.

"Jack…" The word emerged a barely there whisper, a question, an admission. Yearning.

As if he understood, he shifted toward her, his eyes gone darker with intent. "One kiss, Ronnie. I need that."

God, she needed it more. Anticipation sizzling, heart swelling, she met him halfway over the console.

His mouth grazed her cheek, so very softly, leaving a trail of heat along her jaw, her chin. "You have incredible skin."

Skin? Who cared about her skin? "Kiss me."

"Yes, ma'am." As his lips finally met hers in a bold, firm press, his hand, so incredibly large, cupped the base of her skull and angled her for a perfect fit.

Ronnie was instantly lost.

She didn't recall reaching for him, but suddenly her

fingers were buried in his hair and she somehow hung over the center console.

They were no longer poised between the seats, two mouths meeting in neutral ground. She pressed him back in his seat as she took the kiss she wanted, the kiss she needed. Whether she opened her mouth to invite his tongue, or his tongue forged the way, she didn't know and honestly didn't care, not with the heady taste of him making her want more, more, *more*.

Without breaking the contact of their mouths, his seat slid back and he brought her fully onto his lap. Trapped between his body and the prod of the steering wheel, she could barely move, but what did it matter? She managed to get one leg on either side of him, straddling his lap, squeezing closer still.

The side of the console dug into her knee, but she easily dismissed the discomfort. Same with the driver's door handle.

Jack slid one hand down to her backside; she didn't mind that at all. Then his other hand trailed to her waist, over her ribs where he paused, his thumb brushing over her, before he continued up to cover her breast.

With a low groan, he stroked her.

Yeah, that she *wasn't* comfortable with.

Drawing back, Ronnie stared at him, her breath coming fast. God, he looked hot. Very turned on. If she weren't so lacking…

He held her stare, unmoving, unapologetic, not retreating.

His hand remained on her, no longer caressing but still *there*…where she didn't have much to tempt a man.

A new kind of flush covered her skin. Much as she hated to admit it, it might be…uncertainty. "Jack…"

Her voice seemed to galvanize him and his fingers got back to lightly exploring, cupping, gently squeezing. His thumb drifted over her pebbled nipple, making her breath catch.

"No bra," he murmured, his tone approving.

"Do I look like I need one?" The sarcasm wasn't as sharp as usual; hell, with the way he touched her she barely had oxygen enough to speak.

"You look pretty damned perfect to me."

Liar. She didn't want him spinning tales just to make her feel desired. She didn't need that. "I know I'm flat-chested. You don't have to pretend—"

Shifting, he pressed an impressive erection against her backside. "Do I *feel* like I'm pretending?"

As if she'd miss that? Ronnie shook her head.

"Good." He lightly tugged at her nipple, making her gasp and arch against him. "If you put stock into what Marge said, I might just turn you over my knee."

Oh, now wait a minute. Was that a joke or some sort of sexual insinuation? "Don't think—"

He tugged again, rolling her nipple at the same time, and the pleasure was so acute it wrought a low groan. "You surely realize Marge was jealous, right?"

Jealous? Of *her*? A woman Marge considered scrawny?

Head back, eyes closed, Ronnie whispered, "Are you deranged?" She pressed one of her own hands over his, stilling the provoking torment. "Not even."

"I'm a man, Ronnie, and I know women."

"Braggart." She kissed him again, ready to get back to business. She hoped to tempt him away from a discussion on her lack of curves.

He indulged her, crushing her close, kissing her long

and deep until they'd fogged all the windows. Just as she touched the buttons on the front of his shirt, he broke the kiss.

"What—"

"Shh." By levering her back, he was able to touch both breasts. "I need you to understand, Ronnie."

"I do."

He shook his head, denying that. "Marge is big and bold, her figure overblown."

"Yeah. She draws a lot of attention."

"Which is what she's after. But you don't need giant tits to draw a man." Smiling, his gaze dipped down to where his hands covered her. "*Everything* about you is noticeable and attractive, including the way you carry yourself, your attitude, and self-confidence. Believe me, when I first saw you, after I'd looked you over, I didn't see a single lack."

Unable to squelch the curiosity, she whispered, "What did you see?" Then she held her breath.

Dark lashes lifted and his mysterious gaze delved into hers. "A scorching hot lady with an obviously defensive attitude that sharpened her sex appeal."

"Oh." She'd been obviously defensive? *Damn.* "You want to know what I saw?"

The smile turned into a knowing grin. "An easy conquest and a way to kill some time?"

Well…yeah. But she'd also seen more. "Temptation."

"Then let me get back to tempting." He leaned forward.

A knock sounded on his window.

Jumping, Ronnie almost smacked her head on the ceiling. She stared through the rainwashed glass at a petite woman with long curly brown hair frazzled by the weather, fighting an umbrella that tried to blow away.

Jack quickly rolled down the window. "Charlotte?"

"Hate to interrupt," she said, her teeth chattering against the chill, her blue eyes soft and teasing. "I waited, but since it didn't seem like you were heading in any-time soon… I thought you should know your basement is flooding."

CHAPTER FOUR

THE INTERRUPTION THREE days ago had been a blessing. At least, that's how Ronnie chose to see it. She'd been about to buy into Jack's sales pitch, ready to do the nasty with him right there in the cramped space of his front seat, which, on the face of it, would have been fine.

Sex with Jack? Count her in.

Except that he hadn't yet turned down the job. And she didn't do long-term stuff. The job, maybe, since she'd been there a year now. But anything else? Dates? Romance? Family?

No, no, and no.

She'd learned the hard way that one-night stands, very temporary pleasure, and fleeting involvement served her better than trying to make something last. Dates? Why bother when she could eat wherever she wanted, see any movie she wanted, when she enjoyed her own company just fine—and one-night stands were never hard to come by when the mood struck her? The cold, detached, *lonely* arrangement worked for her, had been working for her since... Well, she didn't want to think about that, so instead she focused on the other thing she no longer did.

Family.

Hers had denounced her long ago, and since multiple attempts to reconnect hadn't worked, she'd decided good riddance. She didn't need them. She'd proven that in a dozen different, painful, hard-won ways. She'd learned her lessons, thank you very much.

Class was over.

Now, though, as she prepared to meet Jack for another pickup, her thoughts raced. She'd been in a funk since leaving his house that night, but as far as she was concerned, pretty little Charlotte's propitious timing had saved her from making a grave tactical error.

Jack had raced into his house to fix the flooding problem, Charlotte had taken his car to drive Ronnie back to her car, and she'd been left with the task of telling the brothers their meeting was rescheduled. One second she'd been melting under Jack's compliments, and the next he'd sent her away with a complete stranger.

He could have invited her in to help—not that she *wanted* in his house.

He could have asked her to wait while he sorted out the problem—but she probably would have come to her senses in the interim.

He could have…what? Acted half as caught up in the moment as she'd been? Clearly he hadn't felt the same, and that, for sure, was a problem.

Damn it, she knew better than to give anyone the upper hand. Down that road lived nothing but heartache.

So the next morning when Jack had called, then texted, she'd ignored him. The days had passed and she'd be ignoring him still if she could—but duty called.

Hoping he'd refuse, she'd texted Jack a brief message last night, stating the particulars for a pickup in Lexington and that they'd have to leave by 10:00 a.m. Fifteen minutes had passed before he texted back, Count me in.

So far, nothing with him was easy. Par for…her life.

Ronnie stared into the mirror over the hotel room

dresser as she threaded a third earring into her ear. To match her mood, she wore all black. Black jeans, black boots, another black top, this one a three-button thermal Henley. Her makeup was equally austere, but to keep busy, she'd done a little more styling with her hair. She'd have to remember to keep her restless fingers out of it today.

Stepping back, she reached for the contents on the dresser—and a knock sounded on her door. Wariness narrowed her eyes as she glanced at the clock. She had a few minutes yet before she needed to leave to meet Jack. It was too early for housekeeping, and besides, they knew not to enter when she was away. She didn't let anyone alone with her belongings.

She reached for her purse. "Who is it?"

"It's me. Open up."

Her jaw loosened, then her feet shot into action, carrying her angrily across the floor. At the last second she paused, put one eye to the peephole, and after verifying that it was, in fact, Jack, she jerked open the door. "What the hell do you think you're—?"

Leaning in, he captured her open mouth in a soft, quick kiss, and then ducked her swing when she automatically tried to slug him.

"Whoa." Laughing, he held up both hands in the universal sign of submission. "Sorry, but I missed you."

How could she maintain her new resolve for no hanky-panky when he led with his lips? That brief kiss left her mouth tingling and her thoughts scattered. He stood there looking *so* damn good in another button-down shirt and brown slacks, his expression comically submissive.

As if.

"Ass," she growled. She looked up and down the hallway to ensure no one had seen him, then hauled him inside and began securing the door. "Don't think you can just—"

As she turned, he kissed her again, and this time he pressed her back to the closed door and pinned down her hands. "Missed." He turned his head for a deeper fit, giving her one small taste of his tongue. "You."

Yup, that melted her bones and her resistance.

He breathed against her ear, "I just wanted you to know." Then he stepped back, leaving her there, limp, confused.

Hands in his pockets, casual as you please, he glanced around her rented room.

An unsteady but deep breath helped a little. Pushing away from the door, Ronnie said, "You shouldn't be here. I made it clear that I'd meet you at your office."

"Honestly," he said, eyeing what she had on her dresser, "I didn't trust you to show. Not after you refused to answer my calls or texts."

"I was busy." Busy being butt-hurt, but whatever. He didn't need to know that part. She took the file with her notes and put them carefully into the big pocket lining her purse, then snatched up her keys and dropped them in, too. Lifting the wicked blade that held most of Jack's attention, she sat on the foot of the bed and, pulling up the leg of her jeans, fit it into the sheath inside her boot.

Since she wasn't looking at him, she felt more than saw Jack's curiosity. Would he question her, say something dumb about her weapons of choice?

"That's dangerous."

Yup, very dumb. His attitude should throw some ice on the fire he'd started. "I know how to use it," she assured him, pleased with the steadiness of her voice.

"I meant you on a bed." He leaned back on the dresser. "In a hotel room."

Her gaze shot to his. The fire blazed to an inferno.

Dark eyes both teasing and hot, he smiled. "Especially when I'm already half hard and you aren't exactly saying no."

"No!" Saying it as much to herself as to him, she jumped to her feet and grabbed up a sweatshirt. The storms were over and only fluffy white clouds dotted the sky, but she no longer trusted the weather. And because she didn't really trust herself either, she reiterated firmly, "Not unless you refuse the job." She went to the door and opened it, giving him an expectant look to let him know it was time to go. Past time.

Still smiling, Jack came forward. "You know, I'm confident that I can win you over *and* keep the job."

"You can't." *Could he?* No, she wouldn't let him.

He said nothing else as they left the ancient building via two flights of stairs, nothing as they stepped out into the bright sunshine and crisp, dew-rich morning air.

Nothing when he walked her to his car, parked at the curb, or when he needlessly opened the passenger door for her—and quietly accepted her eye roll—before strolling around to the driver's side.

Once they were on the road, though, he said, "I like your hair."

Self-consciously, she reached for it but dropped her hand before she made contact with the thick, unruly locks. "It's easy," she said, by way of a thank-you.

"I like your style overall." He glanced at her, then away. "The earrings, the makeup, the tight jeans."

In case he thought otherwise, she explained, "It's who I am, and it's *not* for your benefit."

"I appreciate it all the same." He pulled up to a stop sign on the main road out of town. "I've been extremely distracted since I left you the other day."

Jerk, she accused in her brain, but refrained from saying it out loud. "No problem. You had something more important to deal with."

He denied that as he waited for a few people to cross the road. Seemed Red Oak, Ohio, woke up early. "Not more important, Ronnie. Don't think that. But damage was being done—"

"Hey, I get it," she cut in, not wanting to hear his half-baked explanations. And not wanting to risk buying into them. She had to protect herself, because no one else would. So she shrugged it off and said, "You barely know me. Fending off home repairs definitely ranks above a casual hookup."

"I hadn't planned it to be all that casual."

Stop, she told her thumping, stupidly hopeful heart. "Yeah, well, too bad because all I do is casual." She *had* to drive the point home. It was too important for him to misconstrue. "One and done, that's my motto." Though the words sounded flippant, they were now her life— out of necessity.

Pretending she hadn't said that, he explained, "I've been remodeling the house for a while now. I haven't done much to the basement yet, but stuff is stored down there, stuff I'll use in the different rooms once they're finished. If it got ruined, I'd be stuck replacing it."

"No problem." She really did understand. Jack was busy nesting, while she'd continue to roam. He had it together, and she…probably never would. "It's better that we got interrupted since I don't plan to—"

"Mrs. Gershlick would disagree."

"Mrs. Gersh-who?"

He laughed. "She's a local who runs a dog rescue, and once a month she finds forever homes for as many of the dogs as she can. We, Mustang Transport, do free delivery for her when the owners aren't close enough to come get the pets themselves. I had this little schnauzer I had to take to Columbus yesterday. Mrs. Gershlick had to give me the address three times, because my mind kept wandering."

Ronnie closed her eyes and clenched her teeth, but there it was, forever branded into her brain.

He delivered homeless dogs. For free.

Goddammit, why did he have to be so freaking awesome in so many ways? Why couldn't he be a supreme dick or a sexist ass or...or at least not so good-looking?

Trying for derision but mostly sounding snotty, she waved a finger and growled, "We need to plop a friggin' halo on your head, don't we?"

His voice lowered. "If you knew all the things I thought about doing to you during the drive, even while the dog continued yapping, you'd know it wasn't a halo I deserved."

Diabolical, that's what he was!

She was already using every ounce of internal fortitude she had to resist him. Over and over she reminded herself that it would be a colossally *bad* idea to get involved with anyone.

And he went and said that.

Now *she* was thinking things, and she'd be willing to bet her thoughts were even hotter than his.

This should have been easy—but then again, when was anything easy for her? Out of pure frustration, she had to give it one try.

She pinned him with a look. "Whatever you thought about, we can do it. Deny the job and it'll happen tonight. Right now if you want." He could pull over to the side of the road on one of the treed, quiet sections, and they could get started right away.

And then she could get the hell away from him and the risk he posed to her emotional refuge.

"Here's the thing," he said, his tone too careful, too modulated. "I want more than one night." When she started to speak, he interrupted, "I'm not asking you to marry me, Ronnie, so relax."

Her eyes flared wide, that *M* word literally freezing all the air in her lungs. *How dare he say such a thing?* Like she'd even think about that level of commitment? No one had ever asked her…to do *that*, and she was pretty damned sure no one ever would.

Because she wouldn't allow it.

"Not asking you to move in either, or even be exclusive," he continued, as if he hadn't just gone off the deep end of extreme. "But we'll be working together—"

"Not if I can help—" she tried to protest, but again, he spoke over her.

"—and there's so much chemistry between us, we'll both combust if we don't give in. I'm on the verge already." He glanced at her. "You?"

Yes. God, yes. She had a feeling that if she loosened her shirt or unzipped her jeans, steam would escape.

Looking at him wasn't helping, so she turned her attention to the window, sightlessly staring out at the passing landscape and clenching her hands. Her silver rings bit into her fingers, and she realized what she was doing: showing too much reaction. By small degrees, she composed herself, loosening her fingers, relaxing her shoulders.

Emotions were weapons that could be used against her.

"Why you?" she asked, hoping her tone was as polite and casual as his had been. "You're a damned stuffed shirt and all spiffy style and I'm...not." She'd always been the opposite of that, a direct contrast to him. A direct contrast to her entire family. "We have nothing in common."

"Oh, I don't know about that. We both like your hair."

How did he think that counted?

"And we both like this job."

She'd prefer that he didn't.

"We both carry knives."

She...*what?* Pivoting fast, Ronnie gaped at him. "Is that a joke?"

Appearing pleased that he'd finally regained her attention, he said, "No."

Against her will, her gaze tracked all over him. She'd learned the art of searching for weapons, noticing any telltale lumps under clothing, any obvious straps, holsters, or sheaths. On Jack, she saw no evidence of a knife anywhere on his person. "You're hiding it well."

"Same place as you, actually—which I guess counts for another thing we have in common." Reaching down, he lifted one pant leg to show a low-profile black sheath strapped just above the top of his sock.

Momentarily distracted, Ronnie lifted her brows in admiration of the weapon. "Nice. It's completely concealed."

"The skeletal frame is flat. Makes it easier to hide.

The wrap sheath fits in a pocket or hooks on my belt. I prefer my ankle, though."

Skeletal meaning the handle was basically an outline made of steel, but she noticed it had a rubber coating, making the grip more secure. "You any good at throwing it?"

"Decent. You?"

"I'm good," she said without modesty. And at least with this topic, she was at ease. "Odds are if I need my knife, I'm up against someone who could physically overpower me, so getting close wouldn't be smart. If a gunshot is too noisy, or a gun is too noticeable, a knife makes more sense."

As if troubled by that idea, the muscles of his jaw tightened, but his tone remained neutral when he asked, "Have you ever stabbed anyone?"

With a flinch she hoped she hid, Ronnie shook her head. "No." *Thank God.* But she'd done worse, and now, if she needed to, she definitely could use her knife and that's what mattered.

Carefully, with deliberate negligence, Jack suggested, "Maybe you can come by my house again and show me your technique?"

She shot him a narrow-eyed look, just in case he wasn't talking about knives.

"I have a few targets, a big private yard, and I could use the practice."

Crazy, but knife-throwing with him sounded almost as much fun as the horizontal boogie. Yet she was nothing if not stubborn, so she said, "If you quit, we'll go our separate ways. I won't be around town anymore."

Keeping his expression and tone neutral, he said,

"Good thing I have no intention of giving up the job then, right?"

Lord, was that relief she felt? Was she really that hungry to find common ground with someone? *Anyone?* How pathetic would that be? How desperate?

She refused to accept it.

"I'll still see you less often, since I won't stay in the hotel much longer. My visit there was just for convenience. I only live forty-five minutes away and I'll be returning home soon." Home to her small, empty apartment...with loads of security and more anonymity than she could find in a town this size.

"So we're both homebodies, too. Another trait we share."

Since talk of home was a touchy subject, she said with renewed resolution, "You know what? Let's talk about all the things we *don't* have in common. How about that?"

"Such as?" He drove out of town, heading toward the interstate on-ramps. "Besides the style differences you've already driven into the ground."

Driven into the ground? "Facts can't be overstated. You're a fancy-pants and I'm a—"

"A what? Powder keg of attitude in a small, sexy package?" He smiled at his own analogy. "A woman who knows what she likes and goes after it?"

Everything he said held errant admiration, making her feel guilty for the name-calling. She didn't know how to reply. For her, compliments were few and far between and she remained uncomfortable with them. Insults she could deal with. This nonsense from him...not so much. "What about family? You're obviously a family guy."

A strange expression fell over his profile. "My brother

and I are close. You probably already picked up on that. And you met Charlotte."

The woman who'd driven her home? "Yeah, I met her." She wasn't sure what else to say about that. Charlotte had looked sweet and kind and Ronnie had been pretty damned surly.

Getting rejected because another woman showed up didn't sit well with her, whatever the reason for the interruption. She didn't know who Charlotte was to him, and she damn well wouldn't ask because it didn't matter. It couldn't matter.

That didn't stop it from hurting.

He glanced her way. "The two of you didn't talk."

"So?" Conversation hadn't gone anywhere because Ronnie had been too intent on stewing in anger and Charlotte had concentrated on driving the short distance in the nasty weather. "Were we supposed to?"

Using his mirrors, Jack switched lanes. "Charlotte said you were distracted."

Distracted? More like furious. "She complained about me?"

"No. But she said she didn't get a chance to explain who she is."

Oh, now that was interesting. "No one owes me any explanations." For her own sake, she needed to keep it that way.

Of course, Jack explained anyway. "Charlotte's been working with us since she was sixteen. She's an office wizard and keeps everything in order, but she's more than that, too."

Perfect. Just what she didn't need to know. "She looked really...wholesome."

Taking the description as an insult, Jack sent her a

look of reproach. "Her mom died when she was eighteen after a long illness, and my mother stepped in where she could."

Ronnie almost groaned. So they were all do-gooders? Clearly they were nothing like her. Shame made her mouth pinch. "I'm sorry to hear it."

He flashed a rare, very genuine smile. "You'd like Mom."

Good God. When it came to mothers—including her own—she batted a big fat zero. And he thought she'd like his? "Why?"

Surprise made him pause. "Why what?"

"Why do you think I'd like your mom? Just because she birthed you?" Ronnie shook her head. Meeting his family would only complicate things further.

"Well, there is that." This time his smile was the practiced, too-polite gesture she'd already grown used to.

And she hated it. It meant she'd insulted him and that hadn't been her intent. Not this time. It was just… "Nothing against your mom, Jack, but mothers and I don't mix."

Confusion sharpened his expression. "I'm not sure what that even means—"

Good. The less he knew about her and her many failures, the better.

"But Mom is genuine. You could trust her, Ronnie, and I have a feeling you don't trust easily."

With damned good reason. Feeling self-defensive always brought out the worst in her, making her tone sharper, her replies harder-edged. He had no business digging into her psyche, analyzing her and what she did or didn't need. "One minute you tell me you want to fuck but nothing more. Then you throw your mom out there like she's bait I can't resist? Is that how you seal the deal?" Her laugh sounded as ugly as she could make it.

Annoyance carved a frown into Jack's usual complacent expression. "You know I didn't mean it that way. She's a nice person. Everyone likes her. Everyone confides in her."

His mother sounded like a martyr to her, and Ronnie wasn't interested. "What makes you think I want a confidant?" She didn't. She *couldn't.*

He took the ramp onto the highway, silent as he checked the traffic and moved into the passing lane. Finally he said, "Everyone needs someone to talk to."

"Maybe you like a good shoulder to cry on, but not me." She'd cried enough tears over the years and they'd gotten her exactly nowhere. Never again would she allow herself to be that weak.

Something shifted in the air, spurred by the sudden quiet. Had she hit a nerve? Was it her insinuation that he was a mama's boy, her indirect insult to his mother, or her refusal to share?

Could he be tired of her being a bitch? Probably.

Throat thickening with an emotion she didn't want to name, Ronnie turned away from him. Good. Let him despise her. Maybe that was the trick to make him back off.

Then she could get on with her life.

Alone.

Fifteen minutes later, she acknowledged that the problem, at least for her, was the closeness in the car. Mustangs, while being very sharp vehicles, especially Jack's 2005 GT, weren't exactly what she'd call roomy.

Ronnie could almost swear they shared breath. She definitely felt his heat, scented by his big body. Hell, she could almost hear his heartbeat, the slow, steady thumping that her own heart gradually matched.

Little by little, her skin prickled with responsive awareness.

No other man had affected her so strongly—and she knew why. Jack wasn't only good-looking. Only sexy. He was also friendly and funny, open and caring. Pushy and protective. She wanted him…and she liked him. She couldn't help herself. He both tantalized and threatened, drawing her while making her equally determined to get away.

For now, she was stuck. Sex wasn't an option, and neither was escape. So what to do?

Not the silent treatment. That was a loser since it clearly tortured her more than it did him.

Grasping for the first topic to come to mind, she said, "I like your car." Weak, but she couldn't think of anything else so she forged on. "How long have you had it? Did you spiff it up yourself?"

He remained quiet just long enough to make her think he wouldn't answer, and it stressed her horribly. She usually didn't offer olive branches for this very reason—she despised being rebuffed. Never again would she deliberately set herself up for—

"It's a complicated story." His gaze shifted over her in what felt like quick judgment, then returned to the road. "But I don't mind explaining if you actually want to hear it."

"I asked, didn't I?" *Damn it, Ronnie, stop sniping.* Something about Jack Crews brought out the absolute worst in her. Maybe it was sexual deprivation. She didn't like being denied. More likely it was the sharp contrast he provided. The man had close family, an upbeat disposition, a home, and job he loved. He didn't have to prove his strength to anyone. His confidence wasn't contrived. She doubted he'd ever felt alone. Or afraid.

Had she really sunk so low that she resented others for having what she couldn't? That would make her a pretty miserable person—a person she didn't want to be.

Feeling like a spoiled brat and hoping to salvage his offer, she sighed. "We have a long drive ahead of us yet. Might as well chat."

"Might as well," he agreed, always polite.

That damned politeness also got on her nerves, to the point she wanted to growl. "Great."

His small smile proved he wasn't fooled by her fake enthusiasm. "The long and short of it is that my dad gave each of us a car for our eighteenth birthdays."

Wow, nice gesture. When she was eighteen, her "dad" had his revelations…and it wasn't a car she got.

"But if you knew my dad—" there he went again, with the family introductions "—you'd know it's no surprise that I didn't get the car until I was twenty-four."

Her brows jumped. "Wait. If you were twenty-four, then how was it for your eighteenth birthday?"

"Exactly what I said. Dad claimed he'd lost track of time."

"For *six* years?" She couldn't claim to have great math or an error-free memory, but that defied all logic.

"I wanted to tell him to take his gift and disappear. Again." He shifted, his hands tightening on the wheel, muscles in his jaw flexing. He was the one growling when he added, "Mom talked me out of it. She's always made excuses for him."

Whoa. So there was trouble in paradise? Something about his life wasn't golden? She could honestly say she wasn't happy about it. Hell, she *didn't* want to see anyone be unhappy. But it did make him feel more…relatable. Less like a hot, shining example of perfection.

It was like a layer of protective ice melted away from her heart. Studying his stern profile, Ronnie said, "I'm not sure I'm following."

"Dad never could remember our birthdays." Jack ran a hand over the back of his neck as if rubbing away an unpleasant memory.

And of course, being the base creature she'd become, she noticed the flex of his biceps, how his shirt pulled taut against a flat middle.

She also noticed that this was difficult for him, which told her he didn't share the story often. Crazy enough, that made her feel…special.

Ronnie forced herself to focus on the topic. "So he might've forgotten the exact date. I'm not great at noting memorable occasions either. But still, *six* years?"

"Half the time he forgot *me*, so yes, a birthday wasn't a big deal to him." Jack gave a small shake of his head, denying the importance. "Dad was—*is*—the complete opposite of my mom. Much as she mothered Brodie and me, Dad only remembers us when he needs something. Otherwise, he's an absentee father. Worse, he was a perpetual cheater, always chasing something better, younger, freer."

Freer…meaning, a woman free of kids? *His* kids? What a prick! Frowning in commiseration, she shifted toward him. "That must've been tough on your mom." Ronnie related to this glimpse of his life, the disappointments and imperfections. Now that he'd started talking, she wanted to hear more. Unusual for her because she tended to avoid anything that even resembled "getting to know each other."

"You know what bugs me the most?"

Why it felt so natural playing his confidant, Ronnie didn't know, but damned if she didn't like it. Encouraging him, wanting, maybe needing to know how despite the problems, he had such a seemingly happy life, she guessed softly, "Not having a dad?"

Using one of her favorite expressions, Jack snorted.

The sound almost made her grin. "No?"

"I can't say we ever missed him much. Mom made up for any lacks."

But his mother was only one person and given his apparent bitterness, he had felt the lack. All Ronnie could think to say was, "I'm glad."

"It wasn't that he'd leave for long stretches, or the string of other women he'd drag around when he finally remembered to visit, which was only when he needed something. And it wasn't that he'd claim bragging rights when Brodie kicked ass in football or I scored high honors in school."

Funny how he used those two examples to describe his and his brother's different youthful accomplishments. Brodie *was* more physical. And Jack obviously prided himself on being smart.

Staring ahead with stony irritation, he said, "It's that he always tried to cozy up with Mom. The bastard would have some young thing tagging along, and *still* he'd try sweet-talking her in front of us, finding reasons to touch her like he actually cared. Acting as if she hadn't booted his ass to the curb."

Wow. What a weak-ass. Caught up in the story despite her usual resolve to stay detached, Ronnie asked, "How did she handle it?"

A slow grin chased away the darkness. "Mom would drag him away because she didn't want us to see them fight, even when we were older. But when she's pissed, there's no mistaking it. She'd give him holy hell and by the time she finished setting him straight, he'd be dragging around like a sad sack."

Okay, damn it, she was starting to like his mom after all. How could she not? "Why didn't she just chew his ass in front of you?"

Jack shook his head. "She always encouraged us to accept him for who he is."

Floored, she stared at him in disbelief. "An asshole?"

He surprised her by laughing. "Basically, yeah. She claimed Dad did the best he could and we should enjoy the good times with him while they lasted."

That was a little too much roses and sunshine for Ronnie. "Doesn't sound to me like you're enjoying him much."

Another laugh. "No, not much." Then he added, "You know what will surprise you? She was always nice to the women he brought along. They really were young and sometimes didn't realize where he was headed. I think that's what infuriated her more than anything. Mom is all about respect, and Dad doesn't show it often."

Ronnie was pretty sure she couldn't do the same, so yeah, major props to his mom for having such a big, understanding heart. "Younger women liked him, huh?"

"Mom claims he's still good-looking."

Ronnie eyed him. "Do you look like him?"

His mouth quirked. "Brodie and I have Mom's eyes and her coloring, but we got Dad's nose and shoulders, his height and strength." Jack glanced at her. "Mom's a shortie."

She smiled, too. "What about your brother? How does he deal with your dad?"

"Overall, Brodie seems okay with him. Whenever Dad comes around, Brodie steers him away from me as much as he can."

Always the big brother, she supposed. That was nice. How different would her life have been if she'd had someone like that around? Someone who looked out for her, no matter what?

This new closeness with Jack, talking to him about important stuff, learning more about him, had the dual effect of softening her guard while also reminding her of things she didn't have, and never would.

"At least your dad gave you a sweet ride." She ran her hand over the black leather seat. "It's in great shape."

"It is now," he agreed. "I did the work myself, with Brodie helping on occasion."

Surprised, she took in the details in the car more closely. It looked as factory-perfect as a car could, with flawless workmanship. "What do you mean, you did it? It wasn't like this when he gave it to you?"

Jack grunted. "Not even close. He gave us beat-up cars on the pretense that we'd do the work together, but of course that never came about. Not that I waited on him anyway. Once Mom convinced me to keep it, I got to work on it and had it pretty cherry within a year."

A whole year? Admittedly, Ronnie didn't know much about restoring a car, but that seemed like a really long time. "A project like that would require a lot of dedication."

"True, but the one useful thing Dad ever taught us

when we were younger was how to work on cars, inside and out."

"You like working with your hands?"

The knowing look he sent her way gave a new meaning to her question, but his answer was bland enough. "Yes, I do. I told you I'm remodeling my house, too. It, much like this car, was in terrible shape when I got it."

"The land is great." She'd love living in a private, wooded area like that. Free to be herself. "It's like your very own refuge."

"Which is why I bought it." Sunshine reflected off the windshield, prompting him to take reflective sunglasses off the visor. He slid them into his place, hiding his eyes—but not his satisfied smile.

This, too, then, was something they had in common. He valued his land every bit as much as she would.

Feeling relaxed for the first time in…well, forever, Ronnie watched the movement of his hands. It was an odd, very unfamiliar feeling to let down her guard.

"Your turn," he murmured.

"Hmm?" The sunshine warmed the car, making her drowsy. His seats were comfy, the ride smooth on the highway. "My turn for what?"

"To tell me about your family."

The statement ripped away the feel-good moment, leaving her raw and tense all over. "I don't think so," she said, with a little too much emotion leaking through.

"Why?" He reached over to brush his knuckles along her cheek. "Got something to hide?"

CHAPTER FIVE

JACK MEANT THE words as teasing, but one glimpse of her frozen face proved he'd failed. For the flash of a moment, her gray eyes reflected a hurt so deep, it had left her wounded. His instinct was to reach out, to take her hand, and tell her things would be okay.

She'd probably sock him if he did. Sympathy was not something she'd want, definitely not something she'd accept.

Yet.

Understanding her wasn't easy. More often than not, she behaved like a pissed-off junkyard dog…who'd taken abuse one time too many. Snarling, snapping, ready to bite if he got too close, rather than risk being hurt again.

At unexpected times, though, she lowered her guard— like while he'd spoken of his dad. She'd listened intently, with a sort of understanding that left him guessing about her past.

What type of upbringing had helped mold a woman so unique? Had she been coddled, given independence, or left to her own devices? Had her parents been strict or lenient?

She looked younger than his thirty-two years, maybe twenty-five or six. Had she always been such a strong personality? Or had circumstances made her that way?

Gently prodding, he asked, "Siblings?"

Her narrow shoulders lifted with a slow breath, almost as if she prepared herself. "Sister." Then she flagged a hand. "Half sister, I guess."

She guessed? "Were you raised together?"

"Yes."

The clipped answers and reluctance to talk might have dissuaded him from pushing, except that Ronnie never pulled her punches. If she didn't want to answer, she'd tell him to fuck off. Maybe, even though she'd deny it, she could use a sounding board.

Maybe she actually needed one?

He knew he'd felt a sense of relief to unload about his father to someone totally unbiased. His mother didn't deny him many things, but she always countered his complaints about his dad with explanations and excuses for the man. Since she'd been married to him, Jack didn't want to say too much in case she thought he questioned her judgment.

Brodie liked him well enough, so Jack couldn't bitch to him.

But Ronnie had listened, her reactions honest.

And that, he realized, the honesty, was one of the things he enjoyed most about her. She didn't make him guess on her thoughts, didn't hedge on her reactions. That pure, unrefined, almost brutal honesty was so damned refreshing.

Especially since she was honest about wanting him.

"Is your sister older or younger?"

Her shoulders settled back against the seat and she looked out the window at the surrounding traffic. "I'm twenty-seven," she said, confirming he'd guessed close, "and Skylar is twenty-two."

Yet Skylar didn't share both parents with her. Jack asked, "How are you related? Mother or father?"

"Mother." Then under her breath, she murmured, "Guess there's no mistaking that."

Thinking she meant they shared similarities, he teased, "So she's as cantankerous as you?"

"Who?" Her gaze swung back to him in surprise. "My mother? Skylar? No way. Mom always says the right thing in the right way. Or…" A dull flush crept over her face. "I mean she usually does."

That wasn't embarrassment heating her skin, more like genuine upset.

"Skylar follows suit. She's the perfect daughter." In a defensive gesture, she folded her arms. "My family's *refined*."

And Ronnie wasn't. He wondered how, or why, she'd turned out so different. "Is your mom widowed or divorced?"

Mouth flattening, she shook her head. "Neither."

Yet she had a half sister? "Then how—"

Her shoulders curled a little closer to her ears, forming a weak barrier between them. She withdrew, physically, emotionally. Jack regretted asking her and was about to back out of the conversation when she turned toward him.

"When I was eighteen, Mom and Dad were arguing about his new secretary. Mom didn't like her because she was too young and pretty, and I guess Mom thought he'd be tempted. The argument got ugly. Dad accused Mom of petty jealousy." She forced her soft lips into a derisive smile. "Out of the blue, Mom announced that she'd cheated. Dad was shocked. He didn't believe her. Or maybe he just didn't want to believe it."

Jack waited, dread holding him still.

"I guess Mom was determined to prove it, because she said that I...that my dad wasn't really my dad."

What the hell? Shock bolted through him. He couldn't even imagine how she might have felt. "Maybe your father was right. Maybe she just made it up."

"No." Her eyes went a little glassy and her mouth tightened before she said, "In a weird way, once she said it, it actually made sense. To all of us. I'd always been so different, like a changeling." Lips trembling, she looked away, and her voice softened. "I'm not sure who was more shocked, me or Dad."

Jesus. "She shouldn't have thrown that on you with no warning." To deliberately hurt her daughter like that... it was unforgivable.

Seconds ticked by before she spoke again. "Dad blew up, saying he'd always suspected." Nervous fingers twisted the rings on her right hand. "It was like from one minute to the next, he hated me."

Rage churned inside Jack, so hot and turbulent he had a difficult time tamping it down. Rage wasn't what she needed, so he sucked in cleansing air until he knew he could speak without growling. "Are you certain your mother didn't say it just to hurt him? People sometimes do crazy things when they're angry."

"Dad insisted on a DNA test right away. Mom didn't lie." Ronnie shook her head. "I thought they would get divorced over it, he was so furious."

"But they didn't?"

"No. Things are still strained, though. Doesn't seem like it'll ever be like it used to be." She smoothed her hands out over her thighs. "Skylar blames me."

So she'd had extra hurt heaped on? No wonder she was

bristly. "Your sister was…what? Thirteen at the time? Too young to be rational. You can't—"

"She blames me now. *Still.*"

That spiked his anger all over again. "Then she's a fool. How the hell would it be your fault?"

Wide-eyed over his tone, she explained, "If I'd tried harder to be more like them, like the rest of the family, it wouldn't be such an issue."

"I happen to like who you are."

She blinked, then frowned. "You don't really know me."

"Doesn't sound like they do either."

The frown evened out and she sighed. "Dad always said I was the black sheep of the family, and he's right. I never completely fit in." She gave a wry smile. "They're all tall, with honey blond hair and dark blue eyes." She ruffled a hand through her hair. "Even without bleaching it, my hair is far lighter than theirs."

"That happens. People can inherit physical traits from grandparents, or even great-grandparents."

Putting her hands over her chest, she said, "I didn't inherit *this.*"

His gaze flashed to her chest. At her hands on her breasts. He felt like a complete bastard for stirring at the sight.

"Mom and Skylar have much bigger boobs, as did all the women in my family."

Disgruntled, Jack scowled. "Women put too much focus on that."

"Ha! Only because men focus on it—and don't deny it."

"No, I won't." How could he when he was presently

focusing way too much on where she touched herself? "I like your breasts, Ronnie—exactly as they are."

Snorting a laugh, she dropped her hands. "I didn't mean to turn this into a discussion on boob size, but if you're insistent on keeping this job—"

"I am." Now more than ever. From jump, he'd figured Ronnie was worth the extra effort. The sexual chemistry was strong enough that he hadn't minded the challenge. Now it wasn't just physical.

It was a hell of a lot more.

She'd probably deny it, but they had a connection—in bed and out.

"—there's something else you should probably know," she finished.

"Okay." Once she got it all said, he could think of ways to reassure her. "Let's hear it."

In an awful rush, she blurted, "I ran away when Dad told me he *wasn't* my dad. I mean, I was eighteen, so able to leave, but I just booked without telling them where I was going or anything. I figured they didn't care anyway. It was really stupid. I had about a hundred bucks to my name and a part-time job at a grocery. Not exactly independent, you know?"

After what they'd put her through, she was hurt and lashing out. "I get it."

"Anyway, I wasn't sure where to stay, so I figured I'd spend the night in my car and work it out the next day."

She'd probably assumed her family would come after her, that they'd see the move as a desperate cry for understanding…because that's how he saw it. "How'd it go?"

"Not great." She hesitated for an extended time, struggling, her breathing more shallow, her color intensifying, then she whispered, "I got grabbed off the street."

Jack went rigid from his feet to his hairline. Knowing he couldn't continue this conversation while driving, he glanced in the rearview mirror, made some quick maneuvers, and took an upcoming off-ramp.

Ronnie didn't seem to notice. Turned toward him, one hand gripped the top of the seat, the other fisted on her thigh. "It was a warm night so I had the driver-side window down. I was about to doze off when this crazy dude literally reached in and grabbed me."

Jack curved a hand over hers, their linked fingers resting on her leg.

"When he dragged me out, I tried to scream, but I couldn't seem to get enough air. Then he shoved me into a trunk and no matter how much I pounded and yelled, he just kept driving and driving. Honest to God, it felt like he drove forever."

She paused, her bottom lip tightening, blinking fast. In a whisper, she said, "I figured I was dead meat, you know? But while I was in that damned trunk, praying like crazy that he wouldn't rape me, kill me, or both, I decided I didn't care if I had a dad. I didn't care if I had a mom or a sister either." She drew in a shuddering breath. "I just wanted to *live*."

He pulled the car around back of a gas station, jerked it to a stop, and turned it off.

With sudden realization, Ronnie looked around. "What are you—?"

Already out the door, Jack stalked around the car, snapped open her door, clicked off her seat belt, and drew her up against him, crushing her close.

She was so damned small, so fragile in his arms—but warm, vital, and *alive*. Thank God she'd gotten away.

"Er… Jack?" she mumbled against his chest, her lips a tease.

He counted himself lucky that she wasn't throwing punches or shredding him with her sharp tongue. Cupping the back of her head, he pressed her cheek to his shoulder. And held her. Just that, nothing more.

After a brief bit of confusion, she went pliant against him. "You're comforting me?"

He nodded. "And me." Crazy that she sounded so confused. When was the last time anyone had offered her comfort? True, every inch of him thrummed with awareness. He ignored it to focus on the rare pleasure of her acquiescence.

Silky hair teased his mouth as he kissed her temple. A lot of things were starting to make sense now: her insistence on one-night stands, the stark need for independence, the surly defensiveness whenever he got too close.

Only she wasn't surly right now, and he planned to take advantage of that. "Will you tell me how you got away? Did you know about the interior latch?" Law required an interior latch on trunks, but unfortunately, most people didn't know about them.

The way she burrowed closer surprised and pleased him. "I found it by accident, really. I was so panicked, that at first all I did was cry." With disgust, she sneered, "*So* useless."

Would she keep ripping out his heart? "You're allowed to cry, Ronnie."

"It's a waste of energy." In an abrupt effort to change the subject, she pressed back to look up at him, then over him. "God, you're big." She tested her fingers against his chest. "Hard, too."

Much more of that and he'd be looking for a room.

Emotion already had a stranglehold on him, putting him on edge. Adding in lust would push him right over the edge. "Before you start seducing me—"

"I wasn't!" A smile teased the side of her mouth. "Not seriously, anyway."

"Will you tell me the rest?" Somewhere he hoped to hear a happy ending, like perhaps she'd been reunited, if even briefly, with her family.

As if she didn't want to, Ronnie wrinkled her nose. "It's not an uplifting story."

Jack stroked her hair, encouraging her anyway.

With a sigh of resignation and a mock frown, she said, "I can't, not while you're holding me. You're too distracting."

Letting her go wasn't easy, but he made a show of opening his arms and taking two steps back. "Go."

She leaned on the car, arms folded. "I found the latch by accident and when the trunk opened, I saw we were in this remote area I didn't recognize. A narrow gravel road in the woods, loads of trees everywhere, and I didn't see any houses. He'd already been driving slower, but as soon as the trunk opened, he hit the brakes. I damn near fell out, so it didn't take much for me to hit the ground." Her gaze held his. "I knew he was coming. I heard his door open."

Keeping his distance just about killed Jack. He wanted to touch her, soothe her. More than that, though, he wanted her to share. So he held quiet, encouraging her by listening.

She smirked. "I was pretty sure I couldn't outrun him. I wasn't very athletic then and I'd been cramped in the car for a while. I knew I had to do something, though, or back in the trunk I'd go, right?" She paused, gathering her thoughts. "With all the trees, branches were on the ground everywhere. I grabbed one. I remember that it was really heavy, too heavy, but I swung it…" Her voice trailed off.

"I hope you fucking killed him."

His low tone brought her back and she half grinned in a display of unconvincing cockiness. "Close. I still don't know quite how it happened, but I smashed in his face." She swallowed, shook her head. "He had a gun, did I tell you that?"

"No," Jack whispered.

"He went down so fast he didn't have a chance to use it. My first thought was to run, but I couldn't see the end of the road, not with the way it wound through the woods. I didn't know where we were, if maybe he was meeting other people who might show up at any minute." Stepping away from the car, she paced, behind him, back again—this time standing closer. "The car was there, still idling. I didn't want to drive forward because that's the way he was going and I didn't know what I'd find there."

Jesus, even panicked and terrorized, she'd been a critical thinker.

"There wasn't a lot of room to turn around," she explained, "but I finally managed. And I kept… I kept thinking he'd wake up, that I should have taken his gun, that I'd run into someone on the narrow road and be in trouble all over again."

"You must have been terrified." He took a step closer, too, close enough now that they almost touched.

She didn't move away.

"I think I was on autopilot, you know? I just kept driving until I found a small town. I remember it surprised me when I realized my purse was in the front seat with my phone. I didn't even know he'd taken it, but I jumped on it like a lifeline and called my mom."

Not the police? It was a telling reaction.

"I was babbling and stupidly crying and probably not making any sense. Mom didn't realize that anything was really wrong. She thought I was hysterical over the stuff with my dad and I couldn't seem to make her understand. But then a cop saw me and stopped and..." She shrugged, pasted on a smile, and announced, "That's it."

Jack bent to press a firm kiss to her mouth, startling her. "Not even close."

She frowned. "Close enough."

"Ronnie," he chided softly. "You've come this far. Why not tell me the rest?"

Put out, she groaned dramatically. "Fine. The cop talked to Mom and told her he was with me and that I had some bruises and he'd figure it out and get back with her. He was so nice, Jack. He took me to the police station and stayed with me while other cops went to check it out. The guy was still there, and his face was..." She gave a small shake of her head, then moved against him.

Automatically, Jack's arms came around her, but he resisted the urge to crush her tight. "Dead?"

"No. But I'd broken parts of his face pretty badly."

"Good."

When her shoulders trembled, Jack hoped it was with humor and not remembered horror. When she lifted her face he had it confirmed. "Yeah, I didn't feel any remorse, not over that part anyway. The cop, who was one of the kindest people I'd ever met, found out that the dude had a long criminal record. Not kidnapping or anything, but assault, robbery, stuff like that. It was lights-out for him for a good long while, and then he got extended jail time."

"I hope he rots."

"Me, too." The softest expression he'd ever seen drifted over her features. "You're like a magician or something. I've never talked about this stuff with anyone, but here I am in a gas station, spilling my guts."

Jack cupped her face. "I'm impressed."

"That I'm so long-winded?"

That self-deprecating humor made him kiss her, just a quick, firm press. "That you're such an amazing survivor." He had a million questions yet, all of them centered on her family. If it weren't for the exhaustion in her eyes, he'd keep her standing right here for another hour, getting answers while he could.

With any luck, there'd be time enough for that later.

"Want to grab a drink or something while we're here? I might as well fill up the car, too."

"Sure." Her hands slid up and over his shoulders. "This is all pretty damned weird for me. I don't..." she gestured "...*share* with people. I don't talk about the past. I don't cuddle."

She didn't let anyone in—yet she'd opened up for him. "I know. Give it a chance and you might find you like it." *You might find you like* me. "What do you think?"

Going on tiptoe, she put her mouth to his.

Jack struggled not to take over as she expertly teased him, building the kiss little by little until their mouths were open, tongues stroking, familiar heat rising between them.

Against his mouth, she breathed, "You sure I can't convince you that sex would be better than the job?"

Sex would be infinitely better, but he wanted more

than one night to see where things would go. With any luck, he'd get both the job and a satisfying sexual relationship. "You are an incredible temptation, more so than any woman I've ever known, but I'm not turning down work."

After thumping her forehead twice to his chest, she stepped back. "You're going to regret that," she predicated, but she sounded more resigned than angry. "Okay, so let's do this."

"This?" His dick jumped as if sure she meant sex now. His brain hoped she meant something more.

"I'm thinking maybe…maybe we could give the whole working together thing a try."

"And the sex?"

"Don't push your luck." She snagged her purse from the car and turned for the station. After two steps she looked over shoulder. "But I'll keep my options open."

Jack grinned. Hell, at this point he'd take what he could get.

IT WAS THE most torturous four hours of her life. Ronnie wished she had half of Jack's discipline. He didn't appear to be suffering. No, he just sat back and let her set the tone.

They finished the trip in companionable conversation with Jack telling her about his house renovations and her telling him more about the brothers who employed her.

As if that satisfied either of them.

He hadn't even balked at their pickup item, a discarded mannequin. The oddity happened when wasps built a nest around the head, leaving the whole thing misshapen and bizarre. The wasps had since moved on, but it looked truly horrifying and she knew the brothers would love it.

Other than insisting on transporting it in the trunk, he hadn't said much about it. The man had nerves of steel.

They were headed back when she got the call from Drake Dolby, one of the brothers employing them.

Jack held silent while she listened to Drake's request in his deliberately low, dramatic voice. "Let me make sure Jack's free. If not, I'll take care of it myself. Just a sec." She covered the phone and asked Jack, "You mind backtracking for another pickup?"

Without asking for details, he said, "Sure. There's nowhere I have to be."

Putting the phone back to her ear, she told Drake, "We're a go. Does the buyer expect us?" After she'd gotten the address, she disconnected. "Sorry, we're heading to Louisville now. Drake—he's the oldest of the twins by a few minutes—is afraid of losing out if we don't do the deal today."

"No problem." He glanced at the clock. "I'm meeting them afterward?"

She shook her head. "That'll have to wait. Drake also said that he and Drew are heading out of town for a few days. An oddities and curiosities expo or something. They go to those a few times a year."

"Got it."

His easy agreement grated on her nerves. Here she was, aware of every little thing he did and he just went along for the ride. A few hours ago, she'd have given a few jibes guaranteed to annoy him.

But now…? She couldn't help but savor this new camaraderie. It felt fragile, and oddly special, so she was hesitant to ruin it.

For the briefest moment she wondered what her mother would think of Jack. He was not only handsome but polite to the point where he could drive her nuts, and he carried himself like a leader. Lean, hard, confident.

It struck her that she liked him. *Really* liked him.

Crazy.

How had she let that happen?

One day she'd been fending off literally everyone, and then boom. Jack Crews was in her life, refusing to leave, kissing her silly, making her smile. Instead of walking away, she'd actually confided in him. Dangerous.

He kept her from retreating by continuing to chat, about anything and everything. He had such an easy way about him that she found herself replying without thinking about it too much. She even laughed a few times.

By the time they arrived, she'd lost track of time and was surprised to realize he'd slowed to pull down an overgrown gravel drive that led to a mobile home. Not a nice one either, but a rusted heap surrounded by discarded tires, an ancient tractor, and an empty trailer.

Though he didn't do anything obvious, Ronnie knew Jack was more vigilant. It was there in the set of his shoulders and neck, the intensity in his watchful gaze as he pulled up to a widened parking area next to a beat-up truck.

A man stood off to the side, facing away from them. He held a gun aimed toward a trash bin. It took Ronnie only a second to recognize the weapon.

"BB gun." Not a threat.

Jack nodded. "Stay in the car."

She replied pleasantly, "Screw you," and stepped out.

Before Jack could join her, she put two fingers to her mouth and gave a piercing whistle.

The man with the BB gun jerked around, eyed them both, then turned back. "You here for the carcasses?"

Ick.

Jack asked, "Carcasses?" To his credit, he managed to sound only mildly curious.

Yeah, she hadn't exactly explained, but then again, he hadn't asked. Ronnie nodded. "Yes, we are."

"Be with you in a second." The miserable little man again took aim at the trash bin.

And that's when Ronnie saw it.

Frantically scurrying against an overturned, half-rotted stock tank, unable to find an exit, a tiny ball of fur cried out.

A kitten.

Her heart melted, followed by a surge of rage so powerful it infused every muscle, organ, and bone in her body. Her world narrowed to just the asshole aiming the gun and before she even gave it conscious thought, her knife was in her hand.

"Stop." Her harsh command echoed over the area. Heart hammering, she strode forward.

Behind her, she heard Jack curse.

The man turned again, spat a stream of tobacco toward her, and *laughed* at her knife. "Put it away. I don't need no help."

She barely suppressed a growl. "Shoot at the cat again and no amount of help will save you."

A dark scowl twisted his features. "You're threatenin' me?" He pivoted and pinged another shot that sent the kitten scrambling as the BB ricocheted.

Ronnie drew back—and felt her wrist caught in an implacable grip.

"No," Jack whispered softly.

She started to turn on him, but he pressed her to the side, blocking her with his body.

Then she saw why. The douche had aimed at *her*, was *still* aiming at her.

"Coward," she yelled, not in the least afraid. She'd take a piddling BB or two to save the little animal.

"Bitch," the man snarled back, unrelenting—but he did spare a cautious glance at Jack.

Yeah, big bad Jack. Ronnie seriously wanted to kiss him.

He was about a head taller than the hillbilly tormenting the kitten, and instead of a beer belly and bowed legs, Jack was all solid, imposing muscle.

Voice as calm and polite as ever, Jack stated, "I would appreciate it if you'd put that away."

It was the wrong tone for a man in a dirty wife-beater and greasy hair. "Or what?" He spat again, and this time the disgusting tobacco juice hit the toe of her boot.

"Why, you—"

Wresting the knife from her hand, Jack suggested, "See if you can corral the kitten."

His complacent tone pricked her temper even more. "While you do *what*?"

He smiled. "What I'm hired to do."

CHAPTER SIX

FROM HIS PERIPHERY, Jack watched as Ronnie pulled off her shirt. His breath caught and held—until he realized she wore a form-fitting cami underneath. Though this was no time for distractions, she momentarily stole all his attention.

The cami clung to her upper body, revealing her small, round breasts, a narrow rib cage and narrower waist, and ended shy of the waistband of her jeans, leaving a strip of flesh for him to see. She paid no attention to the cool weather, putting all her concentration on using the shirt like a net to catch the kitten, while avoiding sharp claws.

"What the fuck do you think you're doing?"

Drawn back to the more important issue of an idiot with a weapon, Jack said, "She's rescuing the animal you were using for target practice."

Another stream of tobacco squirted from the man's mouth. "My cat, my gun, my property." He curled his lips back over stained teeth. "You and your bitch should mind your own business."

Jack crowded closer. "I strongly suggest you refrain from insulting her again."

A loose chin jutted up. "Or what?"

God, he hated infantile shows of machismo, especially by little weasels who couldn't back it up. At least when Brodie put on a show, he finished it in style. "You already owe her an apology," Jack pointed out.

"Like hell!"

"And," he stressed, "you'll take care of that as soon as you retrieve the—" it was all so stupidly tragic and sad "—carcasses that we came for."

"Fuck that." Filled with petulance, the weasel slashed a hand in the air. "Deal's off."

Jack didn't believe that for a second. This man—and he used that term loosely—wanted the payment.

Whether or not he'd get it remained to be seen.

"Fine." Jack rolled a shoulder with indifference. "I'll just report you to the authorities who can sort it out for me."

Bloodshot eyes widened, then squinted with malice. "You wouldn't dare. I'd tell 'em you threatened me and you'd be in as much trouble as me."

"I can handle trouble. Can you?"

The idiot started to spit.

Jack stepped closer, looming over the man, using his size to his advantage. Violence vibrated in the air. "Spit, and hand to God, you'll regret it."

The man gulped, and judging by the sudden green hue to his skin, he'd swallowed his chew.

The coward before him liked to prey on animals that couldn't defend themselves. Rarely did Jack allow himself the satisfaction of basic instinct. Now, in this moment, for Ronnie, he was happy to unleash his inner barbarian.

Color leeched from the man's face as he scented danger.

Now you know how that kitten felt.

Jack didn't allow himself to be brutal very often. But

for Ronnie, it'd be a pleasure. With the tip of the blade he'd taken from her, he touched the man's chin. "Just so you know, I detest anyone who mistreats animals. After we finish our deal here, I *will* be notifying authorities—those who deal with animal cruelty."

Another gulp had the man's Adam's apple bobbing.

"Consider yourself on notice. If I hear of you ever doing anything like this again, if you even think about spitting your disgusting juice toward an animal, I'll be back. Only you won't know I'm there—until it's too late."

The man's mouth worked, yet nothing came out.

And Jack felt it. Her gaze, penetrating his awareness like hot steam. He cast a glance to the side and found Ronnie staring at him, lips slightly parted, brows up.

As he watched her, she slowly smiled.

"You know," she called, "if I'm not allowed to stab him, neither are you."

Jesus. Jack shook off his temporary loss of control, drew a calming breath, and returned his gaze to the man still immobilized by the knife. Another second or two and the idiot would collapse.

Regaining his normal composure, Jack withdrew the knife, but also took the BB gun from the man's limp hand. "How about I just hold this for you?"

"It ain't right," he mumbled, "stealin' a man's toys."

"I'm having doubts that you could distinguish right from wrong."

"Jack?" Ronnie stood now, hands on hips, that secret smile playing around her mouth. "If you're done goofing off, could you lend a hand? She's so scared, I can't get her."

"Just a second, honey," he called to her. It was a hell of a time for him to take advantage of her, but then, he'd always been about opportunities. Right now, with her both preoccupied over the kitten and amused by his caveman routine, seemed like propitious timing to test his boundaries.

He knew he was right when instead of giving him hell for the endearment, she replied, "Well, hurry it up. We're going to need something to put her in."

Ah, so he and Ronnie were to become pet owners. He'd call that progress.

Jack turned his hard gaze down to meet wary eyes. "I need a crate or a box." When the man hesitated, Jack emphasized, "*Now*, please."

Turning away, the man grouched, "Fucking bastard, comin' here and orderin' me around like dirt. Takin' my gun and stealing my cat." He kicked around the refuse cluttering the area, knocking aside an old clay flowerpot and almost getting his foot stuck in a rusted rake. Finally he unearthed an old animal cage.

Jack examined it. Dried leaves and a few twigs were inside, and the handle on top had long since fallen off, but it closed securely. "This will do. While I help with the kitten, fetch our product—" he wouldn't keep saying *carcasses* "—and we'll be on our way."

"*After* you pay me."

"We're not the villains here."

"Meaning?"

Rolling his eyes, Jack said, "We will, of course, pay you the agreed amount."

"Okay, then." Scratching his protruding gut and still grumbling, the man ambled into his trailer. It squeaked with his weight, the entire thing trembling with his heavy footfalls as he traveled somewhere inside.

Trusting the man would return shortly, Jack stuck the

BB gun in a pocket and turned to survey the situation. He flipped the knife in his hand as he noted that the kitten couldn't go anywhere. Not only did Ronnie have it cornered, but the tiny thing couldn't climb out of the feeder.

"What," Ronnie demanded over her shoulder, "is taking so long?"

Always so prickly. She and the hissing kitten had that in common. "I'm considering how we'll transport our new pet."

She shot him a look that said *our pet?* but immediately turned back to the animal.

Jack took only a moment to locate an old sweatshirt in the trunk of the car, kept there for emergencies. He stuffed it inside the cage so the animal would have something soft to sit on.

Trying not to make too much noise, he approached woman and cat.

Ronnie crouched low, her voice soft and even as she tried to coax the kitten into a more agreeable mood. "It's all right, sweetheart. It's going to be okay. You're just a little peanut, aren't you? Shhh, shhh. You're safe now. Jack dealt with the prick."

How she whispered *prick* in such a sweet voice almost made him laugh. "Here." Jack handed the knife back to her as he slowly knelt at her side. He could see the wild fluttering of the kitten's chest, the panicked white around its eyes. A pink tongue showed as it alternately hissed and panted.

"At this age," he murmured to Ronnie, "she's all claws and teeth. If you'll hold the cage, I'll get her."

"Don't hurt her," Ronnie said without taking her eyes from the animal.

"You should already know me better than that."

After a second, she nodded. "Yeah, I do."

They traded, him now with her shirt and her with the open cage. He spread the shirt like a net, but she was so small it didn't give him a lot of room for error. "By the way, try to keep an eye on our seller. I don't trust him."

"I wish you'd have hit him."

"I might still." Lightning fast, he caught the kitten, bundling it in the shirt. Horror-struck screeching turned to plaintive yowls once he got it inside the cage. Though he'd managed it without a single scratch, the kitten wasn't at all impressed with the rescue. She hunkered down in a corner and panted even harder.

"Poor baby. We'll have to get it a water dish right away." Large green eyes and puffy gray fur seemed to be the most substantial things on the cat. Lifting it had been like lifting dandelion fluff—weightless, except for the panicked wriggling.

The obvious emaciation, the ticks and burrs, enraged Jack all over again, but he kept his tone even when he said, "Food, too. God knows when she last ate."

He'd take care of both water and food on the drive home. He didn't want that kitten to do without for a single moment longer than absolutely necessary.

"I want to kill him."

That broken whisper, raw with empathy, drifted over Jack's skin, then sank in, making his heart lurch. He knew Ronnie meant the abuser, because he felt the same.

Again, he suffered the urge to soothe her, even knowing how she'd react to it. He did allow himself one touch to her silky, disheveled hair. Always disheveled. She seemed to like it that way. And honestly, so did he. Being mussed suited her, somehow softening her otherwise cynical persona.

Liquid silver eyes met his.

Tears? From Ronnie Ashford, self-proclaimed badass, woman with a laser-sharp tongue and an independent streak a mile wide?

"I have questions for you," he stated, because he couldn't handle that expression on her. Not right now. Hell, a second more and he *would* kill the bastard who'd caused it all.

The tender moment faded as she frowned in her familiar way. "Questions about what?"

He went with the first thing to come to mind. "Where is your family now? And have you ever met your real father?"

That came out of nowhere, surprising even him, and she blinked. "What the hell brought that on?"

Jack shrugged. "No idea. Just curiosity, I guess." That wasn't a lie. He wanted to know each tiny detail about her, her past, her hopes for the future—what drove her now. But as usual, timing was everything and for a second there, they'd both been caught in an emotional vortex. Knowing he couldn't do anything he really wanted to do—like strip her naked and kiss her all over, or pull her in his arms and coddle her until she no longer felt alone, or be her white knight and demolish the bastard—distraction seemed like the only option.

With a rude snort, she said, "You are so damned weird sometimes."

Glad that she sounded more like herself, Jack smiled. "Thank you."

"And you can rot on your curiosity."

He was about to prod her when the man reemerged with a large paper bag.

Touching her shoulder, Jack said, "Since I'm not sure

what we're buying, do you want to handle the transaction?" *With me very close by.*

"Sure." The gleam in her eye now was pure malice. "But let's put the peanut in the car first."

Cute name she'd chosen. "All right." Jack carried the cage, holding it out from his body and ensuring his fingers didn't become bait to tiny sharp teeth or claws. Luckily, the kitten had worn itself out and now just sat in a tight little ball in the far corner, its face hidden.

After opening the driver's door, Ronnie pulled the seat forward and Jack wedged the cage into the back seat.

"Just a minute, sweetie," Ronnie crooned gently to the cat, but as she straightened, gentleness washed from her expression, leaving only her usual aggression. "Let me do the talking."

"Do you promise to talk with your mouth, not your knife?"

"No." She stalked forward in that take-charge way that belied her petite size. "But I'll try."

Amused, Jack said, "I'll take what I can get." Close enough to ensure her safety, he listened while Ronnie handled the deal.

"Let me have the bag." She reached for it, but the weasel held it away.

"Not until I get my payment."

Ronnie moved so quickly, it surprised even Jack. She snatched away the bag before the crude bastard could counter her. "You'll get paid when and if I confirm the items." She looked inside, wrinkled her nose, and closed it again.

"Carcasses?" Jack asked, disliking that word more and more.

"Yes, both of them, I think."

"Both?"

"A two-headed snake, and a one-eyed rat. Just as we agreed." The man took a step back as Ronnie's furious gaze drilled through him. "I didn't kill 'em," he said quickly. "That's exactly how I found 'em!"

Jack placed a hand on her shoulder. "Peanut is waiting."

A sound something like a snarl whispered from her, then she shoved the bag at him. "I didn't name the cat that. She's just as small as a peanut." From her big satchel she withdrew the payment and shoved it at the man, not waiting for his hands to open before she dropped it. Bills fluttered to the ground, and greed bent his knees as he hurried to collect it.

Still touching her, something he wouldn't mind doing more often, Jack steered her toward the car. When she didn't shrug him away, he lowered his hand to the small of her back. His pinkie finger grazed bare skin above the waistband of her jeans.

It shouldn't have been a big deal. Yes, her skin felt incredibly silky, warm to the touch. At thirty-two, he'd touched enough women that something so simple shouldn't have felt like foreplay.

But this did.

Given what he carried in the bag and the fact that Ronnie still sizzled very close to violence, it was crazy for him to be thinking along those lines. He couldn't gauge whether or not she might suddenly explode.

It wouldn't surprise him if she did.

And yet, he noticed other things, like the softness of her skin. Around her, he couldn't seem to keep intimate thoughts at bay.

Veering around to the trunk, he asked, "Care to explain?"

Her hand swatted the air, but her annoyance remained in the way she crossed her arms and how she dropped a hip to rest against the side of the car. "He had a neighbor as fucked up as him. The dude thought demons were after him when he found the two-headed snake first, and then later the one-eyed rat. It didn't help that he was always high on something. Eventually he overdosed."

Would the brothers have sent her out to this remote location alone if he hadn't taken the job? The idea unsettled him, but also gave him ammunition for convincing her that he was an asset, not a liability.

After all, how would she have gotten Peanut without him?

Refusing to think of what could have happened to her, Jack asked, "So how did our weasel come by them?"

"There's a shed where he stored stuff." Her chin tucked down but her gaze stayed glue to the man now counting his money. "Behind his trailer, between the two properties. I guess our marksman here grabbed them to sell."

"What the hell would possess a man, even a louse like him, to steal dead animal bodies?"

Tension gathered, and Ronnie cracked her neck to the side. It was such a guy thing to do, Jack marveled.

With admiration.

"Guess he knew they'd be worth a few bucks. He offered them up, the brothers wanted them, and here we are."

Closing the trunk, Jack sealed the purchase inside. Out of sight, but not out of mind.

"I need my gun back."

Jack turned to consider the creep, standing there in his dirty clothes, money clutched in his sweaty hand, his existence utterly grim. A human who took pleasure in being inhumane.

He said to Ronnie, "Go ahead and get in the car. I'll be right back."

Her brows lifted. "Will you hit him?"

"No." Jack strode to the man, closing the distance even when the miserable bastard backed up. He pulled out the gun, but held it out of reach. "It's yours, so I'll return it. But the very first thing I'm going to do once we're out of here is report you for animal cruelty. You better not torment anything, not even a mosquito. Do you understand?" He shoved the gun to the man's chest. "We have your name. Your address. And you better believe, if animal control doesn't do anything, I will."

The man nodded and Jack turned away. The sooner he made good on that promise, the better he'd feel.

To his surprise, Ronnie had done as he'd asked and was in the car, likely just to talk to the cat, but still…

She grinned as he got behind the wheel and turned the key.

Far as Jack was concerned, they couldn't get out of there quick enough. But when they reached the main road, he pulled over to the curb.

Drawing her attention off the cat, Ronnie looked around. "What are you doing?"

"This." He unbuttoned his shirt, one button, two, three.

She watched the movement of his fingers, her attention ripe. "Er…why?"

It sounded ridiculous, even to him, but she deserved the truth. "Seeing you like this—" he nodded at her bare arms and shoulders, the expanse of chest, the hint of cleavage…hell even her collarbone "—is making it difficult for me to keep my hands off you." He shrugged the shirt off his shoulders and offered it to her.

Sitting a little straighter, she scowled. "Well, thanks a lot! Am I supposed to be immune to *that*?" Her gaze moved hungrily over his upper body, making him feel naked even though he wore an undershirt and pants. "Because news flash, Jack, I'm *not*."

They stared at one another, a clash of wills, until the kitten mewled.

"We need to get Peanut a water dish and some food. Since I have to drive, me ogling you isn't a great idea." It was the soundest logic he could come up with under the circumstances—the circumstances being a semi-erection, a half-starved feral kitten in the back seat, a lunatic collector of freakish corpses behind them, and a long drive ahead.

"Fine." Lacking graciousness, she stabbed her arms into the sleeves and pulled the shirt closed around her. "I was cold anyway."

It felt like his hair stood on end. He put the car back in gear and drove away. "Why the hell didn't you say so?"

Shrugging, she pulled the collar toward her nose and breathed in. "Smells good." She gazed at him through lowered lashes, a smile playing on her lips. "Like you."

God, such a tease. He liked the idea of his scent being all over her. He liked that *she* liked it, too. "Damn." To make good on his promise, he requested that she report the goon while he drove.

Ronnie looked up the number, called, and gave a calm, detailed report of the man. Neither of them were surprised that he'd been in trouble before. He'd be checked on routinely after that. There wasn't much more either of them could do.

Ronnie had no sooner finished that call when her cell phone vibrated again.

"Sorry." She glanced at the screen and groaned. "It's the brothers."

"Which one?"

"Both." She accepted the call. "Hey, guys. What's up?"

Jack held silent, listening as the kitten rustled around in the cage and as Ronnie shifted in her seat.

"Okay, just a sec." She covered the phone. "Drake wants it on speaker." She lifted the phone, touched the screen, and said, "Go on, Drake."

"Mr. Crews," came an eerily disembodied voice.

Jack had no idea which brother spoke, so he said only, "Mr. Dolby. Something I can help you with?"

"As a matter of fact, there's something you can both do. We felt like we should only have to say this once, so we hope you're both listening."

Up to that point, only one man spoke, not two, so the whole *we* thing was weird. "Sir?"

"Do you two think you could conduct one exchange without infuriating someone?"

Ronnie said, "Hey, neither time was our fault."

"And do you think," said another male voice, apparently the other brother, though Jack didn't know if it was Drake or Drew, "that you could refrain from threatening sellers?"

Deadpan, the other one added, "It's bad for business."

"And gives us an unnecessary reputation."

Jack glanced at Ronnie, unsure what to say. He knew

what he *wanted* to say, but he didn't want to get her in trouble with her bosses.

That imminent explosion he'd predicted earlier detonated.

"You," she accused, "are the ones who sent us to pick up dead animals from a fucking asshole who gets his rocks off by tormenting kittens."

"Animals? It should be a snake and a rat."

"Animals," she stressed again. "And *you* are the ones who told me to make sure I got the goods no matter what."

"Now, Ronnie—"

The tenor of her voice lowered even as the volume got louder until she almost sounded demonic in her rage. "Well, I *have* your rotted creatures, and I'll gladly hold on to them until you return, but don't you *ever* expect me to turn a blind eye to animal abuse, because that's not happening!"

Dumbfounded and doing his utmost not to grin, Jack kept his eyes glued to the road ahead, grateful that they hadn't yet met any traffic. He didn't dare look at Ronnie or he'd completely lose it.

The silence stretched out until one of the brothers cleared his throat. "So… I'm glad we had this talk."

"Yeah, me, too," she snapped.

Jack had to flatten his mouth, hard. But the humor was bubbling up until it almost strangled him.

"We have a few more deals in the works," the other brother intoned in dramatic fashion, as if Ronnie hadn't just chewed their asses. "Until then, your time is your own."

After she disconnected the call and literally threw the

phone into her purse, Ronnie turned on him. "Just what do you think is so damned funny?"

"You," he choked, unable to hold back a second more.

She poked him in the shoulder. "Knock it off."

"Can't." He tried, coughing and choking in his effort, but the hilarity broke free.

She slugged his shoulder, then turned away in a huff. He continued to laugh for a good solid minute before he realized she was quiet. Too quiet.

Ah hell. Had he insulted her? It occurred to him, be-latedly, that Ronnie might have felt an affinity to the abused kitten. She, too, had been trapped, tormented with ill intentions, and then treated with disregard by the very people who should have protected her.

Sympathy and understanding stomped the humor, and he got himself under control. "Ronnie?"

Staring out the window, she gave a noncommittal "hmm?" She didn't sound insulted, exactly. More like introspective.

"You never cease to amaze me."

"Yeah?" Though her head rested against the seat back, she lazily turned to see him. "Me refusing to take shit is a big surprise?"

"No, I just... I had the feeling you liked your job too much to risk it."

"Please. I like them more than I like the work. But where else would those two find someone as reliable as me to do their bizarre bidding?"

Jack could just imagine the job description. "I see what you mean."

"I'm a catch and they know it."

"I'm glad that you know it, too." Jack sensed the intensity of her gaze as it moved over him, stroking some places—like his shoulders—more than once.

"I used to underestimate myself." Her fingers drifted idly over her denim-covered thigh, toying with a worn patch. "I thought I needed certain things. Certain people." Her voice had taken on a mellow note, as if the rage she'd expended left her relaxed. "Now I know I can get by on my own, that I can defend myself if I need to."

Not wanting to ruin the moment, Jack didn't point out all the ways she could still be hurt if she wasn't more careful. Instead he noted the positives, saying, "You're strong. Self-assured."

She nodded. "Never again will I be a victim. Not for anyone."

A warning? Had she lowered her expectations to ensure no disappointments? He didn't like that idea. "No one goes through life without getting hurt a little." He tried a smile, but it didn't feel too effective. "That's called living."

No objection—but no agreement either.

After a heavy silence, Ronnie studied a fingernail. "So."

Uh-oh. That tone sounded different. "So?"

"You cracked a little back there."

Jack felt his shoulders tighten, his neck stiffen. "I don't know what you mean." He knew exactly what she meant.

When he'd threatened the weasel, and enjoyed doing so, she'd stared at him in rapt fascination, as if she'd known exactly how he felt.

"You cracked, and I liked it." Satisfaction curved her mouth—a mouth he wanted to taste. "Much better than that freaking polite, nauseating niceness all the damn time."

We all have our defenses, honey. Though with Ronnie, he was constantly tempted to be himself. "I didn't realize I was being *nauseatingly nice.*"

"Yes, you did. You do it on purpose. I get bitchy and you counter it by acting like nothing could shake your manners. I didn't mean it as a complaint. It's just… I'm having fun." She wrinkled her nose. "Isn't that strange?"

Glad to divert her from talking about him, Jack said, "No, because I'm having fun, too."

Earnest, she half turned in the seat. His shirt swam around her, her fair hair in disarray, but she *did* look happy, and somehow it was sexy as hell. "I mean, we have a gross two-headed snake in the trunk, right?"

"Very true."

"And that seller was seriously warped."

Jack still wanted to demolish him. "An abusive bastard."

"And the poor kitten is probably traumatized." She glanced in the back seat, contentment lowering her voice. "But she's sleeping now."

Just as quiet, he said, "I'm glad."

"Yet here we are. Still talking, even joking. And I feel good. I don't understand it, and I feel a little guilty for it, but it's true."

"Look at it this way. You did your job, you saved a sweet little animal, and you got to raise hell. That's a good day in anyone's book."

Ronnie grinned. "I guess you're right. But my favorite part…"

"Yes?"

She rolled a shoulder, looking almost shy. "I think my favorite part is *you.*"

CHAPTER SEVEN

NOT MUCH SCARED Jack Crews, she'd give him that. Not disgusting little men who sold weird critter bodies, and not bold, outspoken women who admitted to liking him a little too much.

Or…maybe he hadn't understood her meaning when she'd explained why the day was so enjoyable?

He hadn't replied to her comment other than to smile, and his smiles were so devastating, they made her want to throw off her clothes and straddle him. He was, by far, the most unique man she'd ever met.

Was it any wonder she only now began to worry about his lack of response?

Though she wasn't an expert on these things, his smile seemed like acceptance, which was a damn sight better than horror, right?

Right. But seriously, just once she'd like to rattle that infuriating, unshakable demeanor of his. He'd lost a bit of his polish when dealing with the creep. Witnessing that primitive side of him had left her mesmerized.

What would it be like to see him totally cut loose?

Finding out in bed would be the most fun…but she'd stupidly ruled that out. At least to *him*, she had. Didn't mean a woman couldn't change her mind. She'd wait and see how the rest of the day played out.

The past half hour of the drive they'd made a list of

things the cat would need. Jack insisted on calling her Peanut, and by the time she'd looked up a pet supply shop and they'd driven slightly out of their way to it, the name stuck.

Peanut had either worn herself out or she was too tired to continue her complaints, because she slept for the majority of the ride until Jack parked in the lot.

After removing his seat belt, he turned to look in the back seat. "We don't actually know how feral she might be. A domesticated kitten, under the circumstances where we found her, would probably act just as wild."

Even though he could be right, Ronnie wouldn't chance it. "I don't want to open her cage unless the doors are closed. If she got out, we could lose her forever."

"Agreed. Plus, I don't want to unleash a wild cat in a car where we can't avoid claws." When he reached back toward the cage, the kitten cowered. "Poor baby," he crooned. "You'll feel better when you eat."

Ronnie sincerely hoped that was true. "How are we going to do this?"

In the end, he carried the entire dirty container into the pet store. Customers stared at them like they were monsters, and no wonder with the kitten doing her Tasmanian devil impersonation. Jack held the cage securely, but still the kitten managed to rock it.

It didn't help that Ronnie still wore Jack's shirt, too, which left him in an undershirt and slacks. Never mind that it was late October and chilly, he still looked mouthwateringly good, and plenty of people noticed.

Jack paused at a counter and explained the situation to a pretty female clerk who, with sympathy and admiration, offered them the use of a grooming room to move Peanut to a brand-new carrier.

They lined it with a soft pad and fresh blanket, attached a food dish to the corner and filled it with soft canned food, then added a drip-style water bottle so the kitten could drink but the water wouldn't spill. Before attempting to move her, Jack also purchased a litter box and litter, harness and leash, and a few toys. He didn't buy any flea and tick meds because the kitten was so young; he said he'd feel better taking her to the vet first.

It occurred to Ronnie to wonder, was the kitten hers or his? If he kept it, that'd suit her. Wouldn't it?

She ignored the yearning in her heart and reminded herself that the important thing was for the kitten to be safe. It didn't have to be *her* kitten.

What use did she have for a pet anyway? Her apartment didn't allow them, so it'd be more convenient if Jack claimed Peanut as his own. He knew more about loving than she did, anyway.

And if he didn't keep it?

If necessary, she'd get a new place. *Home* had no real meaning for her, so moving wasn't a big deal. She did it often. All she required was a place to sleep and shower, and she could get that anywhere.

One way or another, she'd ensure that the kitten was safe, well cared for, and if she looked deep enough, she could probably find some love to—

A nudge to her side brought her out of her thoughts. Jack stood looking at her, an indulgent smile on his face. The clerk stared only at Jack.

With no idea what she might've missed, Ronnie scowled. "What?"

"We're going to attempt to move Peanut now," Jack explained.

Ronnie glanced around. The carrier was ready, looking much more comfy than the rusted cage. The cat sniffed the air, already aware of the food.

Shaking off her thoughts of the future, Ronnie asked, "What do you want me to do?"

"Just hold the carrier steady. I'm going to tip the old one forward and hope Peanut goes inside for the chow. Betty Jo will close and latch the door."

Betty Jo? So now she and Jack were familiar?

Ronnie eyed the young, pretty, *shapely* clerk with a touch of dislike, but all she said was, "Thanks."

Overall, the maneuver went off without a hitch, namely because Peanut launched forward and attacked the food as if it might disappear, each bite accompanied with a low growl of relish. *Growl-rowl-mmmrrowl-growl.*

With sheer enjoyment, Ronnie watched as Peanut's little belly grew round and the dish grew empty. She didn't know much about animals, definitely not kittens so small, but neither Betty Jo nor Jack seemed concerned.

"Ahhh. Poor thing was starving." Betty Jo looked up at Jack adoringly. "It's so wonderful that you saved her."

Paying almost no attention to the woman, Jack retrieved Ronnie's shirt from inside the old cage. "Actually, it was Ronnie who saved Peanut."

Refusing to be drawn into the adoration, Ronnie crossed her arms. "I spotted her, but you did all the work."

Jack smiled down at Betty Jo. "Do you think you could discard the old cage for us?"

"Of course. Be glad to."

Seemingly oblivious to Ronnie's rising antagonism—though Ronnie didn't buy it—Jack looked around at everything he'd bought, then rubbed the back of his neck.

The raised arm sent his muscles flexing in obvious strength.

Damn him, even his underarm was sexy, with the soft tuft of hair and paler skin there.

Jack said, "I'll need to make two trips to get this all in the car."

Betty Jo breathed to his bulging biceps, "I can help."

His smile could've blinded a person. "You wouldn't mind?"

Was he *flirting* with the clerk? Right in front of her? Okay, so Jack was always smiling, always friendly. Did he have to be *that* friendly?

Disgusted by the possibility that she might be—*ugh*—jealous, Ronnie grabbed the plastic bag of canned food in one hand, the handle of the carrier in the other, and stalked toward the door without a word.

"Or not," Jack mused behind her, grabbing up the litter and cat box. She heard him say, "Thanks again, Betty Jo."

She closed her ears to anything the woman might have replied.

Though she had the heavier load, Jack didn't try to take anything from her. Good thing, too, because she might've kicked him.

Instead he stepped around her and opened the car, putting his load on the back seat. Ronnie avoided eye contact. She didn't want him to know that for a minute there she'd felt…what? Not just jealous, but *possessive*?

What a joke. She knew better than to—

Instead of moving out of her way, Jack leaned in and put his mouth to hers in a firm, quick press of lips that took her completely off guard. Letting their foreheads touch, he said, "Whatever I did, I'm sorry."

Damn it, he *sounded* sorry, which made her second-guess her pique, and that only pissed her off more. Brows crashing down, she snapped, "Don't you dare—"

He kissed her again, this time softer, slower. Deeper. Longer.

She didn't realize he was taking the carrier from her until his body moved into hers. All that heat and muscle, the delicious strength, pressing to her much smaller frame. He made her feel as tiny as the kitten, and for once, it didn't bother her. She *liked* the contrast.

It was enough to muddle her brain.

Tilting his head, he took advantage of her daze to slide his tongue over her bottom lip, then nip it with his teeth. His hot breath warmed her cheek and his scent invaded her head.

Ronnie gave a low groan and used her free hand to clutch at the sleek, firm biceps another woman had admired.

Mine.

It was a terrible thought to have, one that frightened her down to her soul for all it implied. Weak. Possessive.

Needy.

She pulled back, gulping air and trying to ignore the fact that her palm still rested against the hot, solid steel of his arm.

His dark gaze, framed by those crazy thick lashes, dropped to her lips, now wet and swollen. And wanting more.

He made a low, intrinsically masculine sound, then murmured, "Don't slug me, okay?"

"Okay." She wasn't sure she could anyway; it took all her concentration to keep from reclaiming his mouth. God, every kiss with Jack was a revelation, as if each time she learned what kissing should be…but had never been before.

Cautiously he took a step away, putting a foot of space between them and causing her to lose the heated contact of her palm to his arm. "If you did," he warned, "I might drop Peanut."

No, he wouldn't. He had better reflexes than that, and he cared about the cat, too much to harm it, even accidentally.

"Ronnie?"

She swallowed. Was he really expecting her to attack? "I won't." No, she might jump his bones, but she wouldn't hit him.

After one more wary glance, he said, "I could kiss you all day. Your mouth… I already feel like an addict." Frowning, as if puzzled by that, he shook his head and turned to arrange things on the seat so he could situate the cat, taking a moment to talk to her, to reach a finger inside the cage and stroke her back.

Ronnie watched the stretch and roll of sinew and muscle from his shoulders to the waistband of his slacks. She had to curl her hands tight to keep from reaching for him.

He straightened, and she finally got her gaze to Peanut.

Sated now, the kitten ignored them both while licking one dainty paw.

Introspection was a bitch, involving all her brainpower so that she barely paid attention as Jack stepped back, the ultimate gentleman, while she got seated. She licked her lips and tasted him. The feel of his body teased her.

Even more disturbing, having his shirt draped around her ensured that she inhaled his dark, rugged scent with every breath.

They drove away from the pet store and still she couldn't seem to sort her thoughts into any type of order.

After a time, Jack asked, "Why were you mad?"

She wanted to deny all sorts of things. Her response to him. Her fast temper. That idiotic jealousy. He read her so well that it'd all be useless, so instead she shrugged. "It's dumb."

"Tell me anyway?"

Why not? She wouldn't cower from a madman, so why would she cower from the reality of her own feelings? "You were flirting and I… I dunno. It pissed me off." She stabbed him with an accusing glare. "Not that I have any claim on you or anything. But we needed to focus on Peanut."

His mouth didn't smile, not exactly, but some small, subtle change happened near his eyes and she knew: she'd amused him.

Hell, he was *always* amused. Infuriatingly so.

"FYI," he rumbled, somehow making his tone both neutral and knowing, "thanking a person for helping isn't the same as flirting. Not even close. You, I've flirted with. Betty Jo, no."

Ronnie crossed her arms and slumped in her seat. Apparently one-night stands hadn't taught her much about men and all their weird vagaries. "Looked like flirting to me."

"Maybe because you're always so blunt, you don't get the art of it. In the future, I'll try harder to show you the difference."

Great. If he ramped up the temptation, she was a goner for sure.

"Also," he continued, "I'm not an ass who would come on to one woman while I'm with another."

"You aren't *with* me," she protested, though the idea enticed.

"With me, as in nearby," he clarified.

Well, thank God she'd been *nearby* then. To cover those feelings, she complained, "You're so freaking polite to everyone."

That gave him pause. "You already know how I dislike the way my father treats my mom." Far too serious, he promised, "I would never disrespect you that way."

Before she could get too confused by that, he shook his head, saying, "I wouldn't treat *any* woman like that."

Way to make it clear I'm not special.

That sentiment certainly wasn't new. Not that she wanted to be special to him, anyway. She didn't.

Uncomfortable with her own uncertainty, Ronnie refocused on the insight he'd just shared. So that's why he was always so mannered? Made sense, now that she thought about it. God knew, relatives could have such an incredible impact. His father was an inconsiderate person, so Jack went overboard to be polite.

"As long as we're having this heart-to-heart, will you answer about your family?"

Ronnie groaned. He'd let enough time lapse between the question for her to let down her guard, and now she wasn't certain what to say.

For years she hadn't spoken of her family. There'd been no reason because no one had gotten close enough to ask. Somehow, Jack Crews had dug in from the start. How he treated her was…somehow special, and how she reacted to him was equally so.

If she were honest with herself, and she always tried to be, she wouldn't mind reclaiming that settled feeling she'd gotten after telling him the gist of her history.

Maybe holding the truth inside, protecting it in her heart, insulating it, wasn't the right answer.

Maybe, just maybe, that's why those dark nightmares continued to torment her.

Eyeing Jack, she saw his emotional stillness as he waited, as if he sensed her indecision and didn't want to do anything to tip the balance the wrong way. He'd done that from the get-go, understood her better than most. Accepted her in a way few had, including her family.

Sighing, giving up without much fight at all, she rested back against the seat. "What do you want to know?"

JACK SLOWLY RELEASED a breath he'd held too long. He'd felt her weighing the risks, just as he'd felt the moment she decided to trust him.

She might not see it for what it was, but he did. Ronnie needed someone she could rely on, and he planned to be it.

Usually his cordial attitude was easy to maintain. Around Ronnie, not so much. She made him feel things, think things, to an unfamiliar and uncomfortable degree.

It wasn't as easy as usual, but he managed to moderate his tone so that he sounded only casually interested when he asked, "Have you ever met your real father?"

She shook her head. "Naw. What would be the point? Mom says he knew she'd gotten pregnant, but they both had families and he didn't want his disrupted. What they'd had was a fling, not a commitment, so I get it." A pensive silence interrupted the emotionless explanation, and afterward her voice held a tentative note of regret, along with acceptance. "She told me once that if he'd been interested, she might have left Dad. He wasn't, so she didn't, and here we are."

"Why did she do it?"

"The affair?" Ronnie looked away. "Who knows? Guess she didn't love Dad, not enough anyway. Or maybe she was bored. I have no idea."

"Cheaters cheat," he said, hoping she didn't take offense. "I learned that with my dad. I was talking about the big reveal. I know you said your parents were arguing, and that your mother was jealous. But still. Seems like that'd be a secret you'd keep."

Ronnie tilted her head. "Is that what you'd do?"

"I would never cheat in the first place." He let Ronnie absorb that, wondering why it mattered so much for her to believe him. "But if I did, and I had two grown kids, I'd take it to my grave, not use it as ammunition in an argument." Doing so made the woman selfish and cruel, the complete reverse of how his mother had raised her sons.

Ronnie folded the shirt around her, then smoothed it out again. The movements were nervous, a way of giving herself time to think.

Jack didn't rush her. Better than most, she understood the repercussions of someone being unfaithful.

Finally she stilled. "I don't think *cheat* is the right word. It sounds insignificant, like you swindled someone at cards. It's more than that, though." Her voice lowered. "It's the worst sort of deception. It steals a person's faith and their pride. It steals…trust."

"Agreed."

"I wouldn't do that. Ever." He felt her studying his profile, and he felt her searching for the right words. "It's cowardly."

And she was never a coward. "I believe you."

It took her a second, and then she nodded. "Thank you. I believe you, too."

To Jack, it felt like he'd just gotten past another door. Little by little, Ronnie let him closer. "Do you see your mom?"

Again she took her time replying, carefully weighing her words. "I haven't in a long time. They live in Indiana. Not far away, but not close enough that I run into them."

He wondered if that was deliberate. "You don't want to?"

She snuggled into the shirt like she would a blanket. "When I left, I didn't know how long I'd be gone. But no one really…came after me, or asked me to return, so the time just stretched out until now, I see more reasons to stay away than return."

"That can't be true."

Her lips did that funny little quirk that was part sarcasm, part defense mechanism. "Last I talked to my sister, she said things were better with me away. Mom calls every so often, and she said without me there as a daily reminder, Dad has either forgiven her or chosen to look beyond the affair for the sake of their marriage."

Only with one child missing.

Turning her nose, Ronnie sniffed the collar of his shirt, her eyes closing in a look of pleasure.

Or comfort.

Did she try to hide the fact that she was sniffing his shirt, or did she think he wouldn't notice? He could have told her he noticed everything about her. All the time. He'd never been more aware of a woman.

"They're wrong to treat you that way. You realize that, right?"

"Mom's apologized," she said, as if that would help. "I believe her when she says she regrets what happened. She claims that Dad loves me, but he can't come to grips

with the idea of another man touching her, that it's because of her, not me, that he's cut me out." Her narrow
shoulder lifted. "Results are the same."

Yes, results were the same.

Given the way they'd dismissed her so completely,
Jack wondered if she really might be better off without
them in her life. "Are you curious about your real father?"

"Not really." Her lashes, thicker and longer thanks to
her makeup, shadowed her gray eyes so that he couldn't
tell if she said the truth or only tried to convince herself.

What did she look like without all the camouflage?
He wanted to find out. He wanted to see her fresh from
a shower, no makeup, no jewelry—without her usual
masks.

"What's one more person who doesn't want me?" The
second the words left her mouth, she laughed. "God, that
sounded pathetic, didn't it? I didn't mean for it to. I'm
satisfied with my life. I feel stronger than I ever have."

Stronger—but more alone.

It was times like this, when shades of vulnerability
blunted her in-your-face personality, that he wanted her
the most. She looked seductive without trying, female
to his male, delicate but with a woman's will of iron.

"I've learned a lot," she continued without his prompting. "Now I know I can make it on my own. That's a lib-
erating feeling."

Hoping he hid his thoughts, Jack nodded. He, too,
could make it on his own. That didn't mean he wanted to.

Yes, he supported himself, handled all his own business, and lived independently. He'd been doing so since
he graduated high school. But how awful would it be to
lose his mom or Brodie? Charlotte was like a sister and

he loved her dearly. And now Mary, his brand-new sister-in-law, held a piece of his heart.

It wasn't about needing anyone. It was about family who helped buffer disappointments, who celebrated accomplishments. Who had your back on those occasions when things went south, as they sometimes did. It was someone to listen, and someone to give you shit, each at the appropriate times. It was laughter and bickering, holidays together, and visiting just because.

It was *family*, and hers had treated her with cruel disregard.

Needing to touch her, to feel that electric connection again, Jack reached out, offering his hand.

Her silver gaze went from his hand, up his arm, over his shoulder to his profile. He could literally feel her sorting out the insinuation in the offer.

Scoffing, she said, "Hand holding? Are we in high school?"

In a deliberately lofty voice, he explained, "Gestures of affection aren't relegated to adolescence."

The scoff turned to a laugh, and she relented. "You probably know better than me." Her small palm slid over his, adjusting until she could lock her fingers in his, their wrists resting on the console. "You're feeling affectionate?"

"Yes." Affectionate, aroused, possessive... So many emotions blended together in a potent combination, he felt bombarded by them.

"Is this safe? Shouldn't you have both hands on the wheel?"

"If we hit any dicey traffic, yes. But we're smooth sailing for a while now."

With her free hand, she explored the back of his, tracing one delicate fingertip over his knuckles. "Do you work out?"

That came out of nowhere. "Sometimes, when I can fit it in. Other times I jog to unwind. Why?"

"You're so big all over. Not as bulky as your brother, but your strength shows even in your hands." Her butterfly touch drifted up to his wrist, trailed back and forth through the hair on his forearm, then over his biceps.

Exploring him as if it wouldn't make him nuts.

He stayed quiet, not wanting to dissuade her.

"You're impressive, Jack."

Impressive enough to take to bed? He couldn't press her, not yet. He'd already made his preferences well known. "I'm glad you think so."

She snorted. "I'm sure most women think so. Betty Jo sure did."

Squeezing her fingers, he said, "Let's forget Betty Jo, okay?" Before Ronnie could argue, he added, "Dad is an ass, but he's as tall as me, almost as solid."

"And your mom thinks he's good-looking?"

Jack scowled. Maybe he shouldn't have told her that part. "Apparently he is, given the women he brings around."

"You said your mom is short, but is she pretty?"

"I think so. She's short like you, but according to her, she's chunky—though I don't see it." To him, his mother was perfect. Always had been, always would be.

"She must have very *pretty* eyes."

Her emphasis made him laugh again. "Are you insulting me?"

"You have to admit, your eyelashes would make a lot of women jealous."

He'd heard that before so it didn't bother him. "I imagine there are things about you that make men jealous."

Her chin tucked closer to her chest and her gaze sharpened with mock offense. "Such as?"

"Your bold confidence. Your courage. You have your own strengths, Ronnie, and they're obvious. Don't tell me you haven't met a man or two who wasn't threatened by them."

Pleasure softened her voice when she said, "Not you."

Since he had his own confidence, he could easily admire hers. "I don't scare easily."

That made her smile, but only for a moment. "When people look at me, none of that is what they see first."

"Of course not. People, men especially, would notice all the physical assets first, and you have plenty." Enough to make him nearly obsessed. "But it wouldn't take more than a minute to see the rest, and makes you one hell of a catch."

"Thank you," she said, lifting her chin in challenge. "But just so you know, the thing I excel at most is *not* being caught. Not ever again."

CHAPTER EIGHT

ANYONE LOOKING WOULD see only a distracted college boy driving an inexpensive car. No reason for alarm, no reason to be wary.

Which was how North Runde planned it when he arranged the rideshare with the obtuse young man.

From the back seat, North scoured his computer for info on the woman he surreptitiously followed. She'd taken something that belonged to him. A cardinal sin that would demand the sweetest kind of retribution.

"Do you need me to turn up the air?" his driver asked.

"I'm fine." Eyes narrowing, North studied her image on the screen. Women, he'd found, were more enjoyable than men, more easily controlled. The size of the man now with her didn't particularly bother him.

Even big men could be brought to heel.

But a woman, her skin so soft, her bones so fragile... They frightened more easily and it was that fear that he enjoyed the most.

"You sure, dude? You look a little sweaty."

North forced his mouth into the semblance of a smile. "Fine. Adjust the air."

"Sure thing."

No reason to tell the brainless sheep that it wasn't heat glossing his skin. No, it was the craving that had built and built until he felt it expand with every breath he took, the excess oozing from his pores, leaking from his eyes, making his mouth water...

Using his shoulder, he mopped at his temple while keeping his attention on the screen.

Veronica Ashford. He tasted the name, savoring it.

Careful not to make contact with the touch screen, he brought his fingertips close to her features, tracing around the gray eyes, the unsmiling mouth. Soon, very soon, she'd be within reach.

For a while now, he'd been studying her, familiarizing himself with her acquaintances, learning her habits. In a day and age where people put their entire lives on social media, she didn't have a big online presence. That had slowed him down a little. He believed in doing his homework to avoid errors.

In the end, finding her had proved to be a challenge. But he liked challenges, and he'd more than like getting his hands on her.

It had been a risk, asking others about her. Yes, he'd worn a disguise, but an astute person would have seen through it. He tsked quietly, recalling the guileless fools who'd all but handed him her address. No one used the caution they should, probably because they didn't know *him*.

They didn't understand his craving.

He eyed the sheep in the driver's seat, considering him...but no. Using him would only whet his appetite and leave the hunger stronger than ever.

Perhaps the oversize whore who ran the bar? He could use her as an appetizer.

"No." North shook his head, reining himself in, controlling the urges.

"What's that?" the driver asked.

Ideas, images, formed in his head, painting his vision crimson red. Red like his desire. If he was patient, he might find a different use for a conniving, mercenary woman like the bar owner. Yes, he liked that idea better. Kill two birds with one stone, as the saying went.

He glanced up in time to see the yellow Mustang switch lanes. "You can take this exit," North instructed, ensuring he didn't lose sight of them.

"But I thought—"

"Slight change of plans." It wouldn't do to get too close, just close enough to see where she was going. He'd missed his chance at the hotel today, once the big man had shown up to her room.

Not that he was afraid. In his line of work, with the tools he employed, size didn't really matter. But his interest began and ended with Veronica.

She owed him. And that meant she'd eventually have to pay.

BRODIE WAS IN the yard at the offices when they arrived, allowing Howler to water the grass. The second the big dog spotted them, his angular butt, all bones and spindly tail, started swaying. Jack grinned.

As Jack parked and opened his door, Ronnie fretted. "Maybe we should wait until your brother takes in the dog."

"No need. Howler is gentle."

She didn't know the dog well enough to understand, so of course she still worried. "It's just that he's so big and clumsy. Even if he didn't mean to hurt her, he could—"

"Won't happen, honey. Trust me." There, he'd gotten in another endearment without pissing her off. He was making all kinds of strides today. "Howler's like a big mother hen. If anything, he'll make the kitten feel safer. You'll see." He shut the door on her protests and headed around to her side of the car. He understood her worry, but showing her would probably be easier than trying to explain.

Already out and blocking him, Ronnie insisted, "Still. It's not worth taking a chance."

Jack thought about kissing her. So far it had proven an effective method to getting his way. As he considered it, he looked at her mouth, at the soft pink lips slightly parted, and he completely forgot that his brother and Howler were around.

Until the dog almost knocked him over as he shoved past Ronnie and into the back seat.

Howler's entire body went still, poised in surprise and glee. Jack had a feeling the dog even held his breath. Slowly, oh so slowly he lowered his haunches to the ground while sniffing the carrier.

"Once," Jack said softly, "he tried to befriend a baby raccoon. He was heartbroken when the mother raccoon showed up and gave him hell."

Ronnie laughed. "You're serious?"

"He tried the same with an adult skunk. That didn't go too well either."

"Oh my God, a skunk?"

"Anything smaller than him, he instinctively tries to protect it. He'd make a miserable hunting hound."

Giving a soft whine, Howler looked back at Jack in question, but only for a split second before he returned his attention to the carrier.

Brodie stepped up. "What do you have in there?"

"A kitten." Very briefly Jack explained to his brother what had happened.

"Bastard," Brodie said low, anger coloring his tone.

"The cat doesn't need another fright," Ronnie said.

"Agreed." Seeing the concern still in her eyes, Jack couldn't resist a kiss, but he kept it short since they weren't alone and he wasn't into torture. "Try a little trust, okay? You know I wouldn't endanger her."

Shifting her gaze from his face to Howler to Brodie and back again, she gave one quick nod.

In so many ways, she pleased him. The compassion for a kitten, her acceptance of Howler, and ultimately the trust she afforded him, all felt very special—because she was special.

Jack touched her cheek. "Thanks." He turned to the dog. "Back it up, Howler, and I'll get her out."

The dog sprang away as if launched from a trampoline. Excitement rounded his eyes comically as he went to his stomach, his knees poking up along his big body, his face on his front paws, his tail wildly flagging the air.

"Good boy," Brodie praised. "Now be gentle."

Jack lifted out the carrier and set it on the ground.

"What if she runs away?" Ronnie fretted.

"Howler won't let her." In a gesture of comfort, Brodie draped an arm around her shoulders. "Just watch."

Jack frowned at the familiarity, but what could he say? Nothing. Yet. Soon, though, he'd have some rights. *Hopefully.*

He opened the latch on the door and swung it wide, freeing the kitten.

To everyone's surprise, Peanut tottered straight to Howler without a speck of shyness or reserve, almost as if she recognized him—or at least recognized another animal and, perhaps, a protector.

For his part, the dog held perfectly still, only his eyes

moving, as the kitten sniffed his nose, head-butted his snout, and tasted his ear.

"Such a good baby," Brodie crooned in the ridiculous voice he reserved for Howler, earning an incredulous stare from Ronnie. "What? He is a good baby."

Ronnie snickered.

Stepping away from her, approaching cautiously, Brodie lowered to his knees near the animals. "You're such a good dog, Howler, yes you are."

Howler whined, sniffing the kitten's butt and knocking her over in the process. His ears shot up as if horrified by what he'd done, and he watched her closely.

"She's not hurt," Brodie assured him. He didn't reach for the kitten, instead stroking the big dog until his fingers got closer and closer to the little ball of fur.

Jack and Ronnie stood together, watching the proceedings with shared awe.

"He's so patient," Ronnie leaned in to whisper, her gaze still glued on the animals and Brodie.

"We all love animals." Jack brought her closer still with an arm around her waist.

As Brodie won over the kitten in infinitesimal stages, Jack did the same with Ronnie—until finally she stood in front of him, leaning her back to his chest, both his arms around her.

Damn, it felt good to hold her like this.

"You guys," Charlotte complained quietly as she came from the office. "Why didn't you tell me there was a kitten?"

Brodie said, "Hey, Charlotte?"

She paused. "What?"

"Jack brought home a kitten."

"Ass." Shaking her head, she said to Ronnie, "Do you

see what I put with up?" As if, because they were both female, they should have a natural rapport.

In Jack's experience, that was usually the case, but Ronnie didn't seem to get it. She pressed back as if retreating, confusion making her frown.

In her ear, Jack whispered, "Siblings give each other shit all the time."

Putting her chin to her shoulder, she replied just as quietly, "I got that—although it's not something my sister and I did."

"Maybe women are different." The softness of her cheek drew him and he couldn't resist pressing his lips there. Then to the tender skin below her ear. And her ear lobe.

With her eyes going heavy, she pointed out, "Charlotte's a woman."

"But she was practically raised with us," Brodie said, proving they hadn't been quiet enough, though he didn't look at them.

Later, Jack would have to thank his brother for his discretion. In the yard with his family around wasn't the right time for advancing his pursuit, but he couldn't seem to keep his hands or his mouth off Ronnie.

"I've learned to give as good as I get," Charlotte quipped, before crouching next to Brodie. Her gaze immediately went soft with delight. "*Ohhh*, it's so tiny."

Just then, Howler licked the kitten from butt to neck, raising her small hind legs off the ground and leaving the fur along her back wet and standing on end. Owl-eyed, tail in the air, the kitten turned—and laughter resounded everywhere.

Peanut looked to be permanently caught in a heavy wind gust.

Jack was amused by the sight, but more than that, he enjoyed the way Ronnie so freely shared her humor. The woman didn't do anything half-assed, including laughing.

Hugging her a little tighter, Jack nuzzled the soft skin at the side of her neck, left more available by the open collar of his shirt. She instantly quieted.

God, he needed to get her alone, and soon.

Charlotte, who had fallen against Brodie in her hilarity, wiped her eyes. "She's precious."

"She," Jack said, "is Peanut."

"Well, amusing as Peanut has been, I came out here to ask if either of you could do a job."

"I'm leaving in fifteen," Brodie said.

Tilting her head, Charlotte caught Jack's gaze. "Mrs. Anderson, who doesn't live that far from you, is having a party, but you know she doesn't drive. Her nephew was going to pick up some catered food for her on his way over, but he's stuck at the airport, so she's hoping we can make it happen. Everything's ready, just has to be picked up and taken to her house."

Several reasons came to mind for why he didn't want to do it, but he'd known Traci Anderson since sixth grade when she'd been his favorite teacher. Once she'd retired, she'd gotten as popular as Freddie's with her regular hosting of neighborhood groups. Mrs. Anderson helped organize everything from the Strawberry Festival to the annual parade down Main Street. Unfortunately, her eyes were bad enough now that driving wasn't a good idea.

She was a very dear lady, so of course he'd help, but first he needed to figure out what to do with the cat, and then he needed Ronnie.

Alone.

Pulling away from him, arms crossing in that now-familiar way, Ronnie said, "We're done for the day." Her tone claimed indifference, but in her eyes he saw the disappointment.

She wasn't thrilled to call it quits for the day either.

"It's not our usual job," Jack explained, "but Mrs. Anderson is a sweetheart."

"*Your* sweetheart?"

For anyone in earshot, it was impossible to miss the sharp crack of her jealous suspicion.

Brodie gave a bark of laughter. "Good God, I hope not, because she's *eighty-five*." He drew one fingertip down the kitten's back, smoothing her fur back into place. "Plus she likes me more than Jack."

"Bullshit," Jack said, going along with the joke to spare Ronnie more embarrassment. "She thinks you're too bossy."

"Whereas *you*," Charlotte chimed in, "use your well-mannered civility like a weapon, bludgeoning people with it."

Ronnie jumped on that. "What a perfect description! He does that all the time and it's annoying as hell!"

"Right?" Charlotte winked. "Kittens have claws, and Jack has diplomacy."

Brodie was back to laughing again.

"Shut up, you asshat," Jack growled.

Brodie shook his head, unable to stifle the humor. "She compared you to a kitten."

Charlotte turned on Brodie. "And you're a big cuddly bear."

With a snort, he muttered, "Better than a kitten."

Jack started to respond, until he noticed Ronnie grinning. Now seemed like a good time to push his agenda.

"I don't mind doing Mrs. Anderson a favor—if you'll ride along?"

The smile dimmed. "Me?"

"Sure. Why not? Did you have somewhere else you had to be?"

Instead of answering that, she asked, "How long will it take?"

"Depends." On whether or not she'd let him into her room once he took her back to the hotel. "Are you in a hurry?"

As if in thought, Ronnie pursed her mouth to the side, then turned to Charlotte. "Will I be able to grab a sandwich at this food place?"

Charlotte's knowing gaze bounced back and forth between Ronnie and Jack before she settled into a conspiratorial grin. "Sure. Brewer's is known for their catering, but they also do individual service."

"Okay, then. Why not?"

"Great." With that taken care of, Jack only had one other consideration. Laying a heavy hint, he said, "Now I need to figure out what to do with the kitten."

Brodie looked up. "Who's keeping her?"

Stepping forward, Ronnie said, "I can, but since I'm in the hotel I'll need a few days to figure it out."

"Or I can keep her," Jack offered, even while noting that the kitten kept getting closer and closer to Brodie. "But I'd have to do some cleanup to the house first to ensure she doesn't get hurt on any of the tools, exposed nails, or drywall sheets still lying around."

With infinite care and a lot of fretting from Howler, Brodie lifted the kitten for a few gentle strokes while looking her over. "She seems okay overall. I'd check with Rodney, though, to be sure."

"Plan to," Jack said, and then to Ronnie, "Rodney is the vet Brodie uses for Howler."

The kitten squeaked a few meows and poor Howler looked ready to perish. He circled Brodie, trying to sniff Peanut from different angles. Brodie put her back on her little paws. "Tell you what, since Howler's attached, I could keep her while you get set up."

Ronnie shook her head, laughing softly as the kitten crawled onto Howler's back paw, getting as close as she could. Now that she was there, Howler settled down, curling around her so that he practically hugged her with his whole body.

Charlotte stood and dusted her hands. "Howler is often around the office, and you can't take both a dog and a cat with you everywhere you go, so I could watch her during the day when you guys are busy."

"Perfect," Jack said. "Glad that's settled."

RONNIE'S HEAD SWAM with confusion, and no wonder. It had been disorienting enough to see Jack and his family all working together to care for one pocket-size ball of fur. She'd stood there among them and, honest to God, she'd *felt* the love. It was as perceptible as the warmth of the sun or fog on a rainy day.

At first, she'd tried to convince herself that it couldn't be real. No family was that close, that comical, that *caring*.

But the camaraderie had pulled her in, making her a part of the circle when she'd tried so hard to stay emotionally apart. She'd experienced it…so she couldn't deny it. Yes, they liked to needle each other, but it didn't matter because the love was so heart-crushingly obvious.

And that big dumb dog. The big, sweet, *adorable* dog.

God, he'd almost melted what was left of her heart with his innate tendency to protect something smaller, needier.

Much like Jack.

The similarities had chipped away at her defenses, even as the contagious humor slipped past her guard, causing her to laugh with the others.

For a little while there, she'd been a part of something. A part of *them*. She'd gotten a taste of something she hadn't even known she wanted, had never dared to hope for. Like she imagined an addict felt after getting a hit of a potent drug, she immediately wanted more.

As if Jack, on his own, hadn't been appealing enough? This family, together, was overkill.

"What did you think of Mrs. Anderson?" Jack asked.

Ronnie had eaten her own meal on the way to the woman's house, and then helped Jack carry in the platters of croissant sandwiches, fruits, vegetables, and dips. Mrs. Anderson, who was so tiny she made Ronnie look like an Amazon, had bustled around the kitchen, directing the placement of everything while offering gratitude left and right.

When she'd finally slowed down enough to notice Jack's shirt was on Ronnie, she'd stopped, lifted eyeglasses from a chain around her neck, and ended her intense study of them both with a decisive, "Well."

Jack had teased the older woman, saying, "You were young once, right?"

For a reply, she'd sighed as if reminiscing. "Indeed." Looking over her glasses, she told Ronnie, "But I wore my own clothes."

A dozen smart-tongued replies had tripped through Ronnie's brain. No one chastised her anymore. But Mrs.

Anderson had been so sweet, she ended up saying a lame, "It's not how it looks."

Brows rising up to her gray hairline, Mrs. Anderson asked, "How does it look?"

Jack had snickered, Ronnie had squirmed, and then she just explained. "It looks like we saved a kitten from a jerk who wanted to harm her. The kitten used my shirt on the ride home, so Jack gave me his and I haven't yet been back to my room to change."

Mrs. Anderson's faded eyes blinked, and a web of wrinkles filled her cheeks as she smiled. "That's not nearly as titillating as I'd hoped, but I appreciate the kindness you showed that poor animal. Here, have a cookie."

Far as rewards went, that was a sweet one.

And so they'd eaten their cookies with coffee while indulging in a fifteen-minute visit—which was all the time they had before guests were due to arrive.

Now that they were back in his car, she couldn't stop thinking how nice it had been.

"Mrs. Anderson?" Jack prompted again, when she didn't immediately answer his question.

Ronnie decided to answer honestly, instead of with her usual snark. "She's a character. Very spry for her age, obviously intelligent, and amusing."

Brows lifting, he said, "You liked her?"

She hedged the question by saying, "What's not to like?"

"Well, I adore her. She was my teacher ages ago. She was always strict but fair."

Ronnie choked on a rude sound. "I bet you were her pet pupil, weren't you?"

He grinned. "Yes."

Before she knew it, he pulled up to the front of the

hotel. Damn, the day had gone by too quickly. She hated for it to end because she continued to enjoy herself. Whether taking on a creep, purchasing malformed snakes, saving a kitten, or visiting with his family and friends, Jack made her feel good. Better than good, he made her feel normal. Like she could be anyone.

Anyone other than herself.

With him, she could talk about her life, her past, her family, and it didn't hurt. The memories didn't dig in to plague her or cause her to relive all the moments of regret.

Wondering if she dared to extend the day, she kept her gaze averted and opened her seat belt. "Jack—"

He turned off the car and angled toward her. "Invite me up, Ronnie."

Those words grabbed all her attention, swinging her attention around and locking her gaze with his. His eyes were so dark, his lashes so thick…and damn it, he looked like a man who intended to get what he wanted.

Did he really want *her*? The punching of her heart made it difficult to think. She knew what *she* wanted, yet the instinct to protect herself remained. "We talked about this."

"Yes, and you said you'd leave your options open." He gently slid the rough pads of his fingertips over her cheek, his thumb touching the corner of her mouth.

He might be a stuffed-shirt to those who didn't know him, but the appearance was an illusion. Everything about Jack, from his work-worn hands to the strength in his upper body to the knife in his boot and that overpowering confidence, made it clear he was as elemental as a man could get.

And every bit as appealing.

Husky encouragement lowered his voice. "Tonight is an option, Ronnie. Take it."

He may as well have said, *Take me*, because that's what she heard. It's what she *saw* as she stripped him in her mind and put him on her bed. On *her*.

In her.

Lord, she could almost feel the incredible sensation of it all and before she could censure her decision she said, "Okay."

Triumph filled his eyes, but it was the promise in his slow smile that made her nipples tighten and ache.

"Come on." In her haste to be proactive—or so she told herself—she practically fell from the car. She'd barely closed her door when he was there beside her, his nostrils flaring, his incredible eyes nearly black with anticipation.

Leaning down, he breathed into her ear, "Hurry."

Didn't have to tell her twice. Ronnie fumbled in her purse for her keys. The hotel was so old that they hadn't yet changed the room locks to cards. Their single elevator was also slow as molasses and with the jackhammer pounding of her heart she didn't think she could wait on it.

Instead, she went straight for the stairs, aware of Jack right behind her.

Two older men sat in the lobby, one reading a newspaper, but they both looked as she and Jack bolted up the steps. When they reached the third floor, Ronnie paused to laugh around her huffing breaths.

Spinning her to the wall, Jack pressed his body to hers. "I'm dying here and you think it's funny?" He took her mouth before she could answer, his tongue thrusting in, his hands clasping her ass and grinding her closer.

Lost. Ronnie felt utterly, completely lost.

A noise down the hall alerted him and he stepped away just as quickly, grabbing her hand and saying, "Let's go."

They passed a maid who gave them the stink eye, as if she knew what they'd been up to, and that made Ronnie laugh again.

"It's funny," she explained quickly, allowing him to snatch the key from her hand. "And fun." Because it was Jack, because he made her feel things other than lust—and honestly, she'd never known lust like *this*.

A one-night stand with an attractive stranger might appease a need, at least partially, but it didn't come close to this, to the combination of want and need, understanding and, yes, amusement. All together, they created a powerful, *wonderful* tsunami of sensation unlike anything she'd ever known before.

Watching Jack work the old lock as he tried to get the door open made Ronnie happy from the inside out. "Is it weird that I'm enjoying this?" More than she'd enjoyed anything since leaving home at eighteen. "I've never been in a mad race to my room."

"Good," he growled, finally getting the lock to open. "There's more to come."

What a promise. It didn't surprise her that he liked knowing he was different, whether she wanted him to be or not. "Even knowing this is probably a mistake—"

The door swung in and he turned on her. "I am not a mistake."

Her eyes widened. "I didn't mean—"

Jack bent his knees, scooped her up, and tossed her over his shoulder as if she weighed nothing at all. Carrying her inside, he kicked the door closed, then turned the latch. One large hand splayed over her ass as he strode to the bed.

But he didn't dump her. Or even lower her.

She felt him breathing, his broad chest expanding heavily, exhaling slowly. It was sexy as hell, knowing she'd caused that level of need, but now they were here, and she was more than ready to get on with it.

"The blood is starting to rush to my head."

His hand moved over her behind, squeezing one cheek, and he turned his face into her hip. "I love your ass."

Okay, so maybe her head could take it a little longer.

But no, he turned and gently laid her crossways on the bed, then knelt over her, his powerful arms braced at either side of her shoulders. "I want you naked, Ronnie."

Um…she had hoped to do some kissing first, maybe lose the clothes gradually—after he was so blind to lust he wouldn't pay much attention to her lack of curves.

She wasn't ashamed or anything. She'd bared herself to plenty of guys.

But what they'd thought hadn't mattered. She'd used them to appease *her* urges, and if they enjoyed her body, fine. Their approval hadn't been necessary. In fact, she hadn't worried about anyone's approval in years.

His gaze sharpened. "Stop thinking so much and relax."

Was that an order? She scowled. "I'm relaxed." Actually, she was so wired she felt like a virgin. "*You* relax."

Grinning, Jack dipped his head to her neck, his open mouth against her skin. Warm, damp. Tantalizing.

Eyes closing, Ronnie tipped her head to give him better access. He kept his upper body levered above her, but his lower body…at that point they made firm contact. She felt him, fully erect, against her belly and she couldn't help shifting, sliding one leg out to the side, then hooking it around him.

Jack gave a low groan, his hips flexing so that his erection moved against her. He trailed his mouth up to the shell of her ear, his warm breath making her toes curl before his tongue dipped.

Who knew ears were so erogenous?

Lightly, he bit her earlobe and then brushed his lips over her jaw before taking her mouth with raw hunger that devastated her senses.

She forgot about her meager boobs, instead focused only on how his mouth consumed, the way his tongue claimed…oh, and how his hand just tunneled under her cami to stroke a hot path over her bare skin on his way to her left breast.

Ronnie would have held her breath in anticipation but his kiss kept her too involved to do more than press up eagerly into his open palm as it covered her.

Her A-cup breast was small enough, and his hand more than large enough, that he completely enveloped her, his fingers curling to cuddle and shape.

If he felt any disappointment, he hid it well with a low sound of pleasure.

Suddenly Ronnie wanted her clothes gone. His gone, too. She wanted to feel him skin to skin, but finding the words to tell him wasn't easy, not with the flood of pleasure making her breathe too deeply, clouding her vision, and turning her body into one aching need.

In an easy shift, he turned, putting her atop him and at the same time drawing her knees forward so that she sat on his abs. Ronnie stared down at him and tried to orient her scattered thoughts. The longest part of her hair swung forward, covering one of her eyes. As she reached to tuck it back, he caught both shirts in his fists—the shirt he'd lent her and her camisole—and pulled them up and over her head, leaving her naked to the waistband of her low-riding jeans.

His gaze burned over her, taking in every small detail with carnal fascination. His hands clasped her hips, his fingers flexing. "You are so fucking sexy," he breathed.

All Ronnie could see in the flush of his cheekbones, the heat in his eyes, and the deep breaths he drew was appreciation.

His hands touched her again, this time oh so gently, his fingertips skimming over her from her collarbone to her shoulders, back to her upper chest where he spread his fingers and slowly, *slowly*, brought them down to her breasts.

She saw his throat work as he swallowed, and his gaze narrowed when he lightly fingered her nipples, playing with them like he would delicate flowers.

Ronnie wasn't sure where to look—at his face so she could see every emotion passing over his features, or at his tanned, masculine hands, so large against her smaller frame.

Her breath caught as he lightly tugged on nipples already too sensitive.

"Come down here," he growled, reaching for her shoulders and bringing her closer so he could latch on to her breast, sucking softly…then not so softly.

The tug of his mouth sent a river of wet heat through her body. She couldn't resist the roll of her hips against the solid ridge of his erection.

"Be still," Jack said, then switched to her other breast.

Another order? Fine. Whatever.

But how could she be still? She *knew* lust, damn it, and this…this was something else.

She needed more. Now.

While she struggled for breath, she laid a hand to his jaw, now shadowy and rough. Basic. Elemental. Beneath her fingers, she felt the flex of suction as he pulled at her nipple.

"There's only me." Her words came out huskily, almost as a soft gasp, but they got his attention.

Slowly drawing back, he released her with a curling of his tongue that she felt everywhere. He looked first at her body, at the wet nipples, now aching, then up into her eyes.

She knew he didn't understand, she wasn't sure she did either, but of course, Jack being Jack, he wanted to.

"For you," she said, spreading her fingers over the hot, sleek skin of his shoulder, feeling the contraction of incredible muscles. "You wanted me, and here we are."

"I want you," he agreed, and he smiled slightly. "Finally, here we are."

She couldn't bear comparisons, so she made it clear. "I don't care who else you've been with, or how good it was. Right now, you're with me. *Only* me."

Jack took her elbows and brought her down flat against him, then surprised her with a hug, those strong arms closing around her with affection in the middle of the lust.

"There was only you yesterday. And the day before," he said. He turned again, this time putting her on her back while he moved to her side. One-handed, he worked on the closure of her jeans. "From the second I walked into Freddie's and saw you, it's been only you."

Oh God. It was the same for her, with one exception. She realized now that she hadn't been living. Hadn't truly been *feeling*. Not since her abduction and the estrangement with her family. All that accumulated time of insulating numbness—gone. She felt raw, swamped with sensation. Glorious, wonderful, *terrifying* sensation.

She was in over her head, knew it and accepted it, but no matter what, she couldn't stop.

Opening the snap and lowering the zipper to her jeans, Jack pressed his hand inside. Over the flat of her stomach and into her panties, he curled those long fingers over her.

Wanting his touch, she widened her legs…but he didn't move, didn't do anything else except look at her, her eyes, her breasts, back up to her mouth. He lowered his head for a gentle kiss—when she wanted something *more* than gentle.

"Stop."

He froze, his mouth still touching hers for several heartbeats before he raised his head. Muscles of restraint corded his neck and across his shoulders, but his voice was infuriatingly polite as he asked, "Stop?"

Ronnie scrambled out from under him but didn't leave the bed. "Remember, I have a knife in my boot—"

"No reason to stab me," he said deadpan, falling to his back.

"—so it's safer if I get them off now." She cast a look over his supine body, completely filling two-thirds of the bed, all stretched out and tense, his erection a very noticeable ridge in his pants.

All for her.

If this didn't happen soon, she might possibly implode. "Hustle up and get your clothes off, before I'm tempted to use force."

CHAPTER NINE

"THANK GOD." IF she'd called a stop at that point, pretty sure he'd have died of perpetual, unfulfilled horniness. Rolling to his feet, Jack toed off his shoes and opened his belt. All the while, he watched Ronnie as she laid the knife from her boot on the nightstand.

Maybe she wasn't joking about force.

And why did that make his dick jump in interest?

Hell, *everything* she did spiked his already savage hunger. Her bossiness? A crazy kind of turn-on. If she wanted to take over in bed, he'd gladly suffer the pleasure of it.

But deep down, he thought it was something entirely different that she needed—and he planned to give it to her.

Her platinum hair swung with her movements, coming down to hide her face, catching the light as she tucked it behind her ear.

Anticipation gathered along every nerve ending. Yes, of course he'd had other women. Plenty of them. He'd been with vain women and women who'd made him laugh. He'd had women who hoped for more in a relationship, and women who were no more interested in commitment than he was.

But he'd never had anyone like Ronnie Ashford. He'd

never *wanted* anyone like this either. It was unsettling but also stimulating.

Bare except for her jeans, her unflawed skin creamy and pale, she removed her boots and tossed them across the room. He admired the graceful lines of her tapered back, supple waist, and flat belly. Her arms were slight but with a woman's strength, her neck long and elegant.

Those firm breasts that fit perfectly into his palms had little to no sway with her movements.

His attention zeroed in on her rosy nipples, still drawn tight, glistening wet—from his mouth.

Fuck, he needed her.

Oblivious to his scrutiny, or uncaring if he watched, she ripped off her socks, balled them up and threw them in the direction she'd sent the boots.

Going to her back on the bed, she lifted her hips and shoved down her jeans and panties, then kicked them off.

Something powerful—emotion, lust, or a combo of the two—stalled his breath in his chest and he stood there with his pants gaping open, the waistband in his hands. He couldn't tear his gaze away from her.

Brazen as always, unselfconscious in her nudity, she turned on her side toward him, elbow bent, her head in her hand, and asked, "Need help?"

Posed for him, she made the most beguiling picture he'd ever seen. Proud shoulders swooped down to an exaggerated dip for her waist, before slightly flaring up again to her hip. Beautiful legs, long and lean, and surprisingly small, feminine feet. *She painted her toenails.* Considering her rings and makeup, the sight of purple polish shouldn't have surprised him, yet it did.

She *was* a true blonde. Not platinum, no, but still fair.

"I don't mind if you look…but I'd rather you touch." Her lips curved with invitation. "Or taste."

His pants were off in a heartbeat. For once, he didn't worry about folding them. He just drew his wallet from the pocket and then kicked them aside. After setting out two condoms, he stretched alongside her, drawing her slight body into his, making full contact with the heat and silk of her skin. "God, you're perfect."

Snorting—an odd sound for foreplay—she pushed him to his back to half loom over him. "I'm just me. Too thin and not real shapely, but you…" She straddled his thighs, making his cock swell more as she looked him over.

Jack didn't mind that—he wasn't overly modest either—but he wouldn't let her get by with insulting herself. Relishing the open view of her splayed thighs, he insisted, "I'm a good judge of these things. I've seen enough naked women to know, and I'm telling you—"

Smashing her fingers over his mouth, she shook her head. "I don't need that, Jack. You're here, so you obviously want this. That's good enough for me."

He bit her finger. Not exactly gently.

Snatching back her hand, she scowled. "Hey."

"Keep it up and I will retaliate. Each. And every. Time." He clasped her hips, narrow, yes, but with more than enough curve to push him to the brink of control. "I'm so hard right now, I hurt. I've never wanted anyone like this, so if you claim to be so plain, explain what the hell is wrong with me."

"Are you kidding?" She looked at his body with open greed. "Nothing's wrong with *you*."

When she started to touch, he shook his head. "That

emphasis—was that to say something is wrong with you? Because if it is—"

"Fine!" She leaned down to kiss him. "You want to pretend the flat-chested look is in, feel free—*oof*!"

Using his hold on her hips, Jack flipped her to her back, then immediately flipped her again so she lay face-down. In the short space of time where surprise held her still, he stroked the small satiny bottom that swished just right when she took her long-legged strides.

"You're beautiful, Ronnie."

She reared up. "What the hell are you—?"

His palm landed a light swat that had her stiffening in outrage.

But she didn't move away.

Instead, very slowly, she turned her head to fry him with her glare. Her expression…

It was all Jack could do to keep from grinning, but he kept a stern face and repeated, "You're beautiful. Sexy." He stroked her cheek, now slightly warm from his smack. "Sleek. Soft."

"So." She eyed him curiously. "I had no idea you had these kinky tendencies."

Kinky? If she considered this kinky, she wasn't as experienced as she tried to let on. Or, more likely, Ronnie made sex a very short-term contract. Wham, bam, thank you…sir.

It sounded like her MO.

It would *not* be like that with him.

"Admit you're sexy."

She got comfortable, resting the side of her face on her folded arms. Reeking of challenge, she asked, "Or what?"

No, he wouldn't let her get complacent. "Or…" He

flipped her to her back and drew her arms over her head. "I'll have to convince you."

"I know what I know, Jack. I keep telling you. I don't need—"

He bent and drew her nipple into his mouth, sucking softly.

Hips lifting in reaction, she gave a startled gasp.

"I know what you need." He drew her in again, this time sucking harder, drawing on her, testing with his teeth until she whimpered.

Whimpers. From prickly, argumentative Ronnie Ashford. Very nice.

Liking that response, he blew on her wet nipple and saw it tighten even more. "I love the color of your nipples."

She opened her mouth, but nothing came out so she closed it again.

Licking the other nipple, then plucking with his lips, he said, "They're sort of a rose-tinted brown, darker now since you're getting excited." He lifted up to look at her face. "You are excited, right?"

One tight nod was all the answer she gave.

"I better check."

Another of those small sounds of building pleasure escaped her as he trailed a hand down her midriff, over that very sexy belly, and between her thighs. Using just his fingertips, he stroked the soft hair there—and met her gaze. "Will you be wet for me, Ronnie?"

Color rode high on her cheekbones and heavy lids half hid her gray eyes. "Er…probably."

She might've meant the word to be flippant, but it came out too breathy, too eager.

He teased her with his fingers again, sliding one finger along her seam—just enough to make her quicken. "Open up."

One knee angled out.

The quick compliance was nice, but he wanted more. "Wider."

With a huff of frustration, she parted her legs wide, her slender thighs straining, her toes curled.

"Absolutely beautiful," he repeated.

"Jack—"

"Just a second." He bent to each nipple again, sucking briefly, licking so they'd remain wet. As her breath turned choppy, he eyed his handiwork and nodded. "Better. Now this."

He trailed that same finger over her, this time barely grazing her clitoris—which made her hips lift off the bed—and down to her lips, already slick.

Growling his satisfaction, he stroked lightly over her, spreading the wetness…and making himself nuts. "Sexy. So fucking sexy." He pressed into her just the smallest bit, only using the very tip of his finger.

His dick jumped, maybe in jealousy.

"Jack?" she moaned softly.

He forced his attention from his darker hand wedged between her pale legs, up to those smoky gray eyes. "Hmm?"

"I get it," she gasped, her eyes closing. "You think I'm sexy. You don't have any complaints about my body. I'm glad." Her lashes lifted and silver eyes met his with demand. "Now *get on with it already.*"

Smiling, he pressed his finger deep, all the way to the knuckle. She gave a keening cry, her hips rising to meet him, working herself against his hand.

The second he released her wrists, she grabbed him.

He liked that, the urgent way she reached for him. Not some nameless stranger, but *him*, Jack Crews.

He *would* be different to her, whether that's what she wanted or not.

Settling against her, he kissed her throat, her nipples again, that luscious mouth, all while fingering her until he found the rhythm she liked, the rhythm that made her clench all over.

It was an unpredictable thing, figuring out a woman's needs. Each one was unique, liking one thing, needing more of another, wanting a certain touch, needing to rush, or desperate for patience.

Ronnie took the guesswork out of it with the open, honest way she responded, telling him exactly what she liked with a sound or a move or, his favorite, a soft plea.

Suddenly her hands clutched his shoulders and she rolled her hips, her breath catching. "Jack...*there*."

He slid his thumb over her again, saying against her temple, "Here?"

"Ah..." Her whole body stiffened. "Don't stop."

Two fingers curled deep inside her, his thumb gliding over her swollen clit, he devoured her mouth, and she came with a throaty growl and a rush of wet heat that made him fucking frantic.

She was still trembling when he reached over her for a condom, rolling it on with more haste than care.

Sleepy eyes watched him, taking in his body as he knelt on the bed. She murmured, "I usually like to be on top."

But not this time? To be sure, he asked, "Is that what you prefer? Because I don't mind."

Shaking her head, she lifted a limp hand to him. "It doesn't matter."

He thought maybe it did, that there was significance in her preference, but it didn't seem a good time to point it out. Kneeing her thighs farther apart, he moved over her. The urge to thrust into her, to bury himself, pounded under his skin.

She was used to that, though. A quick fuck that didn't mean anything.

Not this time.

He cupped her jaw and kissed her, striving for patience that was strained to the limit. With long sweeps of his tongue, he kissed her until she began moving against him again, one thigh wrapping over his, her finger tunneling into his hair.

Now, *now* she was ready. Balancing on one forearm, he reached down to slick his fingers over her again. Already wet, swollen, and sensitive, she moaned. He put his cock to her, feeling the kiss to the head, then the slow hug that grew tighter and tighter.

Ronnie surged up against him, taking most but not quite all of him. They both breathed heavily. Meeting her dazed eyes, he slid an arm under her to tilt her hips... and sank home.

Her body bowed, head back, nails biting his shoulders.

God, it had never been like this. Sex was fucking great. He loved sex. But this...? There was no buildup, no slow climb to the finish. He was already *there*.

Even better, she was with him.

Chemistry. Crazy, insanely intense chemistry.

And still...something more.

Jack gathered her close, his face in her neck, breathing in the scent of her skin, now a little damp. Musky. *Hot*.

He withdrew, not completely because he couldn't seem

to make himself do it, then ground against her. Half out,
surging back, pressing hard, withdrawing again.

She strained into him, just as desperate.

The reality pulsed in his head, in his cock.

In his heart.

Ronnie. Soft and sweet, prickly and forthright.

Vulnerable but so damn strong.

Here with him now, when he knew she hadn't meant
for this to happen.

He opened his mouth on her neck, cupped a hand to
her breast, and driven by the frenzied rush of her body,
slammed into her over and over. She met each thrust,
trying to hold him closer, tighter. It took everything Jack
had not to come, but he wanted her to climax again first,
and luckily, it happened fast.

Wrapped around him, arms and legs clutching, she
groaned low, her slender body trembling, her sex squeezing his cock as contractions wracked her, until finally
he felt her begin to ease.

Only then did he rise up on straightened arms to
groan out his own stunning release. While looking at
her. Soaking up the sight of her replete body. Seeing
her hair wilder than usual, her makeup a little smudged.

Beautiful. So goddamned beautiful that as he sank
down to rest on her, the heavy thump of her racing heart
echoing his own, he knew he didn't want to let her go.
Not now.

Maybe not ever.

RONNIE FELT THE first disorienting flutters of wakeful-
ness, but she fought it off. Instinctively, she knew reality would bring regrets and she wanted to hold on to the
unusually peaceful comfort enveloping her.

For her, sleep was usually elusive. Her norm was broken rest, darkness and shadows, memories and regrets, pulling her awake every hour or so. Right now, lethargy made her body heavy, as if she'd been out for a very long time.

She couldn't resist searching her mind, trying to pinpoint the source of peace. Without opening her eyes, she took stock of her surroundings. It took only a nanosecond to realize why she felt so comfortable.

Jack was still in her bed. *He'd* chased away the darkness, keeping her safe in the night, his presence obliterating familiar nightmares.

Instead of going to his house so she could make her usual strategic retreat afterward, she'd let him into her hotel room.

And now here she was, in a place she'd promised herself she'd never be: waking with a man's arm around her, feeling...*indebted* for what he'd given her. So dumb.

Damn it, she should know better than to have expectations. Whenever she did, it ended badly. But she didn't want this to end.

Closing her eyes, she tried to think, but it wasn't easy, not when she was so aware of him, his scent, his heat. His strength.

The erratic way her heart began to hammer, she worried that it might wake him. Her breath caught. Her throat tried to close.

She *knew* this feeling. God, she knew it and hated it. Hope.

She'd hoped that someday the only dad she'd ever known would want her back.

After she'd escaped a kidnapper, she'd hoped her family would realize they loved her, that they'd invite her to return to their lives. Beg her to come home.

She'd hoped—and been devastated with disappointment.

Emotions clamored within her as old memories surfaced in vivid detail, bringing with them the misery she'd eventually been forced to accept.

But that was *then*, and this was now.

She was no longer a naive young girl. No longer trusting of fate and all the ways it could fuck her over. She'd carved out a new life for herself, one where *she* called the shots. She trusted no one, so no one could hurt her. Never again would she be a victim, not of her family, not of a kidnapper.

Not to the gorgeous hunk currently taking up too much of the bed.

So they'd had sex. Twice.

What of it?

Yes, he'd positively blown her mind, showing her depths of sexual satisfaction she hadn't known existed, making her feel things she hadn't known were possible. In key sensitive places, her body still pulsed, nerve endings sparking as if asking for more.

More, more, *more.*

Oh, it'd be so easy to get used to him and the things he made her feel, both sexual and emotional. It'd be easy to rely on him, trust him. To hope for more.

But she wouldn't. Hell no, she wouldn't.

Great sex was all well and good, but it'd have to be on *her* terms, not his. And if it happened again, she'd be sure to recommend his house so she could walk out afterward, instead of fading into a satiated sleep.

With that decision made, Ronnie calmed. She drew one small, even breath. Then another.

Hope only made reality more devastating. So she and Jack had set the night on fire? It was sex, and yet it was more—but so what? Maybe it was always like that for him.

Granted, she didn't usually let men get to her. She made arrangements, fulfilled them, and moved on. Done.

This morning she'd do the same.

He shifted, drawing her body a little closer in such a delicious way, his hairy calf tickling her leg, his breath warming her neck. Oh, the urge to relent was strong. It'd be so easy to curl against him, to give into the need to relax her guard.

But she wouldn't. She couldn't.

STRUGGLING TO NOT be affected, Ronnie stared at the ceiling, watching dawn creep in through a crack in the curtains.

That light meant nothing; certainly it meant less than the heat of his body or the comfort of his nearness. Holding perfectly still, she concentrated on the light as she cleared her head.

Until, minutes later, Jack settled back into a deep sleep and the arm around her waist went utterly slack again.

Stealth was not her fortitude, she realized twenty minutes later as she silently dressed in the dark, grateful for the typical hotel noises that drowned out any accidental sounds she made.

Because she'd already been planning to go, she'd packed the day before and only had a few small items in the bathroom that she had to retrieve. Her hairbrush, toothbrush, her makeup case.

She told herself that the lump in her throat didn't matter. It was caused by nerves at the idea of waking him. Not because she knew he'd be upset to wake and find her gone.

The urge to cry wasn't because she already missed him. It was anger at herself for forgetting, even for a minute, that she didn't do shit like this.

When he turned over, she froze, staring at him, hoping he wouldn't wake…while half hoping he would.

His back to her now, he slept on.

Go. She lifted her bag and hesitated one more time. *Stop thinking about it, about him, and get out while you can.*

Right. This never should have happened.

Knowing she looked a fright with her ruined makeup and wrinkled clothes, Ronnie slipped out the door. Her breath remained shallow until she got down the stairs and approached the desk, leaving special instructions as she checked out.

Not until she reached her car did she dare relax. In the early dawn, the main street was quiet, empty, only a few lights showing from inside businesses. It was cold, damn it, but she hadn't wanted to dig out her jacket and risk waking Jack.

He'd have questions, and if she had answers, it'd be better not to give them.

Hands trembling, she threw her single duffel bag in the back seat, got in behind the wheel, started the car, and pulled away. At the first stop sign, she drew a ragged breath of relief.

And crushing disappointment.

Things would be different now. She knew it. She'd

instigated it. She had no one but herself to blame. For lowering her guard. For getting to close.

For hoping.

Jack wasn't a man who'd appreciate being left behind. His ego was as big as hers, just not as obnoxious. Had any woman ever walked out on him? Doubtful. So she'd be a first, a miserable first, and he'd probably prefer that she be the last.

Suddenly the hairs on the back of her neck lifted. Whipping her head around, expecting to see Jack, she searched the street. The *empty* street.

Yet the feeling of being watched grew stronger.

She'd feel better about things if there were people up and about, but other than the lonely strain of a train whistle and the occasional lowing of distant cows, all was silent. Too silent.

The car idling, her heart a jackhammer in her chest, Ronnie hit the door locks. *Drive away*, she told herself. Yet her eyes kept searching…

There! Beside a darkened building, a gloomy shadow shifted, elongating, moving closer, taking on the shape of…a man.

Finally the spell broke.

Lifting her foot off the brake and moving it to the gas pedal, she drove forward, not speeding but more than anxious to be away.

Over the years, since her kidnapping, she'd honed her instincts, learning the difference between being unnecessarily spooked—and sensing danger.

This was danger.

When the rock hit her back windshield, causing it to crack, she nearly screeched. Was the rock meant to make her stop?

Fat chance!

Gripping the wheel tighter, doing her best to regulate her breathing, she drove faster and as soon as possible, she turned a corner, going left. Two streets down she turned right again, and eventually she wound back to the main road. She didn't see anyone following her, but she wouldn't leave it to chance.

Forty-five minutes later, she finally arrived at her apartment. Away from the small, quiet town, it wasn't so vacant. People milled in and around the businesses, arriving for work, prepping for the day. Numerous cars drove back and forth.

She wasn't alone.

Still, she used care as she parked and headed inside, staying vigilant, watching every dark corner, tracking every shadow.

A few people stared at her, reminding her that she'd left the bed less than an hour ago, without a shower, without even brushing her teeth.

Screw 'em. Lifting her chin and curling her mouth into a smile, Ronnie stared back until they looked away.

The hallway on her floor was deserted when she reached it, giving her chills again. Once safely inside her apartment, she stood against the door, waiting to see if it felt secure.

She didn't sense any trouble, but before stepping forward, she withdrew the knife from her boot and kept her keys in her hand. Given the apartment was small, the interior stark without much decor, it took her only a minute to completely assess it, especially checking the single closet, under the bed, and behind the shower curtain.

The room felt empty. Emptier than usual. But that's how she liked it. Right?

While she was in the bathroom, she turned on the shower so the water could get warm. And then she remembered.

She'd left the snake and rat in Jack's trunk.

Well damn. She'd have to go back, if not today then tomorrow. Or at least…soon.

She didn't want to admit it, not even to herself, but now that she had the perfect excuse to see him again, the heavy sense of despondency no longer felt quite so heavy.

A KNOCK AT the door stirred Jack awake. He smiled even before he had his eyes open—until he realized he occupied the bed alone. Turning his head, he checked the clock and saw it was nearly 8:00 a.m.

Coming up to one elbow, his gaze bounced around, but the bathroom door stood open and there was nowhere else in the small hotel room for her to be.

"Housekeeping."

The closet was empty. He sat up completely, checking the floor, but only his clothes remained.

Reality crashed onto his head. "Son of a bitch."

The door swung open and a middle-aged woman poked her head inside. She and Jack locked eyes.

"Excuse me." Her gaze stroked every inch of his chest. She didn't back out. "I was told I could clean the room at eight."

Ensuring the sheet covered all things vital, Jack asked, "Told by whom?"

"Well…the guest who checked out of the room."

And that wasn't him. "When?" It was a small hotel,

run by a local family. Nothing happened here that didn't immediately become gossip for the town.

"A while ago." She stepped in, dragging her cart with her. "You didn't know she was checking out?"

Great. He was about to look like a giant ass. "Of course I did. I just lost track of time." Holding the sheet with one hand, he ran the other over his head.

The maid stood there—waiting for him to stand? Not happening. Jack looked at her name badge. *Lillie Johns.* He probably knew her brothers. "Would you mind, Lillie? I can be out of here in five minutes."

Disappointment turned down her mouth, but she gave a mulish, "I guess." Leaving the cart inside, she stepped out the door, closing it behind her very slowly.

Jack waited until it clicked shut, then bounded out of the bed and turned the lock. He didn't trust Lillie not to come back in *unexpectedly* for a peek.

He hadn't lied about the five minutes. He spent two in the bathroom, splashing his face, gargling with the hotel-supplied mouthwash, which Ronnie hadn't finished, and then pulling on his clothes and shoving his wallet into his pocket.

He thought to check his phone, but no, she hadn't left a message. Frustration clawed at him.

He felt used. He felt…insulted. Not *hurt*, damn it; he was a grown-ass man, not a lovesick youth. He'd had rejections before and barely blinked.

So why did this make his temper boil?

It shouldn't have blindsided him. He knew Ronnie was different, skittish. Everything about her was unique, how she reacted, how she gauged emotions, her motives.

Was he the only one who'd been affected last night?

She probably wanted him to think that, but he knew better. There was no way—

The knock on the door drew him out of his musing. He'd promised Lillie five minutes, and five it would be. Striding around the cart, he opened the door with a ready apology—and came face-to-face with a man.

Casually dressed, neatly trimmed dark hair, and wearing his own look of surprise.

The stranger leaned to the side, looking past Jack into the room, saw it was empty, and something dark passed over his face.

Standing a head taller, Jack scowled down at him. "And you are?"

"I came to see Veronica."

Tension seeped out of his posture. Jack shook his head. "You have the wrong room."

The man, probably midthirties, five-nine or thereabouts, glanced back to see the number on the door. "This is her room. Veronica Ashford?"

New irritation dug in. "Ronnie?"

The man gave a slow smile. "Is that the name she goes by?"

Stepping out and pulling the door shut behind him, Jack towered over the smug prick. Here was a hapless source for his annoyance. "I'll ask one more time. Who are you?"

Not in the least intimidated, the man shrugged. "An admirer." He checked his watch, a utilitarian watch, Jack noted, and murmured to himself, "I assumed she would be back by now."

"You knew she left?"

A superior smile spread over his face. "You didn't?"

Smashing the bastard would do a lot to take the edge

off his escalating anger—but it wouldn't be fair. Jack had him in height, weight, and obvious strength. The stranger, with his unimposing form, wouldn't stand a chance.

And yet, he didn't seem to realize the risk as he turned to go, saying in amusement, "You win some, you lose some. Looks like we both missed out this morning."

Watching him leave, Jack considered following him, maybe insisting on a few answers…until he heard a sound, almost like a moan.

Where had the maid gone? He glanced down the hallway and noticed one door standing open. Thinking to tell her the room was now empty, he walked over and looked inside.

At first he didn't see her, which he thought was curious. Then he noticed a foot sticking out from the far side of the bed. A limp foot.

Entering in a rush, he found the maid on the floor, her face white, blood oozing from a head wound.

CHAPTER TEN

JACK CALLED RONNIE on the way to the hospital. The maid, who'd awakened disoriented, sure that she'd merely fallen and hit her head on the nightstand, didn't need him to be there.

But he wanted to go. He felt somewhat responsible, which he recognized was absurd. How could he have prevented a fall? Yet if she'd been in Ronnie's room cleaning, instead of waiting on him to come to grips with Ronnie's defection...

It was useless to speculate. All he could do was visit Lillie, ensure she had everything she needed, and offer her a ride home if she wanted. The ambulance had left with her minutes ago.

Unfortunately, the nearest hospital was an hour east of where they lived and everyone else in Lillie's family worked at the hotel.

At first Ronnie didn't answer her phone, which made him nearly frantic, a feeling he didn't like. Call it instinct, call it jealousy, but it alarmed him that a stranger had tracked her down to the hotel, a man who seemed to have known that she'd left that morning—but hadn't realized she'd checked out and wouldn't return.

What if she hadn't left on her own?

What if someone had her right now?

Jack waited two minutes, then called her again.

She finally answered with a succinct, "What?"

His jaw ached from grinding his teeth. "I wanted to make sure you're okay."

"Why wouldn't I be? You're hung, but you're not deadly or anything."

Leave it Ronnie to say the most outrageous things. Cutting to the chase, he replied, "A man came looking for you at the hotel."

Silence. It became so prolonged, Jack wondered if she'd disconnected. "Ronnie?"

"What man?"

Oh, she tried to sound casual, but he heard it in her voice, the strain, the concern. "That's my question to you."

She gave an exasperated huff. "I didn't see him, so how would I know?"

Good point—and it assured him that she hadn't invited another man to her room. That possibility had burned his ass big time and accounted for a big chunk of his anger. To be safe, he asked, "You weren't expecting anyone?"

"No." After a second, she mellowed enough to add, "Look, I don't know anyone around there except you and the people you've introduced me to."

"You were at the bar before I got there. You didn't know me either, but you invited me to your room." Which made him wonder how many other men she might have noticed, and who else she might've considered until he showed up. It was possible the wrong guy had caught her eye.

"Yeah, well, you stole the show, ya know? I haven't been back to Freddie's since then."

Relief was an astounding thing, blunting the edges of

resentment. She'd walked out on him, and he'd have to deal with that, but he felt certain it wasn't lack of interest that had urged her to sneak away.

In short order, Jack explained what was said and what had happened to the maid.

Agitated, her worry more pronounced now, Ronnie whispered, "She'll be okay?"

"I hope so." There'd been blood, too much blood, but that was the way with head wounds. "I'm not far behind the ambulance. I'll know more once she sees a doctor."

"Text me, okay? I want to know if she's all right."

Until the moment he'd heard her voice, Jack had been suppressing red-hot rage. Now a sort of relief along with renewed determination gradually chased out other emotions.

Somehow, some way, he *would* figure her out... because he wanted her again. He wanted...too many things to sort out right now.

All he knew for sure was that the next time it happened—hopefully sooner rather than later—he'd find a way to convince her not to run away. How long he wanted her to stay, he couldn't yet say. But he didn't want to wake to an empty bed. He at least wanted an opportunity to...talk.

Shit. Talking after sex, that was a sure sign that this was more than just physical. But then, he'd sensed that all along.

Now to convince Ronnie.

Hoping not to spook her, he kept it casual when he said, "I should be free by lunch. I could update you then."

"Perfect. I'll wait for your call."

He'd prefer to see her in person, so he asked, "You want to get together?"

"Eventually," she said. "I mean, we'll need to."

"Good, because I was thinking—"

"I left stuff in your trunk, remember? That's a big no-no, so don't mention it to the brothers."

How could he have forgotten? "I hope they were… preserved in some way?"

"I assume so. I can swing by in a day or two to pick it up."

Apparently not too anxious to see him. "There are a few things we need to clear up." Like the fact that he wouldn't be used.

"I figured we'd already said everything we needed to."

Her voice was so clipped, Jack could almost see those straight but narrow shoulders snapping back while her stubborn chin lifted. "Not even close, honey." Anger began to leech back in. "You could have woke me before you sneaked off."

"I didn't *sneak*." A nearly audible wince precluded her defensive, "At least, not the way you mean! I just figured it was early, and you'd pretty much exhausted yourself last night—"

"I wasn't at all exhausted." But damn it, he had slept through her dressing and walking out. "In fact, I woke up wanting you again." He wanted her *still*. "Scurrying out without saying goodbye is not only rude, it's…"

He hesitated to call her a coward, sensing that the insult would hit her harder than any other. He wanted her back, not so pissed that she'd never speak to him again.

Luckily, she didn't wait for him to finish that line. "What do I know about morning-after protocol? I don't do the morning after, and with good reason."

"Never?" he asked, stunned by that disclosure. He knew she avoided involvement, but to have never slept over?

"Why would I?" she asked, her tone flippant. "They're called one-night stands for a reason, you know. By definition, they shouldn't include awkward morning-after chats."

Until that moment, the thought of her with other men hadn't bothered Jack. Now, hearing the vulnerability in her voice, it nearly leveled him. "I don't think it would've been that awkward."

"Look," she said, exasperated. "I figured you'd be thrilled to find me gone."

Ronnie was special. She needed to learn that. "Figure out the opposite of thrilled, and you'll know how I felt."

Seconds ticked by where he heard only her uneven breathing.

He wanted to hold her, and he wanted to fuck her. He wanted to argue with her more, and make love to her. He wanted to keep her around long enough to see where the feelings would go, how much deeper might they might get.

It'd be an uphill battle, but he wasn't a quitter, not when he wanted something.

He wanted inside Ronnie's head.

"I'm sorry."

The apology, even grudgingly given, worked as a balm to his mood. "Will you agree I'm not a one-night stand?"

"Apparently not, if we're going to do it again."

Damn it, now was not the time for humor. Thank God she couldn't see his quick grin. "We definitely are."

"Well… I've never heard of a two-night stand, so…"

Her uncertainty was endearing, and it brought out all his protective instincts. Now that he'd gotten her agreement, he moved on before she could change her mind. "The man who came to your room asked for Veronica."

More silence. "No one calls me that except family."

Her father? The man wasn't old enough, but Jack already knew that's what she was hoping. "He looked to be in his midthirties," he explained gently. "Five-nine, maybe five-ten. Average build. Dark hair."

Making light of her disappointment, she laughed. "What, you didn't get his eye color?"

"Green."

She whistled. "Damn, Jack, you're a regular Sherlock Holmes, aren't you? Anything else you noticed?"

"He wasn't afraid of me, even though I was damn near breathing fire." Worse, he was there when the maid got injured.

What if Lillie hadn't tripped and hit her head?

What if…someone had struck her?

"Doesn't sound like anyone I know."

"Not even a past client? Someone you met during a pickup for the brothers?"

"Nope. I'm not as detail-oriented as you, but I'm not without my own power of observation."

Sensing that she held something back, Jack narrowed his eyes. "What aren't you telling me?"

Another long silence, too many of them for one conversation.

"Ronnie, talk to me."

She huffed again. "I will, when I see you again."

"How about later today?"

"How about I'll call you when I find some time?" She rushed on, saying, "I have to go."

Damn it, why did he feel like danger loomed? "Promise me you'll be careful."

"Always. Don't worry about me."

At this point, he didn't think it was something he could control. He cared. Too much, too quickly.

"Jack?" She hesitated. "Sorry for ditching you."

Coming from Ronnie, that was about as sincere as it could get. "Make it up to me over lunch." He heard her inhale, no doubt to deny him, so he finished with, "Tomorrow at the office, at noon. And seriously, Ronnie, until then, watch your back."

For too long now, Jack stewed.

The doctor hadn't been entirely convinced that Lillie Johns had tripped. The injury to the back of her head was too blunt, as if someone had bludgeoned her. The sharp corner of a nightstand would have left a different cut. However, he'd speculated that the smooth sideboard of the bed *could* have caused her injury, as unlikely as that seemed.

The maid still didn't remember anything, but luckily, other than a concussion and a row of stitches, she'd be okay.

The local cops had assured Jack that they were looking into things. But what could they do?

No one else recalled the man who'd come searching for Ronnie. He was so nondescript that he hadn't drawn attention, not from the desk clerk, not from anyone outside.

He hadn't inquired about her room number—but then, the hotel was small and it wouldn't take a lot of surveillance to discover which room she'd rented. Conceivably, someone could have watched from outside as she entered, and then noted a window when a light came on.

As Brodie passed the office, he paused to give Jack

a second look, then shifted his gaze to the clock on the wall. "She's late?"

"Half an hour." After a sleepless night, Jack had updated Brodie on the current problems, but not the intimacy of his growing relationship with Ronnie.

Now that she'd left the hotel, Jack didn't know where she was staying, and he hesitated to call the brothers to find out. Better to let her come to him, but in the meantime he started some online research.

As far as Jack could tell, Ronnie avoided social media. She didn't have a Facebook or Twitter account, and he couldn't find an email address for her.

Apparently, when someone wanted to reach her, Ronnie either answered her phone—or she didn't. Contacting her in any way was dependent on her whim. He respected that.

Yet some things she couldn't control, like the news.

Again Jack scoured over the article that filled the screen of his computer. A photo in the sidebar showed a much younger Veronica Ashford. While she huddled in a chair, a female officer wrapped a blanket around her shoulders. Another officer stood to the side, talking on a radio.

Ronnie's hair was longer, a darker blond. Less makeup defined her features. Devastation, trauma turned her normally bright eyes utterly blank. She appeared so pale, so small and young that his heart squeezed.

He hadn't found an excess of coverage over Ronnie's kidnapping, but the barest facts were there. She *had* been taken. She *had* escaped. And nowhere was her family mentioned or shown.

Since that awful episode of her life, she'd reinvented

herself, morphing into a cast of courage, attitude, and isolation.

Jack knew he'd have to be patient. Never before had the prospect posed such a problem.

"Did you call her?" Brodie asked.

"I talked to her yesterday morning."

Brodie drew up one brow. "And since then?"

Jack shook his head. Twice he'd tried to reach her. She hadn't answered either time. Damn it, he wasn't in the habit of chasing women. So far with Ronnie, that's all he'd done.

He ran a hand over the back of his neck. "She's probably just being stubborn." At this point, Jack hoped that's all it was.

But what if something had happened? What if she couldn't answer?

"Giving you the cold shoulder, huh?" Brodie tsked in an annoying way. "That's gotta be tough on the old ego. Not what you're used to, is it?"

Just then, they both heard the sound of her car pulling up. The little Chevy left a dust cloud behind on the cool but dry day.

Finally. Recalculating now that he knew she was safe, Jack sat back in his chair.

Brodie's eyebrow went higher. "Not planning a warm greeting?"

"Mind your own business." This was the second time she'd been late, and to ignore his calls… Jack looked at his brother. "Did you know her full name is Veronica?"

Brodie shrugged. "Yeah, so?"

Posing his thoughts aloud, Jack said, "She set her first appointment with us as Ron Ashford. Later she told me to call her Ronnie. And then a stranger asked for Veronica—the full name used by her family."

Thoughtfully, Brodie asked, "You think we might be missing a clue?"

Jack wasn't sure what to think. "I mentioned it to the cops. If they talk to her family, she's going to be pissed."

"You don't know that."

Actually, he did—because he knew Ronnie. "It's doubtful they will, though. Overall, they didn't seem to think much of it."

Brodie shrugged. "They probably assume the guy met her at Freddie's and wanted to invite her for breakfast or something."

"Is that what you think?"

"I'm your brother," Brodie said, as if that made all the difference. "If you think something's off, then it probably is." He looked toward the door. "Here she comes."

When Jack stayed in his seat, Brodie muttered, "Dumbass," and stepped out of view, presumably to greet her.

After closing the screen on his PC, Jack stared at the office door. His heartbeat picked up speed, his temperature rising. Two nights ago, he'd had her under him. He could still feel her fingers digging into his shoulders, hear her ragged moans. They'd slept with limbs entwined.

And the next morning she'd slunk away as if none of it mattered, and other than talking to him once, she'd avoided his calls.

Was it any wonder he felt so conflicted? Jack tightened his hand, then forced his fingers to relax.

He heard Brodie say something, heard Ronnie's husky laugh, and every muscle on his body twitched with awareness. That was a reaction only Ronnie had roused. He didn't *twitch* for anyone else, damn it.

The sound of her boot heels coming closer sharpened his senses.

Jesus, he had it bad. He already pictured her in his mind, her fair hair swinging in the same tempo as her slim hips, an excess of silver hoops dangling from her ears, her clothes all black for dramatic contrast, and the way her trim body moved so gracefully in her long, exaggerated strides…

Ronnie stepped into the doorway and Jack lost his relaxed posture, drawn forward by the sight of her in a low cut, midriff hugging beige pullover.

Braless. *Again.*

Stretchy material clung to her upper body like a second skin, outlining her high, round breasts and currently soft nipples.

Yet…maybe not so soft anymore, not with him noticing her. She looked so hot he felt himself reacting, too.

That particular flesh-toned sweater paired with tight jeans emphasized her slenderness, the delicate, female contours of her body.

Fuck. He felt it all again, the satiny texture of her skin, that tight shapely ass beneath his large hands, the sweet wetness of her sex hugging him tight as he'd slid deep.

The taste of her nipples.

As if she remembered, too, her little nostrils quivered with her quickened breath. Her gaze held his and a flush climbed up her neck to her cheeks, turning her eyes to glittering silver.

She assessed him with new knowledge.

Carnal knowledge.

Whether she liked it or not, things would never be the

same between them. She could run all she wanted, but neither of them would forget.

Closing his hands over the arms of his chair, Jack grounded himself so he wouldn't go to her. "You're late."

"Yeah, so sue me." Ungluing her feet, she sauntered the rest of the way in and took a chair, trying to pretend that moment of sizzling electrical awareness hadn't just snapped and crackled between them. "Where's Peanut? I was looking forward to seeing her."

Brodie poked his head into the office. "He's with Mary and Howler."

Ronnie twisted to see him. "He?"

"Boy kitten. Not easy to tell at that age, but I'm pretty sure."

"Oh." Her mouth pinched as if suppressing a smile. "So you…looked?"

"At his junk, yeah. Not like I could tell by staring into his eyes."

Ronnie snickered.

Brodie folded his arms and leaned in the doorframe. "Envisioning it, are you?"

"Sorry, yes." Her smile broke through.

How could one woman be so damned appealing? When giving him hell, when looking sad. When laughing at his brother. No matter what Ronnie did, Jack admired her, her looks, her manner, her big soft heart.

Brodie didn't seem to mind that he was the source of her amusement. "I can get them down here, or you can go up with me to see him." His gaze shifted to Jack. "That is, after your meeting."

She gave him a brilliant smile. "Thanks, Brodie. I appreciate it."

"No problem." Whistling, Brodie withdrew and headed farther down the hall.

When the hell had they gotten so chummy? Jack couldn't recall Ronnie ever speaking to him in that particular, carefree tone.

And damn it, he would *not* be jealous of his brother.

"How's the maid?" she asked, melting into the chair in a posture so casual, it came off forced rather than relaxed. Long legs stretched out in front of her, ankles crossed. She rested her elbows on the chair arms, her laced fingers on her stomach.

If someone didn't know her, they might believe she hadn't a care in the world, but Jack was so attuned to her, he saw the tension in her shoulders, in her exposed neck and the wariness of her gaze.

"Back home with her family." He'd texted her earlier about the maid's mild concussion. Her reply had been short, but at least she'd acknowledged him. *Barely.* "The doctor says she'll be fine."

"Good."

The sight of Ronnie made it difficult for him to talk—especially when he'd rather be touching. How could she *ever* question her physical appeal? "Another day or two off, then she'll be back to work."

Accepting that with a nod, Ronnie looked over her shoulder to ensure the hallway was clear. Leaning forward and dropping her voice, she said, "I hate to ask it, but do you think she could have been hit?"

That she'd come to that conclusion didn't surprise Jack. "I think it's possible, yes."

"Damn." She sat back, frowning in thought.

And suddenly he knew something more was going on. "Ronnie?"

Her mouth flattened as she met his gaze. "I feel like I need to tell you something, but I don't want you to overreact."

Alarm bells blared in his brain. "I'm listening."

She gave him a narrow-eyed frown. "And you better not dismiss me."

Dismiss her? Unable to keep his ass in the chair a second longer, Jack stood and walked around to lean a hip against the front of the desk. He was closer to her now—but not close enough.

They'd both have to be naked, bodies touching, to be as close as he wanted to be.

Tilting his head, he encouraged her.

With worry etching her expression, she leaned in again. "The other day, when I booked…that is, when I left the hotel…"

"Without telling me."

She frowned at the interruption. "I was driving away when it felt like someone was watching me."

Those protective instincts surged. "Did you see anyone?"

"Yeah, I did." Grumbling low, she admitted, "Fucker threw a rock at my rear window and cracked it. I haven't had a chance to get it fixed yet."

He stared at her, equal parts furious at her and afraid for her. It wouldn't help to share either reaction, so he sucked it up and kept his civil facade in place despite the urge to…what? Give her hell?

Yeah, that definitely wouldn't go over well.

"Did you get a good look at him?"

She snorted. "Hell no. I took off."

Jack locked his jaw. She'd left well before 8:00 a.m. two mornings ago. Whoever it might have been—her visitor, or a random prank—the person was likely long gone by now.

Few things really enraged Jack. And even when they did, he could keep it under wraps and be reasonable. Or as Charlotte always accused, he'd be *polite*.

Not today. Not now. The words practically growled out of his throat. "Why the hell didn't you tell me?"

She blinked at his tone. "I believe I just did."

The need to touch her, to draw her out of her chair, out of her nonchalance, had him breathing harder. "Why. Didn't you tell me. *Right away?*"

Though her shrug couldn't have been more indifferent, her gaze skirted away with guilt. For a few agonizing heartbeats, she kept her thoughts to herself and Jack couldn't tell if her temper was winding up or down, if he'd offended her or just pissed her off.

Finally, she looked at him again, and what he saw was…apology. Regret. "I don't count on other people," she explained. "Haven't for a long time. If I have a problem, I solve it."

"Jesus, Ronnie," he muttered low, unsure how to deal with her in this particular mood.

"What?" Her defensive scowl returned. "You think I, a mere woman, should have run to you, the big man, the second something spooked me?"

Definitely pissed. Jack quickly retreated behind manners. "I would have preferred being informed at least, yes."

"Well, like I said, I solve my own shit. I would've eventually solved this on my own, too, except apparently it's spilling over to you and this town, and I don't want that. If it's not just me—"

Those words snapped the tight leash on his control.

Catching her upper arms, Jack drew her from the chair and to her tiptoes. His nose almost touched hers as he said succinctly, "It's *not* just you." He wanted her to understand that she wasn't alone.

She took it all wrong, wrenching away and glaring. "I'm sorry, all right? You think I wanted that maid to get hurt? You think I wanted you hassled by some random stranger? I *told* you not to take the job. I *told* you we should just screw." She tossed up her hands. "I warned you a dozen times."

In the distance, Jack heard Brodie whistling, which was his brother's not-so-subtle way of letting him know he was near, and judging by the sound of his footsteps, coming down the hall.

"Let's go to my house." At least there they'd have privacy—for him to vent, for her to curse...to touch, explain, comfort, convince, and share.

Brodie walked on past, studiously pretending they didn't exist.

"Why?" Ronnie sneered, her gaze locked to Jack's, oblivious to everything else. "You want to spank me again?"

The whistling stopped. Brodie leaned back to look into the room, his gaze wickedly amused.

Jack ignored him.

Ronnie never even realized he was there.

With a grin, Brodie moseyed on...but he no longer whistled, probably because he hoped to hear more.

Damn it. Jack didn't need this right now. Belatedly lowering his voice, he said, "I didn't spank you. It was one playful smack to get your attention." And talking about this was getting to him.

Ronnie poked him in the chest. "That's why you want

me at your house, though, right?" With a teasing purr, she asked, "So we can do the nasty again?"

"It wasn't *nasty.*" He hated the way she put that, making it sound so base and insignificant, as if she could find the same satisfaction with any other man.

Like hell.

"I won't deny wanting you." This time he slowly brought her closer until they touched from knees to chest. Looking down into her beautiful gray eyes, seeing only the color and clarity, not all the kohl and other paint, he softly insisted, "But there's more than sex going on between us and you know it."

A taunting smile curved her lush lips and she nudged him with her belly. "Unless you've taken to carrying a gun in an odd place, I think that's your dick between us."

Jack inhaled sharply. Yes, he was getting hard and it infuriated him. He didn't want her to have such an undeniable effect on him, not now when he needed to make an important point.

Fighting back the need to take that smiling mouth, to soften it with a kiss that'd curl her toes, he said, "There are things we need to discuss before we get off track."

Her gaze shuttered, then focused somewhere around his collarbone. "I'll agree to sex," she muttered, one hand resting against his shoulder. "But the other stuff... I've already talked too much."

Finally, with Herculean effort, he got his polite mask back in place. He'd need all his self-possession and then some to deal with Ronnie when she was dead set against him.

He almost let the importance of talking slide away. Sex with her again... He'd awakened wanting her, and he wanted her still. He had a terrible suspicion that the craving wouldn't go away any time soon.

Only the mutinous look in her eyes kept him from agreeing. She expected him to give up on her—because that's what everyone else had done. Even after she'd escaped a madman, her family hadn't welcomed her back.

In many instances, he'd be suspicious of the person rejected, wondering what behavior had caused that break in love and respect.

When it came to Ronnie, she'd been little more than a kid, and there was never a good excuse, no viable reason or sound logic for anyone, most especially her family, to treat her so heartlessly.

He'd grown up with his mother making him and Brodie top priorities. He knew without a single doubt that his mom would have fought the devil himself to keep her sons safe. Whenever he'd screwed up, she'd given him hell with the same enthusiasm that she doled out affection. She'd taught him respect by demanding it for herself, showed him that he could make mistakes by admitting to her own. They laughed a lot, disagreed on occasion, and loved unconditionally.

Ronnie had been denied the same, and it broke his heart for her.

In his experience, people who suffered emotional wounds either became needy, clinging to one and all in their pain—or they withdrew behind walls of ice to ensure they'd never be hurt again.

Ronnie had fought for her independence, to make it on her own without needing anyone for any reason.

Now he'd have to fight to win her over.

"Ahem."

They both looked up to see a crowd at the door. Given

the grins his mother and Charlotte wore, Brodie had shared what he'd overheard.

Great. Just freaking great.

Ronnie took an instinctive step away from them, squeezing into his side before realizing what she'd done. Squaring her shoulders, she thrust out her hand and took a big stride toward his mom.

Face composed, chin up, she said, "Hi. I'm Ronnie Ashford. I hired Jack as a driver."

"I'm Rosalyn Crews, Jack's mom." She took Ronnie's hand in both of hers and didn't let go. "I brought the boys lunch. Come join us, okay? There's plenty." Not giving Ronnie a chance to refuse, she tugged her out the door while adding, "I *love* your hair. That cut is amazing. And you have stunning eyes. Charlotte told me so, but I couldn't quite envision it all."

Charlotte carried Peanut, which meant Howler trotted anxiously beside her.

There went his afternoon alone with Ronnie.

Brodie gave him a hard nudge. "Bet I can guess what you're thinking."

Unlikely, since Jack barely understood his own thoughts.

"I had no idea you were into that stuff."

Jack rolled his eyes. "Shut up."

Brodie just grinned. "Hey, to each his own." He started to walk away.

Jack drew him back.

Maybe his brother would be a good sounding board. "Hold up a second." Leaning out the door, Jack called to his mother, "We'll be there in just a minute."

She stuck her head out of the breakroom to wave him

off. "Take your time. We ladies will get to know each other."

And…maybe that wasn't a bad idea either. His mother had more than enough affection to go around, and God knew Ronnie could use a dose or two.

Closing the door, Jack turned.

Brodie's grin widened knowingly as he took a chair. "Tell big brother all about it."

CHAPTER ELEVEN

NORTH TOOK HIS time setting up the room. A narrow cot, recently purchased, was positioned in the farthest corner but didn't touch either wall. It was chained to the floor by an imbedded grommet. Here in the secret room of the basement, with cracks that crawled along each surface, damp permeated everything. He didn't want Veronica's bed ruined.

Not until he ruined it himself.

If only she'd stopped when he'd struck her rear window, he'd have her now. She'd be there, on that bed, one leg shackled. Helpless.

The timing had seemed perfect, but instead of confronting him, as he'd expected her to do, she'd chosen to flee. Smart girl.

He'd also assumed she would return to the hotel room. He'd planned to surprise her, to chat amicably until the right moment when he'd stab her with the syringe...

Oh, but the surprise on the big man's face had almost been worth his own disappointment. How had he missed the yellow Mustang? It wasn't like him to overlook such important details, but the hunger had swelled in him, beating like a pulse in his brain.

He'd thought he was close to having her.

He'd thought he was finally able to feed the hunger.

Oh, that little witch. North chuckled. She'd evaded him for now, but in the end, she'd pay for all the trouble.

Excitement bled through his veins, feeding his need with an adrenaline rush. Drawing a shuddering breath, he ruthlessly suppressed it. It wasn't yet time…but *soon*.

No more assumptions. Now he needed detailed planning.

In the middle of the room, where Veronica couldn't miss it, he'd opened his table and arranged his tools. Before he ever used them, they often had the desired effect of weakening a person's will through sheer, unadulterated terror.

He adored that pale, stricken expression, the loss of hope, the consuming panic that peeled eyes so wide, they were surrounded by white.

He'd read enough about Veronica to know she was a fighter. He, however, wouldn't take any chances. He had plans to wear her down long before she ever entered this room. He didn't like hiring out the fun work to others, but sometimes it became necessary. He would plague her to keep her off balance and if she got wounded… Well, ultimately it would make her more malleable.

And in the end, he could fully enjoy the payoff.

Shivering with anticipation, he needlessly straightened the arrangement, touching each instrument with reverent delight.

She'd give back his property, oh yes, she definitely would, but first he'd have his fun.

With one last look around the dank, windowless room, he knew he'd found the perfect victim.

Now to bide his time…until she was finally his.

AFTER GIVING BRODIE a bare-bones breakdown on Ronnie's family history, Jack explained how they'd met.

"She comes across like sex is no big deal, but she has so many misconceptions—"

"Like a friendly little spanking?"

"Damn it, I didn't—" Jack growled and ran a hand through his hair.

"Whoa, sorry. No reason to rip yourself bald." Brodie gestured. "You were saying?"

Feeling like he'd somehow betrayed Ronnie, Jack scowled at his brother. Talking about it wasn't easy, not because the topic was that unusual. But the woman most definitely was.

Fuck it. Brodie was his brother, and under the circumstances, his needling didn't matter.

"This doesn't go any farther."

Brodie's expression darkened. "Since you're *distraught*, I'll let that slide. Doubt me again, though, and we're going to have problems."

Laughing at Brodie's affront, Jack scrubbed both hands over his face. It wasn't funny. Not a bit. And still his brother could lighten his mood. "I saw how Mom and Charlotte looked. You said something—"

"No, doofus. They were grinning at *you*, not her. The way you look at the girl almost embarrasses me, and you know that's not an easy thing to do. It's obvious to me *and* them that you're head over ass."

Head over ass…in love? The idea didn't unsettle him as much as it should have. "I don't even know her that well." What a lie. In many ways, he felt like he already knew her better than anyone else did. "It's only been a few days." They'd been apart more than together since he'd met her…was it really only a week ago?

"So?" Brodie made it clear that time didn't matter. "I'm not saying you have to marry her tomorrow or anything. But you definitely need to see where it's going."

Yes, he did—assuming he could convince Ronnie, and there was the crux of the problem. "She tries to distance herself from everyone. Me, included."

Brodie shrugged. "That's never bothered Mom. She and Charlotte are in the breakroom right now schmoozing her. You know that, right?"

"Yeah." Ronnie was probably going to kill him, but she deserved a few more minutes with them first. If anyone could warm her up, he'd bet on his mom and Charlotte.

Sobering, Jack sat on the edge of the desk and ordered his thoughts.

Brodie didn't rush him, but they were both aware of the women waiting just down the hall.

"She's far from inexperienced," Jack said, trying to explain without in any way insulting her. "But she's so standoffish, so determined to avoid even the hint of a relationship, I think her experiences have been...fleeting."

"No good details, huh?"

"Doesn't seem like she's ever stuck around long enough to discover any *details*." The euphemism worked, since foreplay was, by necessity, detailed—with touching, tasting, stroking...and sucking—all in key places. "She treats sex like an appointment with a limited time to get things done."

"Except with you?" Brodie asked.

Jack shrugged. *Except with me.* After they'd enjoyed themselves twice, she'd stayed the night, allowing him to hold her until dawn. And *then* she'd reverted to old habits, sneaking away like a thief.

Or a woman who wouldn't admit her fears.

"With the way things went," Jack said, "I already know she'll refuse to stay tonight—"

"Even though someone might be after her." Brodie stood to pace in the limited areas of the small office. "I saw the rear window in her car. Something big definitely hit it, but you know how it is with rocks. They come out of nowhere sometimes."

"No," Jack denied. "Her instincts are as sharp as mine. If she says someone threw it, then that's what happened."

Brodie gave it some thought. "Well, I have an idea to offer, but it'll be a pain in your ass." He held out his arms. "It's all I got, though."

At this point, Jack didn't think he could be picky. "Let's hear it."

IN HER HEAD, Ronnie pulverized Jack. Twice. Where the hell was he? How dare he dump her off with his mother, of all people?

At least she got to hold Peanut, who was now clean, brushed, and wearing a collar—which made her like Brodie even more.

Thanks to the gentle care the cat had received, comfort and security had replaced the panic. Peanut curled up on Ronnie's knees, allowing her to stroke two fingers along his back. Howler didn't complain, but he laid his massive head over her lap so he could remain close, his worried eyes going often from the kitten to Ronnie and back again.

He hovered, like a mother would hover over her only child.

It was so obvious that the long-boned dog felt possessive when it came to the tiny kitten. Of course Ronnie stroked him, too. He was such a big but gentle beast.

Like Jack.

Remembering how Jack had reacted when saving the kitten, she wondered if Howler, too, could be ferocious when necessary.

"Aw, they both adore you," Rosalyn Crews said. "Animals are a good judge of character, obviously."

Obviously *not*, Ronnie thought, or both animals would steer clear. Her character, she well knew, left a lot to be desired.

As Howler crowded closer, Rosalyn laughed. "You don't mind, do you?"

"No, ma'am." She liked animals. They seldom rejected a friendly hand.

"Call me Ros," she said, while cleaning off the round table. "I insist."

Ronnie bit back another "yes, ma'am," changing it at the last second to "Okay, thank you."

Rosalyn flashed her a smile. Jack's mother was bubbly. And sweet. And down to earth.

A likable woman…who Ronnie didn't want to like. Hell, she didn't even want to know her, but already felt like she did, at least a little. Ros Crews was just that open, that welcoming.

Ronnie had already been drawn in, feeling an almost instant affinity for the older woman, maybe because of her appearance.

Jack's mom didn't have a single ounce of artifice.

A high ponytail held her long, light brown hair away from a face too young to have grown sons. Her jeans were as faded and broken in as Ronnie's favorite pair.

The sweatshirt she wore had probably come from Brodie, given how big and sloppy it was on her.

And her eyes—Jack's eyes, Brodie's eyes—were absolutely stunning on a woman. Rosalyn didn't need mascara, not with those incredible lashes.

Honestly, she could see why Jack's dad kept slinking back. The wonder of it was why he'd ever cheated in the first place. He had to be a complete fool.

Ros caught her looking. "If I'd known we had company, I might have changed."

"You look great. Comfortable."

That made Ros laugh. "I *live* for comfort."

Ronnie nodded. "Me, too."

Holding out the hem of the sweatshirt, Ros explained, "Brodie outgrew this his junior year. It's old enough to be really soft. Especially cozy on cool days like today."

When she began setting out food from a large tote bag, Ronnie said, "I should go," vowing she'd give Jack hell the next time.

"But…" Ros paused, each hand holding a container of food. She managed to look both hopeful and understanding. "Please stay and have lunch with us."

All the niceness unnerved her in its unfamiliarity, or so Ronnie told herself, because denying the appeal of it was easier than admitting that she'd never known this much warmth and easy acceptance.

In truth, it scared her a little.

But the food…the food looked amazing. Fried chicken, potato salad, and more. Hell, she could always eat.

Howler apparently felt the same.

The dog finally gave up his sentinel by the kitten to look longingly at the food. He licked his chops as if already tasting it.

"You big mooch," Ros said with affection. She opened the door and yelled down the hall, "Brodie Archer Crews, come and take care of this animal."

Immediately the office door opened. "Yes, Mom," he sang back.

By leaning forward just a little, Ronnie could see Jack prodding Brodie along—two big gorgeous men with similar traits and unique styles.

Her heart gave a little flip of visual appreciation.

In his hand, Brodie carried a large dog treat. Howler, not being a dummy, ran to greet him.

It wasn't fair. They were both so gorgeous and friendly and…damn it, *nice*. She wasn't used to that, to people who went out of their way to counter her belligerence.

And to have a mom like Rosalyn, a woman who welcomed a weirdo like her without batting an eye…

Of course, Ros didn't *know* that Ronnie was a weirdo. She didn't know about the nonstop nightmares Ronnie suffered, or that her family had thrown her away, that she'd escaped a kidnapping, and…and *what?* That she was so damned dysfunctional, it terrified her when Jack was nice, and still she craved his hot bod and the things he could make her feel?

Yeah, *not* something you could tell a man's mother.

Charlotte breezed back in, carrying several colas. "Who wants what?"

In the chaotic fashion only a family could bring, everyone answered at once.

Before Ronnie could say again that she was leaving, Jack pulled up a chair to her right, cleaned the top of a Coke can with a napkin, popped the tab, and set it in front of her. Brodie took the chair to her left, so close that his elbow bumped hers. He grinned at her when she gave him a sharp look.

Conversation happened around her, all while the kitten purred and Howler returned to chew on his bone beneath her chair. At this point, even if she wanted to push away from the table, she couldn't. Not without tripping over the dog.

And actually…she didn't want to go. Not anymore. Her own family hadn't included her like this, not in a very long time, and it felt…good. While it lasted, even if only for a day, she wanted to soak it in, savor it. She could think back on this day to counter the uglier memories when they returned, as they always did.

Jack set a plate of food in front of her, then, without asking, scooped Peanut away and placed him next to Howler.

She was just frazzled enough that she rounded on him. "Hey, I was—"

Brodie spoke over her. "I keep meaning to ask you, Jack. Think you could watch the animals for a few days? Therman is sending me out of town for a pickup, and I thought Mary and I might make it an overnighter. What do you think?"

Beneath the table, Jack put a hand on Ronnie's knee. The warmth of his grip penetrated her jeans, maybe even penetrated her very bones.

"Sure," he said, "as long as Ronnie can lend a hand."

Charlotte perked up with curiosity, her gaze going from one man to the other as if piecing together a puzzle. She leaned in. "Kittens need a lot of care. I'd offer, but I'm already scheduled with…other stuff."

Their mother busied herself with food containers.

Ronnie scrutinized each face. Brodie appeared sly,

Jack intent, and Charlotte conspiratorial. When she glanced at Ros, the woman tried to compress a smile and kept her gaze on her plate.

Okay, so Ronnie wasn't an idiot. This whole thing was a trumped-up excuse for Jack to get her alone. In part, because, yeah, he wanted sex. On that, she was more than willing.

But he was also worried. *For her*.

Actually, so was she. The man from the shadows… He'd spooked her, especially since she had to assume he was the same man who'd shown up at the hotel. She didn't relish the idea of driving home alone. She flat out dreaded the idea of trying to sleep again after two very restless nights. Plus deep down, she had a real bad feeling about things.

Here was an excuse she could use…if it didn't kill her to let them think she was *that* dumb.

While nibbling on a pickle, she glanced at Brodie. "One night?"

"Actually…" Dark eyes took her measure, gauging what she would or wouldn't accept.

In that moment, Ronnie realized that *he knew* she was onto him. It was there in his small smile, in the tilt of his head. She saw understanding, which almost unraveled her. Also respect, which got him off the hook.

"You know," Brodie said, as if thinking out loud, his gaze never releasing hers, "I think a little longer would be better."

"How long?" Jack asked, playing all nonchalant.

Brodie raised a brow at Ronnie. "Four days? Maybe five?"

Finally, she could pull her attention away. Five days

would be a… Hell, they'd be a lifeline. A gift. A memory she could cherish always.

Silence settled around them. No one ate. No one moved.

All she could hear was the kitten purring and Howler enjoying—like *really* enjoying—his bone.

Decision made, she picked up her sandwich. "I'll have to run home to get a few things."

A collective breath released, and just like that, everything returned to normal. Jack put an arm around her for a quick squeeze.

Brodie leaned in to say near her ear, "Thank you. For multiple reasons."

They had her sandwiched in, caught between all that potent machismo and masculine perfect.

Honestly, it wasn't a terrible place to be.

JACK LOOKED AROUND Ronnie's apartment with keen interest. In some ways, it was exactly what he'd expected. Stark to the point of sad, minimal in both furniture and personal items.

Since they'd left the offices, Ronnie had been distant, drawn into her own thoughts.

Respecting her need for introspection, he'd let her be. Coming with him, staying with him—for however long he could convince her—was a big step for her. Monumental in many ways.

Actually, for him as well.

Yes, he'd had other women stay over, sometimes for up to a week. But that had been for convenience, not out of a need to protect, to claim, to build a foundation of trust…for the future.

Pulling a rumpled duffel bag out from under the bed,

Ronnie expertly packed a few pairs of jeans, socks, and underwear, and a variety of sweatshirts and shirts. Her two jackets hung by the front door so he assumed she'd grab them on her way out.

When she finished packing, very little remained in the closet, or in the drawers of the single dresser. Not because she was taking so much, but because she had so little to begin with.

"You travel light," he noted. She'd gotten everything into the duffel and still had room leftover.

With a roll of one shoulder, she explained, "I move around a lot. It doesn't make sense to accumulate too much."

He glanced at the multiple earrings in her ears, the bracelets on one narrow wrist, and the simple silver rings on several fingers. "Any other jewelry to get?"

She shook her head. "I wear it all."

"Every day?" Yes, any time he'd seen her, she'd worn the same pieces, so he'd just assumed she liked jewelry and had more.

She answered with a shrug. "I've had all of these for a while."

It hit him with sudden insight. "Gifts?"

Using her thumb, she turned a ring on her middle finger. "From my dad, yeah." Smirking, she shook her head. "Back when he was my dad."

And they meant so much to her, she kept them close at all times. Jesus, it was unbearable, wanting to soothe her while also wishing he could crush the man who'd so callously hurt her. "I'm sorry I brought it up."

"No biggie. That all ended a long time ago."

And yet she still wore each and every piece. "If your

dad came back to you, if he apologized and said he realized—"

Snorting, she said, "It'd never happen, believe me. I
stopped thinking about it years ago."

For some reason, Jack felt compelled to press. "But
if it did?"

With her gaze on the empty wall, she turned her head
in thought, sending the longest part of her bangs to tum-
ble forward. "At first, I used to imagine us hugging and
crying and…just going back to normal. What a crazy
fairy tale, huh?"

"I understand wanting that."

Her mouth quirked. "Yeah, well, time for that came
and went ages ago. Now I don't know. Honestly, I'd probably tell him to fuck off. He's had years to care, and now
it's just too late."

Jack didn't believe that, and neither did she. If she
truly didn't care, she wouldn't wear all his gifts.

Every day.

As if she'd read his mind, Ronnie flashed him an
overbright smile and deliberately jangled the bracelets.
"Seems easier to wear it all than store it."

The defensive answer didn't surprise him. Ronnie
spent so much time rallying against her hurts, sarcasm
came automatically for her.

But the photos sitting on the dresser in an otherwise
unadorned apartment told another story. Trying not to
be obvious, Jack studied the image of a younger Ronnie
with her parents and sister at what looked to be a Christmas party, then another at a summer picnic.

Physically, the differences were apparent, of course.
He guessed the photo to be more than a decade old. Everyone aged, matured.

But it was her expression that really dated the photo. In it, Ronnie looked genuinely happy. The carefree smile, the innocent light in her eyes... Somewhere along the way she'd lost them.

Jack wanted to help her find them again.

A photo of her sister sat apart. The young woman in the image was everything Ronnie wasn't—tall, poised, and sedate. Her blue eyes, with only marginal makeup, appeared cool and remote.

He'd take Ronnie's restless fire and brutal honesty any day.

Standing to the side, Jack watched as she went out the door and into the small bathroom to fill her overnight case with makeup, lotion, hair products, and brushes. He liked the contrast of her balls-to-the-wall attitude on life softened by her feminine primping.

Everything about her intrigued him, but it was more than that, too. From the moment he'd laid eyes on her, he'd wanted her. Each time he saw her, the impact seemed more familiar.

And he became more determined.

While she stuffed her products into the duffel, Jack propped a shoulder against the doorframe. "I'm glad you're not packing a nightgown."

She snorted as if he'd shared a joke. "Do I look like I'd own a nightgown? I usually sleep in a T-shirt and my panties." Her gaze clashed with his. "But occasionally, when it's hot, I sleep naked."

That blatant tease hit him like a sensual punch, kicking his heart into a gallop, flashing a visual into his brain, and making his cock stir. "Saying things like that," he warned, "could delay how quickly we get out of here."

Laughing outright, she hefted the strap of the duffel

over her shoulder and started toward him. "Promises, promises."

Jack straightened. He'd show her a promise—

The buzzing of her phone immobilized them both.

Dropping the duffel with a groan, Ronnie fished her phone from her back pocket and glanced at the screen. "The brothers." With an apologetic smile, she said, "Duty calls."

Jack watched with interest while Ronnie listened to the newest assignment. Nodding at whatever was said, she put the phone on speaker, placed it on the dresser, and dug a pen and paper from her satchel of a purse.

"Go on, Drew, I'm ready."

The brothers spoke together, first one, whom she'd addressed as Drew, and then the other, which had to be Drake.

"Go by the bank to withdraw more funds." He stated an amount.

"Sure thing," Ronnie said, writing on a scrap of paper. Apparently bank runs were a norm for her employment.

"Because there have been *incidents* in the recent past," Drake intoned with lofty meaning, "we would like to assure you that all should go smoothly this time."

"Sure," she said without concern. "But it if doesn't, I'll take care of it."

Damn, but Jack admired her spirit.

Silence reigned, until Ronnie asked, "That it?"

Drew cleared his throat and lowered his tone. "The purchase will be for two photos of a crime scene, taken by a neighbor in secret. They're not outstanding, but supposedly you can see a spirit in the background, looking through the windows. Ensure both photos are included in the purchase."

Jack mouthed, *Spirits?* At least they weren't more dead bodies.

Ronnie shrugged. "Got it, guys. No problem."

"We return home tomorrow," Drake said.

Or at least, Jack thought it was Drake. They sounded so similar with their dramatically lowered voices, he'd lost track during the conversation.

"You want me to bring everything to you then?" Ronnie asked.

"Yes, but we'd also like to meet Mr. Crews."

Brows up in query, Ronnie slanted him a look. "You free?"

Since he'd be wherever she was, he'd ensure it wasn't a problem. "Absolutely."

"There you go," Ronnie said.

They arranged a meeting for late afternoon, and then they were on their way.

After giving Jack directions to the bank, Ronnie fidgeted and he could almost hear her thoughts, bold but uncertain as she wound up to something important.

Around Ronnie, he forever had to strive for patience, which usually wasn't a problem for him. He never knew what she might do or say, but he knew it'd often be unexpected and sometimes completely outrageous.

"So," she said, her fingers threading through her hair, tucking it back and letting it fall forward again. "I feel like I should explain something."

Hmm. With Ronnie, reactions were important. Whatever she planned to say, he had to respond in a way that didn't insult her—and sometimes *everything* insulted her. Part of her defense was to deliberately take everything the wrong way.

"We can talk about anything." He glanced at her too-serious, wary expression. "Always, okay?"

That typically mulish facade fell over her features. "I wasn't fooled by the whole 'need to watch the animals' excuse."

"I know." Ronnie wore her thoughts plain in her expressions, there for all to see. "Brodie knew, too. It was nice of you to go along."

"Nice?" she huffed. "Nice doesn't have anything to do with it. Truth is, I'm a little spooked about being alone right now."

Wow. Jack never expected that admission from her. Given her pained air, she probably thought it made her look weak, but he took it as honest, brave, and he hoped, a sign of trust. Since she'd given it, he gave one of his own: "I'm more than a little nervous about things, so again, thank you for playing along."

Her brows rose so high they disappeared under the fall of her hair. "You're worried about being alone?"

Damn. She'd completely misunderstood, and now things got tricky. If he said he wasn't worried for himself, would she feel challenged to deny her own fears?

Going with selective honesty, he said, "You have great instincts, Ronnie. If you feel uneasy, it makes me uneasy for you. There's strength in numbers, right? We're safer together." *She* was safer with *him* to watch over her. "That's what I meant."

"Yeah, well, I'm glad you see it that way."

"And you appreciate my trust?" he prompted. Trust was a biggie for him. Outside of family, he didn't give it often. When he did, he wanted it in return.

Instead of answering, she looked away. "It's just that... I'm hypersensitive to danger now." Her hand moved as if dismissing the notion as ridiculous. "When I sense something is wrong, it bothers me more than it should. More than it would other people."

Jack reached for her hand, enfolding it in his so she couldn't downplay her own reality. "Things that happen to us, especially bad experiences, can sharpen our senses. Your kidnapping makes you more intuitive. I never discount my own instincts, so you can be damn certain I won't discount yours."

Briefly, her hand tightened in his before easing away. "There was something about the way that guy watched me, something different..." Agitated, she dropped her head back against the seat. "I've felt people watching me before."

What? Hoping for an easy explanation, Jack asked, "You mean, like men admiring you?"

She snorted. "No."

That's what he'd thought. "So you've felt someone watching you in a threatening way?"

As if it confused her, too, she rolled a shoulder. "Not really threatening. Not until recently."

Maybe, working together, he could help her figure it out. "Share what you can. When it happened, time of day, location—stuff like that."

The way she jumped in, Jack assumed she'd been anxious to discuss it. "It's been happening over the past year or so. Not long after I last talked to Skylar, and several times since then. She was particularly...unfriendly that last time I called her." Consternation drew Ronnie's brows. "Not really angry, but in a forced, too-obvious way, you know? Like she wanted me to believe she was done, even if she wasn't."

"You haven't talked to her since then?"

"No. I decided I'd let it go—let *her* go. But I've often wondered if she might be curious, if she was checking up on me." Ronnie studied him. "I know I'm curious about her, even though I don't want to be."

"She'll always be your sister, no matter what."

"Right." Her mouth pinched, suppressing emotion. "Do you think she could feel the same?"

Restless, Jack squeezed the wheel while he considered how to answer. Honesty, at least in this case, would be brutal.

"I'm not fragile, you know."

Despite the gravity of the discussion, he smiled. "No, you're not." At least not at the moment. Other times, though…

"So stop looking like I asked you to saw off an arm."

That made Jack almost laugh, but he quickly smothered it. "Here's the thing, honey—family like yours… I don't understand them. Ask me about Mom, Brodie, or Charlotte, and I could say with certainty what they were thinking or feeling because I know them, *really* know them, and they know me. I'm not sure that's true of your family." Because if they'd known her, they never would have let her go. "Trying to guess on your sister is like trying to figure out my dad. I can tell you, at least with him, he's usually self-motivated."

Could her sister have a selfish reason for spying on her, for seeking her out? Again, Jack didn't know enough about her to guess. That is, if it was her sister watching her. Could be her mother, the dad who'd rejected her—or it could be something far more sinister.

Ronnie stewed on that a moment, then redirected the conversation. "Anyway, those times felt different. They made my skin prickle, you know? Like I could feel some-one watching."

"Awareness. It's almost a tactile thing."

"Right, like that. I felt it, but it didn't make me want to run or anything."

"So maybe there are two people," he said. "Or maybe the intention of the person has changed."

After a brief moment of surprise, she blinked. "Just like that? You believe me?" She searched his face, her lips slightly parted. More than a little dubious, she added, "About *all* of it?"

"One hundred percent." And that wasn't just telling her what she wanted to hear. Until they could figure out what was going on, he hoped he could come up with enough excuses to keep her close. "And because of that, I also believe you're safer with me."

Ronnie hugged her arms around herself. "I don't like this arrangement—"

"Relying on me?" he guessed.

"—but I dislike the idea of being alone even more."

Every time he was with her, she stole another piece of his heart. Emotions softening, Jack promised, "I'll make it as painless as possible."

She stabbed him with a sharp look. "None of it means anything, so don't start assuming."

For whatever bizarre reason, when Ronnie got par-ticularly prickly, it turned him on. Maybe he had some masochistic tendencies. Maybe he just relished a good challenge. "Wouldn't dream of it."

"You should know, I'm an insomniac. If you're a light sleeper, you're not going to like having me in your bed… That is, I assume we'll sleep together?"

He hadn't considered any other possibility. "Among other things."

"Well…" Her chin lifted. "Good."

The way she blended belligerence with sex appeal, there was no holding back his bark of laughter. And to Jack's surprise, Ronnie broke down and snickered with him.

CHAPTER TWELVE

"NOTHING, IT SEEMS, is ever normal with the twins."

Beside her on the abandoned porch, Jack repeatedly looked around as if searching for a threat. "I don't like this."

Again he banged on the front door.

Again, silence.

Yeah, Ronnie wasn't crazy about it either. It felt wrong, very wrong. Not just the location, but the very air, the smells.

The fine hairs on her arms stood on end.

A table holding the photos sat to the side of the front door. So far they hadn't even looked at them. It all felt too much like a trap.

"It's strange, I agree." Ronnie chewed her bottom lip while considering things. There was no one to meet, no one to do business with. Just the pictures the brothers wanted, in an envelope on that rickety homemade wooden table. A rock kept them from blowing away, and on the rock, someone had used a marker to write, *Leave the $.*

"But hey, it's *all* strange. Drake and Drew collect oddities, so…"

Occupied spiderwebs, strung from the overhang down to the broken railing, shimmered with a light breeze. Dead leaves blew across the unkempt walkway. Warped floorboards in the small treacherous porch were curled in places, missing or broken in others. It was an invitation to twist an ankle or fall completely through.

Ronnie carefully stepped around the table to peer in through a grimy window. All she saw inside was empty shadows. "It's vacant."

"No shit." Jack took her arm and tried to draw her back. "Let's go."

"Sure." She shrugged him off, determined to show him that although she'd accepted his help—for now—nothing had changed. She was the same capable woman. "No reason to stay. Get the photos and I'll leave the money."

Incredulous, he stared down at her. "You're going to drop a hundred bucks out here in the open?"

"Jack." A tingle along the back of her neck urged her to make haste. "If you think this is the weirdest pickup I've ever done, you're wrong. Not saying it's fun, not saying I don't have the creeps, but I *do* have a job, and despite me trying to convince you otherwise, so do you."

Jaw locked, he replied, "I'm doing my job, but take a look around. The photos were supposedly taken by a neighbor. Isn't that what Drew or Drake said?" His gaze swept over the abandoned area. There was a house in even worse shape across the street, with the remains of a basement next to that, and a long-ago burned structure farther up. "Ghosts, I can believe. But neighbors? How the hell is that possible *here*?"

"No one said it happened here." Wind whistled, making her hunch her shoulders against the chill. The grainy photos looked as if they'd been taken from a distance with a magnifying lens, or with a very cheap camera.

One showed a cluster of cops at the front of a house

while paramedics carried someone out on a stretcher. Another showed a destroyed bathroom, shower curtain down, blood splatters on the white tiled walls and floor. In both, the shape of what could be a pale specter, a puff of smoke with eyes and an oval of a mouth, peered from a window.

Not for the first time, the brothers' morbid fascination with weirdness gave her the shivers. "I assume this is just a safe place to trade them off."

"There's nothing safe about it. It's fucking *un*safe. I feel it and so do you."

"Yeah." She rubbed her arms and looked around. "Does it feel like we're being watched?"

A muffled noise made them both go still. Scraping sounds echoed hollowly, close, but not distinct enough to pinpoint. Jack pulled her back, his sharpened gaze darting around even though he held perfectly still.

Whispering, Ronnie asked, "Where was that?"

He shook his head, the gesture as bewildered as she felt.

With her heart suddenly punching too hard, Ronnie knew they had to go.

Apparently Jack agreed.

He snatched up the photos, then stood in obvious outrage as she withdrew the cash and put it under the rock. With his longer legs, he easily bounded down a missing step on the stoop. From the broken concrete walkway, he reached a hand up to assist her, but as she moved to step forward, a long blade, almost like a machete, jabbed up from the gaping hole where a floorboard should be.

It narrowly missed slicing the inside of her ankle.

Dear God, someone was *under* the porch. Someone had been there all along!

Gasping, Ronnie reared back in an automatic reaction, only to see the long knife appear between another crack, and one more. It stabbed up so quickly, searching for her, that she didn't know where to step.

Suddenly Jack's hands were on her waist and he somehow hauled her up and off the porch, her feet never touching the wood until he put her firmly on the ground behind him.

Immediately, a clatter came from beneath the rotted wood, rocking the entire structure.

For a moment, she thought the whole thing would collapse. From the far side of the porch a body scrambled out. Hidden in a dark hoodie, he took off in a dead run without looking back at them. The deadly blade flashed in his hand as his long legs ate up the ground.

Jack visibly waffled on what to do. Ronnie easily read his indecision. He wanted to give chase, to demand answers with his fists. Yet others emerged from the house across the street.

Three men, all watchful, prepared.

They loomed as dark warnings from the shadows, bodies poised in menacing intent. Jack gave a low curse and hustled her to the car.

"I can walk," she snapped, equally interested in getting the hell out of there in one piece and more fractious than usual because of her fear. "I don't need an escort."

Maybe because the driver's side was closest to the emerging mob, Jack let her veer to the passenger's side so they could both get into the car quicker.

He hit the door locks and started the engine...then sat there, thinking.

"Don't even," Ronnie ordered, alarmed by that particular vicious look in his ebony eyes. She knew he disliked the idea of running, and if he wasn't concerned for her, he wouldn't. He'd stay and confront. That's who he was.

It was who she wanted to be—and wasn't.

But fuck it, sometimes intelligence won out over bravado.

"Move it, Jack." She dug the gun from her purse, just in case.

He put the car in gear. "Keep an eye on them while I drive. You see anyone make a move, let me know."

Thankful that he'd put his macho bullshit aside for the moment, she nodded and twisted to keep her gaze on the men. They remained glued to the porch. "Haven't budged an inch. But if they do, I'm ready."

He glanced at her, saw the gun in her hand, and cursed low. "Put that away."

"Not yet." What if the men chased after them?

"You don't need it."

Because she had *him*? He had been pretty spectacular, sweeping her off the porch that way, as if she weighed nothing at all. Thank God he'd acted so quickly, or that next stab of that long, sharp blade might have gotten her. Her boots would have protected her feet, but it would have gone right through her jeans…and her leg.

Ronnie shuddered, swallowing hard to get her heart out of her throat, and then tried to think.

Briefly, she closed her eyes. This was no time for her to fall apart. *You've been through worse*, she reminded herself. True—and she wanted to know why this shit kept happening to her.

At least this time, she wasn't alone.

"If anyone starts to follow, you can outrun them?"

"Yes." The clipped word, harsh with confidence, reassured her.

When they rounded a corner, then another and finally met with humanity again—people in houses, routine traffic, commerce in the form of a saloon next to a drive-through next to a tattoo parlor—Ronnie finally released a calming breath.

None of that had made sense. Not the location, not the attack. Now what?

As she stored the gun back in her purse, another thought occurred to her. "Damn." She twisted to face him, her heart jumping again. "Did you drop the photos?"

"I have them," he snarled. Like, completely, violently *snarled*.

Wow. Every muscle in his body tensed and bulged until he looked bigger, as big as Brodie and twice as menacing as a mob of three.

So impressive.

Ronnie cleared her throat and hoped it would also clear the fog of intruding desire. This most definitely was not the time to think of hot, frenzied sex. "Can I ask where?"

Reaching inside his jacket, he withdrew the folded envelope and tossed it to her lap.

So…still angry, obviously. Not that she knew what to do about it. She wasn't even sure what to say to him. He'd saved her. If he hadn't been there, whoever was beneath the porch would have stabbed between the boards again and again and she'd have been…trapped.

Possibly *murdered*.

Maybe worse because, yes, there were worse things than dying.

After several minutes passed in silence, she said, "I'm glad you have quick reflexes."

"I'm glad you do as well." He now spoke in his most

annoyingly polite voice—but without separating his teeth.

"I made the *wrong* move," Ronnie pointed out. Lurching backward, farther onto the porch, only put her at worse risk. Oddly, it didn't shame her the way it should have. Not with him.

"You reacted," Jack insisted. "You didn't scream. You didn't panic."

Wincing, she confessed, "Maybe a little panic."

Jack shook his head. He breathed harder, deep breaths drawn in through his nose. His chest bellowed, his muscles clenched even more. And suddenly he jerked the car over to the curb in front of a church. Arms rigidly straight and forearms bulging, his big hands squeezed the steering wheel until his knuckles turned white. "*Goddammit*, Ronnie, you could have been maimed, maybe even killed."

Tentatively, she put a hand on his balled-up shoulder, impressed to find pure steel under her fingers. "Yup. I know." She tried a laugh that nearly strangled in her throat. "I'm rethinking that whole working-alone thing."

No response.

"You came in pretty handy today."

His gaze shot over to hers. "Don't tease. Don't laugh about your life." Eyes nearly black, he stared at her, *into* her. "You *matter* to me. Can't you understand that?"

Fighting off a sheen of tears, she nodded. He meant it. She didn't think anyone had ever meant anything quite as much as Jack meant it now. It weakened her, while paradoxically making her feel stronger, almost invincible. "Yeah. Okay."

They stared at each other until she started to feel uncomfortable. He expected something of her, but what did she know of this emotional back-and-forth stuff? Nada. Zip.

All she knew was that for the first time in years, she liked it. "When I see Drake and Drew, man, I'm going to give them hell."

Dumb. Such an incredibly dumb thing to say. True, but still...not what Jack would want to hear.

His chest expanded with a very deep breath. He dragged his gaze away from hers, checked the rearview mirror, and slowly, very slowly, forced the angry stiffness from his body.

As he pulled back to the road, Ronnie withdrew her hand. They drove in silence for a few more minutes.

She couldn't take it. "I want you."

"Not as fucking bad as I want you."

Huh. That immediate reply sent a tingle chasing over her skin from her throat clean down to her toes. "You don't think it's...misplaced? For me to think about sex right now?"

"Like me, you want to reaffirm that we're okay."

That sounded plausible, though actually, she thought maybe she was just a very base woman turned on by his brutal defense of her. There was something so elemental in the way he'd reacted—like a man who wanted to protect...his woman.

She rubbed the top of her head, unsure what to think about that, how to react. For so long now she'd been on autopilot, her reactions so constant they happened by rote, without her considering them. Now, within a week of meeting Jack, everything was different. She couldn't summon up her indifference, couldn't shrug off his interest.

Because she was equally interested, maybe more so. *Definitely* more so.

Trying to sort it all out in her head, she said, "I know you wanted to stay, to maybe kick some ass."

"I wanted to *kill* them."

The stark statement startled her.

"I'd have started with the son of a bitch—" he swallowed, tightening again "—who tried to hurt you."

"He ran off," she said, before thinking about it.

"I'd have found him." His chest expanded on another labored breath. "But you were the voice of reason. They could have all been armed."

"And probably were," she rushed to point out. "We know the one had a knife."

His jaw clenched. "I'd have fed that fucking blade down his goddamned throat."

"Oh." Yeah, he sounded pretty confident, so she didn't know what to do with that info. On most men, she'd have discounted it as reckless cockiness. But with Jack, she had a feeling he could live up to his own hype and then some.

"The problem would have been if they had guns." He flexed and bulged and overall gave off a killing attitude. "God, Ronnie, if someone shot at you—"

The tortured words worked like a magnet, drawing her closer, sharpening her need to touch him. Opening her hand on his biceps, she stroked up to his shoulder and then kneaded the taut muscles that led to his neck. "I'm fine. *We're* fine." She felt more so by the second.

"I couldn't risk you." Taking her hand, he carried it to his mouth where he pressed a smoldering kiss to her palm. "I'm glad at least one of us was thinking straight."

"Me?" Because honest to God, she hadn't felt all that clearheaded.

"You." He lowered her hand to his thigh, pressing it flat. "Never in my life have I completely lost sight of priorities like I did today. I'm always levelheaded, always calm—"

She choked and tried to turn it into a cough. "Yeah," she said fast, before he got fired up again. "You're usually so damned calm and reasonable it makes me want to shake you up."

"Because you're *never* reasonable," he accused, then added half under his breath, "It's part of your charm."

She had charm? Good to know.

"But this time, we completely flipped roles, and I'm sorry."

Another choke of laughter tried to crawl up her throat, forcing her to swallow convulsively. When she got it tamped down, she asked, "You're apologizing because you…acted like me?"

"I wasn't hired to act like you, now was I?"

"Nope. One of me is probably enough—more than the brothers can handle, actually. And just so you know?"

Stoic, he stared ahead.

With a shrug in her tone, Ronnie stated, "I liked how you reacted. It impressed me." Baring herself was never easy, but he'd just rattled off so much, sharing as if it were easy to do, that she felt compelled to reciprocate. "It's been a really long time since anyone felt that protective of me." She leaned closer, moving her fingers on his thigh in and up. "Sort of turns me on. A lot."

"I have to *drive*, Ronnie," he said, strangled. "Unless you want me to find a quiet place to pull over, you better curb the teasing."

Smiling in satisfaction, she settled back, her hands now safely away from him. "How long till we get home?" That sounded really awkward, and she corrected, "I mean, to your house."

"Ronnie."

That gentle tone made her sit up and take notice.

"We have to call the police."

Ha...*police?* That was... Well, yeah, they probably did. She gave a frustrated and exaggerated sigh. "I don't see how it'll help." At this point, the money was gone, and surely the men were also. "You know there's nothing they can do."

"I'm going to insist."

Damn it. Her good feelings drifted away. "How the hell do you think we'll explain buying crime scene shots?"

Expression grim, he said, "You were only doing your job."

"And you think the brothers won't blow up when cops come knocking at their door? I'll get canned."

He said nothing, just continued to stare ahead as he drove.

Ronnie narrowed her eyes on him. "You're going to make me be reasonable twice in one day, aren't you?"

"I wouldn't *make* you do anything."

Oh, so she'd have to own the decision, every sour sip of it? Folding her arms, she sat back in her seat. "They'll confiscate the photos."

Again he held silent.

"I'll have to warn the brothers first."

"I'd like to talk to them anyway."

Yeah, she'd just bet he would. "Fine. Get off in the

next town and find me an office supply store, or some place I can make copies."

Jack glanced at her. "The photos?"

"I have to salvage something." After withdrawing her phone, she held it out, staring at the screen while trying to decide what to say. "A good offense always tramples defense, don't you think?"

"Sounds about right to me." He reached for her thigh to give her a squeeze. "It's sexy when you strategize."

"Now who's teasing?" With her plans decided, Ronnie put in the call.

Drake answered on the second ring and before he could finish a proper hello, she jumped his ass. "We were attacked by a machete-wielding Jason-wannabe at the abandoned house where you sent us." In one long run, she detailed it all, sharing all her outrage, going into grisly detail about the blade spiking up from the broken boards, painting a visual of a demented thug skulking beneath a rotted porch with the evilest intent. By the time she finished her hands were shaking.

Because damn it, it was all true.

Finally, when she paused to suck in necessary air, Drake whispered, "Dear God."

"Are you all right?" Drew asked.

For once they spoke in normal voices, instead of the affected, dramatic tones.

"We both survived," Ronnie said, "but how, I don't know."

Jack rolled his eyes at her. He probably wanted her to give him credit, but she wouldn't.

"And to think," she continued, "you guys promised this one would be easy."

Drake, finally finding his voice again, snapped, "Call the police."

Whoa. Holding the phone out to see it, Ronnie glanced at Jack, but he didn't know what was said. She remedied that by putting it on speaker. "We can both hear you now, so say that again?"

"Go immediately to the police."

Jack's brows rose. "You're serious?"

"Something more is going on here than a single unstable seller. Something more sinister."

The possibility meshed with Ronnie's uneasiness, but still… "How do you figure that?"

"It was an elderly *woman* who contacted us," Drew explained. "She asked if you could meet her on her *quiet street* because she was retired and didn't get out much anymore."

Drake added, "There was no mention of an abandoned house or men. That means you were sent there on purpose. Both of you."

As if he'd suspected all along, Jack popped his neck and squeezed the wheel. "We were set up."

Ronnie had already suspected something amiss, but it didn't reassure her to have a consensus on it. "I have the photos. They look genuine enough."

"But God only knows how they were obtained. Since there was no neighbor to witness the crime, maybe the seller…" Drew paused.

"Initiated the crime," Drake finished in an ominous whisper.

Drew gave a soft groan of distress. "You *swear* neither of you are hurt?"

"We were both a little rattled," Jack said. "Near misses

can have that effect. But you know Ronnie. She reacted like a pro."

"You're due a vacation," Drake announced with dark, magnanimous drama.

"No." If they put her on vacation, if she and Jack didn't have any combined runs to make, she absolutely could not stay with him, not around the clock. And that meant she'd have to return to her apartment.

The thought sent icy dread up her spine.

"I don't need a vacation at all." *Good. She sounded bored.* "You heard Jack, we're fine. But we agree about the cops." Ronnie hated to distress the brothers. For all their peculiarity, they'd actually been good to her. Indulgent with her attitude, respectful of her ability. Friendly, in their own eccentric ways. "You guys know the cops will probably want to talk to you as well, right? You made the arrangements for the pickup. You talked to whoever it was who tried to sabotage us."

"Of course," Drew answered. "Have no fear, Ronnie. We have nothing to hide."

Right. They had a *lot* to hide…unless they meant they'd stash their more ill-gotten gains?

Drake said, "We'll meet tomorrow as planned. If the police want to speak to us, explain that we'll be home then."

"Well, just so you know, I'll make copies of the photos first, in case the cops take them. I'll keep you posted on anything else that comes up."

In the background, Drew murmured, "Isn't she darling?"

"Always looking out for us," Drake agreed.

Jack shook his head.

A little embarrassed by the praise, Ronnie scrunched

her nose. "Yeah, I'm a regular cream puff," she said with sarcasm. "Gotta go, guys. Later." She disconnected on whatever else they tried to say. Even she had started to snicker, and she couldn't let them catch her being *too* soft.

"Cream puff, huh?" Jack's hand drifted on her thigh, his thumb brushing in a way that made her hold her breath. "Sounds tasty."

Him, tasting *her*? Oh, unfair! Immediately, her body warmed at the thought, *wanted* at the thought. She'd felt his mouth on hers, on her neck, and at her breasts.

How would it feel if he kissed her *there*?

Oh Lord, her body gave a quick clench in reaction to the thought, and her nipples suddenly felt far too sensitive. She'd always avoided anything other than straight-up sex. Nothing too involved. Nothing too…familiar.

Just strangers, sharing a quick screw.

Thinking it now, it sounded ridiculous. How could sex *not* be familiar? Probably an attitude thing. Sex for her had been about relief and respite, a way to dodge her nightmares without admitting to a weakness. A prescription that eased her ills. It had never been about any particular man, not beyond the short time it took to complete the…well, the act.

It struck her that, minutes after meeting Jack, she'd forgotten that protocol. Meeting him had somehow been as life altering as being kidnapped or kicked out of the family.

Only far more pleasant—physically and emotionally.

Every damn minute with him had been nice, even the minutes where she'd tried hard to make him retreat. With Jack, it seemed to be all forward momentum.

God, she had spent so much of her life looking back.

Could she, for the first time in forever, look to the future? A different future than what she'd expected?

"You okay, honey?"

Her gaze went to his face, seeing lines of anger still carved beside his mouth, the tension around his narrowed eyes. And yet, the hand on her thigh was so gentle. Possessive, bold, but careful... The way he'd always treated her.

Now, in this moment, was a terrible time for her heart to start to crumble. She drew a steadying breath—and glanced at his lap with renewed interest. "Just thinking."

Thinking of you going down on me. Yeah, she had little modesty, but she couldn't put that into words. "You've had a lot of sex?" she asked instead.

Surprise overshadowed the residual anger, lifting his brows and softening the strain. "Where did that come from?"

She shrugged. "You're touching me." When she said it, his hand tightened. "Are you dodging the question?"

"I don't know how to answer it."

Tilting her head to study him, Ronnie saw his honest confusion. "I'll simplify it for you. How many women have you banged?" As the seconds ticked by in silence, her irritation grew. "Need a calculator?"

"It's not that," he said without rancor. "First, I wouldn't call it that." He chastised her with a quick look. "And second... I've never kept count."

"So make a guess." Why she pressed it, she couldn't say. But damn it, now her curiosity was so ripe, she had to know.

"Maybe twenty?"

Her jaw tightened. "You don't know?"

"Some were more memorable than others."

An emotion—*not* jealousy—clouded her vision and she looked away, letting her fingertips toy with the fine stitching on the leather seat. "You do a lot with these twenty or so women?"

"A lot?" His laugh was short and rich with a flash of insight. "To save us both from awkwardness, why don't I just say that, all experiences combined, there's not much I haven't done, but there's no one I've ever wanted to experience it all with more than you."

An experience, not just an act. She liked the sound of that, especially since it mirrored her recent revelations.

"Well, just so you know, I'm willing." *God, that sounded dumb.* She cleared her throat, trying to ignore the heat in her face and the happiness surging through her blood. "I mean, usually I like to get right to the point, you know?"

"Yes, I've noticed your direct approach."

Was that an insult? Had she disappointed him? The idea horrified her when, in the past, she hadn't given a flip what anyone thought about it. Long as she got hers, it was up to him to get his. Not her problem.

Then she remembered Jack's release, how...well, *incredible* he'd been. The heat in his dark eyes, the delineation of every muscle, how his throat worked, and the husky sounds he'd made.

Ronnie shivered.

Maybe that explained why she'd found his anger so appealing, too. Release and rage had both stripped away his polite regard, leaving only real, raw, basic male.

She cleared her throat again. "So we can try a few things?"

Jack shifted, straightening one leg and tugging at the material of his pants. His voice was gruff when he promised, "We can try anything you want, but I don't think I can talk about it anymore. Not right now. Not if you expect me to keep us on the road."

Ronnie felt the pull of a slow, smug smile. *We can try anything...* An exciting promise, prompting her to wonder about different possibilities.

Him going down on her, a definite yes.

But would she enjoy repaying him in kind?

A visual of his naked body filled her mind. He'd been bigger than she expected, lean and hard all over. Totally gorgeous.

But it hadn't just been his physical appeal that made her one experience with him so memorable. He'd been so thorough in touching her—and while she normally would have rejected that much attention, with Jack she'd felt powerless to do anything but *feel*.

Damn, she wanted to feel like that again.

Into the throbbing silence, Jack asked, "Has it really only been two days since I had you?"

She answered honestly, saying, "Feels like a week."

"At least." He smiled, then promised, "Only a few more hours."

This type of lust was new to her, sharper edged since she wanted Jack specifically, not anyone else. But she wasn't a wimp. She could hold out that long, right?

First they made copies of the photos, which Jack put under a floor mat, concealing them *just in case*, he said. From the parking lot of the office supplier, he called the police—and was asked to come in.

They found the station without any problem. After locking her gun and both their knives in the glove box, they walked in.

The station was small and from what they were told,

short on resources. A detective, probably in his fifties, large and solemn, led them to a windowless room. He pulled up two extra chairs to an old metal desk, gesturing for them both to sit.

His chair creaked as he lowered himself into it. Sitting back, he regarded the photos the cop had given him, now in a protective plastic sleeve. "Two officers are riding out to the address you gave, to see if they can find anything."

"They'll be long gone by now," Jack said.

"Most likely."

Three piles of folders littered the desktop, one dusty, the others scattered as if someone had recently gone through them. The painted cinderblock walls boasted framed photos and exposed pipes, in equal number.

Frowning, the detective put the photos aside and turned to pick up their detailed statements. He'd already skimmed them twice.

"Why," he asked aloud, "would someone try to hurt you when you'd already left the money? If they thought you had more, why not mask up and rob you at knifepoint?"

"He'd have a broken neck if he'd tried that," Jack said without inflection.

The detective glanced at him, made a sound, and refrained from commenting.

Ronnie wanted to smack them both. "Clearly, it wasn't about the money."

"Do you have enemies, Ms. Ashford?"

"None that I know of." She briefly explained the rock that cracked her rear window, and the strange visitor to the hotel room. "Do you think they're related?"

He shrugged a heavy shoulder. "Rocks ricochet from tires. Men try to pick up women."

"And vice versa," Ronnie said, staring him in the eyes.

"And vice versa," he agreed. "So who knows? But it bears noting." He was jotting the details onto a paper when his phone rang.

Ronnie shared a look with Jack. He was keeping it together for the cop, but tension still radiated from him. Tension, and more.

The detective spoke briefly to his caller, nodding a few times and giving short replies before hanging up. "Officer Inman said they didn't find anything there, no thugs, no money, no table, not even a rock. Only abandoned houses."

Figured. "So are we done?" Ronnie asked.

He regarded her. "It sounds to me like you were lured there for some other reason." He gestured at the photos. "This was just an excuse."

"Sounds like that to me, too," Jack said.

"Unfortunately, in that area, it's not uncommon. Gunshots, drug deals, prostitution, robbery." He eyed them both. "Could be it's random, someone using your bosses' hobby to grab some easy cash. Could be the intent was to further rob you." He glanced at Ronnie. "Or worse."

The idea of *worse* had her throat going tight.

"In another station, this might get a ton of attention, but here..." He held up his hand. "We have more than our fair share of violent crime, without the manpower to deal with it all."

"Well." Ronnie smacked her hands onto her knees and started to stand. "Thanks anyway."

His stare kept her in her seat. "Overall, I'd say you were lucky to get out without any physical harm. That's not an area to visit, if you get my drift."

Jack agreed, leaving Ronnie to scowl at them both.

"Without a description of the man you say attacked you, there's not much to go on." The detective lifted the photos. "My advice is to stop playing dangerous games."

As Ronnie had feared, he seemed more concerned with the brothers' hobby than with the criminal attack.

"You realize these are likely photoshopped, right?"

"I figured." Not that it mattered. Drake and Drew had bought other fakes when they were interesting enough.

"I'll call your bosses and arrange a meeting," the detective continued. "We'll see if we can lift any prints off the photos, but I wouldn't expect much to come of it."

At that point, they all stood. To Ronnie, the detective looked tired and that softened her annoyance over the inconvenience. She remembered the last time she'd dealt with the police. After her kidnapping, those detectives, too, had looked tired. Tired of crime, tired of senseless death, tired of not enough hands to get it all done.

In the scheme of things, an attempted foot-stabbing probably fell pretty low on the chain of priorities.

She stuck out her hand. "Thank you, Detective. We appreciate your time and I'm sorry we had to burden you with this."

His brows lifted before he folded her hand into his. "I'm glad you came in. It's why we're here." After a gentle squeeze, he accepted Jack's hand, too.

"If you need us for anything else, we'll make ourselves available," Jack said.

"Appreciated. You both take care now." As they left, he added, "And stay out of that area."

By the time they arrived back at the office, the sun hung low in the sky, sending one last splash of crimson over the horizon. They only had to collect the animals and her car…and then she and Jack could be alone.

For once, as darkness blanketed the landscape, the concern of nightmares didn't touch Ronnie. She didn't even think about rock-throwing thugs or knife-wielding creeps hiding under porches.

Instead, thoughts of Jack filled her, body and soul. What he'd do to her, what she'd do to him, and the overwhelming, wonderful, indescribable things he made her feel.

CHAPTER THIRTEEN

THANK GOD ONLY Charlotte had been around when they arrived. Jack didn't think he could take another delay. Ronnie's curiosity, combined with the way she'd looked at him, had stoked his lust to a fever pitch.

He'd had to concentrate hard to keep from sporting wood.

Brodie, who would have recognized his predicament right off, would have detained him just for fun. His mother, who God willing would *not* have realized why he was in a rush, would have wanted to visit with Ronnie to make her feel more welcome.

So all in all, putting up with Charlotte's knowing smiles wasn't so bad—especially since she already had everything ready for him. He got both animals, along with everything they'd need in the coming week, loaded into his car in only a few minutes. He led the way out to his house, with Ronnie driving her car close behind him.

After everything that had happened, Jack would have preferred to put Howler with Ronnie as extra protection, even though she was only a car length behind him. When riled, Howler could make a professional killer turn tail and run. But Jack didn't want to load her down with both animals, and the dog kicked up such a fuss at the idea of being separated from Peanut, howling so pitifully, it had almost sounded like a human's wail. No one had the heart to separate them.

It was comical how such a big-boned, massive mutt wanted to mother the tiny kitten. It was also really sweet. Not for the first time, Jack said a silent prayer of gratitude that Brodie had rescued Howler from the abusive dicks who'd kept him chained in the yard. Howler was now a part of the family, and he was well loved by all.

Constantly checking for Ronnie's headlights in his rearview mirror, while also watching the road and staying alert to trouble, meant it took Jack five minutes longer than usual to reach his house.

The porch light, which came on automatically at dusk, lit up only a part of the yard. Most days Jack never gave a thought for the shadows. But today wasn't most days. He hadn't yet been able to shake the bad feeling from earlier. Even after they'd left the street, the lingering sense of menace plagued him.

And of course he knew why.

Whoever had set them up had specifically targeted Ronnie with that long lethal blade.

It didn't take a genius to come to that conclusion, and he'd be surprised if Ronnie didn't realize it. She was sharper than most, definitely more alert. It all added up—unless she didn't *want* to see the truth.

If taking them both out had been the plan, it would've made a lot more sense to start with him. Because of his size, he was the bigger challenge, and yet that knife had stayed hidden until he'd left the porch—and then the stabbing had begun.

A deep enough cut to the foot or ankle could immobilize a person. Without Jack there, she'd be a sitting duck.

So why not go after him first?

Maybe capturing Ronnie had never been the plan. Maybe the ultimate goal was just to frighten her, to put her on notice that someone was after her.

Her family? From everything Ronnie had told him, Jack didn't trust them at all. Yet Ronnie didn't seem to suspect them.

Did they want rid of her permanently? Hard to imagine, when he only wanted to get her closer.

After studying the shadows for any shifts and seeing nothing out of the ordinary, Jack left his car—lights still on, animals inside—and strode to where Ronnie had pulled up behind him.

When she stepped out, he waved her back.

Hitching her purse strap over her shoulder, she asked, "Changing your mind already?"

How could she even think that? Never in his life had he felt this urgent burning need to protect, as if he protected his very world.

Not having her close would be torture.

"You know I'm not." He held her door so she couldn't close it. "Wait in the car for me while I have a quick look around. Keep the doors locked."

That order had her searching the area, too. "Something's wrong?"

"Just a bad feeling."

Her eyes widened. "If you think someone's here, I'm going with you." She plunged a hand into her purse, no doubt to retrieve her gun. "I can watch your back—"

Jack stayed her hand. God love the woman, *she* wanted to protect *him*. If he told her he'd be better off alone, she might take it as an insult to her capability. Truth was, his focus went askew around her. They were both better off if he knew she was safe in the car.

"I don't think anyone is here," he explained. "If I did, I'd have us both out of here already. But a lot happened today and I won't take chances with you. Stay inside and if I'm not back in five minutes, drive away."

Her brows climbed up. She shoved her hair to the side, gave him a frown, and walked around him.

"Ronnie." He caught her arm. "This isn't a game."

"No kidding." She pulled free and wrapped her arms around herself. "But how about I wait in your car with Howler instead?"

It took him a second to realize she didn't want to wait in the dark alone.

And there went another piece of his heart.

"A much better idea," he confirmed, closing her door and striding with her the few feet to his car. Howler whined, unsure what was going on. The kitten stared wide-eyed through his carrier.

As Ronnie got behind the wheel, she spoke softly to the dog, reassuring him. "He'll let me know if anyone comes around, right?"

Jack nodded. "Howler has incredible hearing and is a ferocious defender. Trust him." After disconnecting the house key, he handed the ring back to her. "Keep her running and keep the doors locked. I'll be right back."

"Maybe you should take my gun."

He'd rather she keep it—just in case. "Stay put, Ronnie." Locking the car door himself, he closed it and turned to go.

A brisk chill settled in, made sharper by the breeze. Keeping his arms loose, Jack searched the area as he walked to the door of his house, but he didn't creep along. He was too anxious to get back to Ronnie.

As he unlocked the door and pushed it open, he

stepped back, waiting a couple of seconds before reaching inside to hit the lights, both interior and additional exterior.

A soft yellow glow lit the yard, the tree line, and beyond. Two deer looked up, and then ambled away. A good sign, since deer tended to be skittish around humans.

His living room was the same "work in progress" shambles he'd left it in.

A carefully cleared path led from the right of the couch to the kitchen, another straight from the couch to the television. In and around that were stacked cans of drywall mud, tools, sawhorses, and other various construction needs. During the remodel, he'd opened up the room enough that there was nowhere to hide. Skimming through the house, he checked doors and windows, looked in closets and under the bed, but found nothing amiss.

Relieved, mostly that Ronnie could have a relaxing night, he headed back out to her.

It impressed him that she'd waited inside the car, doors locked, until he reached her. Yes, she was sometimes rash and always too brave but clearly not foolhardy. He should have realized she was too smart not to take precautions.

He let Howler roam around the yard, sniffing and piddling at random, while Ronnie got her duffel and he unloaded the kitten's carrier. It took a second trip to get the cat box and litter and the rest of the paraphernalia essential to the animals.

Once they were settled inside, Ronnie announced, "I'm starved. Do you have anything to—?"

"Don't say it." Jack quickly nodded at the dog, who'd been circling the kitchen, nose to the ground, but paused to look at her as if he'd sensed the topic of food.

Laughing, Ronnie cupped Howler's massive head in her small hands. "You are so clever, aren't you? Clever, sweet, and beautiful."

Howler narrowed his eyes in bliss and his tail thumped hard against the tiled floor.

"I'll give you the first two," Jack said, "but Howler prefers to be called ruggedly handsome."

"Does he?" She kissed the top of the dog's head. "Ruggedly handsome, it is."

Next she picked up the kitten, cuddling his downy softness to her cheek. "And you, you little Peanut. Look at how much you've changed already. No more hissing and heartbreaking cries, just purrs."

"Love and care," Jack said, "makes a huge difference." He hoped that would prove true with Ronnie as well. If she saw differences in the kitten, well, he saw similar differences in her. Though he'd happily have skipped them, the risky circumstances they'd experienced had worked to strengthen trust, and time together built familiarity. She was more relaxed, her guard not as tall or steely.

And then there was the mutual, volcanic sexual attraction—honestly, his favorite part.

"Peanut deserves time to play, to grow and learn without being threatened." As did Ronnie. "It was the same for Howler before Brodie took him in."

Her gray eyes shifted to look at the dog. "You said he was mistreated?"

"Chained in front of a drug dealer's house in the broiling sun. No water, underfed." Jack's hands automatically clenched into fists with the memory. "Brodie was in the area to buy car parts from a nearby garage."

Wearing a soft expression, Ronnie knelt by the dog.

She put the kitten in her lap so she could hug Howler. "Brodie couldn't ignore that."

"Hell no, he couldn't. He put Howler in his car, then went to the house to tell the miserable bastards that he was taking him."

Eyes rounding, Ronnie looked up at him. "He went into a *drug dealer's* house?"

Good thing the subject was so grave, because having Ronnie on her knees in front of him sent his imagination into overdrive. "He didn't know their…*occupation* at the time." The memory brought a reluctant grin. "He interrupted some business, guns were drawn, and Brodie had to fight his way through things." With dark satisfaction, Jack said, "Didn't go well for the bastards."

"Wow." She looked at Howler again, this time with a sympathetic frown. "You poor baby."

Howler soaked it up, rolling to his back to instigate a belly rub, his massive paws held limply in the air.

Her gaze still on the dog, Ronnie asked, "Would you have done the same?"

"In a heartbeat." He couldn't stand abuse of any kind. What good was it to be gifted with a big, strong physique if you didn't use it when you could?

In a whisper so low, he barely heard it, she asked, "Is that what we're about?"

Her tone, her averted gaze, bothered Jack. "What do you mean?"

Shaking her head, she got back to her feet. *Still* she didn't look at him. "Never mind."

"Wait." Jack caught her arm and turned her toward him. She resisted getting too close. "Ronnie?"

Reluctantly, she lifted her gaze to meet his. With a

world of hurt and uncertainty in her eyes, she asked, "Do you feel sorry for me, Jack?"

Shit. Is that what she thought? She wasn't wrong, but what he felt was a hell of a lot more complicated than mere sympathy.

To ensure she couldn't rush off in a huff, he caught her waist, lifted her, and plunked her down on the counter.

"Hey—"

Stepping between her legs, Jack braced his hands at either side of her hips, caging her in. "Yes. I feel sympathy." Her brows pinched down and she opened her mouth, no doubt to blast him. "You were kidnapped, babe. I'd feel the same for anyone, man or woman, who'd been through what you have. I also have crazy respect for you."

Her frown eased into skepticism.

Jack kissed her forehead to soften it more. "You're beautiful, smart, gutsy, and so fucking sexy I can't believe we're having this conversation when you could be showering to move things along." He threaded his fingers through her silky platinum hair, tipped her head, and kissed his way down to her ear to whisper with suggestion, "Unless you want to skip the shower?"

Her short nails dug into his shoulders. "So tempting."

When he traced her ear with his tongue, he felt her nails again as she tensed in delicious reaction.

"How," she breathed, "can an ear be so sensitive?"

That innocent question was a perfect example of all the nuances to sex that she didn't know—and he couldn't wait to show her.

Pressing back, she gave him a mock scowl. "Save all your sexy tricks for after my shower."

"Only if you promise to hurry."

With a smiling sigh, she looked him over. "All mine—
for the next few days at least." She patted his chest,
pushed him back, and slid off the counter. "Given we're
both in a hurry, how about you play the nice host and
just surprise me with some simple—" she glanced at the
dog "—*nourishment* while I get ready?"

The idea of her in the shower, *his* shower, kept Jack's
need front and center, but her timing was perfect. He'd
been hoping for an opportunity to call Brodie, and this
seemed like his best bet.

Unable to resist, he slipped a hand along the back of
her neck and drew her in for one last kiss. Her skin was
soft and warm, her silky hair sliding over his knuckles.
Even after their long day, she smelled sweet and fresh,
like the outdoors, flowers, and warm woman.

"I'll have something ready in ten minutes," he murmured, before taking her mouth.

Here, now, kissing her was different. There was significance in having her in his home, not just for tonight,
but for an indefinite time. They were locked safely inside, guaranteed privacy, and he planned to make the
most of it.

Having her here felt right in too many ways to count.

Though Jack kept it short, when he looked at Ronnie, her eyes were closed, her lips parted, and she leaned
into him.

He could have her now, forget the shower and food,
but he knew enough about Ronnie to understand that she
needed to do this her way.

As he released her, Jack said, "If you need more
time—"

"I need you." Her hands, which she'd knotted in his
shirt, loosened as she smoothed the material, stroking

his chest underneath. "I don't think I'm as good at being patient as you are."

"It's a struggle, honey, believe me." Obviously, more than she realized.

Putting some space between them, Jack busied himself by filling the animal's food dishes. He put Howler's, with a bowl of water, along an out-of-the-way space against the kitchen wall. Surprisingly, the dog waited politely until the kitten's dish was down, too, before digging in.

Ronnie lingered, making him wonder if she was nervous about being in a strange house.

"Everything okay?"

She nodded at the animals. "Where will they sleep?"

And now she expected him to be coherent? He popped his neck to the side, trying to free himself of the sexual tension. "Usually Howler goes wherever he pleases when he stays over."

"He's spent the night before?"

"Several times. He's stayed with Mom and Charlotte, too. Usually Brodie can take him along when he has to travel, but not always."

"That's nice."

She was definitely stalling. Jack just didn't know why. "I assume he'll stick close to Peanut, and I planned to block him off in the spare bedroom. The closet there is empty so it's a good spot for his box." He wouldn't close them in. Instead he'd use a small gate to ensure the kitten stayed put, knowing Howler could easily get past it if he found it necessary.

"Sounds like a plan." She laced her fingers together. "Guess I'll get to it."

"Use the bathroom off the main bedroom, end of the hall. Towels are in the cabinet." Jack watched her walk, loving that long, confident stride and the slight sway to her slender hips. "Let me know if you need anything."

She went into the bedroom, but then leaned out to say, "I need all sorts of things, Jack, count on it. But they can wait until after I've showered, changed, and been *f...e...d*."

Slowly grinning, Jack acknowledged how well she *fit*—around the animals, with his family...and in his life.

When he heard the shower start, he called Brodie. While he set up the cat box and dog bed, he explained everything that had happened.

"You're meeting the brothers tomorrow?" Brodie asked.

"Late afternoon." With the prep done for the animals, Jack returned to the kitchen to start on food. "I'll feel them out then, but they seemed honestly concerned when we spoke earlier."

"I'll talk to Therman," Brodie said. "See if he knows them."

Therman Ritter, a wealthy collector of murderabilia, seemed to know every serious collector in the tristate and beyond. Elderly and in a wheelchair, Therman now counted Mary and Brodie as part of his eclectic family. There wasn't much he wouldn't do for them. Add in his extraordinary wealth, and he was liable to get answers the brothers couldn't. Hell, he might even get answers the cops couldn't.

"I'd appreciate it." Jack peered into his fridge, wondering what he should fix for Ronnie to eat. "I've got a bad feeling about things."

"About her employers?"

"Not necessarily. Thing is, I can't pinpoint where it's

coming from. I just…feel like bad shit is going to happen."

"You know, that could be because you're happy with her. It feels right, so you're worried something will go wrong."

"Maybe." It was definitely a new sensation, feeling committed to a woman. And not just any woman, but Ronnie Ashford, unique, ballsy, and with more baggage than any woman should have to carry. "You have to admit, a lot of shit has happened. My gut tells me it's all related."

"Well, damn." Brodie no more discounted gut instinct than Jack would. "I'll get back to you soon as I hear anything. And hey, if you need me, I can be home in only a few hours."

Withdrawing cheese, butter, pickles, and condiments, Jack stacked it all on the counter. "We're good for now." He planned to spend the night showing Ronnie everything she'd missed in bed. "But I appreciate it."

"No problem. I'll be in touch." Brodie hesitated. "Watch your back."

After disconnecting, Jack got out a skillet and made two grilled cheese sandwiches. He'd just finished putting them on plates when Ronnie came down the hall, damp hair brushed back, face clean of makeup, wearing a big white T-shirt with panties…and nothing else.

Jesus, she was even more striking like this. Her gray eyes were huge, framed by brown lashes and slightly arched eyebrows, the delicate bone structure of her face more obvious.

As she walked, a thick hank of damp hair fell forward, half covering one eye. He loved the cut, how it complemented her uniqueness and played up her delicate features.

The oversize shirt hung off one shoulder, showing her collarbone. It fell to mid-thigh, draping her body, displaying as much as it concealed. Her nipples, small and tight, pressed against the fabric.

She'd removed all the jewelry and… Jack was already hard.

He looked at the food, then back at Ronnie.

Smiling, she held out her arms. "Deal with it." Then reached around him and grabbed a plate. "I'm starved."

RONNIE HAD ALWAYS considered herself pretty good at reading people. Until Jack. Half the time she had no idea what he was thinking.

This, fortunately, was not one of those times.

All through the quick dinner of sandwiches, dill pickles, and chips, he'd watched her like a starving man. For once, his polite manners abandoned him and he managed only stilted replies to everything she said.

At first, she'd worried what he would think, seeing her completely undone.

From all indications, he *couldn't* think. He just kept devouring her with his gaze, sexual greed stark in his expression. It emboldened her…and heightened her own need. She didn't have enough imagination to play coy, so instead she'd concentrated on eating.

When she'd finished off the very last bite, they loaded the dishes, then stepped out back together, her holding the kitten, to let Howler take care of business.

When Jack led the dog to an empty bedroom, Howler's only concern was Peanut. Once Ronnie set down the kitten, both animals settled in to sleep on the big plush doggy bed.

After Jack set up the gate, they headed toward the bedroom. "They're so cute together, don't you think?" Ronnie asked.

Beside her in the dim hall, Jack's stare burned over her. "I'm going to take a two-minute shower."

Biting back a smile—because seriously, the way he wanted her was too fun—Ronnie nodded. "I'll just brush my teeth."

"Two minutes, Ronnie."

The smile won out. "I heard you." Feeling him watch her, she stepped ahead of him and made a beeline for the bathroom. They nearly collided, her at the sink, him stripping off his clothes as if being timed.

Oh wow. She watched him in the mirror while haphazardly putting toothpaste on her toothbrush.

Talk about new and different experiences.

She'd never brushed her teeth with a naked stud behind her. Never watched as a man adjusted the temperature of the shower and stepped into a tub.

The glass shower door only vaguely obscured all the awesomely carved definitions of his body. One thing she loved—no, scratch that—one thing she *enjoyed* about Jack's body was that he wasn't a bodybuilder type. No crazy bulk and grotesquely bulging parts. His lean muscles were about strength, not looks, naturally built by hard work and enhanced with awesome genetics.

He claimed he got that physique in part from his father. For that, alone, he should thank the man.

Everything about him was so perfectly symmetrical. Long limbs balanced with his height and the breadth of his shoulders. His feet, especially when compared to hers, were big, but not overly. Just enough to provide a good foundation for all the rest.

And his cock, currently jutting out…

Ronnie went still, her mouth full of foam and an idle toothbrush, as he lathered soap in his hand. He didn't look at her, but she could see him roughly scrubbing everywhere, then rinsing, both hands in his hair.

Those arms, that torso, and his thick legs…not to mention the erection that stood front and center.

He shut off the water and she realized she had to spit and rinse.

She'd barely finished doing that when suddenly, buck naked and his skin still damp, he scooped her up and carried her to the bed. "I brushed my teeth in the shower," he said.

"You didn't finish drying."

"I'm dry enough, and now we're both done."

They went down to the mattress together, his mouth already fused over hers, his hot hands sweeping over her body, feeling her through the cotton T-shirt, up to her waist, over her stomach, cupping first one breast and then the other.

It was such a firestorm of sensual onslaught that she couldn't think. He kissed her long and deep, his tongue exploring while he parted her legs with one hairy thigh.

She felt drugged, unable to catch up, her nerve endings sizzling and a pulse beat of aching need uncoiling low in her belly.

"God, you're beautiful, Ronnie," he muttered as he trailed his mouth to her throat, drawing on her skin, probably marking her.

The idea was strangely exciting.

He hadn't shaved since that morning and the rough beard shadow abraded her skin in a delicious way. As he opened his mouth over her throat and shoulder, he moved against her.

It was difficult to think, much less speak, but she asked, "You like me without makeup?"

Groaning, he said, "With makeup, without, I more than like you."

Her heart punched into her throat. What did that mean? "Jack—"

He plumped up both breasts in his hands and then, without warning, his mouth was on her, sucking at first one nipple, then the other, and even through the material it was almost too much.

Oh, dear heaven. She felt the pull of his mouth straight down to her vagina, like a lightning bolt that continued to burn. Her fingers tightened in his hair, ensuring he wouldn't stop. She was so tuned in to the pleasure that she didn't realize he was lifting the shirt until cooler air touched her breasts, followed by the velvet stroke of his tongue. One hand slid into her panties, pushing them down.

Sensation hit her in so many places, everywhere vital, that she couldn't ground herself, couldn't focus on a single impression.

His fingers played over, teasing, touching in key places, but never long enough for her to find relief.

Frustration built in tandem with the heat until she thought she might combust—but she loved it. Every burning second of it.

Finally, after her nipples felt too sensitive and she knew his fingers were wet, he lowered to kiss her ribs.

Her eyes flickered open. She stared at the ceiling without seeing it, all her concentration on his hot mouth… traveling south. Everything they'd talked about, all the ways she'd teased him about new experiences, came flooding back.

Would he—?

He brushed a kiss over her hip bone, tickling a little, making her tense with expectation. While she struggled to ground herself, he slowly worked two fingers into her, testing, pressing, pushing. "So wet," he whispered.

Once those fingers were in her as far as they could go, her body naturally clamped down. When he curled them just a little, touching a sweet spot deep inside her, she released a shuddering breath.

"You smell so good." He trailed damp lips over her stomach, down to her inner thigh. After a soft love bite, he urged quietly, "Open up for me, Ronnie."

For all her sexual encounters, *this* was very different, in part because it was Jack and, for the first time in her life, being with someone mattered. This wasn't just for relief, just for company.

She wanted to be here with him so badly it actually scared her. She wanted Jack. She *craved* Jack.

The bombardment of emotion took her out of her realm, making her anxious but uncertain. She didn't want to be anywhere else, hell no, but here, now, in this perfect moment with Jack, she lacked her usual confidence. It all felt new. Fresh. *Special*.

Hoping she didn't sound ridiculous, Ronnie stroked his hair and admitted, "I've never…"

Jack went still, then looked up at her.

"I've never done *this*."

Savage satisfaction smoldered in his gaze. He gave one small nod. "Good."

CHAPTER FOURTEEN

IT RELIEVED RONNIE that Jack didn't wait for her to move, but easily spread her legs himself, arranging her, lifting her right leg over his shoulder and pressing out her left until she bent it at the knee.

Sprawled was the only word for it as he looked at her, at her exposed sex, with hungry eyes. That, too, was new. Never had she allowed anyone to see her like this. She'd never even considered it. In fact, no one else had asked.

Men, she'd found, were readily agreeable to a quick screw without formalities.

Not Jack. She had the stunning sense that he didn't just want more, he wanted everything.

Bringing those same two wet fingers back to her, he opened her sex, leaned down, and licked.

Ronnie almost came off the bed. Never, not in a million years, had she expected it to feel like *that*. Holy Mother of God, that was…amazing.

"Easy," Jack murmured, sounding all smug and male and incredibly turned on. He flattened his free hand on her stomach to steady her, to hold her still, before returning to lick again, over her, *in* her, again and again.

Hold still? Impossible. Even if she'd wanted to, her hips had a mind of their own.

When he concentrated on her clit in a way that made her cry out, she fisted her hand in his hair. Not that he

was trying to get away, absolutely not, but she wanted
to make sure she saw this to the end. She struggled for
breath, and a rapidly building climax.

"Relax," he growled. "It'll happen."

Right. He sounded sure, but she wasn't. Having never
had this before, she wanted it bad. All of it. Pleasure
spiked through her, wringing out a harsh groan.

"Who knew?" Jack teased.

She managed to reply, "Ah, God, shut up," in an em-
barrassingly broken voice.

"All right," he agreed softly.

There was no more talking. She did her best to keep
quiet, too, but that proved impossible, especially when his
fingers sank into her again, pressing, twisting rhythmi-
cally. Her hips just naturally rode up against those thick
fingers, against his clever tongue, against the very idea
that this was *Jack*, going down on *her*, and nothing had
ever felt so sublime.

Finally, Ronnie didn't care how she sounded, how she
looked, how incredibly desperate she acted. She cared
about his tongue and that sweet suction and…

The orgasm crashed into her, forcing her head back,
screwing her eyes shut and clenching her jaw as the
nearly painful pleasure rode through her, sharp and *real*.

Jack stayed with her, prolonging it, pushing her, until
her hands and legs—her entire frame—turned to jelly.
Tingling jelly. *Melted* jelly.

She was gulping in air, totally flummoxed, as he continued to lick, tongue, and suck, though more leisurely
now, as if savoring the moment.

As if he really, truly enjoyed it.

Unable to take any more, Ronnie groaned and made
a half-hearted attempt to ease away.

After the soft press of a kiss, he rose over her. His beautifully lashed eyes stared down at her with some emotion she couldn't name, but it unsettled her all the same. If she had any energy left at all, she'd have turned away.

"No," he chided in a rough whisper. "There's no going back. Don't hide from me."

Even through her lethargy, she found the need to protest. "I'm not."

"Good." Reaching to the nightstand, he snagged a condom packet, opened it with his teeth, and deftly rolled it on.

It fascinated her, seeing that thin sheath rolled over the solid length of his cock. He was so big, so thick and hard. She'd really wanted to explore *him* a little—but that could wait until later. Because this time, she'd have a later. It was a uniquely satisfying realization.

"I should give you a minute, but swear to God, Ronnie, I can't."

She smiled up at him with a deep sense of…contentment? Yes. That would describe the emotion filling her up. "It's okay."

"Is it?" The sensual mouth that had just shown her crazy new things curled in a smile. "I'm glad." In the next second, he positioned himself and pressed forward, the head of his cock giving her the most intimate of kisses. On his forearms, which he'd bracketed at either side of her head, he covered her mouth with his, steadily thrusting and driving her right back to the peak before she could recover.

When he was as deep as he could get, he lifted his head. Nostrils flared, color high on his cheekbones, he studied her. "I want you closer."

Gasping each breath, Ronnie shook her head. "Not possible."

He held her gaze as he reached back and caught her left leg, hiking it above his hip until she held it there. Now that she knew what he wanted, she drew two deep breaths, and did the same with her other leg, locking her ankles at the small of his back.

He lowered down onto her, his chest pressing against her breasts, her belly to his abdomen. She found his weight deliciously…comforting. She'd rarely let a man over her and now she knew what she'd been missing.

But only with Jack.

The friction grew sharper as he gently, slowly, rocked against her.

Arms tight around his neck, Ronnie kissed his shoulder, now a little salty with sweat. She liked that, so she licked his slick skin, opened her mouth against him, and sucked. Even lightly bit.

This, too, was new—allowing herself to do as she pleased, feeling free to taste and touch. And the indescribable smell of him… She breathed him in, filling her head and her heart. Oh, how she'd love to wrap herself in that particular scent every single day.

They moved together, leisurely at first with a lot of kissing and touching. But each kiss grew deeper, their bodies grew warmer, and that insane tension escalated again.

Ronnie tried to hurry him along, but he controlled the pace and wouldn't let her rush. Frustrated, she freed her mouth and moaned, arching up against him.

His next stroke was firmer, putting her flat to the mattress again, making her gasp with the thrill of sensation. He did it again, and again… So *close*.

When Jack burrowed his face into her neck, she realized he was struggling to hold off, to wait for *her*. And that did it.

Clenching everywhere—her arms around his neck, her legs around his waist, her sex on his cock—she came. Hard. Immediately, he reared up, watching her as he found his own release.

Yeah, she knew sex...but she didn't know what the hell had just happened to her. She only knew she liked it.

Liked him.

Too damn much.

JACK WOKE TO a restless movement in his bed. Though he didn't often have women stay over, his very first thought was: *Ronnie*. Tightening his arms, he held her closer.

He wouldn't let her skip out on him again.

She went so still, she felt frozen. They were still naked, the room was dark, and he'd never been so satisfied. Not just sexually, but in every other way. He felt like he'd just solved a difficult puzzle. Conquered a nation. Scored first prize.

Ronnie Ashford... She was a puzzle for sure. And she had kept him racing to figure her out.

Smoothing her hair, he asked, "What is it?"

There was an odd note to her voice when she whispered, "I need to...to get up for a minute. Just go back to sleep."

Not a chance. He noted that her breathing felt shallow, her skin clammy. Her entire body was tense.

Taking a guess, he asked, "Nightmare?"

She shook her head. "No." After a prolonged hesitation, she whispered, "Memory."

His first thought was *thank God she's with me*. He

gentled his hold, pressed a kiss to her temple. "The kidnapping?"

"It's fine," she insisted in a quiet, desperate rush. "Go back to sleep. Please."

Jack knew he had to tread carefully. Ronnie's faith in him, in *them*, was an elusive thing, hidden behind her bravado and pride. He valued that about her and didn't want to do anything to make her feel more wounded.

Cupping a hand around the side of her neck, he asked, "Does getting up help?"

"I just need a minute." Her voice trembled.

So did his heart. "All right." Pushing back the covers, trying to be as matter-of-fact as possible, Jack stretched. "Should we do this naked or what?"

Ronnie didn't move. He wasn't even sure she breathed until she asked on a huff, "Do what?"

Well, at least he'd distracted her. He flipped on the lamp on the nightstand. They both flinched away from the light until their eyes adjusted.

Still acting like it was no big deal, Jack said, "We can go out to the couch. Maybe turn on an old movie? I'll doze with you." Making the decision for her, he went to the dresser and dug out a pair of boxers. Not naked, but close.

Staring at him, Ronnie slowly sat up on the side of the bed. "Jack—"

"It's only 1:00." Barely stifling a yawn, he walked around the bed and found her T-shirt, then pulled it down over her head. "You know I can't resist you fully clothed, so I hope you appreciate my restraint now, with you all bare-assed and everything."

Scowling, she punched her arms through the sleeves. "I don't need a babysitter."

LORI FOSTER   261

"God, I hope not, considering all the things I still want to do with you." He clasped her hand and hauled her up from the mattress. "Cold?"

Suddenly she looked incredibly lost. So lost, his throat felt thick and it was all he could do to keep from lifting her in his arms and coddling her close, promising her insane things.

In a barely there whisper, she said, "You don't have to do this."

"Ronnie, love." It was a struggle to make his tone light, to hide all the emotion bombarding him. "Here, with you, is exactly where I want to be. I wish you'd believe me."

Her eyes rounded. He found it sexy as hell, seeing her without her makeup, utterly bare—for him.

They both heard the nails on floorboards right before Howler stuck his big head in the door, eyeing them both as if wondering why the hell they were up.

Jack laughed. "Look, more company." Giving Ronnie a moment, he asked the dog, "Where's Peanut?"

Howler's ears perked up comically, then he wheeled around and lumbered away.

"Come on." He grabbed a blanket off the bed and hauled her somewhat resistant body down the hall and into the living room. Settling into a corner of the couch, he pulled her down close beside him. "Better claim your seat before—"

"Umph." Ronnie barely managed to keep her spot when Howler leaped up, gave her a frenzy of doggy kisses that she tried and failed to avoid, and then plopped down with a big sigh, taking up the majority of the couch.

Laughing, Ronnie swiped her shoulder over her face

and then patted his hip with affection. "You big lummox."

He thumped his tail and gave her a big, loose-lipped doggy grin.

Around the corner came Peanut, tail in the air, fur ruffled, as he tried to catch up. The kitten made a leap for the couch and missed. Howler jumped to assist, but Ronnie quickly said, "Stay! I'll get him."

The dog relented with a whine—until Ronnie scooped up the kitten and put him in the curve of Howler's body. He gave Peanut a long lick that almost knocked the kitten over, but then allowed him to crawl up to his scruff and groom himself.

Ronnie laughed.

"What?" Jack asked, busy spreading the blanket over both of them.

In the most natural way, she settled into his side, allowing his arm to go around her. "Look at his face."

Jack leaned around her, and grinned. Howler's eyes were wide, wary, but he held perfectly still so he wouldn't upset the kitten as he got settled in Howler's neck roll.

"Such a good, gentle boy," Ronnie told him, resting a hand on the dog's lower back.

Jack turned on the television but kept it low. Only the glow of the intruding porch lights and the flat screen lit the room. He propped his feet on the coffee table and put his head back.

After a minute, the kitten settled down, and then so did Howler. The two animals dozed back off again.

For a while, Ronnie was silent, introspective. Then she turned her face up to his.

Jack brushed back her long bangs, drifted a thumb over her high cheekbone, and waited.

She turned away again before quietly speaking. "You didn't need to do this."

Inwardly, he sighed. It'd take time for her to understand. He could just state that when she hurt, it hurt him, too, and only being with her helped. If she'd left, he would have felt tortured in the worst possible ways.

She wasn't ready to hear all that yet, so instead he asked, "Aren't you comfortable?"

"Very comfortable." She proved it by laying one leg over his and cuddling closer.

His heart seemed to fill up his chest until there wasn't room for his lungs to draw oxygen. How did you tell a woman you'd only known for a week that she was it, the one, and that everything good and bad was different, better, with her? How did you convince a person who'd been hurt so badly, whose love had been disregarded, trampled by those who should have been there for her no matter what?

For now, his number one priority was to make her feel safe. If he could accomplish that, he'd consider the night a win.

Trailing his fingertips up and down her slender arm, Jack asked, "Is it better, not being alone?"

Her fingertips toyed with his stomach, brushing over the hair that led from his navel to his cock. "Yes."

"Good." If she didn't stop touching him like that, he'd get hard. His touted control seemed sorely lacking around Ronnie. "Sleep if you want. Or we can talk if you prefer." Jack waited, hopeful.

Time came and went. She wasn't as stiff anymore, and her breathing was more even, less strained. Luckily, her teasing hand left his stomach as she hugged around him. "It's just…sometimes in the dark I can almost feel myself back in that trunk. There's not enough air and it's too hot. There was something under my hip, here—" she carried his hand to her side "—and it left a big bruise on me that lasted two weeks."

Jack spread his hand protectively over the spot.

"When the memories come back, it hurts all over again. Like it's fresh. I can't…can't breathe right." With a small gasp, she wiped at her eyes, then gave a shaky, self-deprecating laugh. "Sometimes it puts tears in my eyes, too, just like it did way back then."

God, his heart just completely shattered. His own eyes grew damp. "You're not expected to be a rock all the time." She started to object, but he continued. "Hell, Ronnie, hearing about it makes me want to cry. I can't even imagine living through it."

She gave a choked snort. "You don't cry."

"Ah, babe. Everyone cries sometimes, even badass chicks with loads of 'tude."

Laughing, she tucked her face into his side. "I don't have attitude."

"You have more attitude than a pack of lions prowling through sheep. But I like it, so it's not a complaint."

Once again, she went quiet. They were twined together, him slouched on the couch, feet up, her draped over and around him. Next to them, Howler snored and the kitten purred. Only the quietest hum came from the TV.

"That was a first for me."

Jack smiled. "Coming while I ate you?"

She tucked closer and gave him a smack. "Don't talk about it."

Her scandalized order brought a rumbling laugh from his chest. "You liked it," he teased.

"Shut it." She dared a quick peek up. "I thought my firsts were behind me, you know? But since meeting you, everything is different."

"Different *better*?"

"Fishing for compliments?"

More like fishing for reassurance that she'd stick around for a while, but hell if he'd admit it. Doing so might just scare her off. "I heard you, saw you, and *felt* you, babe. I don't need any compliments beyond that."

She scrunched her nose as she scrutinized him. "I was going to do the same to you."

Lust had no place in the moment, but still it kicked him in the gut. "The same?"

"You know. A blow job." She lifted one shoulder in a shrug. "I was going to try that on you."

How the hell was he supposed to *not* get hard? Though Jack did his best not to visualize it, his breathing deepened. "Yeah, just so you know, I'm on board with that idea."

Looking up at him, she asked, "Now?"

Ah, hell. His dick jumped up with an enthusiastic *yes*, but his heart and mind, always more reasonable, claimed the timing wasn't right. Ronnie was finally opening up, not just with facts but with honest feelings, and that took precedence over everything else.

Trying for a look of mock sternness, he said, "Right now we're talking."

"No, I'm whining and you're forced to listen." She turned away. "I hate being pathetic."

"You aren't and never could be." Jack hugged her, then put a kiss on the top of her head. It took him a second to find the right words. "You can't know what this means to me."

"This?" She peered up at him again, her eyes bright with the unshed tears she disdained so mercilessly.

It was all he could do not to take that soft, lush mouth. Her skin was so smooth and warm, her hair tangled. And she wanted him. Again.

Priorities, he reminded himself.

He smoothed down her hair, brushing it all to one side the way he'd often seen her do. The silky strands fell into place. "This feels like we're building something, like we're getting closer. I want that with you." He lifted her hand and kissed her palm. "I want that a lot."

Their gazes held while she visibly wrestled with her thoughts. "I don't want anyone, especially you, to see me as weak."

"Ronnie. That's not what this is about." Jack threaded his fingers into her hair again, then gave her head a waggle. "Weak is not a word I'd ever use to describe you. Stubborn, yes. Antagonistic. Independent. Resilient, tenacious, strong." So many emotions crossed her expression, he forgot about his erection and her interest in blow jobs. "No one can doubt your strength, honey. I'm just saying that you don't always have to be strong, not with me."

Breath shuddered into her, came out as whimper, and then the tears spilled down her cheeks. Jack felt his lungs constrict as he gathered her up against his chest, rocking her slightly, crushing her as close as he dared.

Howler lifted his head in question, his doggy eyebrows beetled up in worry. "She's okay, buddy," Jack assured the dog, but damn it, he sounded a little choked up, too.

Ronnie gave a watery laugh and turned to see Howler.

"Oh, baby. I'm sorry." She stretched out an arm to scratch under his chin. "I really am okay. Promise."

Howler's gaze went from her to Jack and back again. He licked her hand before dropping his head, closing his eyes, and letting out a long sigh.

Ronnie smiled a little crookedly. "See," she said, dashing angrily at her wet cheeks. "No good comes from crying."

Already her nose had turned red and the skin under her eyes was blotchy. It was enough to dismantle him. "How often does it haunt you?"

She rolled a shoulder that was too small to carry such a burden. "Often enough to piss me off." She choked on the words, sniffled. "Often enough that I...sometimes grab a one-night stand so I don't have to spend the whole night alone."

"I'm not judging you, not in any way," Jack said. "It's important that you know that. But from now on, you'll come to me." Using the side of his fist, he tipped up her chin. "Okay?"

"Long as you're delivering like you did tonight, sure. Be glad to." She flagged a finger between them. "But that goes both ways. Not that you can't sleep at night, but I don't think you should sleep with anyone else."

Did she really have any doubts about that? She consumed his thoughts. Every part of him wanted her, only her. Jack gave a nod and settled on saying, "As long as you're here, no one else exists."

Her lips twitched. "Aww, aren't you romantic." She barely smothered a yawn before getting comfortable with him again. "I don't know what triggers it." Her voice went soft again, with embarrassment, regret. Maybe resentment. "Some days will pass when... Well, I never forget, you know? But a lot of the time it doesn't plague me. It's not front and center. Then suddenly, it's there, more alive, dark and scary. It… I don't know. It smothers me, taking me back to that day, to how panicked and confused I was when he grabbed me. You can't know, can't imagine what it's like to be angrily shoved into a trunk."

"No, I can't. I'm listening, though, if you want to tell me."

She paused, swallowed. "I tried to scramble back out. You should know, even shocked and scared stupid, I didn't just let him do it."

Jack didn't know what to say to that. As a girl, she wouldn't have stood a chance against a grown man intent on harming her.

"I fought him, but he slammed the trunk. If I hadn't jerked my hand back in time, or my knee, he'd have crushed them." She stilled, trembling. "It didn't matter to him. I didn't matter to him."

Jack rubbed his hands up and down her slim back, over her shoulder. He wished he could get his hands on the bastard who'd done this to her.

And on her fucked-up family, too. They'd abandoned her when she needed them the most and he wouldn't blame her if she never forgave them.

"Sometimes," Ronnie continued in a whisper, "it seems like it happened so long ago it shouldn't even be a memory anymore. Other days, though, it feels like it happened yesterday."

"Have you noticed any triggers?"

"What do you mean?"

He couldn't keep his hands from touching her, coasting over her skin and hair. Assuring himself she was okay. "I would think what just happened, being attacked by a thug with a knife, could bring it front and center. You have a dangerous job."

"Not usually."

Too often for him to rest easy. "Do you think that could have anything to do with it? The danger today maybe ignited your memory of the kidnapping?"

"Maybe." She yawned widely, avoiding further discussion. "We should get some sleep."

The finality in that statement told Jack not to push—except he couldn't resist one little suggestion. "I'm comfortable here. How about you?"

Her gaze jerked up to his. "You want to sleep *here*?"

"We're all settled in. Why not?" Jack saw the suspicion in her eyes, as well as the relief. She probably dreaded going back to the bed, but Ronnie would never admit it. So he gave her an easy out. "No reason to disturb the animals since they're already up."

Her gaze searched his. "Yeah, true. You can sleep here?"

"I'm halfway there already," he lied.

"Mmm." She squirreled around, getting situated, ensuring the blanket was over her toes, then said around another yawn, "Okay, then. If you insist."

Because it'd make it easier for her, he said, "I do."

Within minutes, her deep breathing joined that of Howler's snores.

It was a gift, to help her rest, to know that he'd played a part in making her feel secure enough to go back to sleep. Jack stayed awake for another hour, loving the feel of her in his arms. Loving her.

No reason to deny it. Hell, he'd probably fallen a little in love with her that very first day and every minute after that had just secured the feeling. He kissed her lightly on the crooked part in her pale hair, then closed his eyes.

He needed time. Time to win her over. Time to convince her.

Time to show her exactly how good it could be if they stayed together.

As long as she was with him, he had a chance.

That is, if he could resolve the threat against her first.

THE BROTHERS WERE not what Jack had expected. Willowy thin, with straight inky hair that hung to their shoulders and flat blue eyes set against smooth pale skin. They were near-mirror images of each other, with only the subtlest of differences that helped him to tell them apart.

They both stood around five-seven or five-eight, wearing matching black outfits. Drake had a very slight scar in his right eyebrow, and Drew probably weighed twenty pounds more than his brother, evidenced in a slight pouch at his gut. Their deep, modulated voices were no doubt fake, used for dramatic effect. Overall, they seemed harmless. Sad, actually.

It didn't take him long to realize that they relied on Ronnie. She appeared to be their grounding link to the real world.

They urged her in and treated her like she'd only just been assaulted. Of course, she didn't tolerate that for long.

"Knock it off already." Dropping into a padded easy chair, she huffed her annoyance and swatted away their hands. "You guys know how I feel about personal space."

They immediately took two horrified steps back, as if gravely afraid of her temper.

Jack barely bit back a laugh.

Until she flagged a hand at him. "Why aren't you fussing on Jack? He was there, too, you know."

Owl-eyed, both brothers looked at him.

Dryly, Jack said, "I'm fine." He held out a box containing the thankfully preserved rat and snake that they'd collected earlier. On top was the envelope with the photos. "Where do you want this stuff?"

"Oh." Drew stepped forward, his bottom lip in his teeth. "Is it heavy?"

Jack switched the box to one hand. "No."

"Excellent." He accepted it as if handling something extremely fragile. "I'll just go put this by the basement steps."

"Perhaps some coffee," Drake intoned, "while you're in there." He gestured for Jack to sit. "That detective called."

"Yeah?" Taking the chair nearest Ronnie, Jack asked, "How'd that go?" As he spoke, he looked around. The house could belong to a great-grandmother…if the great-grandmother had never updated anything.

"He asked many questions but there wasn't much I could tell him." Drake's gaze shifted to Ronnie again. She stared back until he cleared his throat and looked away. "We're very sorry for the trouble."

Jack nodded his understanding. Drake did look sorry—and fearful that he might lose their services. He could have told the man that Ronnie wouldn't be quitting anytime soon, but Jack decided to leave that up to her.

"Will the detective visit you?" Ronnie asked.

"No. He said the phone interview sufficed but if they're able to lift any fingerprints or anything, they might need us to come to them."

Jack glanced around the old-fashioned house again,

taking in the ancient architecture, glass doorknobs, and cove ceilings. "All we can do going forward is better prepare with some research. That means I check locations before you agree to send us after something."

"Entirely acceptable," Drake promised. "I, um, might already have something. That is, if Ronnie is comfortable with—"

Ronnie snorted. "What, where, who?"

Drew slunk back in with a tray of coffees, sugar bowl, and a little creamer urn. "I brought cookies," he announced solemnly.

Jack got the impression that the brothers didn't have company very often. If collecting oddities did it for you, he imagined it might be difficult to make friends other than the other weirdos who hung out on the message boards doing the same.

Then he thought of Therman Ritter, Brodie's main employer and his sister-in-law Mary's pseudo family. Therman collected murderabilia, which was actually worse than a two-headed snake, but where things differed was wealth. Therman lived in a mansion, not a two-bedroom bungalow in a lower middle-class neighborhood.

As Jack sipped his coffee, he glanced at Ronnie.

She had half a cookie in her mouth and another on her knee while she dumped sugar into her coffee. For a woman so petite, she had a voracious appetite.

After a big breakfast of bacon, eggs, and potatoes, she'd helped him work around the house. He put away heavy tools in the living room while she'd insisted on finishing the paint job he'd only half completed. That freed him up to do some remaining work in the kitchen.

In between letting Howler out and taking a few breaks, they'd accomplished a lot.

Most helpful, though, was when she took another shower before they left, which allowed him to talk to Brodie again.

Therman did indeed know the brothers and dismissed them as harmless. He claimed they were peculiar but not psychopathic, despite the weird presentation. Jack decided to withhold judgment until he toured their basement.

But first… "You mentioned a job?"

"They're stalling." Ronnie grabbed a third cookie. "That's what they do when they know I won't like it."

A flush bloomed on Drake's pale cheeks. "It's true, you might grumble."

"You know how you love to grumble, Ronnie." Drew turned to Jack, saying with dead-seriousness, "She's very good at it."

"I've noticed."

Ronnie ignored that. "Details?"

"Marge called. She has a bargain for us."

Disgusted, Jack briefly closed his eyes.

But Ronnie asked, "What's she selling now?"

"A necklace." Drew nodded. "That's all."

"Uh-huh." Eyeing them both, she sipped her coffee. "What's the significance?"

The brothers shared a look. It was Drake who cleared his throat. "Do you remember the story in the news about the woman who was used as bait to catch men?"

"Yeah, what about it?"

Jack said, "Whoa. What's this?"

Instantly more animated, Drew picked up the tale. "She would sit on the side of the road, appearing abused and lost, but when men would stop to help her, her boyfriend would attack."

"She wasn't really beat up," Ronnie explained. "Crazy broad was in on it with her nut sweetie. They hurt a few men, killed another, but one guy that they kept locked up for a week finally got away. He led the cops back to where they lived."

Jesus. "What does the necklace have to do with it?"

"It was hers." Drake touched his own throat. "Her name was Ginny Musak and the necklace belonged to her. The man wrestled with her when she came into his cell to feed him. He ended up with the necklace in his fist."

"And this necklace is odd, how?" It sounded more like something Therman would want, since it was linked with a crime.

"It's a little glass vial, and it held some of her boyfriend's blood."

"Jesus." Never, not in a million years would Jack understand the fascination. He looked at Ronnie, but she just quirked her mouth and waited to see what he would say.

Knowing she wanted to take the job, he resigned himself to it. "When?"

"Next Friday, early evening." Drew searched his face, anxiously hoping for agreement. "Will that be a problem?"

"No problem," Ronnie said, but then tacked on, "As long as Jack's okay with it."

He could almost hear the brothers' collective shock. Deferring to him was a huge concession on her part. Just yesterday she'd have told him what she was doing, and he could have gone along or not. It felt like a major milestone.

"Marge isn't holding a grudge?" He seriously didn't want to expose Ronnie—or hell, *himself*—to that again.

"Not at all," Drake assured him. "I hesitated also, but she swore she's interested in making money, nothing else."

Jack turned to Ronnie. "You believe her?"

"She does like her green."

"Fine." Jack finished off his coffee. "Now, how about you take me on a tour? I'd like to see what happens with the...*items* you collect."

Ronnie stood with a grin. "Oh, by all means, let me lead the way." She gestured for the kitchen. "You're in for a treat."

Behind him, the brothers beamed in excitement.

Fucking crazy, that's what they were.

But again, he'd trust Ronnie, and if anything, she seemed fond of them.

So how bad could they be?

CHAPTER FIFTEEN

RONNIE HAD TO ADMIT, it was nice having some time off. In the week since they'd seen the twins, her worry had melted away. Nothing else happened to put her on guard.

But plenty happened to nourish that scary, elusive hope.

Sleeping with Jack every night, having nearly nonstop sex—usually at least twice a day—sharing meals and the shower...the whole relationship thing worked better for her than she'd ever imagined.

The sex aspect alone was enough to win her over. So far, Jack hadn't given her a chance to do all the things to him that she wanted, mostly because he spent so much time doing things to her, and during those times, she couldn't think straight. He'd already shown her a dozen different ways to enjoy herself. And oh, she did.

But her favorite, by far, remained good old missionary, face-to-face with Jack, seeing every nuance of his release, watching his thick lashes lower and the clench of his jaw, feeling the tension coil in his big body until his release came in a vibrating groan. She shivered just thinking about it.

The way he looked at her in those moments made her feel more connected to him, as if she were the only woman in existence. It was a link she hadn't known was missing from her life, and now that she did, she dreaded the day she'd lose it.

While she waited for more work from the brothers, she got to show off her skill to Jack. He set up targets in his backyard, both for shooting and knife throwing. She was a decent shot, though he was better.

When it came to her knife, though, she was every bit as good as him. He might have more power behind a throw, but she more than equaled him in accuracy and speed.

To her surprise, instead of viewing it like a competition, he enjoyed her accomplishments. She'd never received as much praise as he heaped on her. Better still, it always felt genuine. Jack even asked her to show him a few things, and God love the man, it meant the world to her.

She also accompanied Jack on other private deliveries arranged by Charlotte. Some were mundane deliveries of important papers and such. Others, though, were more fascinating, like delivering a replacement wedding cake while the bride and groom waited, because their own cake had been dropped.

She still laughed over the woman who'd paid Jack to deliver a bag of sand to her ex, a symbol of the vacation property she'd won in a divorce after the dude had ditched her for another woman.

She loved working on his house with him. Doing her small part, seeing sections come together, was oddly satisfying. She'd never been great with her hands, or so she'd thought, but Jack gave such simple instruction, he made it seem easy.

Didn't matter if she was sanding a wall, painting trim,

or holding a board so he could cut it. It worked, maybe because she and Jack worked.

As a couple.

Short-term, she reminded herself, unwilling to jump the gun. All good things came to an end. She wouldn't let herself forget that.

Jack had handled her freak-out with compassion, a touch of humor, and a lot of understanding. How long could that last? So far, she hadn't had another occurrence, but she would. She always did.

Likely she'd have them for the rest of her life. She didn't think he'd accept having his sleep disrupted in the long-term.

"You're too quiet," Jack said suddenly, glancing at her. "Something wrong?"

Ronnie smiled. Jack always read her so easily, sometimes knowing her better than she knew herself.

Giving him a partial truth, she asked, "Will you miss them?" She reached into the back seat to stroke Howler's muzzle.

It was their last day with the animals. Brodie and Mary had returned the night before and now they were joining them at the office.

Grinning, Jack parked in his usual spot near the entry doors. "You'll see them often, honey. Brodie rarely leaves Howler behind, you know that. When he does, Charlotte or I are the sitters, which means the dog is still around."

"And since he and Peanut are inseparable—"

"Where Howler goes, Peanut goes."

It wouldn't be the same, though. For a little while, they'd felt like…what? A family? She nearly snorted at her own absurdity. Some family person she'd make. For her to even try would be the joke of the year.

Predictably, Howler went completely bananas at seeing Brodie. He wanted out of the car, now, and made it known with howls and barks and whimpers.

Brodie wasn't much better. He was in the yard waiting, and his face lit up when he saw them drive in.

The two of them had really missed each other.

What would it be like to have anyone, or anything, love her that much?

As soon as he parked, Jack released the dog. Howler leaped out, practically doing flips in berserk excitement. To greet him, Brodie knelt, opened his arms, and ended up flat on his back in the dirt while the dog climbed over him, licked his entire face and neck, barked in glee, and finally stretched out over him, panting.

Brodie grinned ear to ear, hugging Howler and saying, "I missed you, bud."

Crazy, but Ronnie felt tears sting her eyes. That's why she should never have shed the first tear. One tear always led to more and God knew, if weakness found a crack in her armor, it could bring down her whole foundation of defenses. She'd worked too damn hard to rebuild herself to let that happen.

To avoid the emotional overload, she went inside, joining Charlotte and Ros in the breakroom. It was past the lunch hour, but they sat at the round table sharing colas together.

"Hey, honey," Ros said, standing to greet her with a hug.

She did that often, even when Ronnie only stiffened. Sometimes, like now, when Ros was so very nice and welcoming, it made Ronnie miss her own mother even more.

That, too, couldn't happen. She'd given up on a reunion. At some point she'd found her backbone and realized that chasing that particular dream only led to frustration and hurt, that if anyone wanted to see her, they'd have come to her.

And they hadn't.

Over Ros's shoulder, Ronnie saw Charlotte's grin.

"You may as well get used to it," Charlotte said. "Ros is a hugger. The whole family is. They already converted me, then Mary, and now they'll wear you down, too."

"Nothing wrong with a good hug," Ros said, squeezing her a little tighter.

Jack's mother always smelled of flowers, something Ronnie couldn't help noticing. Not perfume but maybe floral shampoo, or lotion. She was soft, in a warm, gentle way—though her hugs were always fierce. They stood close to the same height, but Ros had much more generous curves. The brisk fall wind had lightly tangled her hair, which she wore loose today.

She was extremely pretty, in a very natural way, with Jack's and Brodie's incredible bedroom eyes.

Whenever Ronnie found herself in this position, she didn't know what to say or do. Awkwardly, she returned Ros's hug, but without as much enthusiasm.

Ros finally released her and held her back to say, "I just love your hair and makeup. Whenever I see you, you always look so striking."

Mary, with Howler now trailing her, joined them. "It's like an art, right? I can do my regular old makeup, mostly to hide my freckles and flaws, but if I tried your eyeliner, I'd botch it for sure."

Ros said, "I happen to know Brodie adores your freckles—and so do I."

Laughing, Mary took a seat. "Brodie claims to adore

everything, so he doesn't count. And you're always sweet."

Ros started to protest that, but Charlotte chimed in with, "I love your whole look, Ronnie." She wrinkled her nose. "I never quite got the knack for any of it. Whenever I try makeup, I look like a clown."

"You don't need makeup," Brodie said as he and Jack strolled in. He paused to kiss Charlotte on the top of the head, then dropped into a chair next to Mary.

Charlotte rolled her eyes. "Right. Because you think I'm still a teenager."

"You're pretty enough without it," Jack corrected, and he took the seat next to Ronnie.

Honestly, she didn't think anything of that comment. Charlotte *was* pretty in a wholesome, young and innocent way.

The other women, though, all glared at Jack.

"What?" he asked, the perfect face of innocence.

Ronnie was curious about their reaction, too.

"I wear makeup," Mary said. "Are you saying I'm not pretty without it?"

Jack paused. "What? *No.*" He glanced at Brodie for help, then back to Mary. "I don't think I've ever seen you without your makeup, but I'm sure you look great regardless."

Brodie muttered, "Nice save."

"You said Charlotte was pretty enough without it. You think women only wear makeup because they're unattractive without it?"

Jack blinked. "Honestly, hon, I have no idea why women wear it."

"Sometimes," Ros said, "it's just fun to get all dolled up."

"How would you know?" Brodie asked her. "You don't wear it."

There was a thump under the table, and Brodie yelped, grabbing for his leg.

"I don't either," Charlotte said. "But I want to try Ronnie's look." Mutinous, she turned to Ronnie. "Do you think you could show me?"

Ronnie blanched as all eyes turned to her. "Um…"

The men were strangely still and silent, as if afraid to speak.

Mary eyed them with censure, then linked arms with Charlotte. "Perhaps you could show us both. I'd love to spruce up my look a little."

Brodie looked pained, Jack exasperated.

"Me, too," Ros said, after shooting her sons a killing glare. "We'll make a girls' day of it." She reached out and put a hand on Ronnie's arm. "How fun will that be?"

Fun? Ronnie almost strangled on her surprise.

"Mom," Jack warned.

"Hush it," she replied. "You'll be working on your house. We'll stay out of your way, no worries."

Excited now, Mary grinned. "Tell us what we should buy. We'll all bring makeup. Oh, this is going to be fun."

"It's ridiculous," Brodie groused.

"Agreed." Jack sat back in his chair, his arms crossed.

With the women watching her expectantly, Ronnie's temper started a slow rise. At first she hadn't realized the insult, but now she got it.

Tucking in her chin, she stared at Jack. "So tell me why, exactly, I shouldn't do their makeup?" Not that she particularly wanted to, but did he think she'd somehow defile his family? "You told me you *liked* my look."

Harried, Jack said, "On *you* it's sexy as hell." He gestured at the other women. "But it'd be different for them."

Brodie nodded dumbly.

"If Ronnie is sexy, that makes me *what*?" Mary demanded.

"Already too hot for words," Brodie said easily, his gaze roving over her in a way that showed he meant it.

Jack's brother did that a lot, saying overly sexual things about Mary, eyeing her as if she was the most gorgeous woman in the world. Ronnie would write it off as them being newlyweds, but she had a feeling it had more to do with Brodie being himself than anything else. He clearly loved Mary and had no problem sharing that love with the world.

"Then what about me?" Charlotte asked. "Neither of you would ever describe me as sexy."

The brothers looked horrified by the very idea.

Brodie said, "You're pretty."

"And sweet," Jack added.

"Pretty and sweet," Charlotte sneered, as if those were insults. "I'm also *single*, you know, so I need all the help I can get."

Ros laughed. "They'd both like nothing more than for you to *remain* single."

Mary nodded. "Honestly, though, Charlotte, you know that's a choice. You get plenty of interest, you're just picky."

Brodie choked. "Look who's talking!"

"Nothing wrong with being picky," Jack added.

"True." Mary smiled at her new husband. "Look where it got me."

The homey little spat made Ronnie feel very much like an outsider, which she was. "They're grown women," she pointed out. "Charlotte included. She can make her own decisions about her look."

"Fine." Jack opened his arms in a gesture of magnanimity. "Knock yourselves out."

"Oh, son." Ros shook her head in a pitying way. "No one was asking your permission."

Brodie laughed. "Get used to it."

After slanting a look at Ronnie, Jack cracked a smile. "Believe me, I hope to."

Oh crap, what did *that* mean? He hoped to…get used to her being around? Butting into a family discussion? *What?*

Her lungs refused to function, especially with everyone now smiling at her in such a knowing way.

"So, uh…sure." God, she felt conspicuous. "Long as I'm not working—"

"Great, then it's settled," Mary announced.

The women chatted about what they'd need and when they could get together, and so it was that Ronnie found herself drawn into plans for a girls' adventure…when she had no idea what it even meant.

It wasn't until some minutes later, when Brodie spoke to Jack, that they got off the subject of makeup.

Thankfully.

"You finally met the brothers, right? What did you think? Therman's description of them was…colorful."

"They're kooks," Jack replied simply.

Ronnie shoved him with her shoulder. "They're just eccentric."

"Yeah," Jack agreed, "if by eccentric you mean a display room in the basement with the walls, ceiling, and floors painted dark, with only a few lights arranged to selectively highlight their bizarre goods. I almost tripped over a bookshelf that looked like it was made with the legs of a wolf."

Charlotte covered her mouth with a hand.

"It just *looks* that way!" Ronnie pushed Jack's shoulder for misleading them. "They're molded plastic."

"Worse than that," Jack continued, "is their creepy-ass doll collection."

Ronnie groaned as Ros sat forward. "What's creepy about a doll?"

"They're misprints or something." Jack gestured to his own cheek. "Faces on the side where an ear should be, a nose traded for an eye. Eyelashes stuck to a tongue." He gave a mock shudder.

Yeah, she had to admit, the faces were creepy. Still, Ronnie defended her employers. "Those dolls are some of their most valuable pieces. One's an antique."

"Which explains the security," Jack said. "A deadbolt on the basement door, and bars on the two casement windows."

"They have to protect what's theirs," Ronnie stated. The deadbolt was mostly overkill, since the door itself wasn't that sturdy—and seriously, who would want a screwed-up doll or a wolf shelf? Other than the twins.

Intrigued, Brodie asked, "So their shit is as weird as Therman's?"

"We recently added a two-headed snake and a one-eyed rat to the mix, so you tell me."

Brodie's brows shot up. "Yeah, that's pretty disgusting."

Damn it. Ronnie considered shoving Jack out of his chair. She didn't want his family to think badly of her by association. "They didn't *kill* the poor animals. Some other nut did."

Mary choked, which prompted Ronnie to explain the whole sordid thing—and for payback, she embellished Jack's fire-breathing dragon impersonation that day.

He groaned.

She added, "I think he sprouted new hair on his chest, thanks to the flow of testosterone."

That had Charlotte and Ros outright laughing, and Mary attempting to pull on his collar to "get a peek."

Brodie tugged his wife back to her seat. "Well, I for one am glad the brothers made that purchase. Otherwise you wouldn't have found our little Peanut."

Our Peanut? He said that as if including Ronnie in ownership, but clearly the cat belonged to...well, if not Brodie and Mary, definitely Howler. She leaned around Jack's chair to see the dog lounging right behind Brodie. Even now, the kitten slept under his floppy jowls.

"True enough." Thanks to the job, they'd saved a kitten...and thanks to the brothers' insistence on hiring a courier, she'd met Jack. She'd like to keep them both, but she was realistic enough to know she wasn't set up to care for a pet, and someone like Jack wasn't meant for her, not in the long run.

"They're nowhere near as wealthy as Therman." Jack turned his can of cola, tracing a finger through the condensation there.

Knowing the magic of those fingers, Ronnie found it horribly distracting. She sat surrounded by his family, so it was an awkward feeling in the extreme.

"If you saw where they lived," Jack continued, "you'd wonder where they got the cash for their hobby. I know I did. But Drake told me they've inherited estates from not only their grandmother and their parents, but also their only uncle."

Charlotte's eyes widened. "You don't suppose—?"

"No." In this, at least, Ronnie knew her facts. "Their parents died separately, the father in a car accident, the mother with breast cancer. Their grandmother died peacefully in her bed at the age of eighty-nine, and their uncle had a stroke."

"Apparently," Jack continued, "they first got fascinated when they found some bones at a junkyard. They were cutting through the yard on their walk home from school and noticed a hand sticking out—or rather, the remains of a hand."

Brodie sat forward as if fascinated, but the women all wrinkled their noses in distaste.

"When they told their parents, who were still alive at the time, they called the police and it turned out the body was a guy who'd been missing for several months. He'd belonged to a local gang, and a rival gang had killed him."

"What nobody knew," Ronnie added, "was that the brothers had kept a ring they found on that hand."

"A black onyx ring shaped like a bear tooth." Jack rolled a shoulder. "And their interest in oddities was born."

The phone rang and Charlotte excused herself to answer. When she returned, she said, "One of you has to help Mrs. Gershlick tomorrow. There's a poodle she needs picked up from Chicago. The owner passed away and she's promised to find it a forever home."

"I can do it," Brodie offered, "unless Therman has me set up for anything else?"

"He doesn't," Charlotte confirmed. "But you just got home, so I wasn't sure if you'd want a break between travel."

"Thanks, hon, but it's not a problem. Consider it done."

Jack gave him a nod of gratitude.

It didn't escape Ronnie's notice that Charlotte practically ran the office on her own, answering phones, filing papers, and setting appointments with impressive ease. What Ronnie really liked, though, was the way both Jack and Brodie always showed their appreciation. Anyone could see that Charlotte was part of the family, but they didn't take advantage of that relationship.

Every day she found a new reason to admire Jack.

And speak of the devil... Jack rose from his seat. As he said, "We have to get going," he shared a look with Brodie. "We have a pickup."

Brodie gave a barely perceptible nod.

Ronnie looked between the two men. "What was that?"

"What?" they said together.

No, she wasn't buying the naive expressions. "That little nod and knowing look." She mimicked it in an exaggerated way, making Mary snicker. "What are you two up to?"

Charlotte paused on her way to the file room. "It's their secret code, meaning they'll be working together but they don't want to upset the little ladies with their concerns." She showed what she thought of that with a roll of her eyes.

"Brat," Brodie accused, without sounding too irritated.

"Chauvinist," she shot back, before blowing him a kiss.

Mary and Ronnie weren't amused—until Jack said, "Actually, I didn't want to worry my mother."

Ros's eyes went wide. "Too late for that." She, too, stood, arms crossed, expression stern. "So what's going on?"

Brodie scrubbed a hand over his face.

"Brodie Archer Crews..." Ros warned.

Jack held up both hands.

Ros turned on him. "Jack Wilson Crews."

Ronnie's jaw dropped. *Wilson?*

"I wanted Brodie to be backup," he admitted. "That's all."

It was Ronnie's turn to cross her arms. "Backup for *what*?"

"You." At her dark look, he quickly amended, *"Us."* With a scowl, he explained, "After everything that's happened, I'm not trusting the twins. And after our last experience with Marge, I figured it couldn't hurt to have Brodie close by in case things went south. Again."

All of that seemed plausible, if only he'd told her first. "I've dealt with Marge plenty of times."

"And I take it she didn't want to molest you. But if you'll recall, she felt differently about me."

Mary and Roz listened in, and even Charlotte paused long enough to poke her head into the office.

Damn it. He had a point.

Roz said gently, "I'd really rather not have my son molested."

Ronnie wanted to say that she wouldn't let that happen, except their last visit at the bar had been pretty intense. Short of drawing her knife or gun, she wasn't sure she could have controlled things. And shooting people wasn't really something she wanted to do. Not if she could help it. "All right, fine. Let your brother play protector."

Jack said, "Thank you," in that typical, maddeningly polite tone that made her bristle.

"But from now on, don't plan stuff behind my back."

He nodded. "My apologies."

"Well." Roz beamed a beautiful smile. "I feel better knowing there are levelheaded ladies keeping my sons in line. Makes a mother's heart rest easy."

A WRECK ON the road leading to the bar tied up traffic, making Jack more alert as he continually checked for trouble. It didn't appear that anyone was badly hurt, but the two cars tangled together, fender and bumper locked, required more time than it should have to clear them out of the way. To Jack, it felt like they were sitting ducks.

When he noticed Ronnie's frown, the worry amplified. "You feel it, too, don't you?"

Her mouth flattened and her gray eyes darted around. "Something's off."

Good enough for him. He assessed the traffic, looking for a way out.

Ronnie touched his arm. "Wait. There's the tow truck now." Her gaze sought his. "No one would dare try anything here, right?" She gestured at the cop car ahead, at the string of cars behind them.

"I don't know." He only knew that he didn't like risking her. Not in any way.

She twisted to look out the rear window. "Brodie is back there?"

Jack, too, searched behind them. The traffic was such that it took him a minute to spot his brother's red Mustang. "About ten cars back. Behind a truck." Close enough if they needed him, even if Brodie had to approach on foot—which he would.

Either of them would do whatever it took to ensure Ronnie's safety.

"Can he see us?" she asked, not out of concern, but as part of her strategy.

Jack could almost see her brain working as she considered different scenarios, should the unthinkable happen. "I'll ask."

He dialed his brother as he studied the faces of drivers and passengers stuck in their cars. From the center lane, he had people on both sides. Two families with young children, some women alone, a man alone, a trucker. They all looked frustrated, but not threatening.

Brodie answered with, "I see you. Anything going on?"

"Not that I can easily spot." Jack shook his head, the sense of brewing trouble impossible to dismiss. "Both Ronnie and I have a bad feeling about this. Keep your guard up and your doors locked."

"Done and done," Brodie said. "For now, I'll unleash Howler. I can hook him back to his harness once the jam is cleared."

In Brodie's car, Howler had a custom-made harness that secured him in his seat. He traveled often with Brodie, so it made sense. Whenever anyone else had the dog in their cars, he simply lounged in the small back seat.

Jack understood that if Howler was leashed, he wouldn't be able to get free should something go down. Yet if the dog thought Brodie was threatened in any way, he'd injure himself trying. Better to make it easier on him…just in case.

Ronnie glanced at the time on her phone. "Marge is going to be pissed that we're late."

Marge in a good mood was difficult to deal with. Jack didn't relish seeing her annoyed.

"It's probably nothing, though." She folded her arms around herself. "I mean, just because we've had a string of bad luck with pickups, doesn't mean every job is a trap."

Jack watched the tow truck finally clear the way. "There are a hundred things I admire about you, honey. Your intuition is one of them." He glanced at her face, which to him was beautiful, and that trim little body that made him wild with lust. "Maybe not the top five, but right up there with attitude and chutzpah."

That made her grin. "Good to know. But it appears I got antsy for no reason. The cop is flagging people through."

All well and good, Jack thought, as they finally got underway again…except that the edgy awareness didn't leave him, and he could tell by the way Ronnie held herself, she still sensed it, too.

Something was wrong. He just didn't know what.

They were running a half hour behind when they finally reached the bar.

And arrived to utter chaos.

CHAPTER SIXTEEN

PULLING UP TO the curb opposite from the bar, Jack kept the engine running and looked at the mob overflowing the sidewalk and spilling into the street. "What the hell?"

Ronnie craned her neck, staring at the crowds of people clustered outside the disreputable bar, many of them gawking, others taking photos. Lights flashed from an ambulance and two police cars.

Whatever had happened to warrant the display, Jack wanted Ronnie out of there. *Now.*

He was backing up, finding room to make a U-turn, when Ronnie said, "Wait." She rolled down her window.

"Don't," Jack warned, unwilling to take any chance at all.

But she didn't lower it far, just enough to shout out, "Higgs!"

The burly bartender, who'd been standing alone staring at his feet, glanced up. He scanned the crowd and spotted her. Face creased with worry, he started crossing the street and up to where they waited in the running car.

Jack had to keep reminding himself that the last time they'd visited the bar, Higgs and Ronnie had greeted each other like friends. Plus he knew Brodie was close, watching and waiting.

As Higgs got nearer, he removed his do-rag, twisting it in his meaty hands. Who knew he had hair? It was there, just as thick and brown as his beard but cropped short as if by shears. He wore no coat in the chilly weather, but Jack saw sweat on the front of his shirt and at his brow.

Ronnie lowered the window more as he reached them.

Though he glanced at Jack, it was Ronnie Higgs spoke to. "You can't come in today, girl. Not today. She's gone."

Red rimmed his faded blue eyes, stark against his waxy skin.

"Higgs," Ronnie said softly, recognizing the man's upset. "What's happened?"

"She's gone, that's what."

"Who?"

"Marge." He swallowed heavily. "Throat slit."

The shock of those words hung in the air. Jack stiffened. "You're saying someone murdered her?"

Again Higgs glanced at Jack, then back to Ronnie. "I found her myself. She'd bitched that you were late and wanted me to tell her soon as you arrived. A customer mentioned the wreck on the highway, so I went in to tell her, and there she was. Throat slit."

"Dear God," Ronnie whispered.

Jack breathed more heavily. If it hadn't been for the traffic jam, Ronnie would have been the one to find her.

Or worse, she might have walked in while the murderer was still there.

His spine stiffened. *What if that was the plan all along?*

Ronnie spared him a glance, her expression telling him that she had the same thought.

"Cops are questionin' everyone." Higgs looked back over his shoulder at the bar, his hands knotting more fiercely in the do-rag. "You don't want to get pulled into that. Best you just…" He patted the top of the partially opened window. "Just stay away, okay?"

"Higgs." She reached up and covered his hand with her own. "Will you please let me know what they find out? And if there's anything I can do…?"

"Nothing anyone can do now. She's gone. Throat slit."

Higgs kept saying it, driving it home like verbal punches. Jack wanted to shield Ronnie from this, from the reality of losing…if not a friend, an acquaintance. Someone she'd done business with on more than a few occasions.

Yet as always, she handled the situation with a cool head, all emotions under wraps as she squeezed Higgs's fingers. "You need to talk to a doctor. You've suffered a shock."

The sympathetic understanding seemed to shake him and he gave a guffaw. "Get on, now, before someone asks me who you are."

"Wait." Jack agreed that they needed to go, but he had a few quick questions. "Anyone new at the bar today?"

Higgs looked away. "I'll tell you the same thing I told the cops. Customers come and go, some regular, some not. Long as they behave, doesn't matter enough to me to notice."

Ronnie tucked in her chin. "Bullshit. I know better than that. Nothing gets past you, Higgs, so who was it?"

Eyes narrowing and barrel chest puffing out, Higgs asked, "You calling me a liar?"

Of course Ronnie didn't back down. "I'm saying you're hiding something."

"Well, what kind of bar would we run if I took to gossip? You know the area, girl. People gotta trust that their business is private."

Of all the stupid… Jack asked, "What kind of business do you have left with Marge *dead*?"

Higgs's lips scrunched together.

"We're not the police," Ronnie pointed out. "And Higgs? I've had some personal trouble. What if this is related? I was invited here, due thirty minutes ago." She drew in a deep breath. "What if you next hear that *my* throat—?"

"Don't say it," Jack barked, unable to bear the words. He glared at Higgs. "If you know anything, fucking tell it."

For several intense seconds, he and Higgs stared at each other. In the end, the burly bartender softened toward Ronnie.

"You won't talk to the cops?"

"You have my word," she promised.

Jack wasn't sure that was a good idea. What if Higgs revealed something that indicated Ronnie was at risk? They'd need to talk to police.

"Him, too," Higgs said, nodding at Jack. "You I trust, your guy there, not so much."

"He works for me," Ronnie stated. "He won't say a thing. Isn't that right, Jack?"

Well, hell. Jack was divided, but what could he do other than nod agreement? Not a damn thing.

Higgs's big beefy hand rubbed the back of his neck. "There was a guy who stood out. Clean-cut. Average height and weight. Not fat, not skinny. You know the type."

"Unremarkable," Jack said, an ominous vision of the man from the hotel materializing in his brain. "Except that you remarked him. Why?"

"As the girl said, it's my job to ferret out trouble, and

something about him was too slick, too confident. Like he knew something I didn't. Whenever any of the regulars looked at him, the fucker just smiled back, all serene and shit, you know? That ain't normal. Not in this neighborhood."

No, it wasn't normal. It was exactly as the man at the hotel had behaved, smiling at Jack without a care.

"He was alone?" Ronnie asked.

"Had a hooker with him, but she split an hour before he did."

A hooker? "Did he visit with Marge?" Jack asked.

"No, but he kept looking toward the hall that leads to her office. At one point, he asked about her—or about the owner of the bar. I told him to go fuck himself. He grinned like a little prick, but finally left." Higgs mopped his perspiring face with the rag. "Bastard must've come back, though, because the back door was pried open and Wallace, who guards it, was out cold."

Ronnie frowned. "What do you mean?"

"No bruises or blood, but Wallace was limp as a noodle. One ambulance already left with him."

Drugs? Could someone have spiked a drink? Or maybe injected him—

"I have to go." Higgs looked at Jack through the windows. "Get her out of here and keep her away."

Before Jack could offer assurances, Ronnie growled. "You know I look after myself."

"Then use that good sense I know you have and forget you ever knew Marge." Higgs paused. "Mention any of this to the cops, and I'll deny it."

Ronnie's chin shot up.

"But if you have a name," Higgs continued, his eyes

narrowed beneath bushy brows, "give it to me. I'll take care of the rest."

At that, Ronnie deflated. "I wish I did."

Reluctantly, Higgs nodded. "If I can be of use, let me know. Otherwise, I don't want to see you again." With that, he turned back to the bar.

Once he was gone, Ronnie murmured, "This is a problem."

That had to be the understatement of the year. Jack wheeled the car around, anxious to get out of the area. "You realize it's the same man."

"We don't know that." She fretted with the rings on her fingers. "Yes, they sound similar, but going to the police would not only break my word to Higgs—"

Jack snorted, letting her know what he thought of that.

"—but it would implicate us in…" She gestured behind them at the bar receding in the rearview mirror. "Murder."

Jack sawed his teeth together, fighting to keep his composure. "Could this be the same man who attacked you when you were a kid?"

"What? No. He's in jail. I told you that." She lifted a hand before he could question her more. "I'd have been told if he was free."

"You're positive?"

"Yes." Putting her head back, her face filled with strain, she rasped a humorless laugh. "Apparently, I'm just doomed."

"Don't say that."

"What are the odds, Jack? I mean…why me? I know I can be abrasive, but am I so bad that people want to kill me?"

As she'd spoken, her voice had gotten smaller and it both broke his heart and infuriated him. "Listen to me, Ronnie. You're fucking perfect."

She turned her head to stare at him, her eyes wide. "Is that a joke?"

You're perfect—for me. Knowing she wasn't ready to hear it, he shook his head. "None of this is your fault, so don't ever think that." From one second to the next, he made a decision. "I'll hold my tongue."

Looking oddly dubious, she said, "Thank you?"

"On one condition." They turned a corner, Brodie not far behind them, and still Jack felt like he couldn't put enough distance between them and the bar to outrun the fear. "You go nowhere without me. You don't leave my sight."

Her jaw dropped, then snapped shut with an audible, angry click. "Until *when?*"

"Until we know the lunatic responsible is either behind bars or dead." This time he dominated the conversation, cutting off her automatic protest. "Take off, and I swear I'll follow. If I have to, I'll camp in the hallway outside your apartment. I'll sleep on the hood of your car." He knew his voice had risen and he wrestled it back to a moderate tone.

"That's..." Ronnie blinked fast. "Do you even know what you're saying?"

Hell yes, he knew. "Someone is targeting *you*, Ronnie. Someone is after *you*." And he was willing to kill others to get her. Jack slowed the car, slowed his breathing and the growing fear, and he took her hand. "That's my offer. Take it or leave it."

She didn't pull away, and after remaining silent for far too long, she finally nodded in agreement.

NORTH WAS CAREFUL not to smile as he milled with the crowd, staying to the outskirts but managing to blend in. After turning his coat inside out and pulling on a stocking cap, he felt sure he looked innocuous enough. Why not enjoy himself for a few minutes?

It had been so easy, too easy. When Veronica Ashford hadn't shown up for her appointment, he'd let his frustration get the best of him. It was a shame, because Marge might have proved useful again. After all, without meeting him or knowing his motives, she'd agreed readily enough to calling Veronica, to arranging the meeting.

After hiring thugs to terrorize her at the abandoned house—an incident she'd somehow escaped without injury—he'd gotten impatient. That was the problem with hiring others to do those things he'd enjoy himself. Imagining Veronica's terror wasn't nearly as fulfilling as seeing it in person, watching her face pale, her limbs tremble, her eyes fill with tears.

Knowing he couldn't wait any longer, he'd come up with the perfect lure to get her to the bar, and an even better plan to take her afterward.

If only Veronica had shown up.

If only, if only. Always, with that one, she thwarted his carefully arranged plans.

It was her fault that he'd grown tired of waiting, her fault that he'd changed course and entered the bar from the back instead of waiting on her. Her fault that he cut that bitch's throat.

If he hadn't, he probably could have used her again. She was the type of woman easily swayed by money.

Or rather, she *used* to be.

The giddy smile almost came then and he had to bite his lip to keep it at bay.

No, killing the bar owner hadn't given him the rich satisfaction he craved, the satisfaction he needed. Veronica was the one who'd taken what was his. *She* was the one who had to ultimately pay. But like a delicious appetizer, sliding his knife over Marge's throat had taken away the edge of his hunger.

Maybe it was better this way. He'd continue to let the excitement build—for both of them.

Veronica had been out there, looking around in confusion and fear. It wasn't the obvious yellow Mustang that had clued him in. No, it was that every nerve in his body had tingled the moment she'd arrived with the driver.

Staring would have been rude and might have drawn unnecessary attention to him, so instead he'd flicked a casual glance or two that way as they'd left.

Wise of her to run. Futile…but wise.

Veronica would be extra wary now, on her guard as she waited for something more to happen. It heightened the exhilaration for him.

The idea of toying with her, just a little, held a lot of appeal. Yes, he'd get his property back, but until then, as she waited for her reckoning, fear of him would be her constant torment, a living nightmare.

His blood sang with the pleasure of it.

RONNIE PACED AROUND Jack's home, from the bedroom down the hallway, around the living room and through the kitchen. Four days had passed since Marge's murder and they'd barely left the house. She was about to go stir-crazy, both from boredom and from uncertainty. Drake and Drew, who didn't know all the details but were again horrified at the way trouble seemed to find her lately, had insisted they call a halt to all activity until "issues could be resolved."

What the hell did that even mean?

How could something so indistinct ever be resolved? They didn't know for sure if the murder had anything to do with her, and in fact, Higgs reported that the cops were blaming one of Marge's other "associates."

God knew, Marge made a lot of shady deals with a lot of crooked creeps. Anything was possible.

Not that Jack would be convinced. He believed Ronnie was a target and refused to budge from that assumption.

Ronnie didn't know anyone who might want to hurt her. She sure as hell didn't know why. Hadn't she been through enough?

No! Damn it, she would not feel sorry for herself. If anything, it was Jack who deserved the sympathies. She'd brought him nothing but trouble, and now she knew he was dodging other jobs to stay with her, like an around-the-clock freaking sentry.

True, thanks to the way he'd rearranged his time, he was about done with the renovations on the interior of his house. She'd enjoyed helping out, learning new skills, but still…

He and Brodie had a business to run.

And she couldn't stomach being a charity case.

After another day spent on home improvements, Jack had finished retiling the hall bathroom around nine o'clock. She'd heated up a frozen pizza for their late dinner, and then taken her shower while he put away his tools.

Now, dressed in a loose T-shirt and panties, she tried to outpace her discontent while he took his own shower. At least he afforded her that much trust. Ronnie snorted to herself. At first, he'd been like a shadow, staying so close it equally unnerved her, and made her feel… Well, it made her *feel*. Too much. Of everything. Comfort, security. Warmth and affection. Guilt. Worry.

God-awful worry.

If someone *was* after her, what if Jack got in the way?

Of course he would. He thought of himself as a buffer, her own personal bodyguard. She knew he would willingly, gladly, step between her and danger.

And if he got hurt, it'd be her fault.

Ronnie shook her head hard, unable to bear thinking of it.

The house was cool, leaving a chill on her bare arms and legs. She hugged herself while stopping to lift a curtain, gazing out at the well-lit yard. The moon turned every bare tree into a long shadow that shimmered with the wind. A sprinkling of snow was in the forecast.

Before long, the holidays would be here.

And then what?

She was an independent, self-sufficient person used to spending Thanksgiving and Christmas alone. A card from her mom, a call from Skylar was all she expected. No gifts, no visits, no big elaborate meals. An undefined sort of dread tried to bloom in her chest. Jack and his family would all get together. Where did that leave her?

As an interloper?

Yes. That's exactly what she would be at a family gathering, because she wasn't family. She didn't have family.

His or her own.

They'd laugh and hug, exchange gifts and enjoy each other… God, she couldn't bear it. She dropped the curtain and went up the hall, pausing in the living room when she heard Jack emerge from the shower. Rubbing her arms, she waited for him.

"Ronnie?" he called from the bedroom.

Hearing that particular note in his voice, the one that said he was still afraid for her, she closed her eyes. "I'm here."

He came into view looking better than a man ever should, wearing casual athletic pants and nothing else. He'd left the drawstring waist loose and they drooped on his muscular hips.

With one look at her face, he asked, "What's wrong?"

What a joke. *She* was wrong. This *relationship* was wrong.

Her life was a complete mess.

Unwilling to dump all that drama on him, Ronnie shook her head as she gazed at his chest. She loved the soft, springy hair there, lightly sprinkled from one flat brown nipple to the other. It was thicker in the middle of his chest, disappeared as it went down his torso, then resumed beneath his navel where it arrowed down and into his pants.

The things she felt for him weakened her, but she couldn't seem to resist.

"Ronnie."

He sounded so strained, she met his gaze. No, she wouldn't burden him with her uncertainties and indecisions, but she couldn't help asking, "Aren't you *bored*?"

Bored with me, with the wait-and-see threats, with my crazy bullshit?

At first the question lifted his brows, but as his eyes drifted over her, he smiled. "How could I be bored when you look at me like that?" His chest expanded. "Hard, sure. But not bored."

Of course her attention zeroed back in on his junk, and sure enough, he sported partial wood. A hot thrill cut through her morose worry. She'd never get used to the idea that she, Ronnie Ashford, estranged daughter and victim extraordinaire, could turn on Jack Crews with just a look.

How long can that possibly last?

She didn't want to think about it right now.

"So…" Trailing a finger between her breasts, back and forth, Ronnie watched his gaze track the movement. Before Jack, she'd never have thought to do such a thing, but in so many different ways he'd shown his sensual appreciation for what little she had.

Now, thanks to him, she knew, at least in this, she was enough.

If nothing else came out of this brief episode of her life, she'd always have that.

His smile turned wicked. "So?" he prompted.

For now, by his own design, Jack was stuck with her, but he was far from complaining about it. Might as well take what she wanted. "I was thinking about something."

He folded his arms. "I'm listening."

Yes, he was. Jack always listened to her. Better still, he *heard* her, what she said, and sometimes what she didn't say.

God, she would miss that when things ended. And if they didn't? Could she dare to hope for more? Would the disappointment be worse if she didn't even try? Probably.

Ronnie checked that the curtains on the living room windows were still completely closed. Jack had made a point of buttoning up the house each night, ensuring everything was secured.

Ensuring she was safe.

It had been a very long time since she'd had that much concern directed at her. So long, in fact, she'd forgotten the comfort of knowing she mattered to another person.

That's what she valued most of all.

Strolling up to him, she went on tiptoes, hands braced against his chest, to kiss him. She made the press of her mouth soft but sure, lingering for the space of three heartbeats before switching to feather a kiss over the corner of his mouth, along his jaw, then down to the side of his neck.

He smelled of masculine soap and shampoo, but it didn't conceal his own unique scent, a complex combination of earthy warmth and basic man that made her nipples tighten.

She opened her mouth against him, stroked his hot skin with her tongue, grazed him with her teeth, sucked lightly—doing all the things she wanted to do…in another place.

Taking him by surprise, she wrapped her fingers around his cock through the soft cotton of his pants.

On a hissed breath, Jack's hand covered hers, pressing her more tightly to him.

She bit his throat, a soft, delicious love bite.

Cursing, Jack forced her hand to stroke, slowly up and down. "Let's go to bed."

"I like it right here." She licked the spot where she'd marked him, then nibbled her way over his upper chest, down to lick one nipple.

"Ronnie…" His fingers threaded into her hair and he tugged her back. "You can kiss me all you like, but you're wearing too many clothes."

"You first," she said, slowly going to her knees and

tugging down the pants. His erection jutted out, thick and hard, his balls drawn tight. She smiled. "Want me?"

He stared down at her with that fierce expression she loved so much, showing emotion so intense it could be rage or red-hot lust. Either was sexy, in her opinion, since it far surpassed his usually moderate manners, but right now, she wanted the lust.

When she brought her attention back to his cock, he stilled. Ronnie studied him—all up close and personal—without saying anything, letting the anticipation build, until she wrapped her fingers around the base of him.

Dragging in a breath, he tightened his muscular thighs.

"I was wondering…"

He said nothing.

With her hand clenched around him, she slowly pumped, once, twice. "You and Brodie are alike in a lot of ways."

That made him choke. "Jesus, Ronnie."

"Not that I'm interested in your brother or anything." She looked up to meet his glare. "I'm all about you, in case you can't tell." Hoping he wouldn't take that too seriously, she rushed on. "I'm just wondering if this is something you guys got from your father, like a superior 'big dick' gene or—"

His fingers stabbed into her hair and lightly clenched. "Yes, in this, Brodie and I resemble him. But I do *not* want to talk about my family right now, not when I can feel your breath."

"How would you like to feel more than my breath? Like maybe my…" She leaned in and licked him. Not a timid lick. Timidity wasn't in her nature. She flattened her tongue and dragged it up the underside of his erection, all the way to the crested head where she lapped up and over him. "Tongue."

His body rigid, he growled low. Nice.

He tasted salty, especially at the tip where she found a drop of fluid. His scent here was stronger, muskier, and so potent she felt herself getting wet.

Of course she wanted more. After all, this was Jack.

"Or how about my mouth?" She closed her lips around him, drawing in the sensitive head, sliding him in deeper so that the side of her hand and her lips met before she pulled back.

His gaze burned down on her, nostrils flared, mouth hard. "Yes."

Hmm. His voice was pure gravel and she'd barely gotten started. She liked this. She liked it a lot. "Yes to which?"

"Either. Both." He pressed her head forward.

Smiling, Ronnie accepted the encouragement and took him in again. She'd never done this before. Had never had even the slightest interest in putting a stranger's dick in her mouth.

Eew, no.

But Jack? Jack, she wanted to devour, every single inch of him. And since she took pride in her work…

She concentrated on what she did while enjoying the taste of him, the texture, the heady scent.

"Ronnie," he growled.

Letting him slide free again, she sat back on her heels and checked her handiwork. His cock glistened, darker now, throbbing. "Complaint? Suggestion?"

"Not a fucking one." He petted her hair, his big hand gentle. "But I'm a nanosecond away from coming." He tipped up her face. "You have to stop."

"I don't want to stop. *You* never stopped." No, he kept at her, up to, during, and after her climax, pushing her until she couldn't feel her bones, or even her muscles.

"It's not the same." His thumb brushed her cheek. "This is your first time?"

Well, hell. It had been obvious? She made a face. "Consider me eager to learn."

Jack caught her under the arms and drew her up to her feet. "Don't look like that. You were perfect. Too perfect." With shaking hands, he cupped her face. "But let's save that for another time, okay? Right now, I want you. All of you."

Sounded good to her. "Bedroom it is." She grabbed his hand and practically ran with him down the hall.

In the time that she'd been with him, his house had really come together. No longer did they have to dodge around tools and construction mess. With a little decorating, some art on the walls, it'd be a perfect, cozy home.

Whoa. Ronnie slammed the brakes on those thoughts. She didn't know shitola about decorating a house.

Plus, she already accepted that she wouldn't be around long enough to see it all done anyway. Better that she concentrate on the moment, on Jack and sex and incredible new experiences that she knew would be also become favorite memories.

But as Jack tumbled her into the bed, his mouth on hers, his hands everywhere, she knew she'd already started to hope.

And God, it scared her half to death.

JACK FELT THE change in her, the uncertainty that always brought a slight withdrawal, but he didn't remark on it. Sometimes Ronnie was an open book, easy to read. Other times he had no idea what went through her head, but he knew it'd be complicated, wrapped up in her past and all the hurts she'd been dealt.

After he rolled on a condom and settled between her legs, he looked down at her. The T-shirt was bunched up over her breasts, and he'd already skimmed away her panties.

With each small hand, she held on to his biceps as he braced over her.

Her face was precious to him, especially when she was like this, her hair falling back on the pillow, her exotic gray eyes smoky with need, her lips puffy from kisses.

"I will never tire of looking at you."

Her lips firmed, then gave a sad smile. "Never is a very long time."

With Ronnie, it wouldn't be long enough. He wanted to explain it to her, but fire burned in his veins. God, he needed her.

Opening her with his fingers, he said, "I loved having your mouth on me."

"I…loved it, too." She stared up at him, unblinking as he pressed into her, first just the head, then with another rocking thrust, he slid deep. She was already wet, swollen, and hot, and he didn't think he'd ever get used to it, how completely *right* it felt to be with her like this.

Her eyes went heavy in that special, turned-on way. "I'd never done that before. Never *wanted* to do it before. But with you…" She licked her lips, making his blood boil. "You taste good."

He crushed her close, his face in her neck as he concentrated on waiting for her. Thanks to that sexy mouth, he was already primed and she had some catching up to do.

She ran her hands slowly over his shoulders down to the small of his back and up again. "I like this, too, how it feels when you're on me this way." Opening her mouth against his shoulder, she wrapped her legs around him.

Now that she'd given in to her curiosity, Ronnie liked to try different positions, but this was her favorite.

His, too. Having her wrapped around him, holding him tight, he could almost convince himself that she was his. Forever. But with Ronnie, he knew nothing was guaranteed.

There were times it made him frantic, wondering when she'd bail, when she'd find an excuse to leave him. Hell, sometimes he worried that if he slept too soundly, she'd slip away—run from him and what they were building together.

If she did, how would he find her again?

Still moving in her, his thrusts steady, Jack whispered, "Give me your word."

Her body went alternately soft and tense in that way she had as her climax built. Her slender arms tightened, her thighs gripped around his waist. "Yeah, sure," she crooned, her eyes barely open as she kept pace with his rhythm, the roll of her narrow hips following his, always faster, always deeper.

"Swear you won't leave me."

She missed a beat, the lethargy leaving her eyes, making them brighter. "What—"

Jack hammered into her, stealing her concentration.

She gasped, groaned in pleasure.

Softer now, he demanded, "Promise me, Ronnie. Say you won't leave."

Her pale throat worked as she swallowed, her eyes held his…and she smiled. "Okay."

That did it. He was a goner. Wedging a hand under her sweet little backside, he lifted her up, angling her so he could go deeper as he lost control, release storming through him.

Ronnie trembled, cried out, her heels digging into his ass, her petite body arching beneath his with surprising strength.

God, he loved the way she came, the raw sound of her labored breath, the very real twisting of her features.

How she held on to him.

As her moans dwindled and her body relaxed, Jack kissed her. Her shoulder, her throat. Her small perfect breasts.

That stubborn chin he adored.

Her soft, parted lips.

He felt sluggish and sated, satisfied in a way that, sure, had to do with amazing sex, but also with Ronnie and her promise. Sex with her was more of a connection than anything he'd ever known.

Rolling to his side, Jack brought her against his chest. He wanted to tell her that he was in love, that she meant everything to him. A day with her felt somehow fuller than a year with someone else. He breathed easier with her, burned hotter, felt *more*.

The words were there, but he didn't want her to bolt, and despite her promise she might. She'd been hurt, terrified, abandoned…and because of that, she'd forgotten what love was. How could she trust it—even if she trusted him?

With a very real threat still out there, he didn't want to distract her. She needed to stay vigilant.

Hand limp, she patted his chest. "Want me to do the honors tonight?" she asked around a yawn.

"I've got it." They'd fallen into a routine for after-sex bed prep. He disposed of the condom, brought a washcloth to the bed to refresh her, and straightened the covers. It was a small thing, but he liked taking care of her.

"It's always your chore," she mumbled, half-asleep already. "Not fair."

"It's a pleasure, not a chore, so hush." He took only a minute in the bathroom and then he was back, standing beside the bed and looking down at her body.

So small and delicate with her narrow frame, her slim limbs, but he knew that, in her heart and mind, she was an Amazon.

Facing away from him, she rested on her side with one leg bent, giving him a tantalizing view. She could have been a slender model. A very short model, granted, but still, Ronnie clearly didn't see what he did.

If she did, she'd never have another self-doubt about her appeal.

Jack trailed a finger over the rise of her shoulder, down the deep dip of her waist and back up the delicate curve of her hip, along her shapely thigh and calf to her small arched foot.

"Perv," she muttered sleepily, pulling her foot away. "Come to bed."

Jack inhaled and told himself it would be all right. Somehow he'd figure it out. He finished up quickly, and after getting into the bed, he pulled the blankets over them both and drew her into his arms. Here, with him, he could keep her safe.

He knew the threat was all tied together. The man at the hotel, the attack at the abandoned house, the murder at the bar—it was all about Ronnie. About hurting her.

He wouldn't let that happen. No way in hell.

But she wasn't a woman to hide from life, and sooner or later, regardless of what he or the brothers had to say, she'd get back to work.

Ronnie didn't know it, and she might be pissed when she found out, but tomorrow while she did a makeup party with the women, Jack and Brodie planned to research her family.

If they were tied to the trouble in any way, he'd find out.

And then he'd deal with it.

CHAPTER SEVENTEEN

RONNIE HEARD A faint noise and stirred. It couldn't be morning yet. Not when she remained so boneless.

Mornings had never been a problem for her, but then, waking with Jack hugged up to her changed everything. She smiled even before she got her heavy eyes to open. His arm rested across her waist and his hairy thigh prickled the skin of her hip.

Turning her face, she looked at him. In this room, he'd installed blinds, but the decorative transoms allowed in the gray shadows before dawn.

In his sleep, his brows evened out and his lips slightly parted. Jack didn't have a heavy beard, but a new growth of whiskers added angles to his face. Her appreciative gaze traveled over his throat and collarbone, down to the swell of a pectoral muscle. He shifted, drawing her closer, cuddling her before relaxing again.

Even when asleep, he overwhelmed her. Ronnie started to close her eyes, hoping to keep reality at bay, when her phone buzzed. A text? Must be what woke her.

Hopefully Drake and Drew were ready to put her back to work. Yes, she wanted to be productive. Badly. Plus when she worked, Jack worked, so she'd consider it a win-win.

Carefully shifting to her side, she reached out and lifted her phone from the nightstand. With her thumb, she swiped the screen—and found a photo of her sister heading out the front door of her parents' house.

Shock brought her upright.

Jack's voice, lazy with sleep, stroked her hip. "What's wrong?"

"Nothing." An automatic answer, but her lungs couldn't seem to pull in oxygen. *Something* was wrong.

Of course Jack knew. He always realized her moods, sometimes before she did. The bed shifted and then his big body was behind her, his chest supportive, his heat removing the chill of unease from her skin.

"Your sister?" he asked, looking over her shoulder.

"I don't recognize the number." It was a distant shot of Skylar, so someone could have taken it without her knowing. But who? And why?

Drifting a big hand up and down her arm, Jack suggested, "Your father? Maybe this is his way of finally getting in touch."

A little numb, Ronnie shrugged. "That wouldn't really make sense, would it? Why send me a photo of her leaving the house?"

"Nothing the man has done makes sense to me. Maybe you should send a reply?"

Nodding, Ronnie texted, Who is this?

She and Jack waited while the screen blinked, indicating someone was typing. Then she read, You're not home.

Breath strangled out of her.

"What the fuck?" Jack sat straighter, crowded closer.

She texted, Of course I am.

No, you're not. ☺

Her heart hammered. The smiley face only made it… weirder. As she started to thumb in another response, the next messages came through.

But your sister is.

Jack turned on the lamp and pulled her back against him. "That's it. Call the police."

"And say what?" Ronnie stared at the words, tasting the threat, feeling it pulse through her veins.

Her phone blinked, and new words appeared on the screen.

No police. You'll regret it if you involve them.

Confusion vied with panic, and she texted, Who are you and what do you want?

I want what you took from me.

She shook her head, but replied, What did I take?

It will come to you. But don't take too long.

Asshole. Just tell me!

I'll be in touch again. Have a nice day.

She waited, but when nothing else showed up, she turned to Jack in a rush. "Where's your phone? I want to call Skylar but in case he texts again—"

"Here." Jack grabbed it from his side of the bed and

they exchanged phones. He stared down at her screen with the threatening words, his expression lethal.

"Don't reply to him, Jack. Not until I talk with my sister." She didn't wait for his agreement but quickly put in the number.

On the fourth ring, Skylar answered with, "Do you know what time it is?"

"Yes, but you're up."

"Veronica?" she asked, her voice thick with sleep.

So…maybe she wasn't awake. Maybe that photo was from another day. "Yes, it's me."

"Are you nuts?" Skylar bit out, instantly more alert. "It's barely five thirty. I was in the middle of a good dream. And why are you calling me from a different number?"

Ronnie licked dry lips and tried to think rationally. She glanced at the phone Jack held, scanning the words again. With her fingertip, she scrolled back to the photo and made note of the clothes. "When did you work out?"

"I work out every day, you know that." There was some rustling, as if Skylar sat up in the bed. "Why? What's going on?"

"When did you wear black yoga pants, your pink sneakers, and a pink hoodie?"

"Yesterday," Skylar breathed, and then with furious accusation, "Are you *spying* on me?"

"Not me, no."

That only agitated her sister more. "What does that mean?"

"Someone sent me a pic of you in those clothes. You were walking out the house."

"Who?"

Frustration burned Ronnie's eyes and made her stomach queasy. "I don't know." Messing with her was one thing, but involving her sister—a sister who already disliked her? "You need to be careful, Skylar. Don't be anywhere alone, okay?"

Tension pulsed in the silence, and then Skylar burst. "This is because Mom left Dad, isn't it? You're trying to nose around for details. Well, forget it. It's none of your damned business."

Ronnie almost dropped the phone. "Mom… Dad… *what*?"

"Mom threw him out." Skylar sniffed. "Like you didn't know."

Her brain buzzed. "Threw him out, as in…he left? Why?"

"If Mom wanted you to know, she'd call you. Now I need to get back to sleep—"

"Wait!" Ronnie drew in a calming breath. The neverending drama between her parents could wait. "I'm sorry, but someone took a photo of you leaving the house, then texted it to me. Do you understand? Someone was *watching* you. I don't know who, but I know it's meant as a threat."

At least that got her sister's attention. "A threat against *me*?"

"I don't know. Maybe."

That spiked her sister's ire again. "You and that sick job of yours!" Rife with accusation, Skylar said, "You know Mom hated it from the start, but you kept it anyway. It made her worry about you and that made them argue even more."

"Mom and Dad were still arguing about me?" Ronnie shook her head the second the words left her mouth. It didn't matter. "Neither of them really cared about me,

Skylar." Not about her, so why should they care about her job? "You know that."

Skylar stayed quiet, and the old bitterness sank in. God, how Ronnie hated this, reliving it all, having the lack of love shoved in her face one more time.

Jack put an arm around her, silently supportive.

It helped, being here with him. What if she'd still been all alone? She shook her head again. "I have to go, Skylar. Promise me you'll be careful. Don't go anywhere alone and if anyone bothers you, anyone at all, call the police."

"Sure, but you realize it's probably just Dad." She sounded unsure—and a little afraid. "I imagine he misses me since I stayed with Mom."

"I hope you're right." Ronnie hesitated, wanting to tell her sister how much she cared, but they didn't do that anymore. Maybe they'd never done it. "I'll let you know if I find out anything, and I hope you'll call me if you see anyone suspicious. My number is the same."

"Yeah, all right." Skylar hesitated, then added quietly, "You be careful, too. Just in case it's not Dad." When she disconnected the call, Ronnie dropped Jack's phone to the pillow.

Jack wrapped both arms around her. "It's the man from the hotel. The same one who killed Marge."

"Maybe." Ronnie hesitated for a moment, her thumb hovering over the screen, until she made a decision. "I'm going to call him." Maybe, just maybe it would be her Dad, though she had serious doubts.

Doubts that doubled when the call went unanswered. These days, everyone had voice mail—unless they deliberately didn't want it.

More to herself than Jack, she whispered, "I have Dad's number. Maybe I should try it…"

"Let me call him."

Twisting to face Jack, Ronnie took in his rumpled hair, the beard scruff, the alert dark eyes, now hot with possessive anger. She'd awakened him with this mess, and yet he didn't complain.

How? How could he feel so familiar and safe in such a short time? He deserved so much better than what she'd brought to him.

"I don't think so." Ronnie touched his face, feeling the rasp of his whiskers, the warmth of his skin. "I need to do this."

"Ronnie—"

She put her forehead to his. "Don't say a word, okay? I'm almost positive it's not Dad, that he wouldn't do anything to threaten me, but I still don't want him to know I'm with you." She wouldn't take chances. Not with Jack. "Promise me."

"We should call the police."

Of course he was right. It's the advice she'd give to anyone else. Still, Ronnie shook her head. "He said not to."

"Fuck that. Some anonymous coward doesn't get to call the shots."

Oh, how she agreed. It rubbed her raw to think of the miserable puke sitting back in glee while he played his sick games.

But as usual, how she felt didn't matter. "He's threatening my *sister.*" Yes, she and Skylar were estranged, had been for years now. In Ronnie's heart, that changed nothing. Skylar was still, and would always be, her little sis. "He's watching her, Jack. Maybe watching me." *Maybe watching you.* "I don't know, but until I figure out what he wants, I can't do anything to put her more at risk."

Jack's hand tunneled into her hair, fingers spread. "All right. But I want a promise from you, too."

She eyed him warily. "What?"

He pressed a soft kiss to her lips. "Remember that you aren't alone. Can you do that?"

Damn it, her mouth trembled with an excess of relief. Oddly enough, the brief emotional weakness gave her strength. "Yes, thank you."

His mouth quirked. "Don't thank me, babe. Just don't cut me out."

As if she could. Ronnie stared at the phone a moment, hesitating in a maelstrom of emotions. Would her father give her hell? Would he blame her, yet again, for the separation from her mom?

It seemed likely.

But what choice did she have? None. Realizing it galvanized her, and she put in the call to the man who had raised her...and no longer cared.

NORTH SMILED AS he took apart the phone and disposed of the pieces. He was always thorough, never buying his burner phones in the same location, never using the same one twice, making the calls well away from where he lived. Caution in his work was second nature.

As he pulled into his humble home, he went over plans.

How long could he resist ending Veronica? Not long at all.

Thinking about her built the need to a fever pitch, and the only way he knew to soothe himself was by viewing his collection.

After locking up his house, he descended the steps to the basement, went past the false wall, and flipped on the bright florescent lighting overhead. The mementos waited there, forever captive. Proof that he was the best at what he did, the most elusive, invincible.

Eternal.

"Hello, my pets." Strolling the perimeter of the room, North let his hand trace lightly over each photograph with the wisp of hair neatly stapled to the corner. When he reached the last photo, his mouth flattened. The red haze threatened to cloud his vision.

This keepsake was incomplete, something he couldn't abide, but he'd correct the situation soon.

And then, when he finished toying with Veronica, he'd add yet another photo—and with it, a clipping of silky, platinum hair.

NICHOLAS ASHFORD HADN'T answered the first call a few minutes before six, nor when Ronnie called again at seven. Or, after she'd dressed had breakfast, when she called at eight.

But finally, at nine o'clock, her father answered with a slightly slurred, "Hello?"

Until that moment, Ronnie hadn't considered how to start. She couldn't call him *Dad*—he'd forbidden that long ago. Business associates called him Nicholas, friends called him Nick, but she couldn't bring herself to use either name.

Rather than address him at all, she identified herself. "It's Ronnie."

The heavy pause hurt, until he said with enthusiasm, "Veronica? Honey, s'it really you?"

She frowned at the way his words ran together. "Did I wake you?"

"Yes, but doesn't matter. How are you?" Before she

could answer, he said, "Your mother kicked me out, did ya know that? After everythin', she said she's done with me. Took another goddamned lover."

Ronnie blinked. "Skylar told me."

"And so you called." He sighed heavily. "I've been such a bastard to you. It's jus'… I love her, ya know? Love her so much."

Jack was near her in the kitchen, a tall, strong, symbol of strength and support. He tried a casual stance, his hip against a counter, arms crossed over his chest. But he was oh so attentive.

The contrast between Jack, a strong, kind, responsible, *family* man, and her selfish, weak father sent a scalding flush of embarrassment over her skin. How crazy was that? Jack already had a low opinion of the man, but now, for him to be a witness to this… In some way, Ronnie felt like it reflected on her…but Jack wouldn't.

No, Jack would never look down on her for anything her father did. He liked her. He respected her.

Knowing that helped to ease her mortification.

"Veronica?" her father said, in a whine.

For lack of anything else to say, Ronnie asked, "Are you all right?"

"No. I'm not. And she doesn't care. Skylar doesn't either. She's spoiled. That girl goes with the money. But you, Veronica, you're strong."

Praise? The laugh choked out of her, causing Jack to push off the counter and take a step toward her. She got her lips to form a smile, shaking her head to let him know she was fine. Confused but fine. This little phone reunion wasn't going at all as she'd expected.

"Look…" Damn it, what did she call him? "Nick, did you text me a photo of Skylar?"

The silence dragged out so long, Ronnie thought he'd hung up on her or maybe passed out. Hard to imagine since she'd never, not once, seen the man drunk. Slightly tipsy a time or two, but even then, only on a holiday. The drunken slur was as uncommon as the forlorn and pathetic attitude.

In overblown misery, he stated, "That's what yer callin' me now. Nick."

She plunked the phone onto the table and hit the speaker button so she could pace. "What should I call you? Huh?" She flung out her arms, shocked at her own tumultuous response. "You made it clear you're *not* my father."

"Ah, God, honey. I'm so sorry."

"Don't," she warned, anger chasing away the disorienting surprise. How dare he do this to her, now of all times? "We're past that. I just need to know, *did you text me a pic?*"

"No. Other than checkin' on you a few times, I haven't contacted you. You know that." He added, "I've been such an ass."

Ronnie went still, her hand covering her mouth. No, she couldn't have heard him right. "What do you mean? When have you ever checked on me?"

"I thought without you there, *his* child, she wouldn't keep thinking of him, ya know? But it didn't stop her. She's screwin' someone else now..."

"Mom?" Ronnie shook her head. "I can't sort out your marital problems for you, and I didn't call to be your confidant." Even as she said it, she felt...bad. For him and for herself.

"It didn't matter if you were there or gone."

Because *she* hadn't mattered. Damn it, Ronnie

straightened her shoulders, refusing to do this again. "When did you check up on me?"

"I've always known where you were. I wanted to see you, honey, but I didn't know where to start, what to say. And now it doesn't matter." Indulging his self-pity, he sniffled. "You hate me, too, don't you?"

Closing her eyes, Ronnie rubbed at the ache in her forehead. God save her from drunken idiocy. As she dropped her hand she felt Jack's nearness. She looked up, and there he stood, backup if she needed it, in her corner whether she requested it of him or not.

A month ago, even a week ago, she'd have refused to lean on him. But now…? Trying to process everything her father had just said, she dropped her forehead to his shoulder. Jack's hand opened on her back, gently pressing, warm and vital.

It helped more than she could explain.

"I'm here," Jack whispered, as if she needed the reminder.

Ronnie inhaled a fresh breath.

So many times she'd known she was being watched, and now, in a moment of drunken weakness, her father explained it was him. She wasn't sure how to feel about that beyond annoyance.

"Veronica?"

She stepped back to the phone. "Next time you come around," she stated, making her tone firm, strong, "say something." At least that way, when she felt his presence, it wouldn't alarm her. "Can you do that?"

"I'd like to see you. Maybe we could—"

"I have to go." No way was she ready to make up with him, not right now. He'd thrown too much on her at a time when she didn't feel particularly receptive. "Just... be careful, okay?"

"Veronica—"

She ended the call before he could say anything that might sway her. She needed time. She deserved that much.

Jack stayed close, waiting, she knew, to see how she'd react.

She raised her brows and tried to laugh it off. "So. Not Dad."

"No." His hands settled on her shoulders and he looked into her eyes. "Are you okay?"

"Surprised for sure." She twisted her mouth. "I wasn't expecting any of that."

His fingers gently massaged, easing the tension in her muscles. "Good surprise or bad surprise?"

"Both?" She huffed a breath. "God, leave it to him to hit me with another shocker." Some dormant sense of loyalty had her explaining, "He doesn't usually drink that much. At least, he never did when I lived at home."

"Sounds like he took right to it."

The grin came despite her pangs of resentment. "I guess." Groaning out her frustration, Ronnie asked, "Why unload to *me*? And for him and Mom to be split up... I'm so out of the loop with them, I just figured everything was... I don't know. Fine?" Better than fine, actually.

She frowned at her own misconceptions.

"You thought without you, they managed to become a happy little family unit? Come on, Ronnie." Jack stroked his fingers through her hair, something he did quite often. "Happy people don't act like assholes."

She snorted a laugh, always amused when he lost his manners. "No?"

"Definitely not. And they don't abandon family."

"I'm not family," she pointed out.

"Bullshit. Your mother is still your mother, your sister is still your sister, and the man who raised you should *still* be your father, blood ties or not. Family is what you make of it, and if you don't mind me saying so, they only made a mess." He tipped up her face. "That doesn't sound very happy to me."

"No, I guess it doesn't." Happy people were more like his family, sometimes at odds but still there for each other. "It's all so…dysfunctional. I just never realized."

When they heard the car pulling down his drive, Jack gave her a crooked grin. "Speaking of dysfunctional, are you ready for this makeup party?"

"As ready as I'll ever be." Which was not ready at all. "I don't know much about this stuff." She gestured. "Women and friendship and doing the…the girl thing."

"Just be yourself. That's all you need to do."

So easy for him to say. Before the others walked in, Ronnie needed him to know something else. "I'm taking this seriously. The threats I mean. Knowing it wasn't my dad makes it more disturbing. I want to give this guy a day or two, see if he contacts me again. If not, maybe there's nothing to worry about."

"Ronnie," he said.

"I know, I know. It seems like it's all tied together, but we can't be sure." In so many ways it felt like her safe little boxed-off world was unraveling around her.

On the plus side, there was Jack. He'd come into her life and turned it upside down in all the most remarkable ways.

But on the negative, she appeared to be in the cross-hairs of a nut. A person she couldn't identify. A person who would hurt those around her.

"It could just be coincidence, all of it."

"You don't believe that any more than I do."

No, she didn't. Ronnie blew out a breath. "I can't risk going to the regular cops. But the officer who helped me when I was kidnapped? For a year after, he checked up on me. If he hasn't changed numbers, I could... I could maybe reach out to him? That is, if the creep bothers me—"

"Us."

"—again." Ronnie blew out a breath. Good or bad, Jack was so insistent on being a part of it with her.

As the doorbell rang, he said, "We're in this together. I need you to remember that."

Amazingly, he made her feel better about everything. The threats didn't seem as real, and the news of her family no longer felt as emotionally disruptive. Oh, those things were still there; she had to figure out how to proceed, she would continue to worry for Skylar, and her heart would remain divided over family issues.

But for right now, she could enjoy Jack and the lovable chaos of *his* family. A real family...the kind she wished so badly that she had. As far as distractions went, she couldn't ask for more.

On the way to the door, she asked, "What are you and Brodie going to do?"

"Watch?"

"Ha!" The look in his dark eyes told her he was teasing, but still she said, "Absolutely not."

"We'll entertain ourselves," he promised, before growing serious again. "Try to enjoy my family, if you can."

Enjoying them wasn't the problem. Ros, Mary, and Charlotte were so warm and friendly, her only problem would be growing to care for them too much.

Jack put his arm around her waist. "Whoever texted you, there's not much more you can do right now, so for today, just let me do the worrying."

Something in his tone gave her pause, but then he opened the door and Howler bounded in, overjoyed to be visiting. Kneeling to greet him, Ronnie accepted that no one could be downcast while receiving enthusiastic doggy kisses.

Mary came in carrying Peanut, followed by Ros carrying food, and Charlotte carrying a bag of makeup. Brodie followed the women, and the way he and Jack shared a quick look, Ronnie knew they were up to something.

She just didn't know what, and at the moment, she didn't even care.

In Jack's third bedroom, which he'd set up as a small in-home office, he and Brodie scrolled the internet, starting with social media. Ronnie didn't use Facebook, but the rest of her family did.

Did she know she was still included in their photos? That both her mother and sister showed her in Facebook albums and in dated Instagram pics? Occasionally, one or the other of them had reshared an older image. Skylar had done so just last week, with a photo of the whole family together.

"Fuckers," Brodie muttered low.

"I don't disagree," Jack said. If they cared about her, how could they be so callous?

"She's a sweetheart," Brodie said.

"A complicated, thorny sweetheart?"

Grinning, Brodie shrugged. "You'd know better than me." He searched for Drake Dolby and found several, but only one included a brother. "Drake and Drew Dolby. Jesus, they even share Facebook."

Luckily, given their pride in collecting, their profile was public. Jack scrolled the wall quickly, finding a lot of nonsensical posts…and finally an image that interested him.

Ronnie. His heart gave a lurch, but then, he always reacted to her. The sight of her, the sound of her voice, her touch.

Even the thought of her.

He clicked the photo, making it larger.

Ronnie stood in the doorway, sunshine pouring in around her, her eyes up as if in exasperation, holding one of the hideous dolls Jack had seen in their basement showroom. It was an endearing photo, showing her forbearance for the brothers' hobby—especially since her mouth tipped in a slight smile.

The brothers posted many of their acquisitions, and more often than he'd expected, they featured Ronnie clowning around.

In one, she held out a crude painting of some sort between finger and thumb, her nose scrunched in distaste. In another, she struck a pose with Drew, the two of them wearing mock expressions of horror. Between them was a mannequin with an abandoned hornet's nest where a head should be.

Yet another showed her sitting on the couch in the living room Jack recognized from their house. She had her feet up on the coffee table, toasting the cameraman with a can of cola.

"Looks like they're documenting their time with Ronnie, too." Brodie scrolled, but paused on one from several months ago. Smiling, he said, "She's cute."

Normally Jack would disagree, because to him she was scorching hot. But in this pic, she looked adorable. She held a lock of darker hair over her head, her eyes crossed and her lips pursed.

Jack couldn't quite smile. "I didn't realize."

"That she'd made them her family?" Brodie shrugged. "Can't say I blame her. They're odd, but they seem more tenderhearted than her flesh and blood."

Jack studied her face in yet another photo. She looked tired but triumphant, and no wonder, given that the text claimed she'd driven two days straight to get a preserved ostrich egg.

"He said she took something from him." Jack glanced over the various objects again. "One of these things could be it."

"Someone who got outbid? A seller with regrets?" Brodie frowned. "Or just a nut?"

"Take your pick." Ronnie could pretend otherwise, but they both knew everything was tied together—and that it started and ended with her. "If we could figure out what he wants, maybe we could track it back to him." And then Jack would put an end to the bastard.

"I think we need to visit Drake and Drew. They could know the names of other collectors who lost out, especially any who were bitter about it."

Jack agreed.

They were busy making notes of the weirder pieces to ask about when Mary breezed in. She struck a pose in the doorway and batted her eyes.

Wow. Jack wasn't sure how Ronnie had done it, but Mary looked even more amazing than usual.

He elbowed his brother to get his attention.

Brodie glanced up, then did a double take, which wasn't an uncommon result to seeing his voluptuous wife. This time, though, Brodie couldn't even manage to blink.

Jack watched as he very slowly stood from his chair.

Smiling, Mary said, "I take it you like the look?"

Skirting around the desk, Brodie headed for her, his intent clear.

Laughing, Jack reminded him, "Not the time, Brodie."

Brodie pulled up short and growled a low curse.

Cocking a brow, Mary said, "Okay, I get it. It looks better, but don't act like I was a hag before."

"You're always beautiful," Jack promised.

Nodding, Brodie agreed. "Always." He studied her face. "You do look different now, though." Then he rushed to add, his tone low, "But you know my favorite is when you're fresh from the shower, still naked—"

Mary smashed a hand over his mouth. "Ronnie said that instead of trying to hide flaws—"

"You don't have any flaws," Brodie said around her fingers.

"—I should play up my assets." She batted her eyelashes again. "I'm actually wearing *less* makeup, but it does look terrific."

Wrapping a hand around her waist, Brodie drew her close for a kiss. "I'll show you tonight just how gorgeous you are, with or without makeup."

Mary laughed and ducked away. "Return to whatever you're doing. I'm heading back to the kitchen so I don't miss anything."

On her way out, Brodie stroked her behind, making her laugh and skip a step to get out of reach.

"Letch," Jack accused.

"She loves it." Brodie reseated himself. "So when can we visit them?"

"The brothers?" Jack sat back, considering. "I'll give them a call."

On the first ring, Drew's disembodied voice asked, "Is everything okay with Ronnie?"

"Everyone is fine," Jack promised. It struck him again how much the brothers cared for her. "I'm just trying to pin down who's bothering her and you might be able to help me. Do you document your collection with dates and sellers?"

"Dates, always. Sellers, when we can. It's how we secure authenticity."

"Although that's not always possible," Drake added, explaining, "And sometimes not even necessary when something is too fun to pass up."

"Great." *Fun* was not a word Jack would ever associate with their hobby, but he understood Drake's meaning. "Would you mind if we visited to go over everything?"

"We would do anything to help."

A thought occurred to Jack, prompting him to ask, "Why did you decide she needed a driver? Before you hired me, she took care of things on her own, right?"

"Yes, but after that incident…" Drew cleared his throat, and the ethereal tone leeched from his voice. "We couldn't bear the idea of her being alone."

"She's very important to us," Drake stated.

"Incident?" Jack stiffened. His gaze clashed with Brodie's, seeing his brother on alert. Bracing himself, for what he didn't know, Jack put the phone on speaker so Brodie could listen in, and then calmly asked, "What incident?"

CHAPTER EIGHTEEN

"IT MIGHT HAVE been nothing," Drew hedged, and for once he sounded only like a man. An uncertain man. "That's what Ronnie claims. That we're overreacting. It's just that she's been so good to us, so understanding of our...quirks."

Drake said, "We didn't want to take any chances."

"I understand." Ronnie cut out most people, but for the eccentric brothers, she'd opened up, accepting them—because they'd accepted her.

"And still all this has happened," Drew moaned with a return of a dark croon. "Drake and I discussed letting her go—"

"Not a great idea." Jack knew part of what sustained Ronnie was her work, staying busy, taking pride in a job accomplished. It would devastate her to be fired.

"We came to the same conclusion."

"Good." Relieved on that much, anyway, Jack asked, "Can you tell me what happened? What first alarmed you?"

"She was in Cincinnati for a purchase. We don't know if it's related, but there'd been a string of grisly murders in the area. Three I think. No one was ever arrested, but around the same time, we were contacted about a lock of hair."

"A lock of hair?" Holding the phone to his ear with one

hand, Jack grabbed the mouse in the other and scrolled up the screen until he found the silly photo of Ronnie.

He and Brodie shared a look. "Dark hair? You posted it on your Facebook?"

"Yes, that's it. You probably can't tell from the photo, but it's too coarse to be a child's hair, and it's clumped together with a drop of thick glue at one end, so clearly someone meant to keep it."

"Did it belong to someone famous?" Brodie asked.

"We don't know," Drew said. "But it's creepy, don't you think?"

"An oddity to be sure," Drake noted.

Jack did his best to hide his impatience. "What happened to Ronnie?"

"The seller had advertised the piece and apparently we weren't the only ones interested. As Ronnie drove from the neighborhood, another car tried to run her off the road."

Jack sat back in the chair, in his mind, seeing it unfold and wishing he could have been there with her.

"She's an excellent driver, slick when necessary, but her hatchback isn't meant for maneuvers."

"A more aggressive car," Drake predicted with ominous overtones, "would have overtaken her."

"And God only knows what would have happened to her," Drew said.

Ronnie was a slick driver? She'd never said anything to him, although of course she'd touted her overall capability plenty of times.

"How did it end?" Jack asked.

"She managed to avoid a collision, and she said once she made the highway, she lost the other driver."

"Of course, for us," Drew said, "it was a wake-up call."

Drake cleared his throat. "We felt she needed a man with her, someone big enough to be intimidating—although we didn't tell her that part."

If the brothers were within arm's reach, Jack would hug them both. "She'd have had you for breakfast."

"Yes, well." Drew swallowed. "We chose you because you're rather large, and your brother is highly praised by Therman Ritter."

"You did the right thing." And now that Jack knew her, he never wanted to let her go.

Drew asked, "When did you want to go through our records?"

"Just a second." After covering the phone, he said to Brodie, "I'm not sure we need to look beyond the details surrounding that lock of hair, and Drew could just send that to me in an email."

"True," Brodie said. "But I get the feeling Ronnie isn't used to being cooped up so much. She could use a day away, especially if it helps her feel proactive in dealing with this shit."

Jack rubbed the back of his neck, undecided.

"I'll follow again," Brodie promised. "We won't let anything happen to her."

"I'm not sure she'd wait behind anyway." Truthfully, Jack was equal parts worried about someone getting to her, and her leaving him out of some misguided idea of protecting him.

Jack had just finished setting up a meeting with the twins when his mother sashayed in like a beauty queen.

Jack disconnected with Drew and turned to grin at

her. "Well, look at you." Ronnie clearly had a knack for this sort of thing.

With her hair in the usual ponytail, and dressed in a loose, long-sleeved T-shirt and jeans, fancy makeup would have looked out of place. Ronnie must have realized that, too, because his mom just looked like herself, only more so.

Brodie closed out the screen and stood. "If Dad could see you now," he teased, "he'd be crying at your feet."

"Oh shush," she replied, laughing.

Jack scowled at his brother. "No matter how she looks, Dad would still be a cheating, thoughtless dick."

"That, too," Brodie said easily, arching a brow at him.

Belatedly realizing how he'd blundered, Jack added, "You look great, Mom."

Brodie gave him a shove. "She always looks great."

"I look greater," she stressed, "but thank you both." She folded her arms in a pose that Jack knew he and Brodie had probably learned from her. "Now, about your dad—"

Jack scrubbed a hand over his face, then glared at Brodie. "I'm sorry *he* brought him up."

"But you know it's true," Brodie insisted. "Every time Dad is around, he starts slathering after her."

"Doesn't make it a good idea," Jack stated.

"I didn't say it was."

"Ahem." Ros gave them both *the look*, and it rendered each of them instantly mute. "Just so we're clear here, your father will look at me like that until we're old and gray, and probably then, too. It has absolutely nothing to do with actual appreciation. It's more like a habit for him."

Brodie protested. "We can all agree he's a jerk, most

especially to you, but Mom, you have to know how pretty you are. Everyone says so."

She preened. "Thank you."

"You're too good for him all the way around," Jack stated.

"I certainly thought so, or I wouldn't have divorced him." She winked at Jack. "I don't want you boys to ever think I'm swayed by your dad one way or the other. His compliments aren't real compliments at all, and his disregard has nothing to do with me. Actually, it has nothing to do with any of us. Those are *his* shortcomings, and he's the one who will have to suffer them, probably alone."

Jack frowned as the reality of that landed like a brick on his head. For the first time that he could ever remember, he almost felt sorry for his father. The man would be all alone, when he could have had an absolutely amazing wife. One day he'd realize it, and then he'd be alone—and miserable.

Standing, Jack pulled her into a hug. "Just so you know, Mom, even when you think you're a mess, you're still pretty damn awesome."

She laughed and squeezed him tight—until Brodie stole her away for his own hug. "I kind of like it whenever I see the regret in Dad's eyes. He has no one but himself to blame for messing it up, but that doesn't mean he's blind or stupid. He knows what he lost."

"Sadly," Ros said, "it never taught him a lesson." She stepped back. "Maybe neither of you will believe this, but I'd like to see him find someone special, a woman who'd inspire him to change his ways and settle down. You should both wish that for him, too."

Jack and Brodie shared another look. Yeah, fat chance.

Suddenly Charlotte cleared her throat. Loudly.

Jack looked up and there she was, posed against the door, Ronnie right behind her.

Not only did she wear makeup, but her hair was different, too, loose and… Jack eyed it. Fluffier? Sort of… Fuck.

It was sexy.

On *Charlotte*.

The job Ronnie did on his mother and sister-in-law was subtle and subdued, but for Charlotte, it was somehow more. Not garish, but instead of Charlotte looking like an innocent teenager—which was how Jack preferred to think of her—she appeared very much a woman.

Brodie muttered, "Holy fuck," and received a whack on the shoulder from their mother.

"Well?" Charlotte prompted. She tipped up her chin.

Jack wasn't sure if that was an affectation she copied from Ronnie, or if she did it so they could better examine her eyes—which now looked even bigger, softer and more inviting.

"Isn't she beautiful?" Mary prompted.

Ronnie narrowed her eyes.

Jack found his voice before Brodie. "You are, Charlotte. You look…more than beautiful."

"I'll have to make a trip around town to issue warnings," Brodie growled. When his wife snickered, he snapped, "It's not funny."

"Puh-lease," Ros countered. "It's hilarious."

"You can't keep thinking she's a kid," Mary said, her tone soft as if she sympathized. "Men *are* going to notice her."

God, Jack didn't even want to think about it. Charlotte had been a part of their family for so long, she might as well have been a sister. He couldn't love her more if they did share blood. But she was so tenderhearted, in some ways—in most ways—so innocent. "It'll take some getting used to."

"So." Charlotte gave them both a glare. "What was I before? Butt ugly?"

Ronnie said, "You were sweet and young. That's all." She glanced at Jack. "Though you're only two years younger than me."

Two years—and a world of attitude. Jack tried to joke, saying, "I'll be more restrained than Brodie—"

"Aren't you always?" Charlotte asked.

"—but a few warnings wouldn't hurt." Jack reached out to snag Ronnie and pull her into his side. She looked uncertain, and therefore combative. She was stiff against him, but he pretended not to notice when he kissed her temple. "You have a knack."

Her gaze turned up to him. "Yeah? What's that?"

"Taking beautiful women and making them more so."

To that, the women pretended to lift a glass and said, "Hear, hear," with enough enthusiasm to make her blush.

Brodie still just stared at Charlotte in bemused shock.

CRAZY HOW EXCITED Ronnie was about doing something, anything, other than waiting for another sign of trouble. It was a cold morning, a dusting of fresh snow leaving the world sparkling. Her breath had frosted as they'd stepped outside, and she wondered if she needed a new, thicker coat.

Once in Jack's car, he turned up the heat and within minutes it was cozy. And familiar.

Ronnie loved doing this, going places with Jack, riding shotgun as he drove. Talking, listening. *Sharing.*

She liked returning home with him, too, but that wouldn't last much longer. If the twins had the information they needed, she might be able to put an end to the drama. Then she'd move back to her own place, maybe get back to her old life. What would happen with her and Jack, she didn't know. And honestly, she didn't want to think about it. Not now.

They'd just about reached their destination when she found her curiosity from the day before too much to contain. "So."

Jack didn't exactly smile, but a line bracketed his mouth, telling her he was on the verge. "So?"

"Yesterday—"

He immediately reached for her hand. "You did an amazing job. Charlotte was…transformed. It was a shocker." Jack shook his head. "A nice shock, but still, it's just a tricky thing, knowing what to say. If I went on too much about how good they looked, I'd get accused of thinking they weren't pretty enough to begin with."

"True story." Ronnie couldn't help but grin at his plight. She'd witnessed that dual reaction herself and didn't entirely understand it either. Visiting with the women, though, had prompted a weird sort of kinship, and she found herself saying, "Consider how they felt. Women don't want to wear makeup all the time, but it's nice to know it's appreciated when they spruce up."

"Some women," he countered, "don't want to wear makeup at all. Mom rarely has, and until yesterday, Charlotte hadn't."

"But you approve of the look?"

"That's a trick question, right? Because regardless of whether I say I do or I don't, you'll tell me my approval isn't required."

The thought hadn't even crossed her mind, but it sounded like something Ros or Mary would say, so she shrugged. "I'm just curious what you thought."

He lifted her hand to his mouth and kissed her knuckles. "I think you took someone who I wrongly considered a girl, and made it impossible to deny that she's a woman."

Ronnie gave that some thought, decided it was a compliment, and grinned. "Actually, that's not even what I wanted to talk about."

"No?"

She shook her head. "I overheard what your mom was saying about your dad."

"Oh." Scowling a little, Jack released her hand as he slowed and turned a corner.

"The things your mom said… Do you feel sorry for your dad?"

Very carefully, Jack asked, "Should I?"

She twisted in the seat, leaning closer to him. "Probably. I mean, look at what he's missing! You guys are so great as a family. It's nice. *Really* nice."

"Agreed."

"He could have been a part of that, but because he can't get his act together, he's more of an outsider. It's sad, don't you think? For him, I mean. Whatever he has, it can't be as good as all of you."

Jack pulled up to the house where they would again visit with the twins. He stayed quiet as he turned off the car and took off his seat belt. After a very brief pause where he stared through the windshield at nothing particular, he unhooked hers, too.

Cupping a hand to her face, Jack said, "I'm glad you like being with us."

Oh no. Did he think she was laying heavy hints? That she wanted an invitation to stick around? She, more than anyone else, knew the impossibility of that dream.

So she tried to joke it off. "What's not to like, right?" It wasn't her business, and she was uniquely *unqualified* to give advice on family, but she couldn't resist saying, "I think you should forgive him."

With a level look, Jack asked, "Do you?"

Now that she'd brought it up, Ronnie rushed ahead, determined to have it said. "I think when he does come around, if you remember everything he's lost, everything he's stupidly given up, it'll be easier to feel... I don't know. Pity? Compassion? Something combined?"

He leaned in and kissed her. "I love my dad, Ronnie, faults and all. If I didn't, he couldn't piss me off so much. I'd just forget about him."

Yeah, that made sense. "Well...good." She hated the idea that his dad could hurt him.

Jack stroked back her hair. "Do you still love yours?"

The question hit like a snowball to the face. She reared back. "We're not talking about *me*. Besides, I don't even know who my dad is."

"You don't, huh? Well, I do. He's the man who raised you. The man who put his wife ahead of everything else, including his pride. A sad, lonely, drunken fool who, like my father, screwed up the best thing he ever had."

Ronnie's eyes flared and her heart jumped against her ribs. She wanted to act indignant, maybe laugh it off, but the words caught behind a well of emotion.

Jack moved closer, his gaze warm on her face, his smile tender. "In case you don't get it, babe, I mean you."

Ronnie swallowed. Yeah, she'd figured that out on her own. It had the power to level her, that much faith.

"Nowhere else," Jack continued, "is he going to find a stronger, more principled or caring daughter, and now, when it might be too late, he finally knows it."

"I…" That sounded like a squeak, making her scowl. She cleared her throat and managed to summon up some attitude. "It's not at all the same thing."

"The same thing as my dad? No, it's not. But maybe the advice should be the same. Forgive, move on, stop letting it hurt you." He lifted one shoulder. "I'll try if you will."

If Jack hadn't witnessed her on the phone with her dad, she could claim she'd already done that. But he didn't miss much, so Ronnie knew he'd seen everything she felt—years of betrayal and upset. Denial wouldn't work, so instead she said, "Let's deal with one thing at a time." Opening her door, she stepped out to the sunny morning. A bright sun had already done its work against the frosting of snow, turning the walkways damp instead of icy.

Jack caught up to her, his tall body casting a long shadow ahead of them. He adjusted his long-legged stride to match hers so that they reached the front door together.

Suddenly he paused, and Ronnie felt him sharpen with awareness. "The door is open."

"Not open, just ajar. They do that." She started to step around him, but he held her back.

Fury gathered in his expression. "What do you mean, they do that?"

Okay, so she got it. A lot had happened, enough that she shouldn't take anything for granted.

How the hell had she forgotten that?

Because Jack was waiting, she explained, "They sometimes leave it open for me when they know I'm coming over. They're probably in the basement, going through their records for you."

Still Jack didn't move, and Ronnie didn't press him, didn't step around him as she might have done a few weeks ago.

Glancing around the area, he backed up a step, taking her with him. "Maybe you should wait in the car while I—"

"No, that I won't do." Ronnie wasn't about to let him walk into possible danger while she cowered away. "Safety in numbers, right? We can both check it out together." His wariness was starting to wear off on her, and now the fine hairs on her neck seemed to tingle.

Reluctantly, Jack started forward. "Will you at least stay behind me?"

"For now."

With a small push, the front door silently swung open, allowing in a rush of cold air and sunlight. The entry was the same as always, and beyond that, the familiar living room. Nothing seemed out of place to indicate a problem.

"What the hell is that?" Jack tilted his head to listen.

The faint screech of an electric guitar drifted from the general direction of the kitchen, and Ronnie started to relax.

"That's their music, and I'm pretty sure it's coming from the basement." She smirked. "They're metalheads, you know."

"Why am I not surprised?" With his gaze searching everywhere, Jack eased toward the kitchen. He stayed alert, which made her alert as well.

The basement door was wide open, the stair light on.

One chair was moved out from under the small table, as if someone had recently vacated it. A pot of coffee, along with four cups, waited on the counter. Clearly, Drake and Drew anticipated their visit.

Jack paused near the stairs, listening.

Feeling some vague sense of unease, Ronnie hovered nearby, her gaze darting everywhere. What if something had happened? What if the twin brothers had become targets because of her? Despite their fascination with oddities and their exaggerated Goth appearances, they were sweethearts through and through. They were important to her…

And she was important to them.

The music was too loud for them to hear her if she yelled down, and she couldn't bear to wait a second more. When she started forward, Jack said, "Let me go first."

She glanced up at him, and her automatic protest stalled. Jack looked so torn, his breathing deeper, his gaze hard, his mouth firm.

It was the expression of a man who cared. Not just a little…but a lot.

"Jack." Ronnie touched his arm. Did he not understand how much he meant to her, too? Why hadn't she ever made that clear?

She'd been a coward, holding back her feelings, afraid of what might happen if she opened up too much. But she did care, far too much to let him take risks for her.

"Just this once," he growled, "can you be agreeable?"

She should have been offended, but at the moment, she didn't have it in her. "I'm agreeable all the damn time."

"Good. Glad to hear it." Jack moved to the first step. "So let me check it out and once I know it's fine, you can join us."

She threw up her hands. "Fine. Play the hero." Afterward, they could work out the details of who cared the most. "But if you see even a shadow, tell me."

Looking over his shoulder at her, he said firmly, "And you'll call the cops."

Ronnie patted her purse. "Maybe. After I shoot someone."

Grinning, he turned back to the stairs. "It's no wonder I'm so crazy about you."

What? The way her heart floated and flipped, of course Ronnie couldn't form a reply, but the happiness she couldn't contain curved her lips into a smile. Dangerous hope carried her forward, just so she could watch him descend.

What he said might just be a saying; he didn't necessarily mean it the way she took it. But it sounded pretty awesome all the same.

Suddenly the basement door slammed shut hard, shoving Jack forward. Ronnie heard him falling down the steps as a stranger—who'd been standing in the kitchen behind the open door the whole time—slapped the deadbolt into place.

"Jack!" It took all of two seconds for her to realize what had happened, and then the man was on her, snatching her purse away and clutching her close with an arm around her throat.

"Bastard," she shouted as she flailed to escape. She kicked his shin, stomped his foot. *If only I can get to my knife.* Whoever he was, she'd happily kill him…

It was her last thought before a syringe viciously stabbed into her thigh.

She lost her breath for one startling second. *Son of a bitch, that hurt.*

"Shh, now," he whispered, his lips touching her ear,

his arm tightening around her throat so that she couldn't draw in air. "You'll relax in just a moment. It'll make it easier." His crooning voice raised every hair on her body, especially when he added, "For now."

Furious pounding started on the basement door.

Jack?

An odd confusion swamped her. She vaguely heard other voices. Maybe the twins but they sounded so far away.

The stranger let her go and, crazy enough, her legs had gone numb and wouldn't support her. Yet rather than fall, she sank slowly to the floor.

"Ronnie!"

The shout and furious rattling of the door roused her. Struggling to focus, Ronnie looked around, but God, she was suddenly tired. As if outside herself, apart from her own body, she saw the man paw through her purse.

"Ah, yes. A gun. How enterprising." He smiled at her, his eyes completely devoid of humanity. Flat. Dead. She knew she should be afraid, but she wasn't sure why.

As if sharing good news, he said, "Isn't it ironic that I'll use your own weapon to murder him?"

Murder…him?

"Ronnie, answer me!" What sounded like a kick jarred the doorframe.

Jack.

Some deep instinct desperately stirred, prompting Ronnie to remove the knife from her boot. She held it against her leg, hiding it as she swayed and struggled to stay awake.

The reasons were no longer clear, but she knew she didn't want to fall asleep.

The room darkened around her, turning colorless, and

the sounds were horrific. Loud clashes that reverberated through her brain, through her entire body.

After a pat on her head, the man took a stance, aiming the gun at the basement door.

Jack.

Ronnie stared at the man's foot, planted near her. He wore only loafers, and they were damned offensive. The ugliest loafers she'd ever seen. She fucking *hated* those loafers—and all of a sudden, before her hand told her brain what it planned to do, she buried her knife in his foot.

Completely through. Savagely.

Pressure mounted behind her eyes and she felt nauseous, yet she held on to that knife, still pressing with both hands, using all her strength. It occurred to her that she heard screaming, and that something pounded against her head and shoulders. A gun went off, once, twice.

Darkness circled her vision, a tornado of storm clouds that blocked out the kitchen and everything in it. She saw only that loafer, now slick and red.

Then she saw nothing at all.

CHAPTER NINETEEN

With one more heave, Jack splintered the door from its frame and it crashed open, revealing a grisly scene.

Ronnie sprawled on the floor, face down, blood stark in her fair hair. Her small body, utterly limp, was draped around an intruder's feet.

A screaming intruder—whom Jack recognized.

The man from the hotel.

The gunshot had come from the weapon in the bastard's hand.

Volcanic rage carried Jack forward in one powerful lunge to smash his fist into the man's pain-contorted face.

The screams stopped and the man swayed, but Jack held on to him. Standing over Ronnie, belatedly giving the protection she should have had from the start, Jack struck out, hitting the man's jaw, his gut, his temple.

Brodie charged into the kitchen, then drew up short. Drake and Drew scrambled up the steps behind Jack.

He barely noted any of them. Not with Ronnie down. Not with her so still, her…blood. Jesus, no. His chest heaved with pain, and each hollow beat of his heart brought his fist into contact with the bastard's face again.

"Move," Brodie said, kneeling down at Ronnie's shoulder. "He's no longer feeling it and I don't want to get trampled."

While Drake and Drew keened in hysterics, and

Jack stood there praying, Brodie gently turned her and touched her throat.

He looked up at Jack. "She's alive."

Dragging in a great, shuddering breath, Jack released the man with a small shove, watching him collapse back in a heap made more awkward by the fact that his foot was skewered to the floor.

With Ronnie's knife.

White and shaking, Drake rushed forward and pointed. "Look."

A needle lay on the counter, empty.

"Dear God," Drew cried. "He gave her something."

As carefully as he could, Jack lifted her, and still she gave a fretful moan.

"Police are called," Brodie calmly informed him as he looked around. "Bullet holes in the ceiling and wall. I heard the shots and got in here as quick as I could."

Drew ran ahead of Jack and shoved the coffee table away from the couch so roughly that it overturned. "Put her here."

Hands shaking, Drake positioned a throw pillow for her head. "The blood…"

Jack didn't want to let her go, but he had to check her so he lowered her to the couch. Her hand dropped off the side, lifeless, stalling his heart.

"I don't think the blood is hers." Brodie held the gun in his hand. "The bullets missed her. I think that's the blood from his foot." Briefly, he clasped Jack's shoulder. "Stay with her. I'll go secure the prick in the kitchen, just in case you didn't kill him."

Jack didn't care if the man died or not. He feathered his fingers into Ronnie's hair, sticky now with blood.

He felt along her scalp, around her ears. He found a few swollen spots but no breaks in her skin.

"Will she be all right?"

Looking up, he found Drake and Drew, both white as sheets and trembling, staring at Ronnie with liquid eyes.

"Yes." Jack said it, meant it…because it *had* to be true. "She'll be okay."

Not more than five minutes passed before they heard the sirens.

Though Jack didn't look away from Ronnie's face, he was aware of Brodie striding back in.

"He's hanging on, but he's not going anywhere. I left the blade in his foot."

"Fuck him." Jack lifted Ronnie's hand in both of his. "Come on, sweetheart. I need you."

Her lashes fluttered and her lips worked.

"Police are here." Drake moved away, and Jack heard the door open. Drew followed his brother, frantic explanations tripping out without a single nuance of dark mystique shading his tone. For Ronnie, the twins were just…themselves.

Jack bent closer to her, his nose touching hers. "I love you, Ronnie Ashford. Please don't leave me."

He felt her breath and then she groaned. "I think I'm going to be sick."

Hearing her speak, regardless of the words, gave him hope.

"Come on, Jack." Brodie clasped his arm and pulled him away as police and paramedics stepped in. "Give them some room."

The next ninety minutes were the longest of Jack's life. The ride to the hospital behind the ambulance, finding out Ronnie was awake when they got there, only to be told she didn't remember much. Of anything.

She was disoriented and afraid.

Having doctors explain she'd been given a drug that could cause drowsiness, confusion, and even hallucinations made Jack want to put his fist through the wall.

His knuckles were already split but he had little patience for the way his mother tried to cover them with ice. When she was in the room, Charlotte watched him with worried eyes. Whenever he saw Brodie, he had Mary tight in his embrace. Drake and Drew sat huddled together, heads down in misery.

They were all there.

Because they all loved her.

At least this time, by God, Ronnie wouldn't go through it alone. She needed to know that. She needed to understand how much she mattered to everyone.

The man who'd done this to her was also at the hospital. Police had already identified him as a serial killer, a crazed lunatic, a man who had focused on Ronnie as his next victim. Although he'd taken a beating, the bastard would recover. And spend the rest of his life in jail.

Jack was stewing on that, thinking dark things when finally a doctor emerged. He glanced at each of them. "Family?"

"All of us," Jack said, and immediately they were there, clustered around him, standing as one, Drake and Drew included.

Jack didn't waste time contacting her blood family. Far as he was concerned, they could all rot. If Ronnie wanted to reach out to them, then and only then would he bother.

For now, he concentrated on what the doctor had to say, and thank God, the news was all good, far as it went. Ronnie was still agitated, and yes, nauseous, but the effects of the drug had mostly worn off and she was finally lucid.

Jack jogged to the room, pushing through the doors and pausing only when he found her sitting up in a bed, most of the blood now washed from her hair, but some sections stained pink.

She'd been scowling in that familiar way, her slim brows down, her mouth drawn—but seeing him, her expression went blank, then crumpled.

His heart crumpled, too.

In two big strides he reached her, bending over the bed, holding her close with his face in her neck. "I thought you were gone." Jesus, his voice sounded like gravel, but it was all he could do not to break. "Ronnie." He held her back, kissed her mouth, her forehead, then crushed her close again.

Clinging to him, her voice a whisper of sound, she said, "I don't remember."

"It's okay, baby. All you need to know is that I have you and I'm never letting you go." She went still, but Jack didn't care. He kissed her neck and repeated, "Never."

Maybe she didn't believe him, maybe she thought he was just upset, but she nodded against his shoulder. "Will you tell me what happened?"

Jack got it together enough to sit up. "The bastard was already in the house, hiding behind the kitchen door. Drake and Drew had no idea." He touched her face with a shaking hand. "After he knocked me down the steps and locked the door, he gave you a drug. But still, you saved the day."

Ronnie tilted her head and surprised him by asking, "You fell down the steps?"

A smile trembled on his mouth, so he gave it up. "Halfway."

"Are you hurt?"

Again, his eyes burned. "God, Ronnie…baby, I'm fine, but I couldn't get to you and I swear, I died every second that the fucking door held." Old houses were a hell of a lot studier than anything being built today. He had the bruises on his shoulder and hip to prove it.

Her brows pinched. "The door. You were banging on it?"

"Banging, kicking, punching, throwing myself against it." His chest clenched in remembered terror. "He would have shot me and taken you, but you stabbed your knife through his foot and that gave me the time I needed."

Confusion kept her brows together, but she nodded and then wrinkled her nose. "I chucked, twice. And my hair is still sticky, and my head hurts like a son of a bitch."

"I'm sorry." Jack swallowed as tears clogged his throat. "He hit you a few times, trying to get away, and I'm so goddamned sorry."

"It's not your fault." She noticed his hand then and her eyes, smudged with ruined makeup, widened. "Your knuckles!" Oh so gently, she touched her fingertips to the back of his hand. "Jack, we need to—"

"Everyone is here and they want to see you, too."

Diverted, as he'd hoped she'd be, she asked, "Everyone?"

"Mom, Charlotte, Brodie and Mary, Drake and Drew."

Disbelief, despair, and wonder all chased over her features. She covered her mouth, but then dropped her hand. "Who has Howler? And Peanut?"

Leave it to Ronnie to think of the pets. "They're in the

lot. Everyone is on a rotation, taking turns to watch them and keep them company. No one was willing to leave, though." He cupped her face. "No one would leave you."

"Oh." Confusion vied with astonishment. And maybe a little awe. Looking away, she ran trembling fingers into her hair and then winced. "I need a shower."

She'd need time, he decided, to understand and accept how much she was loved. "I'll shower with you. And Mom is probably dying to feed you. Just so you know, Charlotte is going to cry on you. Actually, Drake and Drew will, too." Jack stood and held out his hand. "What do you say, honey? Are you ready to go home?"

With a shuddering breath and a small sniffle, she managed a smile and nodded.

FRESH FROM A shower and well fed, Ronnie curled up on the couch against Jack, with Howler and Peanut right beside them.

She somewhat remembered things now—at least prior to being drugged. After that, it remained fuzzy. "I really stabbed him in the foot?"

"Stabbed is a mild word," Brodie said. He and Mary were across from them, sharing one padded chair. "Don't know how you did it, but you drove your blade straight through bone and tendons and into the floor." He pinched a space in the air. "About an inch or so."

"It's a new oddity," Drew said, and then flushed.

Drake nodded. "Right there in the floor, a deep groove."

They stood together like thin disheveled bookends, all but leaning on each other. Ronnie had never seen them look so morose, and no wonder, considering everything that had happened.

"Your poor house." She hated that she'd brought trouble into their home and that their kitchen had suffered because of it.

"Don't," Drew warned, taking a step forward.

Catching his twin's arm, Drake inhaled. "You could have died." His voice cracked. "We all could have died if it wasn't for you. None of the rest matters."

Jack had confided that he liked them a lot. They were still pale, still eccentric, but at least they'd stopped with the theatrical voices.

Ros stood to again put her hand on Ronnie's forehead. "Are you sure you feel okay now?"

Ducking her face against Jack's chest, Ronnie nodded. "Yes, thank you." Never, not in a million years, would she get used to someone...mothering her. God help her, she liked it.

"The soup settled your stomach?"

"Yes, it's fine now." She rested a hand, now thankfully steady, over her once-queasy stomach.

"Would you like anything else then?"

Ronnie looked at Jack, but he only smiled at her, saying, "She's happiest when she's feeding you."

Ros stroked her hair, then retreated to the kitchen chair that she'd brought into the room, close but no longer hovering.

Charlotte sat on the floor yoga-style. "You're like a superhero, Ronnie. You've now taken out two bad men. It's so impressive."

Impressive? She'd always seen her life as a series of tragedies. Somehow, she'd twice been attacked by cruel, insane men bent on hurting her. It was as if fate had it in for her. Yet these people, all of them, looked at her with admiration. They saw her as brave and resourceful, not pathetic. Not a loser.

Her throat thickened again and she had to draw slow, even breaths. Of course Jack noticed and hugged her a little closer.

"Forget makeup," Mary said. "I want to learn your skill with a knife."

Brodie pretended to drop her from his lap, and when Mary squealed, he hugged her back to his chest, laughing—and got a smack to the chest from his frazzled wife.

"I do, too," Charlotte agreed. "Jack's showed me a few things, but—"

Ros perked up. "He did? When?"

Jack quickly changed the subject. "Sick bastard was obsessed over that lock of hair."

Ronnie still couldn't fathom the depth and scope of it all. Luckily the man, North Runde, had his license on him, and at his house they found an entire cellar full of photos with what the detective called his trophies.

Worse, they'd found another room hidden behind it, set up for captivity—and probably torture. She shivered, wondering how she'd ever sleep now.

Jack's mouth touched her temple. "I'm here."

Right, that was how. Smiling, she nodded, glad for his warmth, for the normalcy of having his big, wonderful family nearby, and for the dedication of the twins. But more than anything now, she wanted to be alone.

Alone with Jack.

He must have sensed that, too, because he said, "It's getting late," and in some miraculous way, they all started filing out. It surprised Ronnie, the way each of them insisted on holding her a few seconds longer than usual. When they wished her well, when they said to let them know if she needed anything…she *felt* the sincerity. They said it and meant it.

They cared.

Holding back another wash of tears wasn't easy, but she despised being weak, so she clamped her trembling lips together and nodded her thanks.

Once they were alone, Jack locked the door, scooped her up, and carried her back to the couch.

"You don't remember, do you?"

Which specific part he meant, she wasn't sure, not that it mattered because she remembered very little. "Not after getting stuck. Whatever he gave me, I'm still tired because of it."

Tunneling his fingers into her hair, Jack gently cradled her head and touched his forehead to hers. "I told you that I love you."

Oh shit. Well, good thing he had such a firm hold on her or she probably would have bolted away. Not in displeasure. Hell no. But disbelief? Fear? Yup, she felt that in spades.

"I love you," he repeated, "and I want you to stay here with me."

God, how she wanted to buy into it. But she understood the reasoning, the emotion, behind his declaration all too well. "You're afraid for me. I get that, since I'm still terrorized, too. But it's not a reason—"

"I *love* you." He clutched her closer. "You, Ronnie Ashford. Whether you're verbally kicking ass, rescuing kittens, schmoozing saloon thugs, or fending off a madman with your knife. I love you when you're scared and when you're heroic. It's quick, I know that, and I understand why you can't trust in it—in me—just yet."

Honest to God, she had no idea what to say. Her heart was pumping too hard and fast for her to be able to think.

"It's okay," he continued. "You're overwhelmed."

Well, that part was true.

"Do me one favor." He drew in a shuddering breath. "That's all I ask."

"I'd do just about anything for you." Yes, it was quick, and no, she didn't entirely trust his feelings. But she trusted her own and she knew she loved him completely.

Jack nodded. "Stay with me. Give it time. Give us time. If at some point along the way you decide it's not working…" He paused.

Then he'd let her go? She turned her face up to his.

His dark eyes glittered. "Then I'll convince you."

The laugh came out of nowhere, and she slapped a hand over her mouth.

Jack smiled, too. "Can you promise me that?"

"If you promise the same, that if at some point *you* decide it's not working—"

His kiss smothered the rest of whatever she might have said. Against her lips, he murmured, "We have a deal."

"CHRISTMAS IS ONLY a few days away," Ros said, settling in at the breakroom table with a cup of hot chocolate. Ronnie had coffee and one of the cookies she and Ros had baked together.

The weather had turned frigid over the past few weeks and now snow blanketed everything, but the heat inside the office, along with the family camaraderie, kept her warm.

Brodie, who'd just gotten back from a trip to New York, snagged a cookie from the plate. "Who made this one?" Of course Howler trailed him, his expression hopeful as he peered from the cookie in Brodie's hand to his mouth.

Ronnie raised her hand. "That'd be me, so enjoy it at your own peril." Her first attempt at baking had been a disaster, but since then Ros had taught her a few things. Hopefully enough.

Being a brave soul, Brodie popped the whole thing into his mouth, chewed, and nodded in approval. "It's good."

Without much success, Ronnie tried to hide her pleased smile.

"Mooch," Brodie accused the dog. He snagged two more cookies, but said, "Not for you, bud. Let's go down to the apartment to get you a biscuit."

Brodie's new house, still under construction, would be finished early in the new year. Until then, he and Mary, along with the animals, lived in the attached apartment in the Mustang Transport building.

At the promise of a treat, Howler nearly did a back-flip in his rush of joy. He was halfway out the door when he remembered Peanut. He circled back in to nudge the growing kitten along. Peanut had doubled in size, though he was still small, and he still adored Howler.

Brodie scooped up the cat and they all trooped out the front door.

At almost the same time, Charlotte entered the break-room to snag her own cookie. "Jack's not back yet?"

"Soon," Ronnie said. "He called to say he's on his way." He'd been delivering another homeless dog that, hopefully, would find a forever family.

Over the past weeks, Ronnie had shopped with Charlotte and Mary, baked with Ros, pitched in at the office, and slept with Jack every night. It didn't matter how many awful nights she had, he never complained. He seemed so accepting, so happy, that she now had a new outlook for the future.

"Mmm," Charlotte said, around the cookie. "This is for you." She handed Ronnie the familiar appointment slip.

At a glance, Ronnie saw that the twins had purchased some new oddity, which would require a trip to Columbus. Now that they'd all recovered, they liked to keep her busy—in large part, she assumed, because it meant they'd see her and Jack more.

In fact, they sometimes visited with Jack's family. The twins had gotten to know them better when she, Jack, and Brodie had worked to repair the damage to their house shortly after that awful attack. Unused to company, they had reveled in the attention, especially when Mary had dropped by with Therman.

Being in a wheelchair, Therman couldn't visit their showroom in the basement, but they paraded back and forth with various favorite pieces. Therman, being gruff but kind, had offered advice along with praise.

Now the twins were back to normal—with a few exceptions.

Gone were the fabricated voices and forced personas. Oh, they still loved black and wore it daily, but they greeted Ronnie with new warmth and believably mellow voices.

Also, when making arrangements for a purchase, caution ruled. They openly welcomed Jack's and Brodie's input. Since they now made most appointments through the office instead of calling her directly, it worked out.

Clutching two more cookies, Charlotte headed out to answer the office phone rather than talk around them on the breakroom line. Business was booming lately, so much so that Ronnie now helped with local jobs, freeing up Jack to do the same.

Minutes later, when the chime sounded at the front door, Ronnie assumed Jack was back. Happiness, as always, was her first reaction.

Anxious to see him, Ronnie downed the rest of her coffee and stood, turning toward the door just in time to see a man in a suit—not Jack—disappear into the office. Clients, both prospective and contracted, sometimes dropped in.

Yet…the guarded awareness blooming in her chest cued Ronnie that this visitor was different. When Charlotte closed the door behind him and stared down the hallway at her, Ronnie knew she was right.

Ros stood, too. "Ronnie? What is it?"

Her tongue stuck to the roof of her mouth. All she could do was shake her head.

Charlotte hurried down the hall, stepped inside, and after glancing at Ros, whispered, "There's a man here to see you."

Ros moved to Ronnie's other side. "Who is it?"

Charlotte slowly inhaled. "He says he's her father."

Ros's arm went around her. "Should I send him away?"

"You could stay in here," Charlotte offered.

Their concern finally jogged Ronnie out of her emotional trance. She smiled, truly touched by their caring and immediate defense. "Actually, it's fine." She'd talked to him twice since the attack weeks ago but hadn't told him what had happened. What would be the point? Their conversations were brief and superficial, not conducive to something so serious.

Besides, he hadn't cared when she was eighteen, so Ronnie had no reason to think he'd care now. Mostly, Nicholas Ashford wanted a sympathetic ear, an ally in his unwanted change of circumstances.

She turned within Ros's one-armed embrace, hugging her tight the way Ros had taught her. Damn, it felt good, and it was just the boost she needed. "I've got this." Next she smiled at Charlotte. "He's lonely and a little lost." But Ronnie wasn't. Not anymore. "I don't mind talking to him."

Both women showed their concern and their support.

"We're here," Ros insisted, "if you need us."

"I know." And that made all the difference.

Without remorse, Ronnie went down the hall to slip into the office. The time had come to face her past. Because of Jack, she didn't experience a single second of dread.

HOLDING HIS SQUIRMING BUNDLE, Jack stuck his head into the office—and immediately noticed his mom and Charlotte standing together, identical worried expressions on their faces, in the breakroom doorway.

"What?" He strode down the hallway, looking for Ronnie, but not seeing her. "What's wrong? Where is she?"

His mom glanced at the furry ears sticking up over the fold of the blanket. Without a single question, she took the pup from him.

"Ronnie's here." She nodded back from where he'd come, to the office next to the front door. "In there."

The women looked so concerned, Jack pivoted to look, too. The inner office door was closed. "Doing what?"

"Her father is here," Charlotte blurted.

What? "And you let her in there alone with the bastard?"

Umbrage brought down his mother's brows. "She's a grown woman. I don't *let* her do anything."

Charlotte added in a rush, "Ronnie insisted she was fine." Looking past Jack, she added, "But they've been in there twenty minutes now."

"Damn it." Jack started to leave but then hesitated. "I'm keeping the dog. He's…skittish."

Ros lifted the bundle to rub her cheek against the puppy's ears. "We'll get acquainted. Go on."

Jack was at the door before he'd even thought about moving. God, he'd been working forever, weeks that felt like months, to earn Ronnie's trust. She needed to believe that he loved her, and she needed to understand that real love didn't change.

He loved her now, he'd love her tomorrow.

He'd love her forever.

Without bothering to knock, Jack swung the door open harder than necessary, braced for anything.

Except for what he found.

Ronnie sat on the edge of the desk, legs dangling, hands braced flat at either side of her hips. *Smiling.*

Her silver gaze swung up at his entrance, and her smile quirked with wit. "Come on in, Jack."

Since he was already in, he merely closed the door behind him.

Sliding off the desk, she came to stand at his side, leaning into him. He put an arm around her and zeroed in on the man who'd abandoned her.

At least he looks sober. Nicholas Ashford also stood. Tall, slender, suited. And now wary. His dark blue eyes studied Jack.

"This is Jack Crews," Ronnie said. "We work together."

"And live together," Jack added.

"And live together," she confirmed, again smiling. "Jack, this is Nicholas Ashford."

That she had to introduce her father so formally spoke volumes. Jack didn't offer his hand...but Nicholas did.

When Ronnie's elbow gouged him, Jack reluctantly accepted the handshake. Damned if he'd lie and tell the man he was pleased to meet him.

"Nick and I have come to an agreement," Ronnie continued. "You know the history."

Yes, he did. As Jack stared at him, Nick had the grace to look away.

"Well, we've discussed it and agreed to get reacquainted."

Jack's gaze shot down to hers. Ronnie wore her most determined, obstinate expression, one that dared him to question her decision.

Knowing he had to tread carefully, Jack asked, "How so?"

She shrugged. "Lunch first." After sliding her hand into Jack's, she added, "I thought maybe I'd fix your mom's famous chicken salad."

Ronnie was fixing lunch? They wouldn't meet at a restaurant? "So you two will visit..."

Unblinking, she hugged closer and ventured, "At home?"

Home. Jack's heart started kicking, and a weight lifted from his chest. Ronnie still had her apartment, but they'd already removed the remainder of her meager belongings. He couldn't imagine she meant to go there, but to be sure he didn't misunderstand, Jack asked, "He knows where we live?"

Tension eased from her expression and she gave him a blinding smile. "I told him."

"Sounds good." Sounded fucking *great*, in fact.

When Jack turned back to Nick, he saw the man's shoulders relax. This little meeting had caused tension all the way around. He didn't give a shit how Nick felt, as long as Ronnie was comfortable.

"I should get going," Nick said. He glanced at Jack—who wasn't about to budge—and then back to Ronnie. Coming to some silent decision, he stood taller. "You've been more than fair. Kinder than I deserve." His voice thickened. "Thank you for that."

"I can afford to be fair. Now." Ronnie released Jack to give the man a brief hug. "I'll be in touch soon."

He nodded, keeping his head down, and made his way out.

Jack waited until the entry door closed, then he turned to Ronnie—and caught her as she launched against him.

"Hey." Smoothing a hand over her hair, thinking he might go after old Nick to teach him a thing or two, Jack asked, "What is it, honey? Are you okay?"

Keeping her face tucked to his chest, she nodded. "I love you, Jack."

He stilled, his heartbeat, his breath, his very existence…and then it all kicked back in with a wild rush. He clasped her shoulders to lever her back. "You love me?"

Her mouth twitched. "You already knew I did."

Yes, he'd known. But it mattered that she knew it, too. "You're sure?"

"I thought seeing Nick again would be different.

Harder, you know? He wants me to call him Dad, but I won't do that."

"I don't blame you." Nick didn't have the right to ask. He didn't deserve the title. Not anymore.

"He asked me to forgive him, too, and I did, but I told him I can't just forget." She exhaled heavily. "Right now, he's miserable. Mom is moving on and Skylar just doesn't care enough."

Jack reined in the surge of emotion to say, "You've always cared." About the wrong people.

"I did. But it's different now."

Damn right it was. Now she had the right people—family who would love her back with all their hearts.

"I looked at him," Ronnie continued, "and I didn't feel hurt or mad or…anything like that. I just felt sorry for him." Her mouth twisted, as if she recognized the irony in that. "We have a history together, good and bad. I'd rather focus on the good."

God, she was such a generous person. Smiling, he said aloud, "An ass-kicker with a big heart." In every way, Ronnie was the most unique person he'd ever met. How could he *not* love her?

She laughed at that description. "When Nick gets his life together, he'll forget about me again, and that's okay."

"No, it's not."

"It *is*," she stressed. "I'd like a relationship with him, sure. I wish I could reunite with my mom and Skylar, too, but Jack." She put a hand to his face. "My life is so full with you and your wonderful family—"

"Now your family, as well."

She nodded. "I know. I adore each and every one of them."

Turning his head, he kissed her palm.

"I love your house, too. It feels like a home."

He agreed. "With us there together."

"And Mustang Transport is such a great business."

"Consider yourself an official employee—with time off to moonlight for the twins, of course."

Ronnie laughed. "I just need you to know. While I love all those things, they're not what's most important. I could get by without them."

"I already know that." She'd gotten by with nothing and no one for far too long. "But you love me?"

"Afraid so. You know what that means?" She didn't give him a chance to answer before warning, "You're stuck with me."

Jack went still, except for the smile he couldn't hold back.

"I've thought about it a lot, and I've decided to get rid of my apartment."

"Yeah?"

Her tongue slipped over her lips, not in nervousness, but with building courage. "I'm staying with you. Permanently."

The way she said that, not as a question but a statement, proved she understood just how much he loved her. Jack hugged her off her feet. "That's good, but you might have to share me just a little—because I got us a dog."

"You...*what*?" It was her turn to lever away.

"Consider it an early Christmas present."

Her lips parted and her eyes stayed wide.

Jack kissed her nose. "I thought about an engagement ring—"

"Jack!"

"But I decided we should pick that out together."

Swallowing heavily, she nodded. "I'd like that."

Feeling like he'd just been handed the world, Jack put her back on her feet and caught her hand. "Come meet Buster."

They found Ros and Charlotte on the floor in the breakroom. Ros held the timid dog in her lap and Charlotte cautiously stroked his floppy ears.

Both of the women looked up with questions in their eyes. Jack winked, a silent signal to say that Ronnie was fine, better than fine.

As if to prove it, Ronnie crooned, "You got us a dog," in a soft, happy voice. Jack watched as she sank to her knees. Amazingly, Buster poked his head out of the blankets. He had unique coloring with a white freckled snout, tan jaws, eyebrows, and belly, and a darker brown coat everywhere else.

"Oh, Jack. He's beautiful."

As if he understood, Buster crept over to her.

Quietly, Jack explained, "He's a young, very shy Lab mix who desperately needs a forever home."

Bringing the dog gently up to her chest, Ronnie nodded. "And that's us. Forever." The dog swung his long tail and tucked his snout into Ronnie's neck.

It was a tender moment.

Ronnie and Buster immediately bonded.

His mom and Charlotte were thrilled to realize they'd finally cemented a future.

And then Brodie showed up. Mary carried Peanut, but Howler, who immediately smelled the other animal, went on alert before excitedly rushing in.

Instead of shying away, Buster emerged, thrilled to find a fellow dog.

Chaos reigned—but in a good way.

Still looking overwhelmed, Ronnie stepped up against

Jack, watching as Buster and Howler sniffed each other most thoroughly. Peanut, fearless of dogs, wanted in on the action.

Charlotte and his mom got into a discussion about last-minute Christmas shopping. Brodie brought Mary down to his lap to steal a kiss.

Jack knew Ronnie was smiling—he felt it in his heart. Bending to her ear, he warned, "It's this crazy most of the time. You already know that, right?"

"I know I'm no longer alone." She turned her face up to his. "Thank you for bringing Buster home. I love him. I love Howler and Peanut, too. I love *all* your family. And most of all, I love you."

From the moment Jack had met her, he'd known Ronnie was worth the effort. He hadn't realized at the time that they'd be fighting a murderous madman, or the awful neglect of her family.

But in the end, he was right—because Ronnie's love made any effort worthwhile, and now they had the rest of their lives together as a payoff.

* * * * *

*Don't miss the final book in the sizzling
Road to Love series by* New York Times *bestselling
author Lori Foster!*

*The last thing Charlotte Parrish needs in her life is a
bad boy. She wants someone responsible and settled...
until she meets Mitch Crews. Mitch is everything she
knows she should avoid but everything she can't seem
to resist.*

*Mitch is starting over. Now that his mother is gone,
he's determined to finally meet the half brothers he's
heard about his entire life. Finding family was his
hope, but finding love didn't cross his mind...until
beautiful, bighearted Charlotte walks into his life.*

Coming soon from HQN Books!

Read on for a sneak peek at New York Times *bestselling author Lori Foster's next novel,* Sisters of Summer's End, *about two very different women who learn that the best families are made—not given—and love is just around the corner.*

IT WAS COWARDLY, Joy knew, but she didn't trust this new version of herself, so instead of heading directly back to the park, she took her son, Jack, to a restaurant for fried chicken and biscuits.

Even though he was thin, Jack was a bottomless pit and he finished off two legs and a biscuit while Joy nibbled on a wing.

Her thoughts refused to veer long from Royce Nakirk.

Now that he knew she was a mother, what would he think?

It didn't matter, but still…

"What's wrong, Mom?"

Joy gazed at her son's big brown eyes and smiled. "Nothing. I just have a busy day yet ahead."

Warily, he eyed her around a third piece of chicken. "Will I get to play?"

Unable to resist, Joy stroked his fair hair. "We play every night, don't we?"

"Could I play longer?"

Oh, that wheedling tone. Jack was at the age where he negotiated everything. She loved each new facet of his growth, watching him expand his horizons. He was still shy, but preschool had helped him to make friends. And thank God for that because while the summer had provided constant entertainment, the park would now be incredibly quiet until spring. If it weren't for school, he'd spend all his days without peers.

For the thousandth time, Joy questioned her decision in moving to the Cooper's Charm resort. At the time, she'd been desperate for work that would accommodate a baby and allow her to be both caregiver and breadwinner.

Because there was no one else.

Cooper Cochran hadn't owned the park long when she'd shown up largely pregnant with a nonexistent résumé and promises that she'd be perfect for the job, vowing that she'd work harder than anyone else possibly could. At that time, promises and determination were all she had to offer. She'd felt so fragile, so utterly alone that when he hired her, she'd broken down into tears.

Badly needing a positive focus, and grateful for his confidence, she'd thrown herself into the job, going above and beyond the requirements, and in that process, she'd found a new love: organizing recreational activities for kids and adults alike. Jack had grown up with the other employees as family—more so than her real family would ever be. She, however, still kept others at a distance.

Trust, once broken, instilled a very real fear.

"Tell you what," Joy said, leaning an elbow on the table and smiling at him. "We'll grab an ice cream with Maris first, then play for an hour if you promise to help me with some of my work afterward." She needed to see Maris anyway…but Jack didn't know that. And she'd found he was really great at sorting craft items, as long as she gave very clear instructions. He liked helping out, plus it kept him busy—and close.

"Deal!"

The way Jack's face lit up had Joy grinning, too. It

wasn't often he got to eat out and have ice cream at the camp store, too. She'd grown up the opposite, indulged to a ridiculous degree. Rarely were there meals at home, and if she'd chosen a diet of jelly beans and milkshakes, no one would have denied her.

Only in hindsight had Joy realized it was lack of interest, not an excess of love, that had motivated her parents. The hard truth was forced on her at twenty-four, and in some ways, it felt like her life truly began after that moment.

Now, without her family's influence, she lived on a shoestring budget—and it didn't matter. Her life couldn't be happier. She had Jack, so she had everything she really needed. She'd give her son the more important things in life, like her attention, guidance, protection and supervision. And yes, unconditional love.

And if occasionally, when in her bed alone, she felt an undefined yearning…well, that didn't matter, either. She wouldn't let it.

Cupping her son's face, Joy put a smooch on his forehead. "You are the most perfect little boy I could ever imagine."

"Mom," he complained, wiggling away as his dark eyes quickly scanned the room, ensuring no one had witnessed her affection. He didn't mind hugs, cuddles and kisses, but only when they were alone.

Hiding her smile, Joy cleared away their mess, and within minutes they were headed back to the park. Of course, with Jack buckled up in the back seat with a picture book, her thoughts returned to Royce.

Why had she let him chase her away?

Or more accurately, why had she let her attraction for him get in the way of her responsibilities?

Since she'd be seeing him more all through October, she had to figure out how to keep her physical reactions to him in check.

Or you could just grab one more indulgence?

Oh, no. Definitely *no.* Royce hadn't shown any particular interest, and when would it be possible anyway? Ruthlessly, Joy snuffed that idea.

But after she parked and she and Jack headed for the camp store, she spotted Cooper Cochran standing near the scuba shack, at the edge of the boat ramp. Two others stood to his left on the shore, their wet suits rolled down to their waists.

One of them was Baxter, the scuba instructor. Joy had seen him and his very fine physique a great many times. She took in the sight of him the same way she admired art—with an eye of appreciation, but nothing more.

However, the other man was…Royce.

Seeing him like that, chest bare, dark hair slicked back, sun glinting off his wide shoulders, caused a very different sort of appreciation. Her heart raced, her stomach seemed to take flight and she couldn't breathe.

She forgot her resolve. She forgot everything.

Good God, she felt…*alive.*

Don't miss Sisters of Summer's End *by* New York Times *bestselling author Lori Foster!*

Thirty years old was too young to be this jaded.

*You're just tired after a long week. Don't analyze it to
death.*

He leaned forward to pull his wallet from his back
pocket, ready to pay the bartender and take his gloomy
self home, when he noticed a stunning vision striding
toward him. He froze, the scene unfolding in slow motion.

Strawberry blond hair washed over slim shoulders in a
waterfall of color, bright against the narrow black sheath
dress draped over her slender form. Electric blue eyes
flashed with determination. She was long-limbed, her
walk confident, and her full pink mouth was set in a firm,
unsmiling line. One eyebrow was arched and she homed
in on him like he was the target and she was a missile.

With his next breath, his energy returned. Lust
slammed into his solar plexus and dried out his mouth.

HDEXPJL0419

Which made no sense.

In those heels, in that dress and with no smile to speak of, it was obvious he was in the presence of a way-too-serious woman. He'd had a close call with a woman like this one in his past, and he'd since decided that cute, bubbly bartenders were more his style.

Even so… Intrigued and more than a bit curious, he shoved his wallet back into his pocket when it became clear that this striking woman was coming right for him.

This one he'd dance with. If only to shake things up a bit.

He'd buy her a drink, turn on the Fleming charm and see what happened. It'd been a while since a woman had snagged this much of his attention. Whether it was the strawberry blond's determination or the set of her small shoulders, he couldn't be sure, but he couldn't tear his eyes off her.

How could anyone look that damned delicate and at the same time like she ate nails for breakfast?

He didn't know. But he was going to find out. Something told him that she'd be worth it, no matter the cost.

Don't miss what happens next!
Temporary to Tempted *by Jessica Lemmon*

Available April 2019 wherever
Harlequin® Desire books and ebooks are sold.

www.Harlequin.com